SNOW GHOST

A PATRICKFLINT NOVEL

PATRICK FLINT
BOOK 9

PAMELA FAGAN HUTCHINS

SKIPJACK PUBLISHING

FREE PFH EBOOKS

Before you begin reading, you can snag a free Pamela Fagan Hutchins ebook starter library by joining her mailing list at HERE.

PROLOGUE: DISAPPEAR

Mount Rainier, Washington
August 25, 1978

Patrick

From the beginning, Patrick Flint knew the summit push would be a lesson in humility. Mount Rainier's Ingraham Glacier in late August still wore its lethal white coat, and every step of the route reminded him this was not his beloved Cloud Peak in the Bighorn Mountains of Wyoming. He felt it in the slow burn of his calves, the acid needle-prick in his lungs, the way the mountain seemed to lean back and watch, unimpressed, as the four-man rope team trudged up its eastern flank.

He liked to think of it as a team, anyway. Patrick, Henry Sibley, and Wes Braten were officially "clients," a word Lewis Zahn spat like a sunflower seed husk. Lewis was twenty-six, grizzled already, with a helmet of sandy hair and skin that looked vacuum-sealed to his skull. He moved over the snow with a speed and confidence that made Patrick feel, despite his relatively youthful thirty-six years and a thousand high country miles, like a Boy Scout on a church hike. Of the larger expeditionary group's three guides, Patrick felt like his team was harnessed to the crotchety mule.

"So," Wes called, his voice ricocheting up the rope. The lab tech and Henry had joined the climb after one of Patrick's original climbing partners had been murdered and the other suffered a serious brain injury. "Anyone else regretting that extra helping of oatmeal at breakfast? Because I am. It's like pulling a bull in a bread-basket up this thing."

Lewis, twenty feet ahead, didn't even look back. "That's the altitude, not your breakfast." His words cut through the wind.

Patrick smiled, or tried to, but it froze somewhere inside the mustache his wife Susanne had made him promise to shave when he returned home. At this altitude—nearing twelve thousand feet—the air was stingy. Each inhalation felt like he'd been shorted on the change. But the view! He snuck a glance. The north face of Rainier swooped away in a parabolic arc, the lower ridges cushioned by pillows of cloud. Above, the mountain's head was lost in shifting mist, haloed by cirrus and the thin filigree of frost blown off the cap. Behind loomed masses of ominous gray that sent nerves flickering along Patrick's neck.

Henry, right behind him on the rope, wasn't talking. Hadn't said much all morning since being plagued by a headache, unless you counted the deep grumble he'd aimed at the snow when his boot broke through a cornice. He had the hunched, stubborn stance of a man used to moving cattle, not tiptoeing over crevasses on a two-inch snow bridge.

But Patrick could feel his friend's unease through the rope, the occasional tug or shudder whenever the wind gusted or a shadow flickered in the periphery. He was, as ever, stubborn and stoic, though. No one would guess his feelings by looking at him.

Patrick felt responsible for his friend but confident in Henry's fitness and competence, enough so that he was still able to marvel at the glacier itself. While covered in debris, it displayed a range of colors up close that were impossible to imagine when seeing the white expanse from afar. The reds and yellows of the rock, the blue and even violet of the ice. He felt privilege close to religious fervor to experience it up close, and he whispered prayers of gratitude as he climbed, with occasional supplications for their safety thrown in.

The team moved in rhythm. Step, pause, drive the axe, move the feet, step, pause, breathe. Lewis set the pace, almost metronomic, and it was Patrick's job to match it, his own movements echoing in the rhythm of the men behind him. There had been comfort in it, almost like the slow strumming of a classical guitar, until the first warning sign. The snow underfoot, solid all morning, suddenly gave with a wet, sucking sound.

Lewis stopped. He knelt on the snow, examining a patch where the surface had slumped. "Crevasse here," he called, voice clipped. "Step light. Cross at the point I'm marking." He chopped at the snow with his axe, scouring out a bridge barely two boots wide. He traversed with feline grace and waited, hands on hips, as the rest prepared to cross.

Patrick glanced back. Wes had his eyes closed, lips moving. Henry just looked at the sky and muttered, "Damn it to hell and back." And then they went, one after another, the rope tight between them, Wes going last.

No one fell. But the mood on the rope was different after the crossing. Everyone was more careful, more deliberate. When the wind finally found them in earnest—a shriek that ripped over the ridge and smacked them with a face full of blown ice—Lewis hesitated. The gray clouds had moved in, crowding closer to them and blocking out the sun. He pulled his balaclava up, turned, and gestured the team closer. "We've got maybe forty-five minutes before this system drops in," he said. "We make the saddle before that, we're golden. If not, we bivvy."

Patrick, shaking snow out of his goggles, nodded. Taking shelter in the small tents they carried for that purpose wasn't what he wanted to do, but it was the smart thing to do. His grim experience hiding from the weather in a cave on Cloud Peak had cemented that point for him a year ago. "Copy that."

"Let's move," said Lewis.

They did, heads down, feet seeking friction in snow rapidly hardening under a film of frozen vapor. The clouds above them moved with seeming intent. Each hundred feet of gain brought less visibility, more wind, the sound of it in their hoods a banshee's wail. Late August on Rainier was as volatile and unpredictable as Patrick had been warned.

He felt a change in the rope. Lewis's movements, always precise, became now urgent. The rope jerked and shuddered, forcing Patrick to follow quickly or risk being yanked off his feet. He gave Wes and Henry their sign of two short tugs but didn't dare risk looking back.

They struggled to the edge of a plateau, where every gust of wind cost them half a step of forward progress. Lewis turned hard right, heading for what Patrick guessed was the lip of the Ingraham Glacier proper, when the world just disappeared.

Whiteout was no longer just a word. It was the only way to describe their reality. The horizon erased. The colors and contours vanished into a matte blankness that made Patrick feel stationary. He knew they were still moving because of the scrape of crampons on ice and the twitch of the rope at his hip. For thirty seconds, maybe a minute, there was no way to tell if they were going uphill, downhill, or sideways.

Then Lewis's headlamp appeared, not ahead but below. The rope pulled him hard, and Patrick's feet slid out from under him. He clawed at the ice with his axe, found no purchase, and began to freefall, dropping, dropping, dropping until a yank by the rope at his waist stopped him. For a second, he hung in space, then something gave. He tumbled down the slope, ice and snow abrading his face, the taste of blood in his mouth. He heard a shout, then the thunk of an axe biting in before the rope went tight.

But the tension lasted less than a heartbeat before sudden acceleration that told him the anchoring had failed. They were sliding, tied together, down a glacier at a speed Patrick could barely process.

"Self-arrest!" Lewis's voice, somewhere above, was faint.

Patrick kicked his crampon points in, drove his axe deep. For an instant, he thought it would hold. Then Henry slammed into him. Axes tore out, the world becoming a carnival ride of snow, ice, and screaming wind.

CHAPTER ONE: LISTEN

ASHFORD, WASHINGTON
THREE DAYS EARLIER: AUGUST 22, 1978

Patrick

THE ROAD TO ASHFORD, Washington, ran like a shallow, meandering stream through the Cascade foothills, every bend shrouded in firs so dark green it could have been a forest in the Brothers Grimm's fairy tales. Patrick drove, hands at ten and two, partly out of habit, partly because he hadn't put new tires on the family Suburban before the journey and after the family trip to Seattle for the King Tut exhibition, and the tread wasn't proving up to the job. Henry slouched shotgun, boots up on the glove box, his eyes doing their usual laconic sweep of the roadside as if every corner might spring wayward livestock or wildlife. Wes, in the back seat, had been alternating between napping and reading Patrick's battered copy of *Mountaineering: The Freedom of the Hills*.

They'd been on the road for a day and a half, and the inside of the car smelled, as Wes pointed out for the fourth time, like "forty bucks worth of anxiety sweat, which is what I spent on gear at our last REI stop."

"Quit yer gritchin'," Henry said, grinning sidelong at Patrick. "Your gear is fine. The question is, are you?"

"Every step up that mountain is going to be accompanied by the sound of Wes's lungs collapsing," Patrick said. "He nearly suffocated on the stairs at the hotel in Spokane."

In reality, Wes was an alpine trail runner who maintained a high level of fitness that rivaled Patrick's, and Patrick had been training for Rainier for over a year. Before that, he'd been running half marathons. If any of them would have trouble, he predicted it would be Henry whose training consisted mostly of wrangling cattle in the mountains, driving posts in steep, rocky terrain, and chopping firewood. Or maybe that made Henry the most suited of the three of them. They'd know soon enough.

"I was conserving oxygen, Doc," Wes said, voice pitched in mock indignation. "Speaking of which, did you know some experts estimate that seventy percent of fatalities in mountaineering are due to hypoxia and poor decision-making?"

Henry snorted. "If altitude sickness causes seventy percent, the other thirty percent is numbskulls falling off."

Patrick gripped the wheel and leaned forward, peering through mist at the wet, winding blacktop. "The forecast is decent. Freezing level's above twelve thousand feet."

Wes raised his hands. "If I'm found frozen and blue on Disappointment Cleaver, I want the record to reflect this conversation for posterity."

"Duly noted," said Henry.

They lapsed into silence, the radio a faint AM hum. The station drifted in and out between country ballads—"What a Difference You've Made in My Life" by Ronnie Milsap was Patrick's current favorite—and news bulletins about Mount Baker, where the steam vents at Sherman Crater were keeping the Cascades geologists up at night, which, as far as Patrick could tell, mostly meant the forest service was closing a bunch of back roads. That and the usual Carter malaise—oil, OPEC, everything getting more expensive except for the things people didn't actually want to buy.

But the negative chatter couldn't dampen his mood. Heck, the sky alone was worth the trip. Clouds rolled and tumbled above them, the flat-bellied cumulonimbus backlit by a sun only sensed in the light bleeding through the rain. Every few minutes, the road would climb out of a valley and spit them onto a flat, where the forest parted long enough to offer a glimpse of Rainier itself—massive, backlit, a blue-white cutout in the horizon.

Wes, who'd never seen it before, whistled. "That's not a mountain. That's a direct personal threat."

"It's more of a suggestion," Patrick said. "She's only dangerous if you underestimate her."

"According to Dr. Patrick Flint, world-renowned climbing expert," Henry said, grinning.

"Says the guy who almost got frostbite on Cloud Peak last month," Patrick shot back.

"That was a gear failure," Henry said, but he laughed.

They wound around a turn and entered Ashford proper. The town was basically a gift shop, a gas station, and the Tahoma Mountaineering Institute, which was comprised of a compound of low buildings and gear sheds backed up against a wall of ancient firs. Rainier loomed so close here that it felt like it was about to swallow the town whole.

Patrick downshifted and coasted toward the TMI sign, which had a cartoon yeti on it giving the thumbs up. He squinted, then jerked the wheel as something caught his attention in the corner of his eye. It was a line of people, men and women and a few kids, all dressed in what looked like full tribal regalia—beaded, feathered, the whole works—moving with stately, measured steps across the gravel lot.

Wes leaned forward over the seat. "You seein' this?"

Patrick nodded. "That's a powwow dance."

Henry rolled his window down. "Listen to those drums."

A group of men at the far end of the lot pounded on taut animal-hide drums. The sound was low and insistent. Two dancers moved in a circle, arms held out, adorned with eagle feathers and holding sticks wound with ribbons. Their faces were calm, but with a kind of rapture that made Patrick feel like he was intruding on a private conversation with the earth itself.

He slowed the Suburban to a crawl to get a better look. Which is how he nearly plowed the car off the shoulder and into a hedge. The sudden deceleration threw Henry's boots toward the windshield and pulled a yelp out of Wes.

"Holy smokes, Patrick," Henry said, grabbing the armrest. "Want me to take over?"

"I was appreciating culture," Patrick said, easing the car back onto the blacktop.

Wes tried to peer backward through the rain-streaked window. "What do you think the powwow is for?"

Patrick considered it. "The American Indians call the mountain Tahoma and consider it sacred ground. Maybe it's part of a blessing ceremony."

They pulled into the TMI lot and parked between a battered Subaru and a lifted Ford with a "Keep On Truckin'" bumper sticker. Patrick sat for a second, hands still on the wheel, pretending he hadn't just embarrassed himself in front of a parking lot full of people.

Wes popped the back door. "Can I just say if we all die on this mountain, it's been a pleasure."

Henry barked a laugh. "We're not dying. We're getting up there, taking our picture, and getting home. You've got a wedding to plan."

Wes's fiancée, nurse Kathy Bergman, had made Wes swear on a stack of medical supplies that he'd return in one piece, with all ten fingers and toes. The funny part of the promise Wes had made her was that he was so good at his job that he could lose half a hand and still operate an X-ray machine. Still, Patrick had heard him call home the night before, and his voice had been uncharacteristically soft and serious.

Out of nowhere Henry added, "And I've got a nursery to set up."

Wes beamed. "Another baby? Congratulations!"

Henry rubbed his chin stubble. "Thanks."

With a history of miscarriage and a difficult pregnancy with their son Hank, Patrick considered Henry's wife Vangie high risk and recognized signs of anxiety in his friend. He shut off the ignition and turned to him. "How's Vangie? She feeling all right?"

Henry rubbed his temples. "She's tired. The morning sickness is really wringing it out of her."

"Hopefully that will pass soon. Make sure she comes to see me as soon as we get back."

"I will."

They grabbed their packs and headed for the main building. The rain, which had held off most of the drive, returned with the stubbornness of a Wyoming winter, dense and cool, a fine mist descending everywhere. Patrick pulled his collar up, but within seconds his hair was plastered flat.

The trio reached the TMI office. It was a jumble of boot tracks and rental forms filled with the musky odor of wet wool. A battered bell hung over the counter, and a lean woman in a TMI fleece vest waved them forward.

"You here for the ascent?" she said, pen at the ready.

"Yes, ma'am," said Patrick.

"Names?"

"Flint, Sibley, and Braten."

She checked the list. "Welcome. After you fill out your paperwork, your orientation will be in the West Room. Gear to the right. Your guides will meet you in there."

Patrick signed waivers with a practiced hand. "Any other teams this week?"

"Two. We've got one group of climbers from Atlanta, and a party of American Indians from," she glanced at her clipboard, "the Muckleshoot tribe. Plus, whoever else is on the mountain with other outfits or climbing without assistance."

They found their guides in the gear room. One stood by a table of helmets and harnesses, ticking off a checklist. He introduced himself as Lewis Zahn. The next was Eric Miller, a rangy man in his early fifties with a beard like a red fox and a handshake so solid it left Patrick's fingers tingling. Pauline Miller was younger, maybe twenty-five, with an athlete's build and an intense gaze.

"My daughter," Eric said, his smile wide and proud.

Wes, ever the icebreaker, said, "Heard you almost lost a client to an avalanche last week."

Lewis smiled without humor. "He didn't listen. You listen, you stay alive."

They fitted harnesses, checked boots, and compared ice axes like cowboys checking teeth and hooves at a horse auction. The Atlanta crew arrived, three men with enough photographic equipment to cover a moon landing. Dunk Elliott, ex-Army from the looks of him with a balding patch and a tattoo of a howling wolf on his neck, grunted, tried to one-up Patrick on knowledge of glacier hazards, but Patrick let it slide. He was here to climb, not win a pissing contest.

The three Muckleshoots arrived next, all in varying degrees of traditional dress, with most of the finery stripped away. Patrick realized they had been part of the powwow. The oldest of the three—silver hair in a tight braid, windburned face—introduced himself as Gill Adams. His handshake was soft, but his gaze was a steel trap.

"We come to walk with the mountain," Gill said.

"We're honored to share the trail with you," Patrick said, meaning it.

After the Muckleshoots had changed in a dressing room, they all gathered for the orientation. The rain drummed on the windows, drowning out the voice of the radio, until someone turned it up.

A DJ with a syrupy baritone announced, "Jury's out in the infamous Bella Crooke murder trial in Wyoming. The country is watching as they're expected to reach a verdict by nightfall. Stay tuned for updates—this is KCTM, out of Tacoma."

Henry's voice was a growl. "I hope she gets what she deserves. Damn near killed us all."

Wes perked up. "I predict they return guilty. Four hours deliberation max."

Dunk said, "Wait. She nearly killed you? Were you the guys that were involved in that case?"

Patrick cleared his throat. "Yes. Wes, Henry, me, my son Perry. She ambushed us, but we survived and turned her in. Her trial is for the murder of a young woman named Whitney Saylor, not for what she did to us. In fact, Whitney was supposed to be climbing with me this week."

Point of fact, Bella might have succeeded in killing Wes and him on Cloud Peak if not for Perry shooting her with a slingshot. Literally, a slingshot, which he'd learned only that week while working on the Sibleys' ranch. They'd been bringing down a bejeweled golden ring and breastplate from ancient Egypt that her husband Ichabod had acquired on the black market, one he'd had on him at the time of his death while climbing the mountain.

As odd as it seemed, Ichabod claimed he wore them on all his climbs. In his diary, he'd written, "I always wear my treasures, one over my heart and the other on my pinky finger. They connect me to all those before me. When I look out from a peak, they make me feel like I am sovereign over everything my eyes can see. A pharaoh whose kingdom is the entirety of the world touched by the sun."

The antiquities were worth a true fortune, and Bella had considered them hers and stopped at nothing to try to acquire them.

Pauline, standing at the front, raised an eyebrow. "I remember her from when she called and signed up. When I realized she'd been murdered, I followed the news about the trial pretty closely. You're *that* Dr. Flint? The one who found Whitney and testified against her murderer?"

Patrick felt the heat climb his neck. "Uh, yeah, although I've gotta say it's a surprise that folks out here have heard of me."

"Everybody at TMI anyway. Besides, people eat up that Wild West stuff." Eric's voice was dry as sawdust.

Wes nudged Patrick's arm. "Guess we'd better ace this climb. You've got a reputation to maintain."

Patrick tried to play it off, but the topic made his mind return to Susanne and their teenagers Trish and Perry back in Buffalo with his father Joe. When Patrick had made plans to climb Rainier a year ago, Susanne had told him to go. The kids would be starting school and her classes at Sheridan College were commencing as well. She'd sworn they'd be fine. He'd chosen to believe her, but with his dad there now and the trial ending, he worried. The old man was only a month into widowhood after the shocking loss of Lana Flint to a burst appendix that she'd endured too long without complaint, a situation that led to peritonitis, sepsis, and her death. Already grumpy by nature, in her absence Joe was himself, only more so.

Patrick couldn't imagine a world without his mother's gentle, loving presence. He was grieving. They all were. Joe's behavior made empathy difficult, however. Patrick decided he would call home as soon as they broke for the day.

Eric regained his attention and began a slide show, which was mostly pictures of previous clients. Triumphant on the summit, huddled outside huts, grinning next to crevasse holes. Eric delivered the lecture with the crisp confidence of a man who'd survived near-death experiences and knew the odds.

"Any of you who think you won't be scared," Eric said, "you're wrong. Being scared keeps you alive."

Wes raised a hand. "What if I'm already scared right now?"

"Then you've got a head start," Eric said, and a few in the group laughed.

They went through the schedule for the next few days, checked all their gear, and finished with a Q&A, then broke for the day after a very full afternoon. Patrick wandered outside, drawn by the sound of drums which had begun to throb faintly again in the parking lot, leaving Henry and Wes arguing with the Atlanta crew about which MREs tasted least like cardboard.

He found the Muckleshoot climbers gathered with their families under a makeshift awning, singing in low harmonies. Gill beckoned Patrick over.

"We do this for strength," Gill said, gesturing at climber Ralph Heaton on one of the drums. Ralph, stocky and square jawed, so far hadn't cracked a smile. "And to remember the ones who came before us."

"Sounds like a great idea. I think my team could learn a thing or two from you," Patrick said.

Gill's face softened into a grin. "Maybe we will teach you after the climb. Dougie is new to the dancing. He needs the practice," he said, referring to the third of the Muckleshoot climbers, who was standing a few feet from him. The wiry young man flashed a grin.

"I'd like that."

They parted ways, and Patrick slipped back inside.

Wes looked toward him. "You good, Doc?"

"Never better," Patrick said. Mount Rainier was his warm-up for climbing the Seven Summits, a dream he'd held for years. Next up was Aconcagua in South America in January. Then McKinley in June. And so on until he'd climbed the highest peak on each of the seven continents.

Patrick joined in the swapping of war stories with Dunk and his two buddies, Connor Patton and Gerald Lawrence. The conversation was lively, and it avoided talk about tomorrow as if it were a bomb wired to the center of the table. Patrick liked the three Atlanta men well enough. He decided that if Connor was Burt Reynolds' handsome and magnetic Bandit of the group, then Gerald was the acerbic Buford T. Justice complete with the mustache but minus the belly. Despite liking them, there was a one-upmanship and swiping between the three men that he hoped they resolved before they took it up on the mountain.

The radio in the corner crackled to life. The same DJ from earlier announced, "No verdict yet in the Crooke trial. We'll have the latest on this and more at ten."

Wes whistled through his teeth. "I guess four hours was wrong. What do you think it means?"

Henry shook his head. "This is outside my area of expertise."

Patrick, unfortunately, had more experience with murder trials than the others. The lawyers had always said that the longer a jury took, the worse it was for the prosecution. He told himself it would be fine. The jury would make the right call. It had to. Otherwise, he didn't know how he'd live with the guilt of choosing Mount Rainier over his family.

CHAPTER TWO: WAIT

BUFFALO, WYOMING
AUGUST 23, 1978

Susanne

THE MORNING SUN was already burning off what little mist lingered over the cottonwoods and willows along Clear Creek. The Flints' living room was thick with the smell of coffee and what Vangie Sibley called cinnamon whack bread, the kind you hammered out of a Pillsbury tube on the countertop. In the kitchen, Susanne Flint sloshed around the last inch in the Mr. Coffee carafe, gauging whether to make a fresh pot. She'd made three since six that morning, which was a dead giveaway to anyone who knew her that she was nervous as a long-tailed cat in a room full of rocking chairs. She decided no and returned to her friends.

Kathy Bergman perched on the edge of the couch, picking nervously at the hem of her v-neck sleeveless top, while Vangie, five feet nothing and full of morning sass, made slow work of licking cinnamon icing off her fingers. The three women were trying not to stare at the radio on the end table, a battered Realistic AM/FM model whose plastic handle had been replaced with one of Perry's old belt straps after the original broke. The dial was set to 1450 AM, which was mostly sports and cattle futures except for the news, and the volume was turned low.

"The jury's probably back in session," Kathy said, glancing at Susanne. "Don't you think?"

"According to Max, they went back in at nine, and the judge told them to cut their morning break in half." Susanne managed to sound neutral, but her voice had that two ticks from a migraine burr she'd developed over the last few years. She'd taken her prescription medicine half an hour before, and she prayed it would do its magic.

"So, it sounds like he wants them to be done by lunch."

Vangie snorted softly. "That's how I scheduled my labor when I had Hank."

Kathy giggled, and Susanne surprised herself by smiling, despite her stress. She liked these women. She missed her sister back in Texas, although they were a few years apart and not especially close. Their sibling bonding involved the side-by-side consumption of mashed potatoes, so Susanne had surrounded herself with a girl posse of friends during her growing up years. After she married Patrick, her mother-in-law Lana actually became her closest friend. Thinking about her brought a wave of sadness.

The move to Wyoming had condensed her relationships to Patrick and the kids, primarily because Susanne didn't have much in common with the ranch-hardened and winter-toughened women she met there. Until she met Vangie, then Ronnie Harcourt who was Susanne's former neighbor and Johnson County deputy and was missing this get together due to work, and now Kathy. There were only so many women in town who would show up for coffee at nine a.m. on a Wednesday to discuss a murder trial, and these were the type of friends to do it, not the least because, like Susanne, they had a vested interest in the verdict.

The trial, of course, was the trial of Bella Crooke. Bella had been her daughter Trish's cheerleading sponsor and the widow of wealthy local rancher, mountain climber, and amateur archaeologist Ichabod Johnson. Most notably, though, she was the accused murderer of Whitney Saylor, a nurse who had been Kathy's close friend. The case had been so lurid that the Sheridan newspaper had gone from weekly to bi-weekly just to keep up with it. But what really glued it to Susanne's nerves was how close it had come to home. Whitney had planned to climb Rainier with Patrick. Instead, Patrick had found her face-down in Clear Creek two months before with a broken neck. For a while, the police had looked at Susanne as a suspect under a jealous wife theory, which had been a horrible experience. Now, Bella was waiting in jail for the jury to decide whether to convict her.

"I wonder if that creepy guy from the back row is still hanging out in the courtroom" Kathy said.

"Probably. He looked like the kind of guy with no job to keep him from attending court every day. Did anyone ever figure out who he was?" Vangie asked.

Susanne shrugged. She hadn't seen the guy with the scraggly grayish blonde ponytail and Grateful Dead t-shirts before he started showing up at the trial. "Not to my knowledge."

There was a sudden thump in the garage, followed by the unmistakable cursing of Susanne's father-in-law. Since he'd been widowed and come to visit, he spent most days puttering around the garage or the detached shop, slowly converting Susanne's life into a catalog of minor complaints and errands that had no end in sight.

"Damned thing must be welded shut," Joe shouted from the garage.

Susanne set her coffee cup down with a click. "Excuse me. He'll just keep at it until he breaks something, or himself."

Kathy looked alarmed. "Do you want me to—?"

"Nope. I've got it. Back in a minute. Don't change the station," Susanne said, and made her way through the laundry room, slipping her feet into the battered Dr. Scholl's she kept at the back door.

She found Joe standing in the garage, hands braced against the overhead door, legs splayed like he was expecting a tornado to rip through the creek bottom. His hair was thin at the temples, and he'd shaved the mustache, but he still wore the same plaid shirts and creased khakis he'd worn since she'd first met him back when she was in high school. Standing with his head cocked observing Joe's spectacle was Ferdinand, the Flints' Irish wolfhound.

"Make room, please," Susanne said, and planted her own hands on the bottom panel. "Lift on three."

He rolled his eyes. "I tried that. I even asked the damn dog to help, which he did not do. Worthless mutt."

Ferdinand wagged his tail.

"You try it with me, old man." She gave him a look, and he relented, moving his hands back to the bottom edge.

"One, two, three," Susanne said, and they both heaved. The door, sticky on its ancient springs, gave a groan and then glided upward with surprising ease.

"All good?" she said.

Joe huffed. "I could have done that."

"You could have," she agreed, "but your shoulder would have been in a sling for two weeks."

He gave her the squint he reserved for politicians and insurance salesmen, but a faint smile played at the edge of his mouth.

"You're welcome," she said.

She left him to grumble at the dog in the garage and made her way back into the house, where the air felt about ten degrees hotter than outside. Kathy and Vangie were exactly as she'd left them, but now joined by the faint, electric buzz of anticipation from the radio they'd turned up.

Susanne refilled her mug, restarted the Mr. Coffee, and went to sit on the ottoman beside the couch. "Joe sure likes to have something to fuss about."

"Same," said Vangie, a wicked spark in her eye. "Except my something is named Henry."

"You think they'll let Bella out?" Kathy asked, tugging again at the hem of her shirt, which was getting stretched out. "I mean, if it's not first-degree, does that mean she walks?"

Susanne shook her head. "Max said they're still pushing for manslaughter if the murder charge doesn't stick. But he thinks she'll get at least second-degree. She's made herself so unlikable it's basically a community service just locking her up."

She'd never liked Bella, not when she'd started showing up at football games in a fur jacket and go-go boots, not when she'd insisted on organizing elaborate, mandatory bonding events for the cheer squad, and definitely not when she'd almost run Susanne off the road last October.

She looked at the clock. "Verdict's probably an hour out, at least based on Max's guess this morning."

Vangie wrapped her fingers around her mug and glanced up at Susanne. "So, how *is* Joe settling in? Really?"

"He's difficult. I'm sure he's sad, but that's not what is coming out of him."

Vangie snorted. "You want me to sneak him one of my apple strudels? It might put him in a food coma for the weekend."

Kathy smiled. "At least you have an extra set of hands for home repair."

"I do," said Susanne. "Though if he keeps 'fixing' the garbage disposal, I'll be the first woman in Wyoming to murder her father-in-law with a melon baller."

This got a laugh from both women. Susanne noticed her headache had retreated a bit. She let herself relax, and her thoughts floated to her kids, who'd started school that day. Trish's senior year, Perry's freshman. Puberty and his natural ferocity had landed him on varsity football roster as the youngest to achieve that honor at the school since the fifties.

"Perry's excited for football," she said aloud. "But you can already tell he's anxious. He keeps pretending he's not, but then he'll come downstairs with all the pads and gear on and just sit there, like he's in suspended animation until the first whistle of the season."

"He's going to do great," Kathy said. "I dropped by practice last week after we were doing athletic physicals at the school. He's quick!"

"The way he hits, he's going to knock himself unconscious before October," Vangie said. "But hey, that's what makes men out of them, right?"

Susanne tried to smile. "That's what Patrick says. Meanwhile, Trish's only interest this year is sending letters to Ben."

Kathy's face fell. "Is he still...?"

"Working in Alaska," Susanne finished.

Vangie made a face. "He's working on a salmon boat and renting a room in a by-the-week boarding house across from the docks." Before he graduated high school, the Sibleys had fostered Ben. Susanne knew they missed him almost as much as Trish.

"Do you wish she'd move on?" Kathy asked gently.

Susanne hesitated. The answer, as always, was yes and no. She wanted her daughter to be happy and safe, not spending her senior year mooning over a boy, especially since it was unlikely they'd end up together. *Although Patrick and I did. High school sweethearts forever isn't impossible.* But she also wanted Trish to know what it felt like to care about someone. Last winter, Ben had been framed for a drug offense in Laramie and run away to Alaska, cutting Trish off when he did, supposedly for her own good. Trish had closed up, barely eating or talking. She and Ben had since reconciled, and he'd been cleared of any charges. If his letters kept her afloat, Susanne figured it was better than watching her daughter slowly waste away.

"She'll be okay," Susanne said. "She's resilient."

The air in the house had grown sticky and close, like rain was about to fall. Susanne crossed to the bank of new windows facing the creek and slid one open. The mechanism was smooth, a point of pride for her. She'd fought tooth and nail with Patrick for months to justify replacing the drafty old ones. Double-glazed, shatterproof, and expensive as sin, but the energy bill was half what it used to be. Perry had even managed to hit one with a baseball bat without breaking it.

"Look at these," she said, unable to resist a little triumph. "You could drive a tank into these windows. I dare anyone to try."

Vangie raised her coffee in salute. "I don't know how you got your penny-pinching husband to do it, but maybe you can teach me your secrets."

Kathy laughed. "You should see what we're dealing with at our new place. Wes won't let me hire a contractor, so every project turns into an episode of the Keystone Cops." The two were remodeling a house to move into together after their wedding.

"I can send Joe over if you want," Susanne offered.

"Over my dead body," Kathy said, then laughed. "No offense."

"None taken," Susanne replied.

She looked out at the backyard through the window, where the creek wound slow and low in its August bed, and the cottonwoods threw dappled shade over the battered picnic table near the creek bank. From here, the world looked almost normal. Butterflies, friends, and small-town rhythms. But Susanne could feel her own anxieties lurking just outside the edges of the frame. Her fall class schedule at Sheridan College, the grant proposal she'd promised Professor Seth she'd finish by Labor Day, and the growing suspicion that Patrick's pursuit of dangerous and time-consuming activities away from their family would never end.

She pressed her palm against the cool glass and willed herself to let it go, just for a minute. "We should celebrate something," she said.

Vangie raised an eyebrow. "What?"

"I don't know. Something. Like we made it to Wednesday without the house burning down."

Kathy's eyes lit up. "Actually, I do have something. But it's kind of... Well, it's a thing. And I don't want to jinx it."

"Tell," said Vangie.

Kathy took a deep breath. "Wes and I set a date. October fourteenth. Just a small wedding, really. Close friends, nothing too formal. But I want you both to stand up with me."

There was a tiny silence, then Susanne and Vangie started

talking at once, their voices overlapping in congratulations and questions.

Susanne was genuinely touched. She'd known Kathy less than two years, but the friendship was the real thing. She hugged her, briefly, then stood back, self-conscious. "You sure you want me in front of people? I'm a menace in heels. I'll probably fall into the wedding cake."

"I want both of you there," Kathy said. "I know it's soon, but if I wait, Wes will have a nervous breakdown. He can barely stand to be away from the hospital, and if I try to make him plan a big wedding, he'll run off to the Peace Corps."

Vangie snorted. "He'd make a very irreverent missionary."

They all laughed.

By eleven, the heat was creeping in, and the coffee was mostly gone. Susanne rinsed the mugs and washed the pot because it gave her hands something to do. Even in the worst days, after Billy Kemecke broke into their house and terrorized Susanne and later nearly killed Trish, Susanne's main response was to make chili and freeze it by the gallon. Now, with Joe shuffling around the house like a resentful ghost and Patrick climbing mountains as if the only way to get perspective was to look at the world from fourteen thousand feet, she felt less like a person and more like a pack mule shouldering everyone's load and all their feelings.

She'd been so deep in thought that she nearly jumped when the phone rang. She wiped her hands on a dish towel and picked it up. "Flint residence. Susanne speaking."

"This is Max. The jury is coming back into the courtroom at noon. Just got word from my assistant. You want me to call after?"

"Please do. But we'll be tuned in to the news on the radio, too."

He lowered his voice. "It's going to be guilty. The only real question is how many years."

She swallowed. "Thanks, Max."

She hung up and turned to the women. "They're coming back at noon. Max thinks they'll have a verdict."

Vangie bit her lip, a small crease in her forehead. "You think they'll lock her up for good?"

"Long enough to keep her away from anyone we care about, I hope," Susanne said, a little sharper than she meant to.

The phone call seemed to take the air out of the room. Even the radio, which until now had been cheerfully advertising back-to-school sales in Sheridan, seemed to get quieter. Conversation grew stilted. Silences grew longer.

At eleven thirty, Kathy gathered her things and hugged them both, promising to keep them posted about the wedding plans. She was on nights at the hospital that week and needed some sleep. Vangie lingered behind, hands folded in her lap, and when Kathy was gone, she cleared her throat.

"I need to tell you something," Vangie said. Her voice was soft, which for her was rare enough to make Susanne take notice. "And if I don't, I'll lose my nerve."

Susanne sat down beside her and reached out, not quite touching her arm. "What is it?"

"I'm pregnant again," Vangie's eyes were wet, but she smiled, big and toothy.

For a moment, Susanne didn't breathe. Vangie had lost two babies since Hank's birth and faced miscarriages before it, too. Each time was a little later, each time a little harder to talk about. A specialist in Denver had warned her not to try again, but she and Henry had never been much for following rules.

"That's wonderful," Susanne said, and meant it.

"I'm terrified." Vangie's voice broke. "But I want to hope."

"Hope is half the job," Susanne said, and hugged her tight.

They stayed that way, quiet, until the reporter's voice came on the radio. Both women leaned forward, barely able to stand waiting for what they prayed would be good news.

CHAPTER THREE: SURVIVE

Buffalo, Wyoming
August 23, 1978

Perry

Perry Flint stood in front of the main entrance to Buffalo High School with his brand-new varsity gear bag slung over one shoulder and his fall schedule in his hand. The doors were a set of wide glass slabs framed in aluminum, their smudged surfaces giving back the distorted reflections of a hundred other kids in bell-bottoms and Wranglers crowding the front steps. Perry, in his cleanest pair of jeans and a faded cloud-blue t-shirt, felt as out of place as a Corgi at the Iditarod.

The varsity bag was more than just a prop. It reeked of fresh vinyl and gym sweat, the latter from the previous owner, who'd graduated last year and left it in his locker. The black electrician's tape on the handles was new, though, and the FLINT across white duct tape on the side was courtesy of his own left hand and a fat Sharpie. Perry shifted the bag, scanned the crowd for any sign of Trish, and considered just sitting on the curb and skipping the whole day. The only thing that kept him moving was the mental echo of his dad's voice, words he'd repeated to Perry over and over. *Wolverines go in teeth first.*

He wiped his palm on his jeans and pushed through the doors. The air inside pulsed with shouts and locker slams and the occasional screech of a skateboard wheel going where it shouldn't.

He headed toward the locker he'd been assigned at registration, counting steps and reciting his combination. Thirty-four, seventeen, forty-one. The hallway was a river of bodies, and twice he had to sidestep. Once because of a couple making out by some lockers and the other because of a cluster of girls wailing over a torn Seventeen magazine. His schedule, already dog-eared, said he'd start in Algebra 1.

He caught his reflection in a trophy case as he walked by. Tow-headed, cowlicked, eyes as blue as his dad's, and looking as nervous as he felt. No matter what his mom said about projecting confidence, Perry wanted invisibility today.

A wall of upperclassmen blocked the stairwell. Perry recognized three varsity linemen. Chuck, Billy, and the terrifyingly huge junior whose actual name was Chad but who everyone called Meat. They were holding court, slapping backs and retelling their summer exploits like war veterans. Chuck noticed Perry and gave him a nod.

Meat shouted, "Look out for the baby wolverine."

Then he saw Larry Childs, one of the starters on special teams. Larry looked away as soon as his eyes met Perry's. Coach Cantrell had been alternating Perry in and out with Larry during practice. There was a slim chance Perry was going to beat him out of the spot.

Perry managed to squeeze past and find his locker. The combination clicked on the third try, and he dumped his gear bag and school supplies in it. He didn't have time to second-guess his route because the warning bell shrieked, and the entire hallway surged toward the classrooms like a herd of spooked pronghorn. Perry let himself get carried along.

At the threshold of his classroom, he stopped. Inside, half the seats were already filled. The smart kids were up front. Perry picked a seat in the third row, just close enough to hear but not close enough to be noticed by the teacher.

As he settled in, his mind replayed the conversation from last night's dinner table.

Trish had barely looked up from her beef stew as she coached him. "Just remember, you're the only freshman on varsity, which means you have a target on your back the size of the end zone."

His mom had said something about be yourself, which Perry was pretty sure meant pretend to be someone else until you get through this year alive.

But it was Grandpa Joe's feedback that stuck. "You want to survive? Don't get soft." Grandpa Joe had not, in recent memory, said anything that wasn't a criticism, so Perry suspected this was as close to love as the old man would get.

His attention returned to the classroom. The teacher was a tall, stringy man with a thin, dark mustache who stalked in and scrawled MR. COKER on the chalkboard. Without so much as a roll call, he launched into the world's fastest syllabus dump, punctuated by chalk explosions and references to intellectual discipline. Perry tried to keep up, but by the time Coker got to the syllabus, the numbers on the board were already blurring. Perry's secret—well, not so secret if you'd seen his last six report cards—was that he stank at math. His dad said it was because he didn't try. His mom said it was because his brain was too creative for numbers. Trish said it was because he was one third idiocy and two thirds pig-headedness. Perry didn't know why, but when he stared too hard at words or numbers, the characters got scrambled up, which made it really hard to get answers right.

Fifteen minutes in, the only thing Perry had written was CH 1: REAL NUMBERS. He looked up and caught the eye of a girl two rows over. She had dark hair, almost black, and wore a white turtleneck even though it was over eighty degrees outside. She noticed him, cocked her head like she recognized him from somewhere, then gave the tiniest possible wave. Perry immediately forgot the entire number line and instead spent the next ten minutes running through every possible prior interaction he might have had with her and coming up blank.

He was still zoning out when the intercom bleeped and a voice rattled over the speaker. "Good morning, Bison! Today is August 23, 1978. Please stand for the Pledge, which will be led by your teacher. Have a blessed first day!"

The entire class lurched to its feet.

Perry was halfway up when Mr. Coker barked, "Sit back down," and everyone froze, mid-crouch.

"Today," said Mr. Coker, "before we start, I want to address the elephant in the room. The trial of Bella Crooke is on everyone's mind. I know it's a distraction, but I expect maturity and decency from this class. If you want to debate, do it with facts. If you want to gossip, do it on your own time."

Perry's heart did a somersault. He sank as low in his seat as physically possible. He could feel eyes on the back of his head.

Coker pointed at Perry without warning. "You. Flint."

Every molecule of oxygen in Perry's body evaporated. "Uh, yes?"

"Your dad testified, correct?"

"Uh. Yeah. For the prosecution. He, uh, found the body in the creek behind our house."

Coker nodded, not unkindly. "Must have been tough."

Perry waited for the class to start laughing, but it was dead silent.

He shrugged. "I guess it was for her family. We, um, we didn't know her very well."

The black-haired girl glanced over, this time with a different kind of look. Not curiosity. Maybe sympathy. Or maybe she was just making mental notes for the next round of rumormongering.

Coker finished his lecture on the syllabus, then assigned chapter one. Perry spent the rest of the hour staring at the blocky blue numbers in his book, wondering what people would remember more, that he made varsity football as a freshman, or that his family was entangled with the murder of Whitney Saylor.

After the bell, he hurried to the next class, which was English. The hallways were even more crowded now, and Perry got squeezed into a tide of upperclassmen heading for the auditorium. At one point, a hand clamped down on his shoulder. He twisted, thinking someone was going to shove him into a locker, but it was only Chuck.

"Hey, baby wolverine," Chuck said. "Nice game at the scrimmage."

"Thanks," Perry said, trying to keep the surprise out of his voice. "You, uh, too."

Chuck gave him a look like Perry had answered in Portuguese, then disappeared into the crowd.

In English, the teacher was Ms. Nelson, who wore an actual tie-dye scarf, like she was a time traveler from Woodstock. The class was about to start when a girl slid into the seat next to him. He realized it was the same girl from Algebra. Up close, her eyes were as dark as root beer.

"Hey," she said. "You're Perry, right?"

"Yeah," he managed.

She grinned, showing braces. "I'm Bijou. Bijou Wuthier. You don't remember me, do you?"

He shook his head, mortified. "Sorry. I'm bad with names. And, uh, faces."

"My family just moved back here. From Laramie. We had a class together in sixth grade, though. You gave me a worm sandwich."

Perry's brain whirled through possible explanations. "That was probably an accident."

"It was on purpose. You said you were conducting a scientific experiment to see if girls would die from eating worms."

He groaned. "I don't do that anymore. I mean, I don't do experiments on people."

"Good," she said, then shrugged. "I'm not a fan of worms."

They exchanged shy smiles. The bell rang, and Ms. Nelson called the class to order.

By the end of the period, Perry had managed to pay attention to half of the reading assignment. It was To Kill a Mockingbird, which he'd already read, thanks to his dad's summer reading obsession, and he'd only thought about the murder trial four times.

When class ended, Bijou turned to him. "I'm headed to the cafeteria. What about you?"

"Me, too," he said.

"We should walk together."

Perry couldn't even muster up an answer, so, he just fell in beside her, feeling a little bit lighter than when the day began.

WALKING beside Bijou through the central hallway changed everything about the experience for Perry. She was funny, quick with a comeback, and easy to talk to.

As they dodged a slow-moving cluster she said, "So, what's the deal about wolverines?"

For a moment, Perry was confused.

"I overheard a guy calling you that in the hall."

"Oh. Uh, that's upperclassmen on the football team teasing me. My parents call me Wolverine." He didn't add that his teammates called him *Baby* Wolverine, due to his size and because his Grandpa Joe yelled at him on the field like he was, well, a baby. "We're scrappy and small, but we bite like hell."

She grinned and pointed at a battered trophy case near the gym. "You're on the team?"

"Varsity. Yeah."

"You guys win a lot?"

"Not last year. But this year? Probably still not."

She laughed. “Are you any good?”

“Good enough. Last night at practice I spun out of a block by Meat Miller and sacked the quarterback."

"Meat Miller?" Bijou wrinkled her nose. "That's a person?"

"Chad Miller. He’s a junior, and doesn't like being shown up by freshmen, so," Perry did his best to shrug like it was no big deal, even though it was.

"Must make for a fun locker room," Bijou said.

"You have no idea." Perry looked down at his hands, thinking about all the hazing that summer, then at Bijou. "You ever do sports?"

"Track, in Laramie. Not great at it, though. I got second in the mile once, but it was only because the girl ahead of me tripped on her shoelace."

Perry tried to picture Bijou in running gear, but mostly he could picture her laughing. She had a great smile.

The closer they got to the cafeteria, the more Perry's stomach twisted. He braced himself as they entered, the smell of chili mac making his stomach growl. The lunchroom was a cinderblock box with bad acoustics. Tables were arranged in loose cliques of football players, cheerleaders, cowboys, nerds, and the ones who wore army jackets.

Bijou surveyed the room, then nodded toward the line. "Should we just go for it?"

Perry hesitated. "Sure. But I'm supposed to sit with football players. Rookie rule."

She pursed her lips. "Is there a penalty if you don't?"

"Maybe. Probably not officially. Want to sit with me anyway?"

"I do." Bijou marched toward the food line without another word.

Perry followed, his new shoes squeaking on the linoleum. The line was long, and the stack of trays was down to two. One with a mysterious green smear and another with a chipped corner. He offered the less gross one to Bijou.

"Chivalry is not dead." She loaded her tray with chili mac, a sad salad, and a milk carton. He copied her but added a roll.

As they wound their way toward the tables, Perry felt the eyes of half the cafeteria on them. He tried not to look at the football table but couldn't help it. They were all staring. Perry looked away, pretending he hadn't noticed.

They found a table in the back. As soon as Perry sat down, he heard footsteps and a chair scrape from behind.

A voice like a cat purring said, "Well, look who it is. Perry Flint, our newest varsity football player, in the flesh. With a girl, even."

He didn't need to turn around to know it was Jillian Tupelo. She was a senior, former cheerleading captain, and, according to Trish, the meanest person in the galaxy. Jillian had hair so red it looked like it might set off fire alarms, and she wore thick eyeliner that Perry couldn't look away from. She plopped into the seat next to Perry, uninvited, and ignored Bijou entirely.

"Uh, hi, Jillian," he said.

She leaned in close, one painted nail resting on his arm. "I watched practice last week. You're good. Tough."

He tried to pull his arm away subtly, but Jillian's grip was like a hawk's talons on a prairie dog. "I like playing," Perry said, wishing he could melt into the plastic chair.

Jillian shot a look at Bijou. "And who are you?"

"Bijou Wuthier," said Bijou, with a smile that was polite but not friendly.

Jillian's eyes narrowed, then she stood up, straightening her skirt. "Well, enjoy lunch, Perry. I'll be seeing you around a lot. At least I hope so."

She slinked away, pausing at another table to unleash the same laser-focus on some hapless sophomore.

Perry exhaled. "She's, uh—"

"She's something," Bijou finished.

Perry nodded. "You can say that again."

Bijou prodded the chili mac with her fork, then pointed at the football table. "Your friends are making faces."

He didn't look. "They're not really my friends. Just teammates."

"Do you always get this much attention?" Bijou asked.

"It's never been like this for me before."

Bijou nodded, then took a careful bite of salad. "Well, you seem nice to me, anyway."

Perry felt a sudden surge of hope. "Thanks. You, uh, too."

They ate in a more comfortable silence after. At one point, Perry saw his ex-girlfriend, Kelsey Jones, saunter into the cafeteria with her new boyfriend, Wyatt, the captain of the football team. She made a point of walking past Perry's table, her hand intertwined with Wyatt's, and shot Perry a look. He ignored it, focusing on the last bite of his roll. She was the one who'd broken up with him, after all.

Bijou said, "Hey, if you ever want to work on math, I'm not great at it, but my dad used to teach, so he taught me some tricks."

Perry almost said no, but then he remembered Mr. Coker's board and the way the numbers had swum around his head like goldfish in a tiny bowl. "I'd like that."

They walked out together, and for the first time all day, Perry felt like maybe he wouldn't get eaten alive before Christmas.

Then Meat appeared in front of them, blocking the hallway with his entire bulk.

"Hey, Flint," he growled. "You gonna show up for practice, or are you so busy making new friends that you're gonna skip, like you did on us at lunch?"

Perry looked at Bijou, then back at Meat. "I'll be there."

Meat stepped aside, but not before giving Perry a shove to the shoulder. "Don't be late, Baby Wolverine." He lumbered away.

Bijou raised her eyebrows. "Let me guess. That's Meat?"

"Yeah. He's actually pretty nice once you get past the part where he tries to kill you."

She grinned. "Sounds like most people, really."

Perry nodded. "I've got social studies next."

"Home economics," Bijou said, tucking her books under her arm. "See you later?"

"Yeah. That would be great."

Perry watched her go, then turned toward his next class, bracing himself for whatever rookie gauntlet the upperclassmen had prepared. Maybe, with some luck, he'd survive his freshman year. He thought about the way Jillian had tossed her hair and the scary way she'd flirted with him.

Or maybe not.

CHAPTER FOUR: DECIDE

BUFFALO, WYOMING
AUGUST 23, 1978

Trish

TRISH FLINT HAD LEARNED to ignore the August heat by dissociation, like the way elk could walk through snowdrifts without caring if their ankles turned blue. On the Buffalo High football field, three o'clock meant that even the track radiated with the smell of rubber, and the aluminum bleachers burned the back of your thighs if you forgot to bring a towel. The cheerleaders practiced in the west end zone, out of the way of the football team, who were on the far opposite end in a chaos of white mesh jerseys and coaches' whistles.

"Okay, pyramid, let's go! Marcy, you're up top!" The sponsor and coach, Mrs. Porter, had a shrill voice. She was actually a PE teacher at the junior high and Bella Crooke's replacement, who Trish didn't even like to think about. *I wonder if the jury has convicted her yet?*

Marcy was the first one into position, eyes locked on the goal post as she stretched. Trish followed, pom-poms limp in her hands, hair in the regulation cheer-high ponytail and tried not to roll her eyes as Marcy actually bounced into a deep lunge. There had been a time, not so many months ago, when Trish would have cared more. Now, she just wanted to get through it without catching an elbow.

The other girls shuffled into place. Cindy braced her squat. Trish dropped her pom-poms and did the same beside her. She hated being the base. She got stuck there because of her height, not her strength. Two other girls formed their base beside them. Then the climbers built the second row.

"One, two—UP!" Marcy counted, and on the "up," Cindy and Trish locked arms. Marcy climbed up their thighs to their shoulders, then up the thighs to the shoulders of the girls in the middle row.

"I did it!" Marcy said, her voice squeaky.

It was, technically, perfect. It was also deeply, deeply painful. Trish's knee twinged where Marcy's foot had grazed it on the way up, and she bit back a hiss as she struggled to stay steady.

"Hold it, hold it! YES!" Mrs. Porter howled, clipboard in hand. "For five more seconds, then down on my count!"

Trish stared straight ahead. The yellow goal posts shimmered in the heat. Just past the fence, she could see horses in a neighboring pasture, tails flicking at flies. She'd rather be there than standing in the sun with girls who had nothing better to talk about than who was cutest on the football team or if anyone had seen Kelsey Jones's tan lines and how skimpy her bikini must have been.

The count came. "One, two—DOWN!"

Marcy landed with a minor stumble, then hugged her own waist and staggered off to the water cooler. The girls in the second row stepped down. Trish stood and rotated her shoulders. She was going to have little sneaker hickies on her thighs and shoulders.

"Great job, Marcy!" called Mrs. Porter. "Trish, keep your base steadier on the next one, all right?"

Trish saluted, not smiling, and then jogged after Marcy, who had her face half-buried in a towel.

Marcy looked up, her eyes rimmed pink. "This has been the best day of my entire life."

Trish rolled her eyes. "Then you have a low bar for happiness."

"Or I'm just good at appreciating the little things," Marcy said, grinning. "You could try it, you know."

Trish re-secured her ponytail. "Yeah, well, maybe next time my little thing can be sitting in the stands with a cherry Coke and not catching a foot in the kidneys."

Marcy flopped onto the grass. "You know what? I'd still take this over the P.E. teacher's weekly mile. But if Cindy yells at me one more time for not smiling with my eyes, I'm going to replace her acne medication with white toothpaste." Cindy had taken over as squad captain when Jillian had been booted off the team.

They both laughed, which felt better than Trish expected. She plopped next to Marcy, the grass flattening beneath her. She could see Mrs. Porter consulting her clipboard, and a few yards away from her and Marcy, the other girls clustered, some in leg stretches, some fixing their lip gloss, all pretending not to be looking at the football team.

Marcy wiped sweat from her temple. "Hey, did you hear about the new girl, Bijou?"

"The one from Laramie? What about her?"

Marcy leaned closer, eyes dancing with the thrill of gossip. "I heard she was hanging out with your brother all day."

Trish raised her brows. "Maybe he'll finally be over Kelsey."

"And that's not all. Jillian was flirting with him at lunch and talking about how cute he is. I guess with Dabbo in jail she needs a new guy. Perry seems a little young for her, though."

"Not my brother!" Trish said hotly. "I'll talk to him. But in case you didn't hear, Dabbo and Jimmy are out of jail on bail until their trial."

"That's the worst. Has Jimmy contacted you?"

Trish didn't even want to think about Jimmy Gross. Jillian had set

Trish up with Jimmy on a double date with her and Dabbo once. That had turned into a nightmare that ended with Trish helping the police catch the two guys for robbing a gas station and a liquor store. "Not directly. But I've been getting hang up calls. And last weekend someone threw a paper bag of horse manure at our front door." She'd seen a blue Scout driving away after it happened, but she didn't know what either of them were driving since their release. She'd have to find out.

"Sounds like something they'd do. I don't know what Jillian ever saw in Dabbo. On to nicer guys. How's Ben?"

"He's gained twenty pounds."

"Twenty? He wasn't exactly a scarecrow before."

"Yeah, he says it's muscle from working the nets."

"Is he ever coming back?"

Trish considered, plucking at a blade of grass. "I'm not sure, but maybe not. My parents are so overprotective of me."

Marcy nodded. "Still, better a hayloft than Alaska?"

Trish grinned. "I guess. I just wish Mom and Dad would stop acting like I'm going to marry a felon and have a hundred kids in a trailer park." Ben had spent half his high school years in juvenile detention after he'd been forced to help his dad and uncle Billy Kemecke kidnap Trish. It had been a weird way to meet each other, but Ben was a good person and Trish loved him.

Marcy stretched her arms over her head and collapsed backward on the grass. "At least you have a boyfriend."

For a minute, Trish let the silence spin out. The only sound was the distant, rhythmic drone of the lawn mower over at the baseball diamond. She looked up at the sky, clear except for a single contrail.

Marcy broke the spell. "Is your dad on Mount Rainier yet?"

"Yeah. I think they start climbing tomorrow. Him and Wes Braten and Henry Sibley."

"Isn't that, like, super dangerous?"

Trish shrugged, though she felt a pinch in her chest. "Dad thrives on that stuff. He can't go six months without finding a way to put himself in mortal danger. It's like he's allergic to being safe."

"My dad's idea of an adrenaline rush is two extra shots of Tabasco on his eggs," Marcy said.

"Can we trade?" Trish said, and they both giggled, maybe a little too loud.

Over at the cooler, Cindy was pouring herself a paper cup of water. Originally Trish had thought she was an upgrade, but she'd turned into Jillian Junior.

As if reading her mind, Marcy propped up on her elbows. "You know, Cindy is already gunning for homecoming queen, and it's not even September."

"She's got to be first at everything," Trish said. "Maybe it's genetic."

"More like chronic."

Trish rolled onto her stomach, chin in her hands. "Sometimes I wonder what the point of all this is. Like, why do we practice pyramids in a town where half the bleachers are empty, and nobody cares if we win or lose?"

Marcy's reply was unexpectedly serious. "It gives us something to remember later, when we're old and have those funky blue veins in our legs."

Trish cracked a smile. "Maybe."

Mrs. Porter's whistle pierced the air, and the girls scrambled back to formation.

"Okay! Time for our timeout routine. I want this one clean, girls. Trish, you're up front."

Trish got into place. "Let's just get this over with," she whispered to Marcy.

They ran the routine—snap, twist, lunge, turn—and Trish gave it the old effort, if only to avoid being called out again. Her arms moved in perfect unison with the rest, her jump was as good as any, and when it came to the "Go Bison!" shout at the end, her voice cracked, just a little.

When it was over, Cindy muttered, "Nice, Trish."

"Thanks," she said.

Marcy high-fived her. "You were almost graceful that time."

Trish felt like all arms and legs compared to the shorter girls. "I'm saving my real disaster for the first football game."

"Not bad, ladies. Dismissed!" Mrs. Porter wrapped it up with another blow of her whistle.

The girls scattered for the bleachers, grabbing their belongings. A few students had been watching from the stands, plus a few parents, including a guy Trish had seen at the courthouse. An old dude in a faded Grateful Dead shirt. He gave her the creeps. But she forgot all about him when Jillian flounced down the stairs with two older guys right behind her. Dabbo had reminded Trish of a shorter version of the Marlboro man when she'd first seen him, but he looked sallow and thinner. Jimmy Gross was pretty much the same as ever with his droopy mustache and blond hair. Her stomach turned over at the sight of him.

"Oh," Jillian said. "I guess you guys won't want to see Trish."

Jimmy sneered. "More like she won't want to see us. If she does, she should hurry back home to daddy or she won't like what she has coming to her."

Dabbo snorted and socked Jimmy in the arm. "I think you're still sweet on her, Jimmy."

"That bitch? In her dreams."

Trish kept her eyes away from them as scooped up her bag and slung it over one shoulder. Marcy caught up.

"Are you okay?" her friend whispered.

"Let's just get out of here." Trish sped up toward the parking lot.

"Look at her run. I don't think she likes us." Jimmy's laugh was diabolical.

Marcy grabbed her arm. Together they hustled away. When they were out of earshot, Trish finally relaxed.

"They're such jerks."

"The worst. Come on. I'll buy you a milkshake," Marcy said, hopefully. "I have a buy-one-get-one coupon."

Trish shook her head. "Sorry. I have to give Perry a ride home from practice. He's not allowed to walk home until he learns to look both ways."

Marcy laughed. "That's not fair. He's all right."

"You're right, but don't tell him I said so."

"I'll ride with you. We can stop on the way, and I'll buy him one, too."

Trish considered it. Why not? "Deal."

They crossed the parking lot, heat shimmering off the cars. Trish's old truck was waiting, the windows rolled all the way up, so the interior felt like the surface of Venus. She tossed her bag in the back and flopped into the driver's seat, and Marcy climbed in shotgun, fanning herself with a crumpled envelope.

Marcy said, strapping in. "Have you told your parents you want to apply to college in Alaska?"

"Not yet."

"Maybe I'll come with you."

Trish, hands on the wheel, glanced over at her best friend. "You? In Alaska?"

Marcy smirked. "I need somewhere to wear all my best parkas."

They laughed, and for a brief second, the tension in Trish's jaw let go. Jimmy, Dabbo, and Jillian receded from her mind. Bella Crooke faded. She started the engine, and the truck growled to life. The football team had already broken up for the day, a horde of sweat and dirt and egos, their laughter echoing across the asphalt.

She watched as Perry came jogging across the grass, helmet under his arm, hair plastered to his forehead. He was talking to a kid in a white jersey who towered over him.

"Here's Perry," said Marcy. "He's so tiny."

"Don't say that where he can hear," said Trish, rolling her eyes. She rolled down the window. "Get in, Shrimp!"

Perry trudged over and threw his helmet in the truck bed. As he was about to get in, Trish got a passing glimpse of a mustached man in big, dark sunglasses and a trucker cap who rushed up to him and jerked him by the arm. Perry stumbled. The guy wasn't much taller than him, but he made up for it with menace.

As Trish watched in surprise and then anger, the man started poking Perry in the chest. "Listen you little shit. You cost my son a starting spot and you'll be sorry."

Perry stammered, "Wha-at?"

The guy shoved him into the side of Trish's truck.

"Hey!" she shouted. When the man didn't stop, she honked her horn at him. He didn't look back.

By then, Perry had squeezed in beside Marcy. He looked at Trish, then Marcy, then back at Trish. "Sorry I'm a little late. Coach made us run extra laps."

Trish checked the clock again, shifted the truck, and accelerated slowly. "I don't want Mom to freak if you aren't home on time. But never mind about that. What the heck was that guy's deal?"

Perry sighed. "I'm not sure, but I think that might be Larry Childs' dad. I mean, like, I don't know him, but Larry is the guy whose spot I may get on special teams."

Marcy patted his shoulder. "That's no reason for a dad to get on your case."

Trish cut her eyes over to him. "Would a milkshake make it all better?"

Perry pumped his fist. "Heck, yeah."

"That's settled," Marcy said. "Now, back to what we were talking about before we were so rudely interrupted, Trish. What school would you go to if you moved to Alaska?" Marcy asked.

"Wait," Perry said. "You're moving to Alaska?"

Trish shook her head. "Not now. After I graduate. For school."

Marcy raised her hand to Perry in the stop gesture. "And the answer to my question would be what?"

"University of Alaska Southern, where Ben is. Not that Dad will even talk about it. He's determined to make me go to UW and join some kind of honors track." She said the last part with finger quotes. "He's decided it's the only acceptable option. 'We need you close to home in case anything happens,' he said, which, coming from a man who is currently risking his life on a volcano a two-day drive away feels a little thin."

Marcy said, "Your parents eloped when your mom was, what, eighteen?"

"Yeah. And now they act like it's the world's biggest deal any time I try to even visit Ben. It's only two thousand miles."

"More like three thousand miles," Marcy said.

"Whatever. Same continent."

Marcy laughed, then got serious. "You should tell him. Just tell him. Maybe he'll surprise you."

Trish didn't reply for a second. "I will," she said, meaning it. "I'm done letting them decide for me. I'll be graduated. It should be my choice." The sun dipped lower, throwing gold onto the cottonwoods that lined the creek. For a moment, it looked like anything was possible. Trish closed her eyes for a half-second and let herself believe it.

They stopped at the Buckaroo and ordered three chocolate shakes. Perry was the first to slurp his down, then spent the next five minutes groaning about his ice cream headache.

They dropped Marcy at her house, which was within walking distance of the stadium. She waved through the window, her milkshake already half-gone. Then Trish headed home, the radio blaring some oldies station that Perry sang along with at the top of his lungs until Trish gave up and joined in.

At the one stoplight in town, Trish tapped the steering wheel, thinking about the conversation with Marcy, the invisible clock ticking down until graduation. She watched the light change, then pressed the gas, feeling the engine shudder.

"Hey," said Perry. "Are you really going to go to Alaska?"

Trish nodded. "I want to."

He was silent for a minute, then said, “I think you should do it.”

Trish floored the truck through the next intersection, the wind roaring through the open window, and for the first time in months, she felt almost giddy.

One way or another, she was going to Alaska. And nobody, not even her parents, could keep her from it.

CHAPTER FIVE: BRACE

Paradise, Washington
August 23, 1978

Patrick

The snow slope where TMI was conducting mountaineering school was neither the steepest nor the iciest Patrick had ever climbed, but it offered all the necessary elements. A hard crust overlaying loose granular terrain, the occasional wind scything down from above, and enough gradient that failing to dig in meant a fast ride to an unforgiving base. The volcano itself rising above, though, was so vast and indifferent that it rendered their training ground a mere snowdrift.

With Patrick at the lead, Wes in the middle, and Henry at anchor, they clomped up the drill slope, the woven blue and gold rope linking their harnesses in a literal lifeline. Each wore a helmet, a rental whose padded band made Patrick's forehead itch. Their ice axes, borrowed from the Institute's inventory, were heavy enough to be lethal if swung in anger. Or, as Wes pointed out, "They're also handy for opening beer bottles in a pinch. Just mind the business end."

Patrick had agreed to lead this section. He checked that their carabiners were locked first. "Ready for a test run?"

"As I'll ever be," said Wes, eyeing the slope as though hoping it would spontaneously level itself.

"Ready," came Henry's reply. His tone was steady, and his toed-in stance showed he'd already run the scenario through in his head. Knowing Henry, probably several times.

From down the hill, Lewis watched, arms folded. His face was impossible to read behind wrap-around glacier glasses, but the set of his jaw indicated a general skepticism toward amateurs, Wyoming doctors, and possibly humanity in general. He called up, "Self-arrests first, then team-arrests. Assume a slip at the marker, not before. You all screw up, you do it again."

"Such motivational coaching," Wes muttered as he set his feet.

Patrick led up ten paces, then pointed with his axe at the red flag planted mid-slope. "At the flag, we'll take it one at a time. I've done it before, so I'll go first."

"Showing off, huh, Doc?" Wes said.

Patrick grinned, crunched up to the flag, then turned, facing down. He imagined the slip. Perhaps a heel catching on a hidden slab, or a balance miss after a hard exhale. He did not have to imagine it for long.

Henry's "Go" came as a command, and Patrick let his feet go out as if swept by gravity.

The sensation was immediate. A lurch, a moment of flight, then the cold slap as he met the snow and flipped into the arrest position, right hand locking the axe head at his shoulder, left hand gripping the shaft, his entire body twisted to drive the pick into the slope. The jolt rattled his teeth. Snow filled his left glove and both sleeves.

Below, Lewis shouted, "Decent. Next!"

Wes, seeing Patrick's position, called, "Looks cozy! Mind if I join you?"

He threw himself down the slope with theatrical ineptitude, somehow spinning so that he went backwards before slewing around, losing his axe in the process. For a split second, he sailed helplessly, the rope going taut as he hit the limit of Patrick's anchor.

"Oof!" he said, coming to a halt in a plume of powder. "My life just flashed before my eyes. It was all cafeteria food and waiting rooms."

Lewis made a note on his clipboard. "In the real thing, you'd all be dead. Reset and try again."

Henry reset, moving up to the flag, his steps measured and efficient. At the marker, he simply fell forward, as if fainting. His axe was in the snow before his knees hit, a perfect, silent stop.

"Good," Lewis said in a grudging tone.

Patrick's forearms buzzed with adrenaline. Even practice brought the edge. The danger wasn't life-or-death here, but he'd seen the consequences of poorly executed self-arrest. Compound fractures, brain damage, worse. Wes, for all his clowning, knew it too. Patrick saw him shake out his hand and regrip the axe with a little more intention on the next go.

Between runs, Henry checked the team's knots, eyes squinted against the blowing crystals. "Want to double check?" he said, offering Patrick a look at his figure-eight.

"I trust you," Patrick said, but checked it anyway. Standard operating procedure.

The guides rotated in. Eric, the red-bearded veteran, ran his team in a different style. He offered encouragement. "Nice form!" or "Perfect brake, just like that!" Pauline mirrored his energy, catching each team member's eye and giving a thumbs-up or tip of her axe.

Their Wyoming team, Patrick noted, was more cohesive than the Atlanta crew. Wearing identical windbreakers, the southerners made it up the hill in precise lockstep, but two of them balked at the flag, only tumbling when Eric gave the order a second time.

Up above, Gill Adams and his Muckleshoot teammates moved with a grace that made the rest of them look like clumsy children.

They barely needed instruction. Their rope team flowed in unison, the self-arrests so crisp Patrick couldn't tell who led the move and who followed.

On the third run, Lewis set up the team-arrest scenario. "This time, leader falls, and the rest of team must arrest. If you don't, you're dead and your team fails."

Patrick looked back. "No pressure, gentlemen."

Wes grinned, teeth bared against the cold. "If you take me down the mountain, I'm haunting you, Sawbones. Forever."

"Duly noted," said Patrick. He knew Wes meant business when he segued nicknames from Doc to Sawbones. Without conscious thought, Patrick patted the six-inch pocketknife he carried on a holster. It had been a gift from Wes and SAWBONES was engraved on the handle.

Patrick set out, gained the marker, and, with a practiced move, threw himself out and down, legs scissoring as if truly lost to gravity. The world flipped, then yanked. The rope snapped tight, then in a heartbeat, Wes was on the snow, axe in, followed instantly by Henry's double-arm lock at anchor. The combined force arrested the slide with a whiplash that left Patrick coughing snow from his mouth.

Lewis said, "Teamwork passable. Flint, try again with less style and more realism."

Patrick spat a fleck of ice. "Yes, sir."

Three more times they practiced, each time with a different team member as the fall man, the others scrambling to brace and dig in. On Wes's turn as leader, he made the error of tripping too soon, not even at the flag. The rope coiled around his boot and he tumbled headfirst, howling. Henry and Patrick braced, but it was like trying to anchor a runaway calf—Wes nearly took them all down.

After the stop, Henry deadpanned, "If you ever do that again, I'll bury you on the mountain myself."

"Promises, promises," Wes said, then flopped on his back, laughing.

The last run, Henry led and, true to form, executed a fall so exactly at the flag that even Lewis looked almost satisfied.

At the bottom of the slope, the guides gathered everyone for debrief.

Pauline said, "Excellent work overall. Remember, these drills could save your life—or your teammate's. I encourage you to keep practicing them in your mind."

Lewis added, "Keep an eye on your gloves. If they're wet now, they'll freeze by tomorrow. Put them somewhere tonight where they'll dry thoroughly. And for the love of God, keep your axe in your hands, not your armpit."

Wes flexed his fingers and said, "Good tip. I lost feeling in my right hand two falls ago."

Eric wrapped up. "This afternoon, we move to glacier drills. Crevasse rescue. Don't eat anything heavy. Trust me."

Patrick, feeling the burn in his quads, helped gather the ropes and axes, then joined Henry and Wes at their packs for a picnic lunch. The air was brisker now, the shadow of the volcano stretching across the valley.

Wes said, "That slope is the most fun I've had outside a Slip 'n Slide in my entire life. But I still say we'd have better odds with parachutes."

Patrick clapped him on the shoulder. "If you want to haul one up to Camp Muir, be my guest. Just pack it yourself."

Henry offered a grunt that, in his language, meant agreement.

The mountain loomed behind, unchanged and unmoved, as if observing them and finding them deficient. Patrick glanced up at the sky, clear for now but already threatening new weather at the horizon.

He couldn't shake the feeling that the mountain was keeping score. And tomorrow they'd move from drills to the real thing.

PACKING up at the end of the day was at the same time the most tedious and the most relaxing part of the day, at least in Patrick's mind. There was something cathartic about the rhythm. Unclip, coil, stow, repeat. Forearm muscles half-frozen, half-raw, he found himself falling into a meditative state as he fed the blue and gold rope into a perfect butterfly coil.

Wes, beside him, used the edge of a trekking pole to knock clumps of snow from his gaiters. Through chattering teeth, he cracked jokes even as he hobbled a bit from a whack to the shin during their last drill.

Henry sorted their shared gear. He checked axes for burrs, made sure every carabiner was accounted for, repacked the first-aid kit with the same intensity he'd use to reload a rifle in a blizzard. "If you miss one of these," he said, holding up a worn locking carabiner, "you pay for it later."

"Can't be worse than the price I'm paying right now," Wes said, collapsing backward onto a patch of packed snow and groaning theatrically. "I have a bruised ego, and I may have frostbite in a place no man should have to mention."

"Cry me a river, Braten," Patrick said, clicking the rope coil shut and slinging it over his shoulder.

Wes sat up, rubbing at his thigh. "Hey, for the record, I flubbed that second arrest on purpose. Wanted to test the team dynamic, see if you guys could keep your head when the chips were down."

Patrick just shook his head, smiling. "If you say so."

"I do, Doc. You think I'd fail to self-arrest in front of an audience by accident?"

"I think you could make an accident look like a vaudeville act," Henry said, deadpan. Then he stood, hoisted his pack, and looked out over the expanse below. "Not a bad view for a day's work."

The sun hung low over Rainier's shoulder, igniting the upper reaches in gold and setting the area around them in deep, wintry blue. The air had that cool cleanness that woke up the lungs and activated the nervous system.

Pauline called over from where she was organizing the Muckleshoot crew. "Pack up and head in, guys."

Eric passed by, giving each man a glance. "Tomorrow's a full day, so eat big and sleep well."

The walk back to their vehicle was a slow, collective spasm, everyone's muscles trying to decide whether to seize or just give up. Patrick could feel the dull thump of exhaustion in his hamstrings, and even Henry, who normally hiked like a metronome, limped just a hair.

"I'd trade today for a night shift at the hospital," Wes said, "and I hate night shifts."

They set their packs in the back end of the Suburban, taking care to knock off any lingering ice so it wouldn't melt and soak through everything during the drive. Patrick started to climb in the driver's side when Wes hip-checked him out of the way.

"Uh, uh," Wes said. "You almost put us in a ditch yesterday with your cultural appreciation. My turn to drive."

Patrick yielded, though with a sidelong smile. "You're sure you can handle it? This isn't a snowmobile."

"I'll manage. Besides, Henry here can coach me if I get confused."

Henry snorted, but he didn't object.

As Wes started the engine, the car instantly fogged. They lowered the windows down for a second, letting in a blast of air that bit Patrick's earlobes. The defrost wheezed and clanked to life. The windows cleared.

Paradise Inn was their ultimate destination. The plan was to carb-load, get some sleep, and start for Camp Muir at dawn. But first they had to return to TMI in Ashford, where Patrick had forgotten his wallet the day before. To their credit, neither of the other men complained.

Wes, with one eye on the winding road and the other on the mountain, said, "I don't know about you guys, but after today I'm nothing but a shell with a strong desire for beer and lasagna."

Patrick stretched out in the passenger seat, massaging his forearm, now an impressively florid shade from wrist to elbow where he had banged it during the last run. He couldn't wait to call Susanne later, even if just to hear her voice and pretend he wasn't nervous about tomorrow.

The dashboard clock ticked past six. He could picture his family. Susanne herding Perry and Trish through dinner and Joe barking like a platoon leader, finding fault in everything. It made him smile.

"I worry about leaving Susanne with my dad so soon after Mom passed," Patrick said, mostly to himself.

Henry's face, in profile, softened a fraction. "She can handle it. Susanne's tougher than any of us, and you know it."

Patrick did know it, but it helped to hear it.

Wes took a sharp turn, then said, "My only regret is that Kathy's going to see the bruises and think I got in a bar fight again. And then she'll tell my mother, and I'll have two women in my life convinced I'm an idiot."

"Three," Henry said, "including Vangie."

The car was silent for a beat, then everyone laughed again. The road rose and fell. Wes fidgeted with the radio, twisting the dial through bursts of static, a few bars of a country song, then what sounded like a fire-and-brimstone preacher, then back to more static.

Patrick said, "Give it a rest. There won't be anything until we get closer to Ashford."

"Let the man try," Henry said, his tone amused.

Finally, Wes hit a clear patch, and a local DJ's voice piped in. "You're listening to KCTM, the Voice of the Cascades, with weather at the top of the hour. Next up, Steve Miller Band with 'Jet Airliner.'"

They all sang along, mumbling through the verses and coming alive on the chorus. Patrick was grateful for the distraction.

Then the music broke off mid-song, replaced by the urgent timbre of the DJ's voice.

"Folks, we interrupt our regular programming for breaking news. This just in from Buffalo, Wyoming—"

Wes's foot eased off the gas, unconsciously.

Patrick snapped upright. He could feel, physically, the way Henry's focus shifted from the windshield to the radio.

"In a shocking turn of events, the jury in the murder trial of socialite Bella Crooke has reached an unexpected verdict. Bella Crooke was found not guilty on all charges in the murder of Whitney Saylor. The verdict, announced just moments ago, came after a day and a half of deliberation. The courtroom is said to have erupted in chaos, with Saylor's family and local law enforcement expressing outrage at the decision."

Wes hit the brake, and the Suburban slowed, nearly to a stop.

"Again, if you're just tuning in—Bella Crooke acquitted on all charges in the Saylor murder case. More details as they come in. Now, back to the music." The Steve Miller band filled the car again.

Patrick stared at the dash, then at his own hands, which had closed into white-knuckled fists on the edge of the seat. His mind was a blur. He replayed the words, looking for a loophole or hope, but none was there.

Wes, always the first to speak, didn't. He simply sat, the car idling at the shoulder, the dashboard lights bright in the dusk.

Henry was the one to break the silence. "They let her walk."

"Jesus Christ," Patrick whispered. Bella Crooke had been acquitted. Was she still in custody, though? Or was she out? *Oh, God, she could be out.* Would she run, or would she seek out the witnesses to her crimes on the mountain? To silence them. To wreak vengeance on the posse who had brought her down to face justice.

Patrick's mind leapt to Susanne and the kids. He thought of the promise he'd made to Susanne that all this, the mountains, the training, the obsession, would never be more important than keeping them safe. And now he was a thousand miles away, useless, with the devil herself walking free.

CHAPTER SIX: DEMAND

Buffalo, Wyoming
August 24, 1978

Susanne

The night after the verdict, Susanne talked to Patrick, then she'd lain awake in her own bed, rigid, worrying about Bella Crooke, alternately sure she was being paranoid and sure she wasn't being paranoid enough. She was so upset about the acquittal that it almost eclipsed her fears about Patrick's climb. The next morning, she woke bleary, got the kids out the door to school, and made coffee, then drove into town in a shirt she realized, too late, was inside out. She was entirely focused on her destination and the conversation she'd have when she arrived.

The Johnson County courthouse squatted over Main, all corners and looming authority. She let herself in the side entrance. She climbed the stairs, her shoes echoing off the terrazzo which still smelled faintly of mop water, and was buzzed into the county attorney's office by his assistant before she even rapped on the glass.

Inside, she found Max Alexandrov at his desk. His shirt sleeves were rolled, tie loose, and a half-empty bottle of Tab in front of him. On the wall behind him, the official oil portrait of President Carter gazed down with the same faint incredulity as everyone else in the country.

He stood. "Susanne, hi. Come on in. You want coffee?"

"I've had coffee." Her voice came out flat.

He motioned for her to sit in the battered green chair across the desk, then resumed his own spot. Max's office looked like it belonged to a man being slowly entombed by paperwork. The in-basket had collapsed sideways, spilling legal pads onto the floor. There were two half-eaten donuts on a napkin next to a pyramid of used Styrofoam cups. At the edge of the desk, face-down, was what looked like a photo of a child in a Halloween costume—maybe from a case. On his credenza was a familiar photo of Susanne's sister-in-law, Patricia, who had been dating Max for over a year, long distance from Texas.

Susanne got right to it. "Bella Crooke. What in the heck happened, Max?"

"I've fielded six radio interviews and three calls from the governor's office. Everyone wants to know how this happened."

"Of course they do. Because from where I'm sitting, it makes no sense. I thought you said the jury was coming back mid-day?"

"I thought they were. It turned out they just had more questions. They didn't return until the end of the day."

"Did you see any of them after?"

Max shook his head, looking tired. "Not a one. They all took the back stairs. I think some of them didn't want to see anyone."

She considered that, but only for a second. "They didn't even find her guilty of manslaughter. Or of anything at all."

He scratched his chin, where a dark patch of stubble was growing in unevenly. His personal grooming always went downhill between Patricia's visits. "They went in ready to convict. I could feel it during voir dire. Maybe defense counsel planted enough doubt about the medical evidence. They claimed the timeline was impossible, implied maybe Whitney fell in the creek and hit her head all by herself. We didn't have physical evidence, or—" He stopped, mid-sentence. "We had Patrick as a witness, but not to the actual murder. And his testimony was tricky. Especially since they could paint a story about your family having a motive."

"A motive," Susanne repeated, letting the words rest on the desk between them like a snake. "I thought we'd done away with that before trial. Patrick did not have an affair with Whitney. There was no illicit relationship to end. I had nothing against her."

He held up both hands. "It's just what the defense does. You see enough of these, you stop taking it personal."

"I'm not here to take it *personal*, Max," she said. "I'm here to find out what you're going to do about it."

He hesitated, the moment stretching uncomfortably. Then he said, "I already requested a post-trial review. We'll go through the transcripts, look for reversible error, but absent that, she's protected by double jeopardy. I couldn't charge her again if I wanted to."

She stared at him, willing him to blink first. "So that's it?" she said, voice rising. "She walks? What about everything she did to my family? What about trying to kill my son? Trying to kill my husband? His friends?"

He looked down. "That's a separate set of charges, and you know it."

"Do I? Because I'll admit I don't understand."

"Bella Crooke will be indicted for attempted murder, likely multiple counts." He paused, then added, "Honestly, Susanne, I thought there was no way she'd ever see daylight again. And now I'm sitting here, eating crow."

"Where is she now?"

"Um, we're not actually sure."

Susanne bit down on her own words for a second, seething. "You said that in the event of an acquittal, there would be a detainer from the sheriff, and she would be held for the other charges."

He winced, just a little. "There was. It's just—" He trailed off, then started over. "Look, it all happened fast. The judge ordered the bailiff to release her. There was a moment, right after the verdict, when it was chaos. Whitney's mother fainted, the defense attorney started shouting about suing the state, and the judge was hammering for order. In the middle of all that, someone, we're not even sure who, escorted Bella out the side door. By the time we processed the new paperwork, she was already gone."

Susanne let the image wash over her. Of course. If you could walk away from a murder trial, why not just walk away altogether? "You mean to tell me she's out there? Just—" she made a vague gesture, encompassing the state, the country, maybe the world. "At large?"

"Not for long. The sheriff's department has an APB out. We know the kind of car she drives, her habits. She's not going to get far."

Susanne was not reassured. "Not going to get far," she echoed. "This is the same woman who—" She broke off. Max knew everything Bella had done. "I think you underestimate her. How long do you expect it will take her to come after my family?"

He recoiled a little. "You don't know that's what she's going to do."

Susanne bared her teeth. "What if she wants revenge. Or to eliminate witnesses. Or both. You're not going to keep her out of our lives by waiting for her to make the next move."

He leaned back, stretching his arms overhead. "Susanne, it's not going to happen. You should go home. If you're worried, lock the doors. If you get any threats, call me. Call the police. But you're going to be fine."

She stood, planting her hands on the edge of the desk. "I'll protect my own. But if anything happens to my family, I'll make it my personal mission to come for your job and to make sure Patricia knows you didn't help me today."

He stared at her, slack jawed. Then he rallied. "How about this. Let's talk with the sheriff. Together."

"How will that help?"

He was already dialing. "Bruce? This is Max. I have Susanne

Flint here. Could we come by and steal a few moments of your time to talk about Bella Crooke?" He nodded. "Thanks. See you then." He hung up. "Can you meet me at the sheriff's department in forty-five minutes?"

"Fine."

She walked out of his office, the portrait of Carter watching her go.

SHE DIDN'T WANT to go home for such a short stretch of time, so, she didn't. Instead, she walked into the Busy Bee, ordered a bottomless cup of coffee, and let her thoughts spool out. The morning regulars were mostly gone, but two men in hats sipped from mugs at the counter and a tired mom was trying to keep a toddler from grabbing jelly packets from the caddy. The radio was tuned to the local AM talk, where a host was taking call-ins about the verdict.

She listened, at first out of self-torture, but then out of morbid curiosity. Nearly every caller said the same thing. "If that woman did it, she should pay."

The waitress, a tall, friendly woman with hair the color of melted chocolate, refilled Susanne's mug.

"Sorry to ask," she said, "but are you okay?"

Susanne nearly laughed. "I am, I think."

"You want a piece of pie? Or maybe a cinnamon roll, fresh this morning."

She did, but only said, "Thanks. Maybe in a minute."

The waitress gave a nod and returned to her rounds. Susanne sipped her coffee and tried to decide what to do next. She'd promised Patrick last night that she would be extra careful. But that was before she'd even known Bella was on the loose. Carefulness now seemed almost quaint. Like double-bolting your door while an arsonist torched the house from the outside.

She drained her cup, left two dollars and a dime on the counter, and headed back to her car. There were things she could do. Maybe she'd call Vangie and see if they could stay the night out at Piney Bottoms. Maybe she'd pull the kids out of school and drive up to a hotel in Billings. Or maybe she'd just go home and keep the kids inside where she could see them and know they were safe.

Maybe she'd do all three. Or none of them.

She started the truck, shifted into reverse, and watched the mirror as she backed onto the street, checking for any sign of Bella's maroon Oldsmobile, or a glimpse of her blonde ponytail, or anything that didn't belong.

Nothing.

But that didn't mean she wasn't out there.

SHERIFF BRUCE WESTBURY'S office was the spiritual opposite of Max's. The air conditioning hummed, a silver ribbon of cigarette smoke drifted from a tray on the desk, and every piece of furniture had a worn-in, denim-smooth quality. The sheriff himself was in his fifties with a crew cut, built like a linebacker gone soft. He stood in the open doorway when Max and Susanne approached.

"Max! Morning, Susanne." He swept a pile of outdated hunting digests onto the floor from a guest chair.

Susanne sat, smoothed her skirt, and locked eyes with the sheriff. "I'm here to request a protection order for my family. Specifically, for my son and my husband. Also, for Henry Sibley and Wes Braten. From Bella Crooke."

Bruce pursed his lips, let out a slow whistle. "Well. First off, let me say I sure as heck understand why you'd be upset. This business with the Crooke woman is—what's the word, Max?"

"A travesty." Max leaned against the door frame with his arms across his chest.

"Yeah. That." Bruce picked up his lighter and toyed with it, thumb flicking over the wheel. "You really think she's coming after your folks?"

"I do," said Susanne, calm but intense. "She's angry, and she's already tried to kill them once. If that's not grounds for protection, what is?"

Bruce frowned, as if trying to add up the logic of it. "Well, normally these things require an active threat. Has she called, written, made any new attempts on you?"

"Isn't the threat implicit?" said Susanne. "But no. She hasn't. She's been in jail."

"Unless she's done something since she was acquitted, we're stuck. No judge is gonna sign off unless there's probable cause. Max, correct me if I'm wrong."

Max interlaced his fingers. "He's right. The standard's pretty high. I can file the paperwork, but unless she's made a move, the judge won't approve it."

"So, you're telling me my best option is to wait until she finishes the job she started in the mountains?"

"I wouldn't put it like that," Bruce said, a little too fast. "Look, Susanne, I know this is a scary situation. But I've got two deputies keeping eyes on your house right now. We're canvassing her usual haunts. We're motivated to find her and serve her with an arrest warrant. She's not the type to blend in. She'll pop up sooner or later."

"Forgive me, Sheriff, but my money is on her."

He bristled. "I've been doing this for a long time. Most fugitives don't get past the county line. They try to run, but they always come home. Always. My guess? She's holed up with someone from her past or maybe gone to ground out near Kaycee, where she's got kin. We'll bring her in within the week to face her new charges, and if she so much as spits in your direction, I'll have her locked up."

Susanne, who had been gripping the armrest so hard her hand tingled, said, "I want written confirmation that your department will be providing security for my family twenty-four-seven. I want you to take this seriously, not just send someone to cruise past our house while they're looking for her and call it a day."

He inhaled through his nose. "We're stretched a little thin. Big county and all, but we'll do our best. I'd recommend you talk to Chief Peabody. He's got more manpower in town than me. That said—" He leaned forward, folding his hands over the yellowed blotter. "You ever see a prairie dog hole? Sometimes the more you try to fill it in, the more they dig out on the other side."

Max nodded, like this was actual wisdom.

Susanne didn't bother to tell him he made no sense. "You're worried about looking weak?"

"No ma'am," Bruce said. "I'm worried about making you a bigger target."

She could have screamed, or thrown something, but she kept her composure. Instead, she stood and said, "Thank you for your time, Sheriff. I'll let you get back to your magazines."

Bruce took the hit. "We'll catch her, you'll see, and your people will be safe."

She gave a tight, polite smile, and turned to Max. "Can we go see the police chief now?"

He nodded. "After you."

The walk from the sheriff's office to the police chief's was short, since they were in the same building, but it felt like crossing the ocean. Susanne rehearsed her argument, each step a new permutation. Maybe she should use tears, or go full angry-mom, or drop names of people she knew in the governor's office. In the end, she decided to just be relentless.

Chief Leonard Peabody met them in the tiny waiting area. Short, careful, with wire-rimmed glasses and a beard that looked groomed by a T-square, he wore a windbreaker instead of a uniform. He ushered them into his office, then closed the door behind them.

"Bruce called to let me know you'd be on your way. Sit, please."

They did.

Leonard opened a folder on his desk, scanned it, and spoke

without looking up. “I’ve read the report of yesterday’s verdict. There’s just no understanding juries. You’d like to request a restraining order?”

“Not a restraining order,” Susanne said. “I want police protection.”

Peabody peered over his glasses. “You believe she poses a credible threat to your family?”

“Do you not?”

He considered. “According to your family, she’s committed violent acts, but the court found her not guilty of murder. We can’t act on the basis of past accusations alone. Has she attempted contact?”

“She’s missing,” said Susanne. “Isn’t that enough?”

His voice was firm. “I can’t see her lingering around here, given that she’s facing further charges. My officers will coordinate with the sheriff’s department and keep an eye out.”

“What if she doesn’t run? What if she tries to finish what she started?”

Peabody folded his hands. “Mrs. Flint, you’re not the first person in Buffalo to receive threats or feel endangered. We have a protocol. It’s worked for years.”

“I don’t want a protocol. I want protection.”

He nodded, perhaps a trace of sympathy in his expression. “We’ll do everything possible. But until she acts again, my hands are tied. I can’t commit city resources on a hunch. Not unless the mayor says otherwise. Do you want to speak with Mayor Ochoa?”

“No,” said Susanne, already rising. “I want you to remember this moment. When she does something, I want you to remember what I said. I want you to remember you could have stopped it.”

Peabody’s face colored, just a bit. “Now, just calm down, Susanne, it’s—"

“No,” she said. “It isn’t. It’s not going to be fine.”

She left, Max trailing behind, his face red.

They reached the parking area before he spoke. “I’m sorry.”

She almost felt bad for him. "I know it's not your fault."

"I should have done more yesterday. I should have had her followed after the verdict. I was so sure the jury would convict that I..." He trailed off.

She got in the truck and shut the door, leaving him outside. He walked back toward his car with a bow-legged, awkward stride.

She sat there, gripping the wheel until her knuckles went white. She'd tried the law. She'd tried the police. It hadn't worked.

But she was armed at home. They had their Irish wolfhound Ferdinand. Grandpa Joe was with them. Patrick had firearms, if it came to that.

She'd handle it, like always. She had no choice.

CHAPTER SEVEN: NOTICE

Buffalo, Wyoming
August 24, 1978

Perry

Perry's morning started with Trish hurling a hairbrush at his head when he walked in on her in the bathroom. He dodged, called her a dork, and went down for breakfast, where Ferdinand had his chin on the breakfast table watching Grandpa Joe shoveling down a stack of pancakes.

"You're dreaming, Ferdie." Perry kissed his mom on the cheek and took a plate from her hands. It held his own stack and two links. He stopped at the table and rolled a pancake around each link. "Pigs in a blanket. My favorite."

Grandpa Joe scowled. "Your mother made you breakfast. You should give her the respect of sitting down to eat it."

His mom waved Perry off. "You should get going before you're late."

He grinned at her. "Bye, Grandpa. Bye, Mom."

He crammed one whole pig in his mouth and grabbed his bags. Speaking with his mouth full, he yelled up the stairs. "I'm in the truck."

"I'm coming," Trish answered, louder than she needed to, as she ran down the stairs.

Then he was out the door. He loaded his bags into the cab of Trish's pickup. Trish climbed in her side, in a mood. He knew better than to step in front of that train, so he stayed quiet. She barely waited for Perry to shut his door before rolling backward out of the driveway, tires spitting gravel. The radio was off. He turned it on and tuned in to hear the weather.

She slapped his hand. "Hands off, Shrimp. You're in my truck."

"I just want to know how hot it will be at practice today," he said.

"Hades hot," she shot back, flicking the wipers to dislodge last night's bug massacre from the glass. "It's August."

Something snagged his attention on their dirt road—an old blue Bronco or Scout or Jeep or something, sitting a hundred feet back from their place. *Weird that it's parked there.* He watched as the vehicle, quiet and unremarkable, idled until Trish's pickup turned onto the road, then pulled out. He waited for it to pass, but it didn't. It matched their speed all the way to the highway into town.

He angled the mirror. "You know that car?"

Trish barely looked. "Which?"

He pointed. "The blue one. Behind us."

Trish craned her neck. "I've maybe seen one like it around, but not for sure. Why?"

He rolled his eyes. "It's just weird. I'm probably just being paranoid since the trial's got Mom all freaked out."

"She *is* coming a little unglued."

"Maybe it belongs to that new guy who moved in next door? Mom said he drives a CJ-5 or something." The house had sat empty for more than a year after former Judge Renkin had moved away in disgrace until someone from out of state had bought it.

Trish paused. "That's not a Jeep, genius. That's a Ford Bronco."

The Bronco continued following them. At the traffic light, it stayed four cars behind. At the high school parking lot, it veered right into the student lot like they did. It was for sure not their neighbor, he decided. His mom had told him that guy didn't have any kids, so he wouldn't have a reason to be at the high school. *Unless he works here?*

Trish nosed the truck into a slot, cut the engine, and started applying lip gloss using the rearview mirror. Perry inventoried the cars around them. There was Meat's battered Chevy, a few others he knew, and a bunch of the staff cars. But there, two rows over, was the blue Bronco. The windows were up, shaded by a sun visor. Whoever was inside wasn't getting out right away either.

Perry pretended to root through his bookbag, but really he was watching for the Bronco's driver. Seconds passed with nothing. *Is he waiting on someone?* Then, just as Perry was about to give up, the driver's door opened.

The guy who stepped out and leaned against the Bronco was not a kid, even though he was shorter than most of the teachers. Not even close. He wore sunglasses and a black windbreaker, the kind Perry saw on the mechanics at the service station, and he had a droopy dark mustache. But he didn't look up at the school or at the students but directly at Perry, as if measuring him up. Did he know him? He looked a little familiar.

Perry got out, too, watching him until he realized the man was staring back. There was a flick, the smallest of reactions, like he'd realized they'd made eye contact. Perry walked around the truck to join his sister.

"Who's that?" Perry asked, low, pointing at the guy, who was no longer looking at him.

Trish didn't even glance in the man's direction. "Probably a pervert who likes fourteen-year-old boys with blond hair."

She was already slinging her bags over her shoulder, so Perry shouldered his own and followed her across the lot. The man had vanished, although the vehicle was still there. They passed by a police car parked at the curb in front of the school, which reassured him a little. He looked over at the officer who gave Perry a salute. Perry saluted back.

Inside the school, the entry was a crush of bodies and the smell of industrial cleaner. Buffalo High had morning energy. Students swirled around Trish, some saying hi, a few giving Perry up-and-down looks. Trish made it three steps into the main hall before Jillian materialized in front of them.

"Oh my god, Trish, you look tired. Are you okay?" Jillian started, but then she saw Perry and launched into high gear. "There's my favorite freshman." She placed her hand on his shoulder, squeezing.

"We're running late. Move please," Trish said.

Jillian ignored her. "Can you walk me to class, Perry, or is your sister making you be her bodyguard?"

Perry's mouth dried up. Jillian had a weird intensity about her. The way she looked at him was different than last year when he'd just been Trish's baby brother. Less like she was joking and more like she was expecting him to play along with a game, but he didn't know the rules.

"Maybe," Perry said, voice croaking a little.

"I'll let you off the hook this once." Jillian leaned in, breath warm and sugary with cinnamon gum. "You should hang out at the north doors after last period. There's going to be a thing."

Perry's brain was still rebooting from her contact and proximity, so it took him a second to say, "What kind of thing?"

Jillian revealed her straight, white teeth with a big smile. "You'll see." She spun away, surrounded by her own clique of girls.

Trish made a noise, low in her throat. "I hate her."

"She's okay," Perry said, which made Trish laugh out loud.

"You only think that because she's flirting with you. Yesterday she brought Dabbo and Jimmy to watch cheerleading practice and practically egged them into being mean to me."

Perry didn't know whether that was a compliment or an insult, but either way, that hadn't been cool of Jillian to do to Trish. "That sucks."

They reached his locker, and Perry twisted the dial.

Instead of continuing on to hers, Trish began riffling through her purse. "You're weird this morning."

He didn't want to bring up the Bronco and the guy again. She'd poo-pooed it before. He closed his locker and faked a yawn. "It's nothing. Just a little tired."

She shook her head. "Suit yourself."

Perry decided to shrug it off. He'd probably never see the guy or the car again.

CHAPTER EIGHT: ASCEND

PARADISE, WASHINGTON
AUGUST 24, 1978

Patrick

IN HIS BED at the Paradise Inn, a lodge perched just below tree line, Patrick opened his eyes with the conviction he'd missed something crucial. The room was dark but coming alive with the sounds of daybreak. A thud and a curse from the hallway, footsteps overhead, the faint reek of bacon climbing through the floorboards from the kitchen. He lay perfectly still for a moment, running a systems check. Head clear, hands good, although his forearm still throbbed from the day before. Feet, not frostbitten or asleep. His jaw was tight, a sure sign he'd had a night of bad dreams and taken it out on his molars. He turned and squinted at the bedside clock. His four-thirty a.m. alarm would ring in seven minutes. He turned it off. The start time for their Rainier summit attempt was in two hours, but he'd only managed maybe three hours of sleep, mostly broken into ten-minute increments.

He pushed the blanket aside and sat up, careful not to wake Henry, who occupied the twin on the other side of the room, snoring with the low rumble of an idling tractor. At the foot of his bed, Patrick found his socks, crusty with sweat from yesterday's drills, and pulled them on, wincing as he hit a raw spot above his right heel. He'd been so consumed by last night's verdict that he'd failed to properly treat his own damn blisters. Some doctor. He'd take care of it after he ate.

He crept into the hallway, padded past the trophy moose, bear, and elk heads and ducked into the payphone alcove just off the main lobby whose wood beams were so massive they looked like they'd been harvested from a Tolkien forest. The phone's coin slot was jammed, and Patrick spent a minute fiddling with it, finally jimmying it open with the blade of his pocketknife. He dialed home, counting the clicks as the rotary spun back. Three rings, then the tape hiss of their new answering machine, and Susanne's voice. "You've reached the Flints. Please leave a message and we'll get back to you as soon as we can." There was a beep, then silence.

He cleared his throat. "Hey, it's me. I know it's early, but I wanted to hear your voice before we head out." He paused, feeling the dead air on the other end. While it was an hour later in Wyoming, it was still too early for her and the kids to be up. "I love you. Tell Trish and Perry the same. And Dad. Give Ferdie a scratch from me." He hung up, feeling neither better nor worse.

In the dining hall, the staff were chopping fruit, clattering pans, and laying out trays of packeted oatmeal and hard-boiled eggs for the climbing teams. Through the big picture windows, Patrick could see Rainier's silhouette in the predawn blue, the summit still lost in the clouds. A few early climbers picked their way across the icy parking lot toward the gear shed.

He found Wes in the corner, hunched over a bowl of Cream of Wheat and a mug of black coffee.

"You look like you got hit by a snowplow." Wes gave him a diagnostic once-over.

"Didn't sleep." Patrick poured himself coffee and grabbed one of the bananas, which was still green.

"The verdict keep you up?"

Patrick looked at the table, where a small heap of empty sugar packets made a hill next to Wes's mug. "I don't understand people. I just don't."

Wes grunted. "Maybe that's why you became a doctor instead of a minister." He shoveled a bite. "It's out of your hands, Doc. Now the authorities have to do their job on the attempted murder case."

"They didn't do their job last time."

Wes pointed with his spoon. "Don't let it drag you down. The mountain wants to kill you. It doesn't care about Bella Crooke."

Patrick couldn't help smiling. "I love your bedside manner."

Henry joined them a minute later, clear-eyed, dressed, and ready to go. He nodded to them both, then sat. "Weather?"

Wes jerked his head at the window. "I'm told it's degraded to marginal. They say the summit wind is a beast. Nothing we aren't used to back home."

Henry ate in silence for a while, then asked, "Anyone call home this morning?"

Patrick nodded. "I just got the machine. I'm surprised my dad didn't pick up, though. He's an early bird. Maybe he's having his morning constitutional."

Henry grunted. "Or plotting to kill the dog."

"For the record, Ferdie is the best dog in Wyoming."

Henry smiled. "Vangie said he offered to trade her a chainsaw the other morning for a .410 to take care of a local coyote problem. He was not talking about coyotes."

"Your dad's gonna outlive us all," Wes said. "Out of sheer meanness."

There was comfort in their banter. Patrick felt some of his nerves recede, replaced by a practical checklist of the climb ahead. He had it in his head, could recite it in his sleep. Clothing layers, first-aid kit, headlamp, helmet, hand warmers, water bottles, gorp. His body was the only wildcard. How well would it hold up after yesterday's drills, how much would sleep deprivation slow his reflexes, would his blister become a liability?

They finished eating, then headed to the boot room to get geared up. Wes and Henry debated the virtues of tape versus moleskin for blister prevention while Patrick applied moleskin to his hotspot. Then he tried calling home again, but this time the phone rang and rang until someone picked up.

"Hall-oh," came the voice, gravelly and a little slurred.

"Dad?" Patrick said, thrown for a second.

"Morning, son," Joe said. "Aren't you supposed to be climbing a mountain?"

"Not for another hour," Patrick said. "Is everyone okay there?"

There was a pause. "Everyone's fine."

Patrick smiled. "Tell Susanne I'm just checking in."

A snort. "She can tell you herself. Here, I'll get her up—"

But before the handoff could happen, there was a shrill bark in the background and a crash.

"Dammit to hell," Joe said. "The dog's got something again. Probably a squirrel. Or maybe one of the neighbor's chickens."

The line went dead. Patrick held the receiver for a second then hung up regretfully.

He found Wes and Henry outside, finishing up their packing. A chilly wind raced down the mountain, rattling the flagpoles and tossing the limbs of the trees on the slope beyond the parking lot. The other teams were gathering in knots around their guides, who were checking harnesses and ice axes.

Patrick tried to focus on his own gear, but his mind kept drifting. He pictured Bella Crooke's sly face. His wife, sleepy and slowly waking. The mountain, waiting, indifferent.

The guide teams called out names. Patrick's team was with Lewis. They formed up at the end of the lot, next to the battered Suburban that would ferry them to the Paradise trailhead.

Eric, the lead guide, ran through the final checklist, then gave them a short speech. "If we make the summit, it will be because we're prepared and we watch out for each other. Leave your ego here. If you're feeling slow, you say so. If you need to quit, you say so. No one gets up the mountain solo." He looked at each of them in turn.

Patrick glanced at Wes, who nodded once, eyes bright.

Henry's jaw clenched and unclenched.

Eric finished, "We've lost friends to these mountains. Everyone put safety first, and we'll all get home safe."

The Suburban was already running, exhaust steaming, and they piled in with the Muckleshoot team along with their guide Pauline. There wasn't much small talk. The weight of what they were about to do pressed heavily on them all.

Patrick found himself staring out the passenger window as they drove, watching the trees flash by. The sky was a dark, heavy blue, but the horizon was just starting to brighten with the pink of a sunrise that promised to be spectacular.

His insides were churning again. He tried to talk himself down from all the reasons for his anxiety about Susanne, about the kids, about the failure of a trial, and about what would happen if he didn't make it back. Dwelling on them only made it worse. Finally, he decided to just sit with it, at least until the climbing started.

At the trailhead, the guides doled out the final gear. They checked and rechecked harnesses, distributed radios and extra batteries, and handed out pouches of trail mix. Wes needled Henry and Patrick about who was more likely to slip and break something vital.

"Odds on Wes being the one to fall in a crevasse?" Henry asked, adjusting his helmet.

"Based on my experience as your mountain partner, better than you making it to Camp Muir without taking a leak every quarter mile," Wes said.

Eric, overhearing, said, "Just don't do both at once."

That got a laugh, the first real one of the day, and it loosened Patrick's chest a little.

And then they set out. The first stretch was a gentle slope through dense fir and cedar, the ground crunching with old snow and the detritus of last year's storms. The sun finally crested the range, lighting up the mountain in a way that was both awe-inspiring and vaguely threatening. Rainier, from here, looked less like a mountain and more like a planetary body, a force that had extruded itself from the core of the earth.

Patrick fell into step behind Lewis with Henry next and Wes at the rear. Their breath came in puffs. The conversation faded, replaced by the steady thud of boots and the whisper of snow brushing pant cuffs.

The trail got steeper. The line of climbers moved in tight single file, the guides moving up and down the column with little bursts of speed, checking for fatigue, dehydration, and the thousand small hazards that could multiply if left unaddressed.

Eric called for the first break at the flattish bench just above the tree line. Here the wind blew harder and the view of the valley below was like looking down on a planet from outer space. Everyone dropped their packs and stood around, drinking water or just staring out at the endless sky.

Dunk squatted down. "What's Phoebe up to this week with you on the mountain?"

There was a silence that made Patrick turn to see who Dunk was addressing. Connor was staring at the ground.

Gerald made a surprised face and tapped his own chest. "Oh, are you talking to me?"

Dunk capped his water and stood. "You're the one married to Phoebe. Connor and I are still living the bachelor life."

Gerald's tone was clipped. "I'm sure she's lonely. Although she's not one to endure that for long."

"We'll be back before you know it, newlywed." Dunk punched him in the arm.

Gerald drew back.

Gill caught Patrick's eye. "You have family back home?"

Patrick nodded. "Wife. Two kids. And my dad, who's more trouble than both kids combined."

Gill smiled. "Good. It helps. The mountain likes climbers with something to return to. Makes them careful."

"I hope that's true," Patrick said. "I take it you've summited before?"

Gill nodded. "A few times. In the end, it's just a mountain. Your family is what counts."

Patrick felt a lump rise in his throat and nodded.

Eric whistled, and the group shouldered packs and set out again. The next section was all up, the angle increasing until every step burned in Patrick's calves. He focused on the man ahead of him, on the bright flags of the route markers, on the simple physics of boot to snow to boot again.

He let the rhythm of it push everything else down. Worry, anger, frustrations with the world and himself. He was here, now. This was the job. Behind him, Wes kept up a steady undercurrent of wisecracking to Henry's grumbling. Patrick smiled at it, even when he couldn't catch the words.

The sun was fully up when they broke into the first true snowfield, the light so bright it made Patrick's eyes water even behind his glacier glasses. The summit was visible now, so close it seemed they could reach out and swipe the clouds off the peak. That, he knew, was an illusion. In climbing terms, their journey to the summit had barely begun.

He looked back at the valley, at the faint ribbon of road they'd come in on, at the trees and the lodge and the ordinary life laid out below. He told himself he could almost see his house from here, could almost convince himself that Susanne was at the window, waving.

He turned back toward the climb, wondering why he was so emotional this morning. Maybe it was the symbolism of taking this major step toward fulfilling his dreams. Maybe it was fear. Maybe it was uncertainty about his choices. Maybe it was his relative insignificance compared to all of *this* around him.

He hefted his pack, re-settled his helmet, and focused on his steps, already planning what he'd say the next time he reached a phone, already rehearsing it in his mind. "We made it. I love you. I'm coming home."

CHAPTER NINE: PERSEVERE

SHERIDAN, WYOMING
AUGUST 24, 1978

Susanne

SHERIDAN COLLEGE in late August buzzed with youth and energy. New arrivals circled the parking lots like hungry birds. Students stood in loose packs on the sidewalk comparing sunburns, summer jobs, and vacation stories in the scent of mowed grass and the shimmering heat. Susanne had heard on the radio during her drive up from Buffalo that record-setting heat was expected that afternoon.

She'd parked in the far lot because she preferred a straight walk to the main complex rather than navigating the chaos of Datsuns and battered trucks. Returning from a quick trip to gas up Patrick's truck after her two classes, she was carrying a brown leather satchel and dressed for the part of her research assistant job in high-waisted navy slacks she'd made herself and a sleeveless cream blouse. She reviewed her morning as she walked. She'd impressed herself by keeping pace with a kid from Montana who said he'd read all of the semester's assigned reading just for fun the summer before. He was, like most of the students, fifteen or more years her junior. It was invigorating being back in the fray.

After stopping at a picnic table to eat the ham and cheese sandwich she brought for her lunch, she headed toward the faculty offices. Professor Seth had called the day before and asked her to meet him, even though she hadn't planned to work that day. His office was in a tan, low-slung building with an entrance camouflaged by a half-dead juniper bush and a POST NO BILLS sign that had been heavily layered with flyers.

She navigated the fluorescent-lit maze to Professor Seth's office. His door was slightly ajar, and from inside came the familiar sound of his manual typewriter. She pictured the memos he produced in the aggressive, all-caps style he used for every piece of communication. He never took advantage of correction tape, and he refused to switch to a Selectric. Susanne had once calculated that, for every typo, he wasted approximately thirty seconds retyping the line.

She knocked. "Hello, Professor Seth. I'm here."

The typing stopped. A pause, then the creak of the chair. "How was your time off?" His voice was dry and a little nasal.

Professor Seth was in his mid-sixties, built like a volleyball post, and wore a rotating wardrobe of linen suits. He'd once spent a year teaching in Cairo and another in Caracas, and he claimed that no one in either city had ever once called him by his actual first name, Rami. His desk was the usual disaster area. Three open books, two uncapped highlighters, a crumpled pack of Doral cigarettes, and the battered typewriter.

In the short gap between the second summer session and the fall semester, Susanne had barely noticed she'd had any time off between their trip to Seattle and getting the kids ready for their new school year and Patrick for his climbing trip. "I'm glad to be back."

He gestured her in. "I was just working on the year's first faculty advisory. You should see what the econ department is up to." He pulled a face. "Apparently, their idea of innovation is 'no exams, all group projects.' This is why civilization crumbles."

Susanne smiled, settling into the visitor's chair. "I hope you're not hinting that I should audit Principles of Micro."

"Perish the thought. You're here for the good stuff." He riffled a stack of manila folders and came up with a brown envelope with her name scrawled on it in blue ink. "Your signed author's copy from the Review of Near Eastern Archaeology. Fresh from the inter-office mail."

She took the envelope, the thin weight of it sending tingles up her spine. She'd seen her name in the byline already, as co-author, technically, with Professor Seth listed first, but this was the official, printed version. "It's real," she said, trying and failing not to sound breathless.

He let the moment linger. "You did all the heavy lifting. I'm just the pretty face."

"Your pretty face got us published," she said. Then, a beat later, she added, "And it didn't hurt that the editorial board used to employ your ex-wife."

He barked a laugh. "Not my ex. My ex-ex." He leaned back, folding his hands behind his head as he regarded her with an affectionate, paternal pride. "It's good work, Susanne. I mean it. The bit about the late-period Egyptian metallurgy especially. I'm going to steal that for my spring seminar."

She beamed. "Steal away. That's what I'm here for."

He started to say something else, but then his face rearranged itself. The lines around his eyes pinched. "There's another reason I called you in."

The smile went cold on her lips. She waited, letting him set the pace.

Professor Seth cleared his throat, then slid a letter across the desk. "The college has instituted an immediate reduction in non-faculty hours. Effective as of next week." He said the word reduction with an edge.

She scanned the letter. The message was clear enough. In

response to state budget cuts, all research assistants, teaching aides, and part-time support were to be phased out, a euphemism that made her want to tear the letter in half and stomp on it.

She felt tears building and somehow held them back. She loved this job. "Does this mean I'm fired?"

He smiled, but it was a sad thing. "If I had my way, it would not be so."

She looked down at her hands. A freckle on the base of her left thumb stood out, a few shades darker than her pale skin. "When?"

"End of the week. I'd hoped the article would buy you a little insulation, but, alas, it did not."

She nodded. "Is there any chance the college will get the funding back?"

He shook his head, once, slow. "Not this year. When and if things improve, I'll be first in line to bring you back."

Susanne swallowed. "Does this mean I can't help with the El-Sadat project?" They'd just begun a case study on the U.S.-Egyptian arms deals, a subject she was really excited about.

He hesitated. "It would have to be unofficial."

"I'm not sure I have time to do it unless it counts for something."

"I understand."

She smoothed the front of her blouse, feeling suddenly childish. "I'm sorry," she said. "It's just... I've waited my whole adult life to feel this sense of purpose about something other than my children. I thought I was making a difference."

"You do and you will," he said gently. "You have the best mind I've seen in years, and I don't say that lightly. Get your degree, get certified, keep researching, and teach, as you've planned to do. Maybe even come back as faculty. Or go on to grad school."

She laughed. "With two kids at home?" But Trish would be moving on to college next year. Perry three years later. Maybe it wasn't entirely implausible, except for the fact that Laramie and the University of Wyoming were four hours away in *good* weather.

Professor Seth shrugged. "You'll figure it out."

She smiled, touched. "Thank you for your confidence in me and your encouragement. It means the world to me." She tucked the envelope into her satchel and stood. "And thank you for letting me know in person."

He came around the desk and put a hand on her shoulder. It felt old-school, not sexual like his predecessor, who had made improper advances toward her and several other female students. "I'll miss having you here," he said. "But you're not gone. Come see me anytime."

She left the office, her feet leaden. She wanted to do something petty and dramatic. Instead, she walked out the west door of the building, into the full glare of the afternoon sun. The heat was intense enough that it steamed the edges of the windshields. Susanne made it to the car, sat for a minute with the keys in her hand, and allowed herself a single, voiceless scream before starting the engine and driving home.

THE HOUSE WAS SHUT up tight, as she'd left it that morning, and the only sign of life was Ferdinand, who lay sprawled in the shade by the front porch, tail thumping as she walked toward the house. She almost envied the dog.

"You have no problems, do you, Ferdie?" She leaned down and scratched under his chin.

The house felt like a hundred degrees inside. When she closed the door behind her, hot air enveloped her in bands, one just above ankle height, another at her waist, and a third hanging under the ceiling like an oven. The closed windows were to blame, but she didn't care. She'd locked everything up tight before leaving, even though there wasn't a living soul for a quarter mile in any direction. After her fruitless meetings with Max and law enforcement, paranoia didn't feel like an overreaction.

She went to the dining room first, where the new windows were supposed to open with just a touch, but today were stuck. She braced both hands and tugged, cursing under her breath when it didn't budge. *Maybe it expanded in the heat.*

"Wonderful," she said, and made a note to herself to get Patrick to take a look when he returned from the climb. She didn't dare ask Joe to do it. If history was any indication, he would complain, curse, and ultimately break the window.

Instead, she used the window issue as an excuse to turn on the air conditioner. Patrick made a great living, but it hadn't changed his miser tendencies. To him, saving electricity was next to godliness. *What he doesn't know won't hurt him.* She breathed a sigh of relief when she heard the system kick on.

In the living room, the curtains were drawn against the sun but even so, the deep color of the light filtering in made it look like the floor was bleeding. She jumped when a rattling snore came from the couch. Joe was splayed out, one leg hanging off, the other bent so his calf was on the armrest. He slept with his mouth open, every few breaths turning into the snore that had just startled her.

She tapped his knee. "Joe. You awake?"

He snorted himself upright in a single motion, blinking. "I wasn't sleeping," he said, voice gravelly. "Just resting my eyes."

She smiled. Arguing with him was pointless. "Just wanted to tell you I'm back." For a moment she considered telling him she'd lost her job. He hadn't seen a reason for it in the first place, so she didn't. She needed to talk to someone, though. Patrick was her first choice. But she couldn't talk to him. Maybe she'd call Vangie or Ronnie later. "Have you seen anyone around today?"

He squinted at her. "Nope. Although I was gone most of the morning. Had to make a trip to the hardware store." Joe loved leisurely trips to argue with other men his age at the hardware store almost as much as piddling in the garage. "Since I got back, it's been quiet. Except for that damned dog." He pointed toward the porch with a thumb. "He barked for twenty minutes straight, like a maniac. Probably another raccoon."

"Did you go outside to see what he was upset about?"

He gave her the look he used on slow clerks. "I don't need to go outside to see a raccoon when I can hear that dog. He's a menace."

She shook her head. "He's not a menace. He thinks it's his job."

"His job," Joe repeated, flat. "Huh."

She changed tack. "So, you didn't see any cars or people near the property?"

He grunted. "Only car I saw was the mail truck, same as every day. That girl who drives it now, she's got more tattoos than the inside of a jail cell. I told her that yesterday, too."

"Let's not run off the mail lady. Please."

She moved into the kitchen, sighing, poured herself a glass of cold water, and leaned against the counter, trying to decide what to make for dinner. There was always the option of breakfast-for-dinner, which made the kids happy, or she could try to use up the last of the produce before it became more soup than salad.

Joe lumbered in behind her. He poured himself a glass of milk. Ferdinand had come around to the back of the house and pushed his nose against the window glass, tail wagging. Joe muttered, "Out of control."

She watched them both for a moment. The dog with his earnest face, the old man with his stubborn jaw. She felt the tightness in her chest loosen, just a little. Losing her job had been a blow. She missed Patrick. She was worried about her family's safety with Bella in the wind. But maybe she was making things bigger than they needed to be. Bella really could be long gone. Certainly, everything here seemed fine.

Maybe she just needed to believe everything would be fine, like Max, the sheriff, and the police chief had told her to do.

CHAPTER TEN: RESCUE

Buffalo, Wyoming
August 24, 1978

Trish

Trish waved goodbye to Marcy as she got into her truck after practice. Perry was going out for burgers with half the team, which meant Trish could spend the next few hours in peace. She could even take a shower that lasted more than four minutes.

Something familiar caught her eye as she started the engine. Something big and blue across the parking lot from her. It could be the same vehicle she and Perry had seen that morning before school. With the sun in her eyes, she couldn't see anyone in it. *Or maybe it's that blue Scout I saw by our house last weekend.* If her theory was right that Dabbo and Jimmy were the ones who had been tormenting her, they might be the drivers of the Scout, back to pick on her again, since they'd been here at the stadium the day before.

If so, maybe they hadn't seen her. She backed out quickly and headed toward home.

She rolled up the drive, gravel pinging off the bottom of the old truck. There was no sign of her dad's truck, which her mom was driving since he'd taken the Suburban to Washington. There wasn't even a Ferdinand greeting committee, which meant the dog was either napping in the shade, or out back trying to dig through to China again. Or maybe he'd finally succeeded.

Trish fished her bags from the floorboard, peeled her thighs off the sticky vinyl seat, and banged the door shut, then walked in through the open garage door and into the laundry room, which was, as always, the hottest room in the house with a detergent smell that hurt her head. She almost tripped over a heap of laundry. It was unlike her mother to let it pile up. She considered tossing it in the wash herself but kept going.

She called out, "Hello," expecting her mom or grandpa to reply.

No answer. Even the dog didn't bark.

She dumped her stuff and went straight to the fridge, hoping for lemonade. All that waited for her was a half-empty pitcher of watery iced tea. She grabbed it and chugged straight from the spout, then left it empty in the sink. Mom's handwriting waited for her on a note stuck to the refrigerator door with a magnet. GETTING GROCERIES. BACK SOON. GRANDPA HOME.

She poked her head into the living room. No sign of Grandpa Joe. There was a slight depression in the couch cushion, like he'd just gotten up. Maybe he was in the bathroom or in the shop out by the barn.

The phone rang. She went back to the kitchen and answered. "Flint residence, Trish speaking."

"Bitch." Click.

She stared at the phone as it began emitting a dial tone, then shivered. That was worse than a prank hang up. Jimmy and Dabbo were trying to scare her. She couldn't let them win. She went to the front door and looked outside. No one was there. Of course they weren't, because they'd just been on the phone to her. She locked the door, then went around the house locking the others. If Grandpa Joe came back, he'd just have to ring the doorbell.

She sprinted up the stairs, two at a time, and stripped down to her underwear in the bathroom. She gave herself a brief once-over in the mirror. Ponytail hopeless, sneaker marks on her shoulders and thighs. She pulled out her hair band and turned on the water.

The shower was divine. She stayed in until the water ran cool. By the time she emerged, wrapped in a towel, she felt almost reborn.

After she was dressed, she headed downstairs. The house was still weirdly silent. Since no one was home, she decided to call Ben. If she kept it short, maybe her parents wouldn't get mad at her when the long-distance bill came. She padded to the kitchen phone and dialed his number, heart starting to thump as soon as the first ring buzzed through the receiver.

The proprietor of the boarding house answered, and she asked for Ben.

There was a clatter, the faint sound of a vacuum or blender, then a muffled shout, "Somebody get Ben. It's Trish. Tell him to hurry!" A pause. Footsteps pounding on stairs.

Then, a minute later, Ben's voice, fuzzy with static and familiar. "Trish?"

Trish's cheeks flushed. It was weird hearing him on the phone, weirder than reading his letters or seeing the smudgy polaroids he tucked in his letters sometimes.

She sat on the floor, knees up, hand twisting the phone cord. "Hey! You have today off, right?"

"Yeah. Wednesday's my only day. You wouldn't believe how much I slept. Almost all morning." There was a pause, then he asked, "How's cheer?"

"It's the same. Cindy is acting like the queen of Sheba, and everyone's already betting on who'll get homecoming queen."

"Who do you think it will be?"

"Marcy wants it bad. But it will probably be Cindy. Or Jillian."

"Or maybe you."

She laughed. "Encyclopedia Flint is not the type to be elected homecoming queen."

They chatted about school for a while, about practice, about the principal's new rule banning tube tops, and the verdict in the Bella Crooke trial.

Ben sounded worried. "I thought she was guilty."

"She was. But the jury didn't think so. Mom is flipping out over it."

"Why?"

"Because they turned her loose. Everybody says she's rich and is probably long gone like to Europe or something. But Mom sees the boogeyman in every corner. She thinks Bella will be out to get Perry and Dad because they caught her and turned her in."

"Be careful. I couldn't stand it if anything happened to you."

"I will. I promise." She smiled, even though she knew he couldn't see it. She loved that he worried about her.

"Did you talk to your parents about UAS?"

"I chickened out."

"I get it. Your parents scare me, too. It would be so great if they let you do it, though."

"Maybe you could even go to UAS with me."

There was a long silence. Had she said the wrong thing?

Finally, he said, "Don't get your hopes up. I like what I'm doing now."

She didn't push him. "Well, anyway, I'm, like, one hundred percent doing it this weekend. No matter what."

He got quiet again, but this time it was more comfortable.

"Are you coming back for Thanksgiving?" she asked, and her voice came out way more needy than she'd meant it to.

"Yeah. I already bought a bus ticket."

She heard a rattle in the background. Then a voice yelled, "Wrap it up, lover boy! It's long distance."

Ben covered the mouthpiece, but she could still hear the muffled, "Shut up."

Trish felt the timer ticking in her head, too. "I should go. If Mom checks the bill and sees this, I'll be grounded for life."

"It's great to hear your voice."

She hesitated, then said, "I miss you. I love you."

Ben exhaled. "Me, too."

His response wasn't satisfying, but she knew he was standing at the reception desk with other people around. "Write me," she said.

"I will. You, too. Bye, Trish."

"Bye, Ben."

The phone felt heavy in her hand. She let the dial tone hum for a few seconds, almost like if she didn't hang up she could prolong the connection. Then the off the hook sound started. Finally, reluctantly, she put the receiver in the cradle.

She was in the pantry for some Fritos and a can of bean dip when she heard a weird thumping sound. At first she thought it was tennis shoes in the washing machine, but then she remembered it hadn't been running. Plus, the sound was coming from a different direction. It was more like someone smacking a wall, then a pause, then another. And was that shouting?

She headed for the back door, where Ferdinand met her on the deck. "There you are. Where have you been?"

The dog whined, tail helicoptering with excitement. The late afternoon sun was blindingly bright. She scanned for any sign of Grandpa Joe but didn't see him. Instead, she heard the noise again. A bang, then a shout. Definitely a person.

She circled the side of the house, the grass so sunburnt it crunched under her feet, yelling, "Grandpa?"

No answer. The thumping had stopped.

Ferdinand spun around into the backyard, nose to the ground. Trish followed, careful to avoid the sandspurs. As she rounded her mom's garden full of bright red tomatoes, the sound returned, louder. Then she realized where it was coming from. The old storm cellar behind the house, a relic from the years when there had been a homesteader's house on this land.

She hustled over to its big metal hatch sitting flush with the ground. Her heart rate picked up. The pounding started again.

"I'm here!" she shouted, dropping to her knees. "Grandpa?"

"Open the damn door!" His voice was muffled and absolutely furious. Ferdinand barked crazily, leaping at the hatch like he thought he could dig through it.

Trish wrapped both hands around the rusty ring latch and yanked. It didn't budge. She tried again, but the thing seemed stuck tight. Inside, she heard another volley of cursing and what sounded like Grandpa Joe thumping the hatch with both fists.

She straightened. "I can't get it to open! It's stuck!"

"Get help!" he bellowed, then coughed. "Or a damn crowbar!"

She ran back to the house in a panic. She didn't know what to do with her mom still gone. Should she call 911? Was it an emergency if your grandparent just locked themselves into a bunker? She went into the garage and surveyed the tools. She grabbed a claw hammer that looked like it might work and dashed outside again.

At the hatch, Ferdinand was pawing and whining.

"Move, dog," she said, nudging him aside.

She jammed the hammer's claw under the lip and pried, hard. For a second, nothing happened, then the whole thing groaned and shifted. She threw her weight into it as Ferdinand barked encouragement. With a shriek, the hatch lifted two inches, enough to catch with her fingers. She stepped on the handle of the hammer and, finally, it swung open enough that it nearly smacked her in the face.

A blast of musty, hot air came up. She lifted it the rest of the way open. Grandpa Joe's head, red-faced and glowering, came into view.

"About time." He emerged blinking, like a very angry gopher. "I was down there for forty-five minutes. You trying to kill me?"

"I called for you and you didn't answer. I thought you went for a walk!" Trish said. "I didn't hear you."

"I was banging," he snapped, brushing at his shirt. "The whole town probably heard it except for you. I was about to start screaming for the National Guard."

"Sorry," she said, then couldn't help herself. "Why didn't you go out the back? Isn't there a door that connects to the basement?"

Joe's face tightened. "There's no door in the back."

Trish puckered her lips. She didn't want to contradict him, but he was wrong. She tried to be diplomatic. "I'm pretty sure there is."

He glared, then stomped toward the house, muttering about faulty hinges and bringing dynamite next time he went down there. She watched him go, then looked at the storm cellar. The hatch was all the way open, so it would be safe to go down there as long as she didn't close it behind her.

Curious, she dropped down the steps, one hand on the cool wall. At the bottom, it was dark and not much to see. A concrete floor, long shelves with old Mason jars, and, sure enough, a small plank door set into the far wall. She jiggled the handle and, with a little effort, it pulled open, revealing the corridor to the house's basement. Satisfied that she'd been right, she closed it.

Trish climbed back out and shut the hatch. Ferdinand was right behind her, tongue lolling. She smiled to herself. Only in her family, she thought, could you manage to lose a grandparent in the backyard. The next time she got home from cheer, she'd check the cellar first. Just in case.

CHAPTER ELEVEN: ENDURE

Mount Rainier, Washington
August 24, 1978

Patrick

TMI's overnight hut was a wooden box jammed with too many bodies and too few places to put them, one of two such luxurious abodes at Camp Muir. The smell of meals past didn't improve the atmosphere. Patrick ducked his head beneath the low crossbeam and made his way to the battered plank table, his boots thudding hollowly on the splintered floor. His fingers were so numb he could barely work the zipper on his windbreaker, partly from the decreasing temperature and partly from swinging them at his sides all day while climbing. He scanned the faces of the group. Everyone looked as tired as he felt except the guides.

Someone had strung a gas lantern from a meat hook in the center beam, and it threw a cold, flickering light across the room, making the windows look like frosted glass. At the table, Henry pressed one hand to his temple, his skin gray and beaded with sweat. His bowl of rehydrated stew was still half full, the plastic spoon resting on the edge.

"You all right?" Patrick slid into the spot next to him.

"Headache," Henry muttered, eyes squinted against the light.

Patrick picked up Henry's wrist with two fingers, felt for a pulse. It wasn't bad, considering the altitude and the amount of work they'd done. "Drink more," he said, and passed over his own dented water bottle. "Force it, even if you don't want it."

Henry took a perfunctory swig. "I do not want it." He grimaced and wiped his mouth.

At the end of the table, the dynamic was degrading. Gerald was making a scene, his voice too loud in the small space. "I saw you, Dunk. You slipped a second biscuit." He stabbed the air with a crooked forefinger, the nail chewed to the quick.

"I'm a growing boy." Dunk's tone was pure challenge.

"I haven't even had my first," said Gerald. "Why are my supposed friends hellbent on taking what's supposed to be mine?"

Patrick looked at Connor, whose face was pinched.

"Boys, let's keep it down." Eric's voice was low but deliberate.

Pauline said, "Ten-minute warning to lights out, people. Big day."

"Big night." Wes slid into a seat next to Patrick. "Unless you want to call midnight a day." He eyed the food with suspicion, then loaded his spoon anyway.

Gill and Dougie were talking in staccato voices as they huddled near the windows, faces blue-white in the lantern glare. Connor kept looking toward the door, like he might decide to run back down the mountain.

Patrick tore open a packet of peanut butter and mashed it into a square of bread. He passed another to Henry, then nursed his own. His stomach felt like a black hole. Today they'd burned a week's worth of calories. Tomorrow would be even more intense. Or tonight, as Wes had pointed out.

"How's the forecast?" he asked Eric, trying to sound casual.

"Could be better," said Eric. "Wind's up to twenty at the rim, but

I expect it to increase. We're likely to get snow, too. Not enough to weather us out, but not insignificant either."

"Fun times."

"What about crevasse bridges?" Henry asked, his voice barely more than a whisper.

"All good," said Pauline, moving down the row with the stew. "That means you can go fast if you want to. Or, if you prefer, slow and steady."

"We go fast," said Dunk, looking at Gerald with a little curl of his lip.

"Slow and steady wins," Gerald retorted.

Connor sighed and looked away.

Patrick wondered what the problem was amongst the Atlanta team. He assumed they were friends since they'd come together. It seemed all Dunk and Gerald did was argue, while Connor was unusually quiet.

Oh, well. None of my business.

He felt his eyes drifting to the window. The glass was rimed with frost, but he could see the outline of Rainier's upper reaches, a black mass against a sky that was losing its light. Somewhere up there, not even ten hours away, was the summit and the reason they'd all come. He tried to imagine himself at the top. What would Susanne say if she could see him now, crammed into a plywood shoebox with a bunch of strangers, all of them betting their lives on a few feet of blue and gold rope.

He knew what she'd say. She'd say she didn't understand how he chose this over time with her and the kids. He felt a flicker of guilt but pushed it down. He had to stay focused and calm.

The lantern flickered, and Gerald's voice dropped. "So, Dunk, you ever summited a real mountain?"

Dunk shook his head, spooning the last of the biscuit through the watery stew. "In Vietnam. But that's it."

Wes perked up. "You were there?"

"101st," said Dunk. "Hue, Khe Sanh, the usual parade of misery."

Wes nodded. "This should be a cakewalk compared to that."

Pauline clapped her hands. "All right, everyone. If you're not already packed, do it now. Harnesses ready, gear checked, boots where you can keep them warm. We'll wake you when it's time for your briefing. You don't want to be the person holding us up, so be ready now."

There was a scramble as bodies shifted. Gerald and Dunk went at it over who'd stowed their gear faster. The others worked quietly. Henry just sat, breathing slow and deep, his eyes hooded.

Patrick finished his food, then slid his mess into the giant tub at the end of the table. He looked for a second at the plastic-wrapped tray of energy brownies sitting on the table. He grabbed two, pocketing one for later. As he returned to the table, he caught Eric's gaze.

"Good job today," Eric said.

"Thanks," Patrick replied. "You think we'll all make it?"

Eric's smile faded, just a hair. "Some will," he said. "But not all. Most trips a few don't even leave the hut. Altitude or nerves get'em. It's normal."

Patrick tried to figure out which of his own crew might not make it. He worried about Ralph who was still floor gazing, and about Gerald, who talked too loud but moved slow, and about Henry, who looked like hell but was still the most stubborn human being on the mountain.

They cleaned up, wiped down the table, and made their way to the bunks. The sleeping area was a single long platform against the back wall, already lined with bags. Every space was filled. Patrick found his spot between Henry and Wes and unrolled his bag. He scraped off the layer of snow on his boots, then slid them into the gap between the wall and the mattress, insulated and near his body heat to keep them warm for the morning.

He felt himself going through the motions, brain fogged, body heavy with fatigue. He brushed his teeth, using the dregs of his water, then spat into a rusted can near the door. By the time he finished, most of the group was already laid out. Connor's snoring had started before the lights even went out, a deep, whuffling sound. Wes was sitting up staring at nothing. Henry lay on his side, curled around his own knees, his breathing shallow.

Pauline extinguished the light.

More snores and night sounds joined with Connor. Patrick suffered through every cough, every shuffle, and every squeak of the wood under someone's shifting weight, realizing how lucky he was to live with a quiet wife in a well-insulated house. He tried counting sheep, but it didn't work. For a while, he stared at the ceiling. His mind drifted to his family. About the verdict and what that meant for all of them. He hoped Bella had been arrested and charged with her other crimes in the same breath as the not guilty verdict had been read. He hadn't enjoyed testifying about Whitney's death. He most certainly didn't look forward to testifying against Bella in the attempted murder trial, or to Perry having to do it.

At some point, Patrick began to drift in and out, each dream more fractured than the last. In every one, he was falling, not off a mountain, but through a never-ending stairwell, the faces of his family blurring past as he plummeted, and always, always, he had a feeling of not quite catching the last rung, of almost but not quite saving himself.

When the lights came on in the middle of the night, faint and blue, he was already wide awake.

CHAPTER TWELVE: MEND

Buffalo, Wyoming
August 24, 1978

Susanne

Susanne unloaded groceries from each bag as Trish brought them into the house from the truck. A pot of water was boiling for spaghetti, but all Susanne wanted to do was put her head on the counter and sleep on her feet. She was more than tired. Mentally and emotionally frayed.

Trish set the last bag on the counter. She whispered, "Grandpa Joe got stuck outside in the storm cellar earlier."

"Unload that bag for me, will you?" Susanne was snapping the spaghetti noodles in half and dropping them into the water. "So, how did that happen?"

Trish started putting items in the refrigerator. "I think the hatch got stuck, and he didn't know about the connecting door from the cellar to the basement."

"Then how did he get out?"

"I pried the hatch up with a claw hammer."

Joe walked in with his best friend and worst enemy trotting behind him, tail wagging. "Dinner's late."

Susanne rolled her eyes, then turned to him, still stirring the noodles with a wooden spoon. "Yes, it is."

"What are we having?"

"Spaghetti. And Trish, will you brown the hamburger meat for me?"

Trish said, "Yes, ma'am," and joined Susanne in the kitchen.

Ferdinand walked up and stood beside Trish, nose eye level with the counter.

"Uh uh, Ferdie. Out!" Susanne pointed and Ferdinand skulked to the dog bed in the living room.

"That's not American food." Joe scowled and crossed his arms.

Whatever that meant. "Well, it's what we're having. I heard you got stuck in the storm cellar."

That apparently wasn't what he wanted to talk about, and he left, grumbling.

Trish giggled. "That's one way to chase him off."

Susanne watched as her daughter emptied the package of hamburger meat into a skillet. "You know, I'll bet Joe couldn't have gotten out of the storm cellar anyway. I keep that connecting door to the basement locked."

Trish shook her head. "It wasn't locked. I opened it from the cellar side."

Susanne froze. With her heightened security concerns, that wasn't good news. "Could you drain the noodles when they're done?" She'd taught the kids how to test them by throwing them against the wall. They loved to do it.

"Mo-om, I have homework."

"Which you can do after we eat."

Trish sighed. "Fine."

Susanne walked to the top of the basement stairs, flipped on the stairwell light, and went down into the cool, musty basement, which was only half finished. One side was carpeted and painted, the other a large open rectangle of concrete, cinderblock, and shelves stacked with canned goods and boxes of clothes the kids had outgrown.

She walked to the unfinished side where a door led to the storm cellar. The lock was a simple slide bolt, and today it was open. For a moment, she considered just locking it and going back upstairs. Trish's story about Grandpa Joe getting stuck in there was running in a loop in her head. She sure didn't want that to happen to her. But she was down here anyway, and with her concerns about security, she might as well make sure everything was okay.

She pushed the door open and reached for the flashlight they kept on a shelf outside the door frame. She switched it on, and after a few protest flickers, it produced a beam. Then she stepped into a dank, dark corridor that led to the cellar.

She rarely went into it. It was spooky to her, and she didn't like the rodents that found their way down into it. Shelves sagged under jars of ancient peaches, rusted cans of green beans, and what looked like the world's oldest bottle of Maraschino cherries. In one corner was a cache of "emergency" supplies. A bright orange survival radio, water pouches, batteries in every size, and several boxes of iodine tablets.

Since the basement was actually much bigger than the footprint of the house and the corridor ran under the back yard, the storm cellar was actually pretty far away from the house proper. It had been right behind the original homestead, which sat much closer to Clear Creek than the current Flint home.

She swung the light across the shelves, seeing nothing amiss.

She pressed her palm to the old metal hatch and tried to lift it. It didn't move. She braced her back and gave it a solid push, but it groaned and refused. Stuck, just like Trish had said. Susanne stepped back, flashlight beam jittering. Well, at least no one was going to get in that way.

She retraced her steps, sliding the lock home with a little more force than necessary at the door between cellar and basement, then back up the stairs, where the brightness made her squint.

She'd barely set foot in the upstairs hallway when the doorbell rang.

The sound startled her, and she was chagrined to realize she was clutching the flashlight like a weapon. She smoothed her hair and went to the door. Through the side window, she glimpsed the familiar silhouette of Kathy. Today, her friend looked like she'd been run through a wringer. Her hair was in a lopsided braid, cheeks splotched red and puffy.

Susanne unlocked and opened the door. "Kathy, are you—?"

"I burned it," Kathy blurted, rushing in. "I burned the whole left side. I—" She stopped, wild-eyed, on the rug, holding a mesh garment bag in both hands.

"Come in, come in." Susanne motioned her to the kitchen, where Trish was wielding two spoons. One in the spaghetti pot, one in the skillet with the meat. "Tell me what happened."

"Oh, hi Trish," Kathy said. "Sorry for barging in on you guys at dinnertime."

"Hi, Kathy. Hey, Mom. Do you want me to warm up the sauce, too?" Trish held the glass jar aloft.

"Sure. Thanks." Susanne smiled encouragingly at her friend. "Now, what happened?"

Kathy dropped the bag on the table. Through the mesh, Susanne could see a mass of white and a faint pinkish shimmer—what remained of a wedding dress, clearly scorched on one flank, the polyester melted like candle wax.

"I was only supposed to touch up the hem. I—I wasn't even supposed to do it myself. But I thought, maybe just a little press, and —" Kathy covered her face with both hands. "Is it a sign? Is it a warning?"

Susanne sat down across from her. "It's an accident, not an omen. And accidents happen."

Kathy looked up. "But what if it really *is*, you know, like a prophecy? What if it's about me and Wes, whether we should even be getting married?" Her voice cracked on the last word.

Susanne reached over, resting her hand on Kathy's. "This isn't the universe telling you not to marry Wes. It's telling you to let someone else help with the dress."

Kathy wiped at her eyes, then pulled out the dress. The scorched spot on the left side was a disaster, the nylon underlayer melted, the outer fabric yellowed and hard. "It was my grandma's," Kathy said, her voice tiny. "My mom wore it, too. I can't believe I ruined it."

"Let's see what we can do," Susanne said. "Maybe I can salvage it. Or we can call in a pro."

"I already talked to Marlene at the dry cleaners. She said it's hopeless."

"What if we find another dress?"

The look on Kathy's face told Susanne she was on the wrong track.

"Or we could transplant the bodice onto a new skirt?"

Kathy hugged herself, shivering. "You make it sound so easy."

Susanne smiled, wishing she had even a tenth of the certainty she projected. "Maybe not easy, but certainly doable. I might even know the right seamstress." That seamstress being her. She lifted the dress and examined it. She could at least give it her best try.

"Really?" Kathy wiped her nose with the back of her hand.

"Really."

"I'll think about it. That may be the way to go." Then her face clouded again. "Maybe it's not about the wedding. Maybe it's about Rainier. Wes was already anxious about it."

Susanne cocked her head. "He'll be fine. Wes is careful."

"He's careful with patients," Kathy said, "but he's reckless everywhere else. I'm not sure what I'll do if he doesn't come back."

"You'll have a hundred people to lean on," Susanne said. "Me, included. But he's coming back. They all are." *I hope, I pray. But why did Kathy have to put this in my head?*

The words seemed to calm Kathy, if only a little. She exhaled, shoulders drooping. "You're a good friend."

The front door banged open, and Perry's voice announced his arrival. "I'm home!" He tromped in, then froze when he saw Kathy and the smoldered remains of her dress. "Uh, hi," he said.

Kathy tried to muster a smile. "Hey, Perry."

He dropped his backpack on the floor. "Do any of our neighbors have a new car? There was a blue Bronco parked on the road again."

Susanne kept her face neutral. "Did you see who was inside?"

"Just some guy, you know."

Kathy turned to Susanne. "Is something going on?"

"Nothing to worry about," she said, even though it was maybe the number one thing on her mind. "We're always security conscious."

Trish said, "Perry and I saw one out there yesterday morning and at school. Hey, do you think it's that guy's dad who threatened you yesterday?"

"What?!" Susanne couldn't believe she hadn't known about that.

Perry patted the air down. "It's nothing, Mom. I may get a starting position on special teams. If I do, I'll be replacing a senior named Larry. His dad is upset about it."

"And he threated you?"

"Sort of."

"Completely," Trish said.

Perry screwed up his lips, thinking. "I don't think it was him. It could be. Maybe. I don't know."

Kathy was sniffling again, but less than before. The disaster dress was a heartbreak, but not unfixable. But Kathy's worry about Wes gnawed at Susanne. It would have been so easy to make a joke, to say "Wes can't die, he's too stubborn," but that was too glib. The conversation had rattled her more than she'd let Kathy see.

"Dinner's ready," Trish said. Then she cocked her head. "You all right, Mom?"

Susanne smiled at her daughter. "I'm fine. Just tired. I'll set the table since you did all the work. Kathy, can I convince you to eat with us?"

"I already ate." Kathy squeezed Susanne's arm. "But thank you. For everything."

"Think about the dress," Susanne told her. "Everything is fixable, I promise."

When Kathy left with her dress, a little steadier than when she'd arrived, the house was suddenly quiet, save for the distant hum of the AC and Ferdinand's paws scrabbling on the porch as he escorted their guest to her car.

Susanne looked again at the kitchen clock. It was nearly seven already. "Joe, food's ready," she shouted. Then, to Perry, she said, "You already ate a burger and fries with your friends, right?"

He grinned. "That was just a snack."

As she set the table and the kids chattered, her mind re-played the events of the last twenty-four hours. The acquittal, learning Bella had been freed and then disappeared, getting fired from her job at the college. Three. Three bad things.

Maybe it was the end of the run of misfortune.

Or maybe with Kathy's dress and fears added to it, it was just the beginning.

CHAPTER THIRTEEN: COMMIT

Mount Rainier, Washington
August 25, 1978

Patrick

The lights snapped on at exactly twelve-oh-one, shattering the darkness of the hut with a retina-burning glare. Patrick's eyes had already been open, pupils fully dilated, brain spinning out contingency plans. The wake-up prompt was almost a relief. There would be no more pretending at sleep.

"Departure at twelve-thirty," Eric announced. "All that are going up, up and at'em."

Every horizontal surface in the hut came alive. Sleeping bags unzipped in noisy flurries, boots hit the floor like cinder blocks, headlamps snapped on and off for testing in sequence. Someone had a battery-powered radio that flickered briefly to life and then was silenced by a hissed rebuke from one of the guides. Patrick squinted against the light, a nervous thrum in his veins. Some climbers bounced on the balls of their feet, others huddled over mugs of instant coffee, inhaling steam like medicine. The Muckleshoot crew, Gill, Ralph, and Dougie were already packed and lined up at the door, faces set and serious, all business.

Patrick rotated shoulders sore from the plywood bunk and fished for the energy brownie he'd tucked into the breast pocket of his windbreaker before bed. It was mashed flat. He ate it in three bites, trying to ignore the sawdust texture. When he slipped his feet into the boots, he flinched. The first real cold of the day was always the worst. His footwear didn't feel completely dry, but he laced up anyway, twisting the knots hard enough to bite into his fingers, then finished dressing.

Henry was still on his bunk, sitting upright but not moving. His hands were cupped around a canteen. When Patrick approached, he saw Henry's face was pale. Less the waxen gray of yesterday, more the pinched, flinty look that came with pure determination.

"You good?" Patrick whispered, careful not to let the question carry.

Henry nodded once. "Better," he said, then flexed his jaw. "Headache's a three, not a ten. And if I'm going to die, I'd rather do it on the summit than in this box."

"You're not going to die," Patrick said. "But you need to hydrate. I have Tylenol if you want."

"Already took two." Henry finished his water, then levered himself up to standing with a wince. His hands shook, but the rest of him looked stable enough. "You check on Braten?"

"Not yet." Most of the hut's population was gathered in the main aisle, but Wes was still in his bunk with his sleeping bag drawn tight.

Patrick crouched and whispered, "You alive in there?"

A muffled groan. "Not really."

"Come on, we leave soon."

The bag rustled and Wes emerged, eyes bloodshot but alert. "Who gets up at midnight anyway?"

"It's summit day," Patrick said. "Time is relative."

Wes grunted and began extricating himself. He'd slept fully

clothed, boots included, and only needed to put on his outerwear, harness, and helmet. "I had a dream. A tornado came through the hospital and instead of evacuating, we all just hid in the walk-in freezer."

"That seems about right." Patrick checked the watch on his wrist: twelve-twelve. They had eighteen minutes to assemble, gear check, and be outside. "Eat something, then hustle."

Wes lifted a hand acknowledging he'd heard. That was all Patrick could do.

He finished his own gear prep. The wind was already howling against the door, rattling it in the frame.

At the table, Gerald and Dunk were engaged in a cold war of body language. Connor had vanished, presumably outside for a bathroom trip. The only toilet was a glorified plywood box perched over a garbage can, and the idea of using it at this time of the morning was both horrifying and, unfortunately, necessary.

Gerald slammed his hand down. "That was funny, what you did with my boots."

Dunk scowled. "What are you talking about?"

"You know damn well what I'm talking about. My boots were right here, inside, and now they're out in the snow, frozen solid. Thanks a helluva lot, *friend*."

Dunk shrugged, then started unlacing his own boots. "It wasn't me. Maybe someone moved them to clear the way since you left them in the middle of the floor last night."

Gerald's face reddened. "That was not someone. That was you. You've had a problem with me ever since we got here."

"I don't have a problem with you," Dunk said, "but I'd rather not listen to you chew me out all the way up the glacier."

Gerald stood, fists clenched. For a second, Patrick thought he might throw a punch. But instead, he took a breath, then turned to the table of guides at the end of the hut. "I am not going up the mountain with this man," he said, loud enough for the whole room to hear. "Not that I can even make the climb in frozen boots."

Pauline glanced at Eric, then set down her clipboard. "You want to sit this one out, Gerald?" Her voice was calm but carried an edge.

He folded his arms. "That's right."

Eric stepped over. "Are you sure?"

"I'm sure," Gerald said.

Pauline exhaled. "Okay. No one's going to make you go, but you need to wait for us to come back, right here. There's extra food."

"Fine."

"There's a guide in the other hut with two climbers who aren't summiting. You can stay with them. They'll have food and radio."

Gerald didn't say thank you, just nodded with his arms crossed. He didn't look at Dunk as he sat back down. Dunk gave him a glance that was pure contempt, then went back to his laces. Connor walked in and shot startled glances between the two. The tension in the room hung for a minute before everyone else got back to their own prep.

Wes and Henry joined Patrick by the door, both now geared up. Wes looked nervous but seemed physically fine. He nodded at the drama across the hut. "I thought this was supposed to be a team-building exercise."

Henry grunted. "I guess out here you find out who your friends are."

Eric addressed the room. "If you're going to the summit, now's the time. Anyone else staying here, let me know." He circled his hand in the air and exited the hut.

Patrick was right behind him. Outside, the wind howled. The thermometer nailed above the door read twenty degrees, but he estimated the real feel would be at least ten below with wind chill. He tugged his hood tighter.

The summit of Rainier was invisible, lost above a slab of dark cloud against dark sky. The snowfield glowed with a faint phosphorescence, lit only by stars and the moon. Headlamps bobbed as Patrick saw Eric and the Muckleshoot trio. They'd already roped together, faces stoic and unreadable.

Lewis motioned his team over. "Ready?" he asked.

"Let's do it," said Patrick.

They went through the routine. Harnesses checked, ropes clipped, knots tied and triple-checked. Lewis led, Patrick was second, Wes third, Henry fourth. The rope between them was thick as a baby's wrist, and every foot of it was a reminder that one man's slip could doom all four.

Lewis clapped his gloved hands. "We'll stay at the back of the train. We stick to the interval, no bunching up, no slack. If you fall behind, shout. If you need to stop, shout. If you have to use the bathroom—" He looked at Henry. "Hold it till we hit Cathedral Gap."

Henry didn't react.

The order was set. Eric's team, then Pauline's with Connor and Dunk, then Lewis's team. Each rope team would be separated by thirty feet, enough for safety but close enough to shout to the other teams if help was needed.

Patrick felt the cold in his face, the air so dry it burned his nostrils. Every exhale came out as steam. He glanced up at the mountain and tried to steady his mind and leave the chaos and tension from the hut behind.

Eric called, "Team one, move out!" and his rope disappeared up the slope, headlamps casting constellations in the snow.

Pauline's team followed. Lewis gave a tug on the rope, and Patrick stepped forward, boots crunching with each step.

They moved in silence, Patrick's world reduced to the patch of snow illuminated by their headlamps and the steady, rhythmic sounds of his feet. The wind bit at his exposed skin. He settled into the pace. Ahead, Lewis was a machine, never missing a beat. Patrick hoped the steady pressure on the ropes meant his friends were fine, because the wind swallowed any sound they made.

After a while, Patrick looked back and saw that the lights from Camp Muir were already a distant dot. They were alone with the mountain, with only each other and the blue and gold rope keeping them from falling into the void.

CHAPTER FOURTEEN: SHIELD

Buffalo, Wyoming
August 25, 1978

Trish

The morning started normally for Trish. Trying to tame her mane of yellow static, Perry already in the driveway shouting that she was going to make them late. He was especially excited for the first Friday of the school year, because tonight was his first varsity football game. She grabbed her bags and joined him outside. He was wearing his new black and gold jersey.

She did her makeup in the rearview mirror while driving. Perry was quiet. She squinted at him. "You okay?"

He shrugged, but he was smiling. "Just thinking about the game."

"Are you nervous?"

"A little. Mostly I just want to know if I'm going to get to play."

"Don't get your hopes too high. Have you looked in the mirror? There's a reason I call you Shrimp." But that wasn't as true as it used to be. He'd added a few inches in height. He was taller than her, and he'd put on a lot of muscle. She wasn't going to tell him that and let him get a big head, though.

"Ha ha. My sister is so funny."

She cranked up the radio, which was tuned to the station that played only the same five songs in rotation. They both sang along, as they'd been doing all their lives with their dad. By the time they turned onto the school road, it was late enough that the early birds had already claimed the best parking spots. Trish had to park near the end of the lot, two rows over from the main entrance.

As they made their way toward the doors, Trish spotted Bijou, the new girl, standing next to the curb while her dad gestured at her from a beige station wagon.

Bijou was shrinking away from the car. Her dad was probably saying something embarrassing.

"Go rescue her," Trish whispered to Perry.

"Good idea." He peeled off toward Bijou, who immediately brightened. She saw Trish and gave a hesitant wave.

Trish grinned and waved back. Freshmen were scared of their own shadows around seniors like her. She was halfway to the entrance when Jillian appeared from nowhere wearing a toothpaste commercial smile and a black-and-gold cheer jacket from the year before.

She zeroed in on Perry, said something to him, and then clutched his arm and leaned in close. Perry looked like he'd been Tased, but he managed to nod at whatever she was telling him. Bijou, meanwhile, stiffened.

Trish doubled back, seeing red. "Hey, Jillian. Early for you, isn't it?"

Jillian beamed at her. "I wanted to catch Perry before first period." She turned to him. "We're having a party at my place Saturday. My mom's out of town, and my dad doesn't care as long as we keep it outside. I want you there."

Perry's blushed. "Uh, I'll ask my parents."

Trish could see the disappointment flicker on Bijou's face.

Jillian put her hand on Perry's shoulder. "Don't bring a date. It'll be more fun that way." Then she flicked her gaze to Trish and, in the way only Jillian could, managed to both smile and dismiss her at the same time. "You can come, too, Trish. If you want."

"I'll have to check my social calendar," Trish replied, then, after a nanosecond's pause, said, "Nope. I'm booked. But, hey, I have a question for you. Do either Jimmy or Dabbo drive a blue Scout?"

Jillian was already pivoting away, targeting her next mark, a pair of football players huddled by the flagpole, and didn't deign to answer.

Trish shot a look at Perry. "You don't have to go, you know."

Perry shrugged. "It might be fun."

Bijou, who had been silent this whole time, suddenly said, "I need to get my books from my locker. I'll see you later."

He nodded, and she darted away, her skirt swishing behind her.

"Nice job," Trish said. "You already have a harem and it's not even September."

"Shut up," Perry said.

They started up the walkway, a cracked stretch of concrete lined with dandelions and cigarette butts, both of them watching their feet to avoid the chewed-up spots where rain and ice had gouged little craters. There was a brief commotion as the bus pulled in, brakes squealing. A dozen kids poured out, all trying to out-shout each other.

It was in that moment, the perfect chaos of the pre-bell rush, that Trish heard the sound.

It was a car, idling low. The sound came from the far end of the lot, near the dumpsters. She looked up and saw the car. Blue, old, big. It was hard to be sure from this distance whether it was a Bronco or one of the similar models like a Scout.

It sat there, lights off, as students streamed by. Trish watched as the engine revved, the vehicle inched forward, then stopped. The driver's window was up. She couldn't see who was inside.

She nudged Perry. "Look," she said, tilting her chin toward the loitering vehicle.

"I hope that's not the same one we've been seeing," Perry said.

"I don't know. But let's go in through the side door. It's closer to our lockers."

They cut behind the bike racks along the shaded side of the building. It was cooler there, the shadow broken only by strips of sun that trapped dust motes in the air.

They were halfway to the door when Trish heard an engine again, this time louder, insistent.

She turned. The car was in gear and rolling, still slow, but aimed at them—not the entrance, not the parking spaces, but them.

A chill pinpricked down her neck.

Perry stopped dead. "What's it doing?"

Trish grabbed his wrist. "I'm not sure, but I don't like it. Let's go."

They broke into a run. Her backpack thumped against her ribs. She could hear gravel spitting under tires as they picked up speed. For a wild second, she thought *this is so dumb, I'm running from a car in broad daylight like an idiot.*

Then the engine whined. Wheels hopped the curb, and the car shot directly at them.

The next seconds unspooled in slow motion.

She shoved Perry hard, launching him toward the door by the gym. He sprawled, landing on his hands and knees. The grille filled her vision—black, dull, and peppered with bug guts. She tried to leap to the side, but the bumper clipped her, and suddenly she was airborne, spinning.

She landed hard. The world blazed white for an instant, then everything muted. She couldn't hear the car anymore, only a ringing sound and the thump of her own heartbeat.

She tried to sit up, but her leg wouldn't cooperate for some reason. There was a taste of copper in her mouth. Above her, the sky was perfectly blue, the sunlight oddly cold.

Perry's face appeared over her, white as milk. "Are you okay? Are you okay?" he was shouting, but his voice sounded far away.

Then the world winked out, as quick and total as someone flicking off a light switch.

CHAPTER FIFTEEN: TRUST

Mount Rainier, Washington
August 25, 1978

Patrick

The glow of Patrick's headlamp was a trembling island in a vast sea of suffocating darkness. Forward and back, up and down were iffy concepts. The only thing real to Patrick was the pair of deep crampon divots left by Lewis, exactly one rope length ahead. He put all of his faith in them, and he followed, panting. Every breath was a hot sting to his throat that instantly froze on his upper lip and mustache. When he slowed to blink ice crystals out of his eyes, Henry's helmet lamp beam jittered past his shoulder.

They'd left the hut in okay conditions, but not thirty minutes up the face, the weather had taken a turn. There'd been talk at dinner of a little storm, but nothing like the shrieking, horizontal snow that worked its way through every zipper, every seam of their shell jackets. Patrick reached up to adjust the tape on his left glove. It was starting to unravel, a casualty of yesterday's mountaineering school.

The weather conditions were making everything harder, including keeping a ten-second interval behind Lewis.

Behind him, Henry never complained, even though he hadn't slept. Every so often Patrick felt a subtle tug on the rope, a Morse code tap that told him his friends were still alive and that Patrick and Lewis should keep moving.

For the first half-hour of the storm, the wind was a curse-inducing nuisance. By the second hour, it was a living force, capable of knocking a man off his feet if he let his mind wander for a second. Each step became an act of will. Drive the crampon in, shift weight, lean with the gust, don't look up, don't look up, don't look up. If he did, he would only see a nothingness, the visual equivalent of a dial tone. And if he let that get into his head, even for a minute, it was damaging to his frame of mind.

Henry's headlamp was wobbling now behind Patrick, casting wild shadows. They hadn't said a word since the last check-in at Ingraham Flats, but Patrick knew something was wrong. Every time he caught a glimpse of Henry, his gait was off, the rhythm wrong. There was a shuffle at the end of each step, and a kind of drag.

During the next interval, it grew worse. Was it the headache from the night before? Patrick forced his way through a blast of snow and half-turned, careful not to let the rope snag his boot. "You good?" he shouted. The wind snatched the words and flung them somewhere over Tacoma.

Nothing from Henry, but the helmet nodded once. That meant nothing. Patrick pressed on, trusting Lewis to hold the pace.

Up ahead, Lewis's ice axe rang once on solid ground. It was guide-code for hold, and the rope team paused in their tracks. Patrick exhaled, his breath fogging the inside of his goggles instantly. He flexed his hands, waiting for Henry and Wes.

Lewis's silhouette loomed out of the darkness and weather, close enough for his words to carry. "Checking for crevasse here. Stay on the line."

Patrick looked back as his friends gathered close. Henry had hunched in on himself, eyes hollowed out behind frosted lenses, snot and ice on his upper lip. In the glare of the headlamp, his face looked paper-white, sick. "What's up?" Patrick said.

Henry's voice was ragged. "I'm a little short of breath."

Altitude, maybe. But they'd all acclimated at Camp Muir. Could be nerves. Could be exhaustion. Could be both.

Patrick risked a glance at Wes, who met his eyes with a look of concern. "Do you want to go back?" Patrick asked.

Henry shook his head. "It's getting better."

Patrick decided to trust him. Henry wasn't known for taking crazy risks. If it had been Wes, then he would have pushed back.

The wind howled, flattening sound. For a long minute, nobody moved. Then Lewis called, "Clear to move. One at a time. Patrick, go."

He stepped forward carefully. Snow had drifted over the crevasse, but the guide rope to his right marked the crossing. He planted his left foot first, making a deliberate show of anchoring the crampon, then eased across, the rope taut between him and Lewis.

Behind him, Henry hesitated a full ten seconds. Twenty. Then he stepped up awkwardly like a man walking on stilts for the first time.

At the crossing, he paused. Then he tried to move forward, but his foot slipped and he pitched sideways, landing hard on his hip. The rope went taut. Patrick pivoted as he saw Wes brace. Then Patrick reached for Henry's arm and managed to haul him upright by the shoulder strap of his pack.

His friend was breathing in big, gasping gulps. He bent, hands on his knees, and didn't look up.

Patrick leaned in, voice low. "Talk to me."

"I don't think I can do it," Henry said, shaking his head. "I feel like I'm going to throw up. Or pass out. I just—" He swallowed, then choked down whatever was in his throat. "I need to stop."

Behind them, the headlamps of other teams zigzagged up the

slope, little fireflies in the storm. They were two hours out from Camp Muir, at least another four from the summit.

Lewis took in the scene with professional calculation. Patrick saw the extra breath, the set of the jaw.

"You want to turn back?" Lewis asked, flat and to the point.

Henry was shivering, but he looked up, torment in his eyes. "I'm not sure."

Lewis exhaled, then swung his axe into the snow and leaned on it. "Listen up. Anyone goes down, a guide has to take them. If you're quitting, now is the time."

Patrick looked at Henry, then at Lewis. "What are our options?"

"Turn back or keep going. That's it." Lewis's face was hard to read in the swirling snow, but the message was loud and clear.

Patrick nodded. "Give us a second."

He pulled Henry aside, putting his back to the wind. "This isn't Everest, but it's bad out here. You want to bail, I won't hold it against you. But you have to decide now."

Henry's face was twitching, and for a second, Patrick thought he'd break down. Instead, Henry straightened and met his eyes. "I don't want to let you guys down."

"You're not. Don't worry about us."

He watched as Henry fought with himself. "What if I wait here? Or at the next stop?"

Patrick looked back at Lewis, who shook his head almost imperceptibly.

"We can't leave anyone alone on the mountain. It's not safe," Patrick said.

Wes moved up behind them, his voice low and steady. "I'm with you no matter what you decide, partner."

Lewis's voice cut through the storm. "If we go back now, we can get you to shelter before the next wave of weather hits."

Henry squeezed his eyes shut. His breathing had steadied. "I'm feeling better. I think it's passing."

Patrick wanted to believe it, but the risk was obvious. Still, it was Henry's call. If it was just nerves, maybe he'd get through.

"Okay," Patrick said, clapping him on the shoulder. "But if it gets any worse, you say something right away."

Henry nodded.

Lewis didn't bother with sympathy. "Move out, same order."

They fell in line, and for the next forty-five minutes, nobody spoke. For Patrick there was only the crunch of his own crampons and the wail of wind.

He focused on his feet and his rope. He tried not to think about the year before on Cloud Peak, when he'd been with Whitney and Loren Freemason in similar weather. That climb had ended with a stretcher and a medevac. *Don't think about that. It's different this time.*

The ridge grew steeper. The storm thickened. They'd just passed another switchback when Henry stumbled again. The rope jerked as he caught himself.

"Stop!" Wes shouted, and they all halted in place, snow swirling so thick Patrick could barely see Lewis.

Henry sagged, hands on his thighs, and then, without warning, lurched to the side and vomited into the snow.

Lewis turned, and for the first time, Patrick saw a flicker of worry cross his face. "We're going down."

Henry shook his head. "Wow. That really helped. I can do this, just give me a minute—"

Lewis cut him off. "If you're puking at ten thousand feet, you're not making it to fourteen."

"It was a migraine from last night. I get them. But it's passing now."

Lewis glared at him for several seconds. "You sure?"

Henry straightened and threw his shoulders back. "Absolutely. I'm already better."

Patrick studied his friend's pale face. For a moment, he considered calling to turn back himself. But then he reconsidered. Henry knew his own self best. They would have to take his word for it.

He just prayed to the good Lord almighty that Henry was right.

CHAPTER SIXTEEN: RACE

Buffalo, Wyoming
August 25, 1978

Susanne

Susanne sat in the fourth row of her Contemporary Theory of Instruction class, barely tracking the words floating out of Dr. Zeller's mouth. She was underlining a phrase in her textbook for the third time—"engagement with material improves memory encoding"—when she heard the door open and students murmuring. Someone had entered the room. The footfalls were measured and slow. She looked up and saw a sweating twenty-something kid in a Sheridan College Student Government shirt.

"There's a direct pipeline from stress to memory impairment—" Dr. Zeller, halfway through the sentence, stopped cold. "May I help you?"

The kid lingered in the space between rows. "Sorry, uh, I have a message from the counseling office for Susanne Flint."

She raised her hand and he looked around until he caught her eye then thrust out a folded slip of paper.

She took it, frowning in confusion a little, and the kid whispered, "They said to tell you it's urgent. Sorry."

Dr. Zeller frowned, looking aggrieved. "Something wrong, Mrs. Flint?"

She read the note to herself. *Emergency phone call. Please report to counseling office immediately.*

Her dread, so well-practiced by now, rose like a geyser. For the last three days, she'd lived with a gnawing certainty that something would go wrong during Patrick's Rainier expedition. She'd gone so far as to memorize the area code for the closest National Park Service office. And since Wednesday, that had been compounded by fear about Bella's disappearance. She'd already told herself that any emergency would start with a phone call, but to actually see the words in black ink made her feel both vindicated and sick.

The note had said "*Mrs.* Flint." That usually meant a call about a spouse. Wouldn't it have said Susanne Flint if it were about the kids?

"I have to go," she said, standing up quickly.

The row behind her gasped in unison as she nearly mowed down the note-carrier.

Dr. Zeller said, "I don't recall giving you permission. Your departure is duly noted, Mrs. Flint."

Susanne muttered apologies and bolted up the stairs behind the kid, out of the frigid lecture hall into the late-summer heat. Her feet found a gallop.

The journey to the counseling office was only fifty yards, but it felt like a thousand-mile trek, every step resounding with the threat of bad news. She imagined Patrick's hand caught in a rope, his skull cracked on a glacial boulder, a rescue helicopter shuttling his body to Seattle.

There were two phones on the shelf outside the counseling office. One beige, push-button, the other a rotary in institutional black. The secretary, a plump, motherly type, was holding on to the beige receiver. When she saw Susanne, she waved frantically, nearly jiggling the cord out of the base. "Are you Susanne Flint?"

"I am. I got a note about a call for me." Susanne struggled to keep the panic out of her voice.

"I'm already dialing the call back number."

Susanne reached for the phone. It rang, then there was a moment of pure white static, a shifting of air and paper, and then a familiar voice. "Susanne, it's Ronnie."

Her own voice was tight, like a bad radio channel. "Ronnie—what happened? Is it Patrick?"

The pause lasted only a second, but Susanne felt the shape of it, the geometry of trauma. "No, no. It's not Patrick. It's the kids. Trish mostly. There was an accident this morning. An incident. Trish is in surgery at Johnson County Hospital. Perry's there too, but he's fine. Scrapes and bruises for him."

For a second, Susanne didn't understand the words. "I—what?" She sat down hard on the bench behind her.

"Trish is in surgery with Dr. John for her leg, but it's not life-threatening. She's stable." Ronnie said the word stable with certainty.

"H-how bad is it?" Susanne's voice felt like it belonged to a stranger. Her body seemed separate from her brain.

Another beat. "It's an open fracture of her tibia. The bone went through the skin."

Susanne hadn't been a doctor's wife for over a decade not to realize how serious this was. Trish could end up with her leg amputated if the bone didn't join or if she developed an infection. Plus, there were the normal risks of surgery. Anesthesia. Nerve damage. Blood clots. The list of ways to die was long.

There were a dozen questions she wanted to ask. Was Trish awake when they brought her in? Did she scream? Was she scared? What happened? Were they in a wreck? And then like a sucker punch, a thought hit her. Was it Bella Crooke? Did she do this to Susanne's children? But all that came out was, "Is—" She had to clear her throat. "Is there anyone with Trish right now? Is she alone?"

"I'm here. I've been here since the ambulance arrived. Perry is down in the ER getting patched up but should be here soon, too."

"What happened?"

Ronnie spoke gently. "A vehicle hit them outside the high school."

"A wreck?"

"No. They were walking into the school."

"Oh, my God." Two tons of steel against the flesh and bones of her babies. She put her fist to her mouth.

"It fled the scene, but we're working on it. Perry was able to give us a description of it and the man driving it."

Susanne's vision was blurred, the world gone glassy and bright. A car hit them. A car driven by a man. "I have to get a message to Patrick. He's still on Rainier."

"I'll do it."

Susanne told her how to get hold of Patrick through Paradise Inn. "I'll be there in forty-five minutes. Or less."

"Do you want me to arrange a ride for you?"

"No. I don't want anything to slow me down."

Ronnie said, "Please be careful. The kids need you here safely."

"I will. Thank you."

She was aware, distantly, that she was shaking as she hung up the phone. Then she was running, faster and faster, as fast as her legs could carry her.

Her kids. Someone had nearly killed her kids. And Trish wasn't out of the woods yet.

CHAPTER SEVENTEEN: PLUNGE

MOUNT RAINIER, WASHINGTON
AUGUST 25, 1978

Patrick

AT THEIR CURRENT ALTITUDE—OVER twelve thousand feet—the air was stingy. Each inhalation felt like Patrick had been shorted on the change. At least the weather was giving them a break, for now.

Henry, right behind him on the rope, wasn't talking. Hadn't said much all morning since being plagued by the headache, unless you counted the deep grumble he'd aimed at the snow when his boot broke through a cornice. He had the hunched, stubborn stance of a man used to moving cattle, not tiptoeing over crevasses on a two-inch snow bridge. Since he had tossed his breakfast, though, he had visibly improved.

But Patrick could feel his friend's unease through the rope, the occasional tug or shudder whenever the wind gusted or a shadow flickered in the periphery. He was, as ever, stubborn and stoic, though. No one would guess his feelings by looking at him.

Patrick felt responsible for his friend but confident in Henry's fitness and competence, enough so that he was still able to marvel at the glacier itself. While covered in debris, it displayed a range of colors up close that were impossible to imagine when seeing the white expanse from afar. The reds and yellows of the rock, the blue and even violet of the ice. He felt privilege close to religious fervor to experience it up close, and he whispered prayers of gratitude as he climbed, with occasional supplications for their safety thrown in.

The team moved in rhythm. Step, pause, drive the axe, move the feet, step, pause, breathe. Lewis set the pace, almost metronomic, and it was Patrick's job to match it, his own movements echoing in the rhythm of the men behind him. There had been comfort in it, almost like the slow strumming of a classical guitar, until the first warning sign. The snow underfoot, solid all morning, suddenly gave with a wet, sucking sound.

Lewis stopped. He knelt on the snow, examining a patch where the surface had slumped. "Crevasse here," he called, voice clipped. "Step light. Cross at the point I'm marking." He chopped at the snow with his axe, scouring out a bridge barely two boots wide. He traversed with feline grace and waited, hands on hips, as the rest prepared to cross.

Patrick glanced back. Wes had his eyes closed, lips moving. Henry just looked at the sky and muttered, "Damn it to hell and back." And then they went, one after another, the rope tight between them, Wes going last.

No one fell. But the mood on the rope was different after the crossing. Everyone was more careful, more deliberate. When the wind finally found them in earnest—a shriek that ripped over the ridge and smacked them with a face full of blown ice—Lewis hesitated. The gray clouds had moved in, crowding closer to them and blocking out the sun. He pulled his balaclava up, turned, and gestured the team closer. "We've got maybe forty-five minutes before this system drops in," he said. "We make the saddle before that, we're golden. If not, we bivvy."

Patrick, shaking snow out of his goggles, nodded. Taking shelter in the small tents they carried for that purpose wasn't what he wanted to do, but it was the smart thing to do. His grim experience hiding from the weather in a cave on Cloud Peak had cemented that point for him a year ago. "Copy that."

"Let's move," said Lewis.

They did, heads down, feet seeking friction in snow rapidly hardening under a film of frozen vapor. The clouds above them moved with seeming intent. Each hundred feet of gain brought less visibility, more wind, the sound of it in their hoods a banshee's wail. Late August on Rainier was as volatile and unpredictable as Patrick had been warned.

He felt a change in the rope. Lewis's movements, always precise, became now urgent. The rope jerked and shuddered, forcing Patrick to follow quickly or risk being yanked off his feet. He gave Wes and Henry their sign of two short tugs but didn't dare risk looking back.

They struggled to the edge of a plateau, where every gust of wind cost them half a step of forward progress. Lewis turned hard right, heading for what Patrick guessed was the lip of the Ingraham Glacier proper, when the world just disappeared.

Whiteout was no longer just a word. It was the only way to describe their reality. The horizon erased. The colors and contours vanished into a matte blankness that made Patrick feel stationary. He knew they were still moving because of the scrape of crampons on ice and the twitch of the rope at his hip. For thirty seconds, maybe a minute, there was no way to tell if they were going uphill, downhill, or sideways.

Then Lewis's headlamp appeared, not ahead but below. The rope pulled him hard, and Patrick's feet slid out from under him. He clawed at the ice with his axe, found no purchase, and began to freefall, dropping, dropping, dropping until a yank by the rope at his waist stopped him. For a second, he hung in space, then something gave. He tumbled down the slope, ice and snow abrading his face, the taste of blood in his mouth. He heard a shout, then the thunk of an axe biting in before the rope went tight.

But the tension lasted less than a heartbeat before sudden acceleration that told him the anchoring had failed. They were sliding, tied together, down a glacier at a speed Patrick could barely process.

"Self-arrest!" Lewis's voice, somewhere above, was faint.

Patrick kicked his crampon points in, drove his axe deep. For an instant, he thought it would hold. Then Henry slammed into him. Axes tore out, the world becoming a carnival ride of snow, ice, and screaming wind.

CHAPTER EIGHTEEN: HOPE

Buffalo, Wyoming
August 25, 1978

Susanne

Susanne was met at the intake desk by a young staffer who must have been waiting for her. "Mrs. Flint, Trish is still in surgery, but I'll take you to Perry."

Susanne was too distraught to remember her name, even though she knew most of the staff. "Thank you," she managed to say, then followed closely behind her.

Perry was in a small, windowless room off the ER. He was sitting on the exam table, shirt torn and blood-speckled, staring at the wall. When he saw his mom, his face crumpled, but he didn't cry. Not at first.

She hugged him, fiercely, then checked him over head to toe, as if she could inventory every possible injury. "Are you okay?" she said, pulling back to see his face.

He nodded, mute. "Just scrapes," he finally said, voice hushed.

He pulled his shirt away from his body. "This is from Trish, mostly. Her leg was bleeding everywhere. She screamed, Mom. I've never heard anyone scream like that. Then she just, I dunno, passed out, I guess."

Susanne felt her stomach drop. "They'll fix her up. They're working on her right now."

He nodded again, eyes on the wall.

Kathy appeared, as if on cue. "Susanne, I'm so sorry about all of this. Ronnie is waiting for you in the family lounge. She can update you about what happened. I can walk with you and fill you in on Trish's condition."

"Thanks, Kathy."

"Perry, you've been cleared, so you can come with us, if you'd like."

He hopped off the table, looking relieved. Susanne kissed his forehead, squeezed his hand, then they followed Kathy down the corridor, mother and son side-by-side. The walls were papered with old, sun-faded prints of mountain wildflowers that needed a refresh.

Kathy said, "I just talked to Dr. John. Surgery's going as well as can be expected. The tibia was an open fracture. She also broke her fibula. They're about halfway done."

If Perry hadn't been with her, Susanne would have asked for more detailed information. "Thank you."

"I'll get you an update as soon as I can."

Kathy knocked on a door, then opened it. Ronnie was inside, still in her uniform, hair pulled back into her usual French braid, face drawn and serious.

"Thank you, Kathy. Hey, Perry," Ronnie said. She stood and held her arms open. "And Susanne."

Susanne fell into them, trying not to cry, as Kathy waved and left. "Did you reach Patrick?"

"I left a message at the lodge. They said they can give it to him when he gets off the mountain. He's attempting the summit today and won't be down until tonight."

Susanne bit her lip. She'd expected that, but somehow her feckless heart had hoped he'd be down already. Her knees felt waterlogged, but she managed to sit, and Ronnie took a seat, too.

"Can I run to the cafeteria and get a drink, Mom?" Perry asked.

"Sure. Take my wallet," she said.

"Do you want anything? You or Ronnie?"

Ronnie held up a coffee. "I'm good with this. There's a coffee pot at the nurses station."

Susanne gave Perry a weak smile. "I'm fine, honey. Come straight back."

He grabbed her wallet and hurried out of the room.

She turned to Ronnie. "Any progress on who did this?"

"No. Perry said it was a man driving an older model blue Bronco. We don't have much more to go on than that, but we've got a BOLO out and officers out looking and combing through vehicle registrations."

Her brain started buzzing. She answered, her words weirdly feeling like she was shouting underwater. "He mentioned a car like that in our neighborhood. So did Trish. They've seen it before."

"That's what he said."

"Could the guy have been stalking them?"

"Do you have any reason to think someone in particular would do that?"

"Perry mentioned a feud with a parent over a position on the football team."

Ronnie's eyebrows went up. "Seems kind of extreme, but I'll ask him about that. Anyone else?"

"I mean, Bella Crooke is out of jail."

"But she's female."

"True. But she could have hired someone."

"It's definitely something to keep in mind. Right now, we haven't been able to find her. We'll keep looking for her, at the same time as we look for the car. It's always possible it was just someone who lost control of his vehicle and didn't want to pay the consequences for what he did."

Susanne knew she was right, but, no matter who it was, she didn't understand how a decent human could hurt her kids and then just run away. "Normally I'd agree except the kids felt a car like this was following them, more than once."

"Absolutely. Perry will get me that information about his teammate's dad. And of course we haven't been able to speak with Trish yet. Speaking of her, have you heard anything about how she's doing?"

"Kathy said the surgery is going well. That's all I know."

"That's great news. When you know she's okay and she's recovered enough, we'll want to see what she remembers, too. How about I get you some coffee or water while I wait on Perry?"

Susanne didn't even have the will to decline. "Water, please."

Ronnie disappeared, then returned with a paper cup.

Susanne sipped then set the cup on her thigh, hands shaking. "I should have been here. I should have—I don't know. I should have done something when Perry mentioned he kept seeing the car."

Ronnie touched her arm. "This isn't on you. Not a bit."

The room was silent. The clock ticked. Outside, a child wailed, the sound hollow and far away.

Kathy stuck her head in. "They're closing up now. She'll be in recovery soon." She disappeared before Susanne could even thank her.

She sucked in a deep breath and let it out slowly, her body vibrating. She wanted to rush the OR, to see with her own eyes that Trish was alive, but she stayed rooted to the chair. She thought of Patrick, somewhere on a mountain, unaware of what his daughter was going through. Of herself, unable to reach him and unable to help Trish. Having no control was the worst.

For now, all she could do was wait, and hope, and try to remember how to breathe.

CHAPTER NINETEEN: UNEARTH

Mount Rainier, Washington
August 25, 1978

Patrick

Patrick's uncontrolled descent ended somewhere in a basin of scoured blue ice and bodies piled, two axes tangled, and rope looping all over. Somehow, though, he'd managed to bury his own axe, and it had been enough to stop them all. His ears rang. His shoulder throbbed, and he was face-down, cheek icy against the surface.

Henry groaned. "You guys alive?"

Patrick made a sound, meant to say "Yes," but it came out more like a grunt.

Wes coughed. "Is this how astronauts feel on re-entry?"

Patrick tried to move. "Axes. Everybody got their axes?" He didn't dare pull his out yet.

Henry raised his. Wes fumbled for his, hand shaking, then waved it. "And thank the good Lord none of us planted them in each other."

Truer words have never been spoken. "Crampons, everyone."

Patrick dug in his own and looked up at the featureless gray above. "Okay. No more of that. Ever."

The wind dropped for a second, as if the mountain was catching its breath. In the sudden relative quiet, Patrick heard Lewis yelling from somewhere up-slope. "You guys okay?"

"Define okay!" Wes hollered, voice echoing.

"We're alive," Patrick called. "We're okay."

"Regroup and dig in," Lewis shouted.

"What happened? How are you up there and we're down here?"

"Must have been equipment failure. Storm's picking back up. If you can, move lateral west to stay off the face. There shouldn't be any surprises there, and it will be less steep."

What a time for equipment failure. Patrick looked at his own hands, blood trickling from his wrist. He dusted off, checked Henry and found only superficial cuts, nothing bad. Each man checked his own carabiners, then they triple checked for each other.

Using his compass, Patrick led the team west, as ordered, moving carefully and deliberately. The mountain had schooled them in a hard lesson they wouldn't soon forget. The whiteout thickened, visibility down to five feet, then three. He walked by feel, the tip of his axe tracing the ice ahead.

They came upon a ridgelet of wind-carved snow, the leeward side offering a little shelter for a break, and dug in with axes and boots, facing up the slope. They could not see Lewis, could not hear him anymore, but they did what he'd told them, trusting in his expertise and in God, to whom they'd been vocally and fervently praying as they traversed the mountain.

It was maybe a minute later that Henry yelled, "Hear that?"

At first, Patrick heard nothing. Then he became aware of a faint vibration followed by a low, rolling sound like distant thunder. He pressed an ear to the snow. It wasn't thunder. It was the voice of the glacier itself. The hiss and rumble of something coming to life beneath the surface.

"I think it's an avalanche," Patrick said, whispering, barely breathing.

"Oh, shit," Wes said.

Henry started praying aloud again.

It was not fast and dramatic. There was no white wall barreling down, no cinematic rush. Instead, the snow above them simply began to move, a slow-motion landslide, one layer shearing off another. Patrick saw it out of the corner of his eye, the way the surface rippled, the snow transforming from ground to river in seconds.

"Arrest and down!" he barked.

They dug in their axes and crampons then threw themselves into the hollow, bodies over axes and packs.

The snow hit them like the wind times a hundred. It rolled them, buried them, then dragged them down-slope despite their attempts to arrest for a terrifying distance. Patrick fought for a breath, his mouth packed with ice, as he tried to tell up from down. Fighting to stay calm, he dug a breathing pocket in front of his face and spit out the ice. After a few deep breaths, he shoved the head of his axe in one direction to no avail, then another, then another, getting lucky on a try behind his back. His arm broke through, and he realized he was facedown but not covered by more than a light layer of snow. He swam to turn over and sat up, face to the sky, blinking in the gray.

Was this real? It wasn't what he'd come for. Not what he thought he'd gotten his two best friends into. But it was, while a living nightmare, *not* a dream.

Wes was struggling up to his left, rope over his torso. He gasped and yelled, "I'm not dead! Holy heaven, I thought I was a goner!"

Henry was clear, too. He coughed and spit, then spat again. "We're all here?" His voice was as steady as ever, but his hands shook as he checked the line.

Patrick said, "Against all odds. By rights we should be buried at the bottom of a crevasse and drawing our last breaths soon."

Wes said "Agreed. And yet, while I hate to be the bearer of bad news—"

"That would be *more* bad news."

"Yeah, more bad news. I've got a problem with my arm."

Patrick hadn't thought he could be more worried. He was wrong. "Which one?"

"Left, fortunately. I can still swing an ax. But it hurts like a sonuvabitch."

Which meant that after they got out of their current predicament, Wes would have to return to Camp Muir.

Patrick eased onto his knees to examine his friend, which was when he saw the hand. It jutted from the ice maybe ten feet downslope, a human hand, blue and shrunken, the nails blackened with deep freezing and time. At first Patrick thought it was a trick of the light. But as his eyes adjusted, he realized the hand was attached to an arm, and the arm to a shoulder, and the shoulder to a face, half-revealed and grinning with the rictus of the long dead.

"Do you guys see that?" Patrick said, pointing.

All eyes moved to the unfortunate soul. For a moment, no one spoke.

"Freeze-dried," Henry muttered.

Patrick was unable to look away as his eyes picked out the rest of the body exposed as the avalanche had churned up debris. A torso, leg, and foot. Gear that was old—leather boots laced with rawhide, a canvas parka in Army green. The face, or what was left of it, looked male and mummified from too long in the sun, the features sunken and blurred.

"Whoever that is, he was lost up here a long time ago," Patrick said. "Maybe decades."

Wes shivered. "You think he died in a fall or was alive and hurt, waiting for someone to find him?"

Patrick shuddered. He didn't want to think about what it would be like to lay injured in the snow, slowly starving and freezing to death.

Henry rose and dusted off his jacket. "Let's make sure we don't join him."

"Agreed." Patrick inched downward until he could reach the man's wrist, drawn by the glint.

"What are doing, Sawbones?" Wes didn't sound on board.

"Maybe if we bring something back, the climber can be identified."

"Be careful, now," Henry said. "No need for unnecessary risks."

When Patrick reached the body, he saw an item that would work.

Wes said, "What do you see?"

Carefully, he pulled the glimmering object up and over what was left of one hand and slipped it in his pocket. "A watch."

Before returning to his friends, he took one more glance at the ice-locked corpse, the empty eyes fixed on a summit never reached. *Please God, don't let this be a bad omen.*

CHAPTER TWENTY: RECALL

BUFFALO, WYOMING
AUGUST 25, 1978

Trish

THE THING TRISH noticed first was the taste in her mouth. Metal, like chewing on the lid of a 7-Up can, only sharper and more bitter. Then, the sensation. Her lips were split and her tongue was dry, which didn't make sense because she remembered only the rev of an engine, the thump against her leg, and the strange sensation of flying. She tried to open her eyes, but the left was sealed shut and crusted. The right opened a slit and saw the ceiling tiles, white with a pock-mark pattern, and the fluorescent lights that flickered at the far end of the room. After a few more tries, her left eye opened, too.

She tried to move and couldn't. She was swaddled, top to bottom, in white sheets and immobilized by a weight across her right leg. Her arms worked. She tested each finger, then the elbows where something dragged, then up to her shoulder, which lit up with a bolt of fire so clean and immediate it made her gasp. The noise summoned movement. A shape out of her peripheral, then her mother's face right above her, hair wild and eyes red-rimmed.

"There you are." Her mom's hand was shaking as she put it on Trish's cheek, avoiding the bandaged gash above her eye. "You're okay. I'm here. It's okay."

Trish tried to answer but it came out as a croak. Her mouth worked again and, with more effort, she managed, "Where's Perry?"

"Just down the hall. He's fine. A little banged up, but the car didn't hit him."

Trish worked her jaw, tried to swallow, and finally said, "My leg hurts."

"You've had surgery. Dr. John said you'll need some time to heal, but you'll be just fine." Her mom's hand stayed on Trish's face, thumb gently rubbing her temple in little, automatic circles. "You want some water?"

Trish nodded. Her mom poured a cup from a plastic pitcher and guided the straw to Trish's lips. The first sip was ice cold and glorious. She took one more.

"Slow," her mom said, lowering the cup. "You just came out of anesthesia. Take it easy."

Without warning, the nightmare began replaying in vivid imagery in Trish's mind. The parking lot, using Perry's backpack to get him out of the way, the roar of an engine. "I got hit," Trish said, quietly, and as soon as she said it, she remembered the car. The blue paint, the thump as it hit her, flying through the air. Landing. The pain. Then nothing.

"Perry said you pushed him out of the way. You kept him from being hurt."

Trish glanced at her leg, covered by a sheet but with a bulge in the blanket. "How bad?"

"Compound fracture," her mom said. Her voice was careful and soothing. "They said you'll be on crutches for a few months."

Trish had not even considered crutches. She was sidelined.

Another face loomed at the edge of the bed. It was Dr. John, his doctor's coat buttoned, his horned rim glasses making his eyes look huge. "Good morning, Miss Flint. Welcome back to the land of the living."

He looked at her eyes, then her fingernails, then clicked a penlight into her open right eye. She winced at the flash but didn't flinch.

"How's your head?" he asked.

"Hurts." She hadn't realized it until he asked.

"Anywhere else?"

She did a quick inventory. "My shoulder is sore. My forehead. My... everything, really."

He nodded, almost pleased, as he palpated her shoulder. "You have ten stitches in your eyebrow, and the leg will need to stay still and elevated for at least a week. The rest I think is trauma. Bumps and bruises. So, no sports for the time being." He winked.

"She's on the cheer squad," her mom said, as if that might qualify her for some special exemption.

"She won't be jumping this fall." Dr. John scribbled something on Trish's chart. "The surgery went perfectly. We did some imaging and it looks great in there. I'll have Kathy check you again in an hour, and we'll see about getting you some real food." He patted Trish's shoulder, not the sore one. "You did great, kiddo."

He turned to her mom and added in a lower voice, "Keep an eye out for confusion or memory gaps. Call me if she says anything strange."

She nodded as Dr. John left, but Trish had caught every word.

"I'm not confused," Trish said.

Her mom smiled, but her hand was a vise on the rail of the hospital bed. "Of course you aren't."

Trish said, "I want to call Ben."

Her mom gave her a look that was gentle, but final. "You can call him when we're home."

That was frustrating, but it wasn't the biggest of Trish's worries at the moment. "Can I see Perry?"

"He was here when you came out of surgery. He's just down the hall, in the family waiting room." She hesitated, then said, "He's worried sick about you."

"It wasn't his fault."

"Of course not. But he was there to see you hurt and in pain. He's got a soft heart, and he loves his big sister."

They sat in silence for a minute, listening to beeps and the sound of someone laughing down the hall.

Trish said, "Do they know who hit us?"

"Not yet. Whoever it was drove off. The police are investigating."

A knock at the door startled them both. It was Ronnie, smoothing stray wisps of hair back into her braid.

"Can I come in?" she asked.

Trish nodded. "Hi."

"Hi, yourself." Ronnie pulled a chair close and sat down, hands on her knees. "You okay?"

"I've been better."

"I'll bet. You up for a couple of questions?"

"Sure," Trish said. "Although I don't know much."

"That's fine. Whatever you have, even just a detail, could help."

Trish closed her eyes, tried to replay the moment. "It was a blue car," she said. "Old. One of those square things like a Scout."

"Perry said a Bronco."

Trish opened her eyes and frowned. "Maybe."

"What makes you say Scout?"

"I'd seen one near our house. I thought it might be it."

"Perry and your mom said you'd seen a blue Bronco, too."

"Yeah. Both."

"Do you remember anything more about it?"

"It had a deer guard, I think. Something black on the front anyway. I think it was a guy driving. I think I remember a white T-shirt."

Ronnie wrote it all down. "What else do you remember about him?"

"I only got a brief look at him. I'd say brown hair, kinda curling up around the ears. Dad aged. No beard."

"A mustache?"

"No."

Ronnie's eyebrows raised. "You're sure about that?"

"I'm sure," Trish said. "Why?"

Ronnie checked her notes. "Your brother said the driver had a mustache."

Trish tried to think. In her memory, the face was blank, almost featureless, but she was sure about nothing above his lip. "No," she said, slow and certain. "No mustache."

"Anything else stand out?" Ronnie asked. "Anything weird about the way he drove, or the car?"

Trish thought for a minute. "He looked right at us. He didn't even try to turn. It was like—" She stopped, feeling her skin go cold. "Like he wanted to hit us."

"Any idea who it could be?"

"Dabbo Kern and Jimmy Gross are pretty mad at me. I think they've been doing stuff to get back at me. Hang up calls. Once someone called me a bitch and hung up. Another time someone threw a bag of poop at our door. That's when I saw the blue Scout."

Her mom looked concerned, and her voice rose as she spoke. "When did all this happen? Why didn't you tell me?"

Trish sighed. "Because I didn't know for sure it was them."

"Still, *someone* did it. I wish those two hoodlums were still in jail where they belonged!"

"You kind of go overboard on things, Mom. It can be tiring."

Her mom's mouth dropped open.

Ronnie cut in. "Was it one of them driving the car that hit you?"

"Not Jimmy. Dabbo has dark hair, so it could have been him, but really it happened too fast and the sun was in my eyes. I don't know."

"I'll follow up on Dabbo and Jimmy." She tapped her pen on her knee. "Perry mentioned a parent threatened him in front of you."

"Yeah. I got a quick glimpse of him when it happened. I'm not sure I'd recognize him again if I saw him. But it wasn't *not* him. I mean, it could have been. Like Dabbo I guess."

Ronnie's face softened. "You did good. That's helpful."

"I'm sorry I didn't see more."

She stood. "We'll find him. I promise." She wished them both goodbye and left.

When the door closed, Trish's mom exhaled. "Let me go get your brother."

Trish closed her eyes. She was just drifting off, when her mom returned with Perry.

He hovered at the door for a second, then shuffled over. "How are you feeling?"

Trish rolled her eyes. "Like dog poop."

"Yeah, it looks like it."

"Thanks a lot, Shrimp." But she smiled for the first time.

"Did you see the guy who hit us?"

"Sort of. Ronnie told me you said he had a mustache?"

Perry frowned. "He did. It was, like, the first thing I noticed."

Trish shook her head. "No, Perry. He didn't."

He looked genuinely confused. "Maybe you're remembering wrong because of the anesthesia."

Trish started to reply but then stopped. Was she misremembering?

Their mom, who'd been pretending to read a magazine, put it down. "It was a fast thing, both of you were in shock."

Perry stared at the wall, arms crossed. "I know what I saw."

Trish knew only one of them could be right, about the mustache and the car, which she hadn't even brought up yet. She hoped the accident and surgery weren't playing tricks with her memory.

CHAPTER TWENTY-ONE: SPLIT

Mount Rainier, Washington
August 25, 1978

Patrick

Patrick and his team didn't have long to stare at the dead man. They needed to get back up to the main trail. Who knew how long that would take in this weather?

Wes was shivering, his helmet half-off, his left arm held awkwardly at the elbow. Henry fished a space blanket from his pack. Patrick wrapped it around Wes to make a sling, then clapped him on the back.

"Let's get moving," Patrick said, and his words came out more brittle than he intended.

The three of them staggered upslope now, heads low. The wind bit, but the rope between them held, solid evidence that they were alive and had each other's backs. When they finally reached a break in the slope, they saw a huddle of bright colors against the storm. It was Lewis and, beyond him, another rope team. The second group's headlamps shone through falling snow, making them look wavey and spectral.

When they reached the others, Patrick saw it was Pauline with Dunk and Connor. Lewis had set up a mini triage, using his pack as a windbreak for the others who were hunkered down.

He motioned them in, voice taut. "You guys good?"

"Mostly," Patrick said. "Wes hurt his arm. It's pretty significant."

Wes winced but tried to grin. "It's pretty much a noddle, more like it."

Lewis gave Patrick a once-over, then scanned the horizon. "You and Henry look okay."

"We are. Patrick hesitated, then said, "You'll want to hear this, though. We found a body."

Dunk, kneeling in the snow, jerked his head up. "A dead body?" His voice cracked. "Like, a fresh one?"

Patrick shook his head. "Old. At least a year, maybe decades if the clothes are any indication. We got caught in an avalanche, and when it was over, the body had been unburied."

"Avalanche?" Connor said. "Jesus. And you're still alive." He uncapped his water and took a long swig.

"Barely, I'd say." Patrick retrieved the watch from his pocket. "I took this off the body. Maybe it will help identify the climber."

For a second, nobody said anything. Even the wind seemed to mute itself, as if listening.

Pauline, from where she crouched with Dunk and Connor, gave a low whistle. "That's the mountain for you. It keeps its history." She stood and reached her hand out for the watch, which Patrick gave to her.

Dunk looked from Patrick to the guides, eyes wide. "You all are acting like this is normal."

Pauline shrugged, her teeth flashing. "Every few years, the glacier spits out someone it ate a generation ago. We keep a log with the names."

Connor muttered, "That's messed up."

Lewis checked his watch. "We'll notify the rangers when we're down. Right now, we have to get Wes off the mountain."

Patrick went into doctor mode, examining Wes's arm again. "Can you move your fingers?"

Wes tried, his face going white. "Yeah, but it's like a static shock every time."

Patrick probed the arm as gently as he could. "No gross deformity. Maybe a radial head fracture, maybe a ligament tear."

"Copy that, Doc," said Wes, and he flexed his good hand, trying to keep the bravado going.

"Do we have anything to splint it with?"

Lewis shook his head. "I have a real sling in my pack. There's more gear down at the huts."

Wes said, "I can splint it with someone's help when we get back there."

Patrick frowned. "If you're sure."

"I am."

Pauline said, "Here's the deal. Wes can't climb, and it will take Lewis and another person to get him down. The other three can push for the summit with me if you're up for it, but if so, we need to leave now."

Henry, who'd been silent, put his hand on Patrick's shoulder. "I'll go with Wes. I think I'm at my limit anyway."

Patrick looked at him, searching for any sign of false modesty, but Henry just stared back, matter of fact. "If that's what you want."

"Go," said Henry. "And then tell us all about it."

Pauline nodded at Patrick. "You coming with us, then?"

He looked at Wes and Henry, both shivering and done. He looked at the mountain, a monster with its head in the clouds. And he looked at Connor, who he had no read on, and Dunk, who had been the center of drama the previous day.

But the answer was clear. This is what he'd come for. "Yes," he said.

Lewis started rigging the sling for Wes's arm. Patrick kept a close eye on the process, but the guide did a good job. Lewis was all business now, voice clipped and urgent. "We'll split here then. I'll shepherd Henry and Wes back to Muir. You'll turn around if you don't think you can make it there and then all the way back down before nightfall?"

Pauline shook snow off her boots. "Yes. Always."

The split was surprisingly clinical. Lewis double-checked the rope, gave Henry and Wes the last of his water, then nodded to Pauline as she clipped Patrick into her rope team. "The window will be small. No heroics."

Pauline smiled, and Patrick saw a glint of something in her eyes, something he could relate to. "Wouldn't dream of it," she said, and gave her rope a jerk.

Connor finished his water, and they set off. Pauline leading, then Dunk, followed by Connor, with Patrick last. The air got thinner and meaner. Each step was a negotiation. Balance, then drive the crampons, then haul. Pauline set an aggressive pace, clearly trying to make up for the lost time. Dunk handled it with energy to spare. Connor, by contrast, moved like a ghost, gliding over the ice, eyes locked on the boots in front of him. At one point, visibility dropped to nothing and they moved by feel, heads down, until Pauline called a halt. She motioned them in, faces almost touching in the wind.

"It's decision time," she said. "We're behind schedule, but we can make it if we pick up the pace."

Dunk didn't hesitate. "I'm here to summit."

Connor said nothing. He looked at Patrick, and for a second, Patrick saw the fatigue in the young man's face. But he nodded. "I'm game."

Pauline turned to Patrick. "What do you think, Doc?" She had picked up on Wes's nickname for him.

He was cold, his calves ached, and the vision of the dead man in the glacier was still floating just under the surface of his mind. Patrick felt the adrenaline spark in his veins, pulling him forward, up, to the top of the world.

"I'm all in," he said.

Pauline grinned. "Then let's giddy up, gentlemen."

Patrick lifted his eyes on the summit. He would do this, then he would get his butt back home.

CHAPTER TWENTY-TWO: START

BUFFALO, WYOMING
AUGUST 25, 1978

Perry

PERRY WRINKLED HIS NOSE. He'd spent the last ten minutes fiddling with Trish's bed's remote and, when that got old, counting the holes in the acoustic tile above her head. He was bored, and he hated the food-left-out-too-long smell of the hospital, but he wouldn't say that in front of Trish, who lay in her bed with her leg in a big brace and an IV tube snaking into her arm. He was going to be the first one to sign when they finally cast her leg in plaster in a few days.

Her face was bruised, a purple ring under one eye, and the stitches on her brow made her look like a repaired Raggedy Ann doll. "You don't have to sit here, you know. You can go get food or whatever."

Perry shifted in his chair. "I already ate." It was a lie.

"Fine."

The door clicked open and a man in a black and gold warmup suit stepped inside, his jacket zipped to his chin.

"Hey, Perry," Coach said. "Trish. How's the patient?" Coach Cantrell had a voice that could vibrate water glasses.

Trish smiled at him. "Not dead yet."

"That's the attitude." Coach clapped Perry on the back hard enough to jar his teeth. He pulled up the extra chair and put his arms on his splayed knees. "I figured I should come check on our Baby Wolverine and his sister. How you holding up, kid?"

"Good," Perry said. "I'm good."

Coach sized him up for a moment. "You know, it was pretty impressive, rolling out of the way like that. I saw the marks on the pavement when I came by this morning. You must've been running pretty damn fast."

Perry shook his head. "It was because of Trish. She pushed me out of the way. That's why she got hit."

Coach said, "That's heroic, Trish."

Trish looked away. "It was instinct."

"I'm sorry either of you got hit, and for what you're going through." He turned back to Perry. "You coming to the game tonight?"

"I want to play," Perry said. "If that's okay."

Coach grinned, the gap in his front teeth on full display. "If you're sure you're not too banged up, it's okay with me."

Trish's eyebrows furrowed. "Don't you want to, like, rest after what happened?"

"I'm fine," Perry said again. "It wasn't even that bad."

Coach said, "That's the spirit. Gonna be a big crowd for opening night. You're starting, you know."

"I am?" Perry asked, unable to keep the hope out of his voice.

"Right out of the gate," said Cantrell. "Special teams."

Perry smiled so wide his cheeks stretched. For a second, he forgot about the hospital, the car, everything except the thought of being on the field under the lights, the whole town watching.

His mom stepped in just then, holding a paper cup. She looked tired, but she was smiling. "Everything okay in here?"

Coach stood, all business. "Just telling your boy he's starting tonight, if he can come to the game."

His mom looked at Perry, her eyebrows raised. "You're up for that?"

"I want to." For a moment, Perry remembered Larry's dad. His words, his threat. He had to shake that off. That was just talk. *Probably. Unless he's the one that ran Trish over.*

"I'm sorry to miss your game, though." His mom knelt by Trish's bed and smoothed her hair. "I'm going to stay here."

"I'm fine," Trish said.

"I know. But that doesn't change my decision." She turned to Perry. "Go have fun."

Coach said, "We better get going. Need to run through a few things before warmup."

Perry followed him out, feeling the heat of pride in his ears. *I'm starting!*

THE RIDE to the stadium in Coach's truck was awkward at first. The air conditioner was off and the windows were up. The cab smelled like BenGay. He looked over the fields, brown and alive with grasshoppers. The mountains in the distance were sharp outlines in a cloudless sky.

"You're a good kid," Coach said, eyes on the road, left arm resting on the edge of the window, wrist dangling. "Not just a good athlete."

Perry squirmed a little. "Thanks."

"You're tough, and you think like a football player. That's rare."

Perry didn't know what to say, so he just nodded.

Couch tapped the steering wheel. "You're crazy, but the good kind of crazy. You hit like you're twice your size."

That lit Perry up inside. He imagined himself running down the field, breaking through the wedge, making a tackle so hard the other team would remember his name. "My dad taught me to always give one hundred percent."

"It shows. Keep it up."

They pulled into the school lot. The sun was turning gold over the gym and the football field. Perry saw the bus for the opposing team, painted Columbia blue.

"You go on in." Coach cut the engine. "I'll be there in a minute."

Perry picked up his bag and walked to the locker room. He was the first one there, so he went to his locker near the showers and started changing. His jersey felt stiff and cold, but he liked the way it made his arms look.

After a while, the rest of the team showed up. The locker room filled with the sounds of metal lockers clanging shut, the stink of sweat, and the buzz of excited voices. The older guys mostly ignored him, except for Wyatt, who said, "Heard you got hit by a car."

"It missed me, but it got Trish."

"Is she okay?" Wyatt had a crush on Trish the year before. He hit on Perry's girlfriend Kelsey when Trish didn't like him that way, which was why Perry didn't have a girlfriend anymore. Perry had to be nice to Wyatt because he was team captain.

"She had surgery for a broken leg. I think she'll be okay."

"Man, that sucks. Tell her I hope she gets better soon."

"I will."

Perry tied his cleats tight and slapped his helmet against his thigh.

When they jogged out to the field for warmups, the bleachers were filling in. As the team stretched at the end zone, Perry looked up and saw a man standing at the chain-link fence on the other side of the field. He had brown hair, curling up at the ears and wore sunglasses, even though the sun was setting. He was leaning against the fence with his hands in his jacket pockets.

Something about him was familiar in a way that made Perry's blood run cold.

He looked again. The way he was staring at Perry, maybe it was

Larry's dad? It was too far away to tell, if he'd even recognize the guy. Their interaction had been so sudden and over so quickly. Perry had mostly been in shock that it was even happening. This guy was probably just a regular parent. Perry didn't know the family of everyone on the team.

Still, his skin prickled. He tried to focus on the drills, but every time they turned and ran, he checked for the man at the fence. Once or twice, he thought he saw him staring at him, but maybe it was just the sunglasses, or maybe Perry was just being stupid.

The man didn't move. He just watched. Perry tried to see if one of his teammates was looking at the guy or waving at him, but he didn't think anyone was. Could it be the guy who'd hurt Trish? He didn't have a mustache. He wasn't wearing a white T-shirt. And there wasn't a blue Bronco anywhere in sight.

Perry had to shake it off. He was just being paranoid. He had to focus and play his guts out. *Like a wolverine.* Then, afterward, he'd be proud of what he did on the field.

He just wished one of his parents could be here to see it.

CHAPTER TWENTY-THREE: SUMMIT

Mount Rainier, Washington
August 25, 1978

Patrick

Patrick, Dunk, and Connor followed Pauline in a diagonal traverse across the upper snowfield, aiming for the saddle above the glacier. It was as if someone had turned the world monochrome and punched a hole in the air where the summit should be. Wind battered them in staccato bursts, although overall it had slowed, as had the snow. Pauline would pause, lean into it, then push forward, always exactly on pace.

The climb changed with the altitude. The body burned in layers, first the calves, then the lungs, then a weird, buzzing cold in the teeth. Even the sound was different up here. Instead of wind or breath, it was a constant, high-pitched ringing. Patrick bit his tongue to stay alert and got an immediate, sharp taste of metal.

After the first hour, Dunk started muttering to himself, low and steady. "Gotta do it, gotta do it." Connor was now listing visibly to the right, each step hesitant, like he was following a trail only he could see. Patrick had assumed he'd be the drag on the rope team, but it was Connor who kept losing the interval.

Pauline called a halt.

They hunched together, axes planted, using their bodies to shield the patch of snow where she drew the route with a gloved finger. "Summit ridge is a quarter mile, maybe forty-five minutes," she said, voice taut but not winded. "Conditions are better, but not ideal." She pointed at the boiling mass building over the summit. "We want to be headed down before that wave reaches us. We stay tight, and we keep the interval. If you don't think you can do it, tell me now."

"I'm good," said Dunk.

Patrick forced out, "Just a little winded."

Pauline's gaze locked on him, then drifted to Connor. "How about you?"

Connor gave a weak thumbs-up, eyes glassy.

She didn't buy it. "Stay close. If you change your mind, you say the word and we turn around."

Connor nodded. "Co-py," he said, his voice thick and slow.

They moved out. The snow was hardpan, crusted from the earlier storm, but under the surface was a layer of slush. Patrick focused on the lines in the snow, on the precise angle of his axe, on the micro-adjustments Pauline made at every switchback. The world had narrowed to a tunnel vision, with no sense of time. One minute, the sky was an encouraging blue, the next it was iron gray.

When they crested the saddle, the wind had dropped to a sustained twenty miles an hour. Pauline signaled another break, then motioned for them to duck behind a cluster of volcanic boulders, the only windbreak on the entire ridge. They took a knee, huddled close.

Patrick felt his body rebooting, blood slamming through his temples. He tried to remember the faces of his family, but all he got was a kaleidoscope of half-formed images. Susanne in the kitchen, Trish reading a book on the porch, Perry bouncing a basketball off the side of the house.

Dunk was first to speak, voice barely audible over the wind. "How much farther?"

Pauline checked her altimeter, then stabbed a finger skyward. "Four hundred vertical, then the summit plateau. This is our last push."

Patrick looked at Connor, who had sunk into a squat, arms wrapped around his knees, lips tinged blue-ish. His hands shook as he fished a granola bar from his pocket and fumbled the wrapper.

"Connor," Patrick said. "You good?"

It took a moment, but Connor managed a smile. "Yeah, man. Just —" He stopped, eyes going vacant for a split second. "Just gotta catch my breath." His words were a little slurry, like he'd had a few beers.

Patrick had seen it before. Altitude can do that.

Pauline crouched next to Connor, making sure to put her face at his eye level. "Hey," she said, voice calm. "You sure you can keep going?"

Connor nodded. "I've got this." But even as he said it, he listed sideways, nearly tipping over.

Patrick's doctor brain clicked in. Connor was exhibiting ataxia, slurred speech, and disorientation.

Pauline spoke up, voice firm, before Patrick needed to step in. "We'll extend the break. If you're not better in ten minutes, we go back. No ifs, ands, or buts. My call."

Connor nodded. "Got it."

Ten minutes later, she re-checked him.

"I swear I'm good," he said.

Pauline looked over at Patrick. He shrugged. It really should be her call, but he didn't object. He was behind Connor and would take care of him. Everyone deserved their chance to summit, and he knew Connor wanted it, too.

They moved out. The last stretch to the summit was a wind blasted ramp, knife-edged with exposure on both sides. Every hundred yards, Pauline would turn and check the line, making sure nobody was slipping. Patrick moved as if on autopilot, but he kept a close eye on Connor.

He felt the summit before he saw it—a change in the pitch of the ground, a sudden flattening, a sound that was almost like applause as the wind scoured the plateau clean of loose snow. They stood, blinking in the weird, half-light, the wind slamming them from the left.

Pauline signaled to unclip. "Stay away from the edges."

The summit of Rainier was not what Patrick had expected. There was no sign, no marker, just a shallow depression in the snow and a drop-off into the white. The sky above was open, a strange blue, but all around them clouds roiled.

Still, Patrick reveled in it. This. This is what he'd set out to do. Reach this pinnacle. Stand on this summit, beat his chest, and howl at the moon. Metaphorically, at least. In reality, he just rotated in a circle with his mouth open like a fool, taking it all in. For this moment, it was worth it. Every second of training, every sacrifice, every blister, every time a truck had slowed down as its driver gawked at him as he jogged the Buffalo backroads wearing an enormous backpack, every tense moment with Susanne. Even the mess with Bella Crooke that he would never have landed in if he hadn't started climbing. They summed to a price he'd been willing to pay, and without them, he wouldn't be here.

Here.

He almost hugged himself.

Pauline dug her camera from her jacket. "Photos, fast."

Her words broke his spiritual moment of accomplishment, but that was okay. This was important, too. Dunk and Connor crowded together, arms over each other's shoulders. Patrick put his arm around Connor, who was shivering hard. Patrick looked at Pauline and tried to smile for the camera. His face felt frozen.

Pauline took three shots. "Let's get the hell down."

Patrick reached out, put a hand on Connor's shoulder. "You good to descend?"

"Yeah," said Connor, but it was a weird, echoing voice. "I'm good. I'm good."

"Time to clip in," Pauline said.

Patrick whispered a goodbye to the spirit of Tacoma, the great volcano and the mountain it had created, then he turned back to the group.

In retrospect, everything happened incredibly fast. Connor took two steps then his boots hit an icy patch. He tried to correct his balance, tripped, and fell. Instead of falling down, he fell forward. Way forward. Over the edge forward, his body limp, like he'd lost consciousness.

As if in slow motion, he began to slide, doing nothing to stop his own descent.

CHAPTER TWENTY-FOUR: HOLD

Buffalo, Wyoming
August 25, 1978

Susanne

Susanne sat at the nurses' station with the beige house phone's coiled cord knotted around her wrist as she punched in the home number. Perry was supposed to be at the football game. Trish was three doors down, leg up and covered in a thin cotton blanket. She hated that she couldn't go to Perry's game and that Patrick wasn't there either. Their son's first start on varsity was a big deal. The only family member left to deploy was Joe.

After four rings, the other end picked up. "Hall-oh," Joe said.

"It's me," Susanne pressed a thumb to her forehead. "Perry's at the stadium. He needs somebody at the game. I can't be at two places at once, so I need you to get over there. Please."

Joe's voice was staticky, distant. "That why you called? You know I don't like to drive at night. Or to be in crowds."

"He's your grandson."

A longer pause, filled by the tick-tick-tick of a wall clock behind her. "I'll go," Joe said. "But only after supper. Haven't eaten since noon. When do you think you'll get here to make me something?"

It took everything in Susanne not to put a fist through the counter. "Trish just had major surgery. I've been at her side all day, and I'm *not* coming home. I'm staying with my daughter. You can make something yourself or buy food at the game. I don't care which." A weight was coming off her as she spoke. She hadn't realized how much her frustration with her father-in-law had built up. "I need you to do one thing for me tonight, and that's be there for Perry, to make sure he's safe and knows he is loved. Is that really too much to ask?"

There was a sound on the other end, a kind of stubborn exhale. "I'll do it, fine. But I don't like—"

"Not another word," Susanne said. "Trish could have died today. Both of them could have died. Some maniac tried to kill my kids. Save whatever you have to say for someone else, some other time."

For once, Joe went quiet. Then, a change of tone. "All right, then. I'll go."

The abrupt reversal startled her more than a raised voice would have. "Thank you, Joe."

She hung up before he could change his mind, then sagged onto a bench and let the weariness settle over her. After a few moments, her eyes flew open. Had she fallen asleep sitting up? She stood, stretching her arms until she felt the vertebrae pop in her back. She headed for Trish's room.

As she turned the corner, she almost walked into a stretcher rolling up the hall at a brisk clip. Kathy and another nurse steered the bed into an empty room. The person on the stretcher was small, female, and wrapped in a blood-spotted sheet. For a split second, Susanne thought it was a child.

But as the cart rolled past, the face came into view, and it was unmistakable.

It was Vangie Sibley.

The blood drained from Susanne's face. She lunged after the

gurney into the room. The nurses were already hooking up the blood pressure cuff and stripping away the sheet. Kathy met Susanne's eyes with a sad look.

Tears were trickling down Vangie's cheeks. "Susanne," she managed, voice almost a whisper.

"Vangie! What happened?" Susanne's hands shook, even as Kathy steered her gently to the side.

"I'm fine," Vangie said, but she didn't look it.

Kathy shook her head at Susanne, a subtle don't push it, but Susanne ignored her.

"Vangie. Talk to me. Are you hurt? Was it a fall?" She checked her friend's hands, then her scalp, then looked over at the sheet Kathy was wadding into a ball.

Vangie's lips trembled. "It's the baby." She started to sob, full-body convulsions.

Kathy pressed a cloth to Vangie's forehead. "Shhh, you need to rest, sweetie. We're going to need to—" She looked at Susanne, hoping for an assist.

"Vangie," Susanne said, kneeling to be eye-level. "What happened?"

Through shudders, Vangie said, "I started cramping this afternoon. I thought it was just gas or something I ate, but it got worse and then I just passed out." She squeezed her eyes shut. "One of the hands found me in the kitchen when he came in for supper, and he called an ambulance."

Susanne put a hand on her shoulder, trying to be both strong and gentle. "I'm so sorry. I'm so, so sorry."

Vangie shook her head. "Henry's on the mountain. He doesn't even know."

Susanne blinked hard. "They can't be reached until they're down. I hope it's soon. I can leave a message for him at the hotel to call you here, if you'd like."

"No." Vangie nodded, wiping her eyes. "I want to wait to tell him face to face. There's nothing he can do until he gets here. I just—I just want to hear his voice." Then she started to cry again, and it was the sound of absolute heartbreak.

Susanne held her friend through the wracking sobs, even as Kathy slipped a needle into Vangie's arm for an IV. Vangie didn't flinch at the stick, didn't even seem to notice.

After a few minutes, Susanne let her friend drift asleep, and she made her sad way to Trish's room. Her daughter slept, mouth open, face softened by the morphine. Susanne sat by the bed and watched her for a long time, remembering every fight, every joy, every time she'd thought she couldn't possibly love her more than she already did. She was so blessed with her two beautiful children and how easy it had been for her to have them. It broke her heart to see what Vangie was going through, had been through, again and again.

Susanne sat back in the chair by her daughter's bed, feeling an ache behind her eyes, fatigue in her bones. She let her mind wander to the last time she'd held Trish as a crying baby, to the night Perry was born, to the little, secret hope she used to hold to have four children. But Patrick had convinced her two was enough.

Somewhere on the mountain, her husband was climbing, step by step, toward an accomplishment he'd convinced himself he needed. She tried to imagine him, the way the snow would cling to his mustache, the way he'd curse the wind, the way he'd keep going even after every part of him wanted to quit.

"We need you here, Patrick," she whispered. "Please come home."

CHAPTER TWENTY-FIVE: CATCH

Mount Rainier, Washington
August 25, 1978

Patrick

As Connor fell, Patrick's first instinct was to reach for him, but the ground beneath his own boots was slick. He barely had time to half-lunge, half-dive, hands grasping for any part of Connor's jacket or pack straps.

He was too late. Connor's momentum had already carried him past Patrick's help, the slope dropping away in a long, perfect chute with nothing to slow him.

Patrick's boot slipped, and suddenly he was sliding, too, accelerating in a wild, uncontrolled rush. He tried to dig in with his elbows, but his gloves just smeared slush off the crust and made his spin worse. Somewhere above, Dunk shouted, but the sound was torn away by the wind. Patrick glimpsed Connor below him, limp but moving faster now, gaining speed with every heartbeat.

Patrick jammed the spike of his ice axe across his chest, shifted his weight hard left, and stabbed down. The first time, it just bounced off the glare ice. The second, it stuck and jarred his sore shoulder all the way to the socket. His body whipped sideways, and he felt the pop of the rotator cuff, but the axe held. For a moment he hung there, two feet off the snow, like a human pennant. Then, in a weird, weightless moment, he flopped down, and the world snapped back into place.

He chanced a look up the slope. Dunk was just a silhouette, a black cutout against the sky. Above him, nothing. Below, only the trail of churned snow where Connor had gone, and then the dizzying white drop.

Pauline was nowhere to be seen. Where was she?

Patrick tried to scramble to his knees, but his left arm ached, and it took him a second to lever himself upright. He fought for a grip with the crampons, finally anchored, and looked downhill. The main slope rolled away for maybe forty yards, then ended in a cornice, and after that it was bad physics and worse luck.

Connor was careening toward the edge, still in a slow spin. He wasn't yelling. He wasn't even flailing, just tumbling.

"Shit," Patrick said, and then, "Shit! Shit!"

He made a choice. He unclipped his own axe and started side-stepping, edging downslope as fast as he could. His left arm resisted at first, but he ignored the pain, swinging the axe in like a pick, then locking the spikes of his boots, repeating the sequence, accelerating.

Twenty feet below, Connor hit a depression and rolled, coming up face-down, arms splayed. His body skidded, caught again, then started to slide the last stretch toward the cornice. The wind was all Patrick could hear now. He tried to focus, trying to plan his route, calculating whether he could get there in time. If Connor went over, he would not survive, and Patrick knew it.

He tried to yell, but his voice came out as a croak, nothing but vapor.

Suddenly, there was a streak of movement. Pauline was there, descending the ridge in a controlled chaos, feet hammering the ice, axe out, crouched low like a linebacker about to blitz. In two seconds, she closed the gap, then, with a move that defied every guideline in the mountaineer's book, she dove for Connor's legs.

For a second both bodies slid together, accelerating, then the mass of them dug a rut in the snow, and Pauline's axe bit, the guide bracing both of them, somehow, despite their speed and weight.

All at once, the motion stopped. Both bodies lay still, half-buried in snow.

Patrick forced himself to keep moving, arm protesting with each swing of the axe. He reached them, breath ragged, and dropped to one knee, instantly shifting to doctor mode.

Pauline was on her side, breathing hard, face as red as if she'd been slapped. She had lost her hat, and her hair was pasted to her forehead in a fan of sweat and ice. She didn't seem to care.

Connor, facedown, was limp.

Patrick positioned himself by Pauline downhill of Connor then rolled him, careful not to torque his neck. The young man's eyes popped open. They were wild. His mouth began working but made no sound.

Pauline's face appeared in Patrick's vision, close enough that he could see her wide pupils. "Check his airway." Her voice was raspy and graveled.

Patrick did. Connor's teeth were clamped, but his tongue was not blocking his air. There was no blood in the mouth, but he was gasping, pulling tiny, ineffective breaths.

Pauline kept a hand on his shoulder, pinning him to the slope.

Dunk arrived, dropped beside them, and added his weight to the barricade that kept Connor from sliding further.

Connor finally spoke. "What... what happened?"

"You fainted. Took a little slide." Patrick jammed two fingers to Connor's carotid. It was rapid, for sure. He looked at Connor's limbs. Miraculously, nothing seemed broken. He had the younger man move each limb, his fingers and toes, his neck. "Can you sit up for me?"

Connor did, wincing. "I'm okay." His words were slurry like before, but Patrick didn't see evidence of a real injury.

"We need to get you down out of this altitude."

Patrick braced Connor under the shoulders with Dunk taking the legs and, together, under Pauline's direction, they crabbed their way back up the slope, using the battered trench of Connor's fall as a guide.

They reached the top of the ridge, where the route leveled out a bit, and Pauline made them stop. She forced Connor to drink electrolyte solution from a squeeze bag, then yanked a bivy sack from her pack and wrapped him tight.

"Can you walk?" Patrick asked.

"Yeah. I think so." Connor was able to half-stand, and together they shuffled the rest of the way to the summit plateau. The wind beat them from the left, and the blowing snow covered their tracks almost instantly.

At the edge of the plateau, Pauline anchored the team with Dunk and Patrick on either side of Connor and Pauline as point. Then she did a quick inventory of everyone's gear and pointed at Patrick. "You're medical. You stay close to him all the way down. Dunk, you cover rear."

Patrick nodded, already feeling the bruises blooming across his shoulder, imagining a possible torn rotator cuff. He was good enough, though. He could manage this.

They started the descent, step by step, every single movement measured and deliberate, like a group of arthritic old men. Connor moaned from time to time but did not resist.

The route down was, if anything, more treacherous than the climb up. Every exposed patch of snow was wind-hammered into ice. Patrick kept his eyes locked on Connor, his mind running through a constant cycle of assessment. Was the lowering altitude helping him? Was he better or worse?

Pauline led them unerringly, her body language telling them when to move, when to freeze, when to brace for gusts. She was a master conductor, each motion tuned to the tempo of the mountain. About halfway down the ridge, the wind dropped, and for a moment they could hear each other's voices again.

Dunk said, "I thought we'd lost you, Connor."

Patrick had, too.

They traversed the slope, one slow yard at a time, until at last they reached a sheltered depression where they could catch their breath. Pauline motioned for a break. They huddled behind a slab of rock.

Patrick went through the drill again. He checked pupils and pulse and asked the basic orientation questions. Connor answered them all. His eyes seemed a little clearer, and his breathing steadied.

Pauline pulled off her glove and jammed a square of chocolate into his mouth. He chewed it automatically.

Dunk looked at Patrick. "You good?"

"Banged up my shoulder a bit," Patrick said, "but I'll make it."

Dunk shook his head, awe or something like it on his face. "I can't believe she did that. Went after him like a damn superhero."

Patrick grinned, then flexed his left hand. "She's the real deal."

Pauline heard. She shot them a look. "We're not done yet. Muir's still three hours out."

She squatted in the snow, re-tied the team rope, and clipped each of them in herself, checking every knot, every carabiner. When she reached Patrick, she held his gaze. "You trust me?"

He nodded.

She looked at Dunk. "You?"

Dunk swallowed, then said, "Yeah. Yeah, I do."

Pauline's eyes were hard and bright, the gold in them fierce as a hawk's. "Good. Because it only gets harder from here."

From the look in her eyes, Patrick didn't doubt her for a second.

CHAPTER TWENTY-SIX: REGROUP

Mount Rainier, Washington
August 25, 1978

Patrick

Pauline had not lied. The descent was harder than the climb to the summit. Patrick would remember it for the rest of his life.

For the last half mile, with Patrick on one side and Dunk on the other holding him up, Connor's head lolled and his feet dragged. Dunk was essentially carrying the weight for both of them. Patrick was spent, his own left shoulder pulsing after the self-arrest, but he forced his muscles to comply.

When the battered foursome staggered into Camp Muir, they looked like survivors of a failed moon landing. Their faces were rimed with salt and windburn, their eyes raw and their jackets torn.

Eric was first out the door. He stared at Connor, then said, "You guys need help?"

Dunk said, "I got him," and guided Connor toward the nearest flat surface, a bench made of two-by-sixes and snow. Connor sat and almost toppled, but Dunk kept a grip on him.

Patrick joined Wes and Henry. Wes looked pale but composed. "How's the arm?"

Wes flexed his fingers and winced. "Not great, but I've had worse." He tried to smile, then failed. "Maybe not worse, but close."

Patrick smiled. "You guys were great today."

Henry gave a huff that could have been a laugh. "If puking and nearly quitting three times is great, sure."

"But you didn't. And you took care of Wes," Patrick said. "I'm proud to be your friend."

Henry finally smiled.

Pauline debriefed Lewis and Eric with a rapid-fire exchange of guide jargon. The words were lost on Patrick, but the meaning wasn't. All attention was on the battered, the injured, and the missing.

Missing. That word reverberated in Patrick's mind. Who was missing? He looked around. He saw the Gill, Dougie, and Ralph as well as Wes and Henry. Along with the guides, that was eleven people, and there group had started as twelve. One person was not there.

"Where's Gerald?" Patrick asked.

For a beat, nobody answered. Then Dougie said, "He's not here. Not in the other hut either. No one's seen him for hours. We hoped he'd gone to meet up with you guys."

"We didn't see him." Dunk snorted. "God, that Gerald. Why is he always causing trouble?"

Eric raised his hand. "It's time to go down to Paradise."

Henry slumped onto a bench. "Can't believe anyone would be dumb enough to walk out of here alone like that."

Pauline said, "People do dumb things at altitude."

Eric huddled the guides together. The conversation was a muted staccato. "Search and rescue—" "They won't get here until it's dark

—" "He could be fifty yards away and we'd never see him." "Have to wait until morning." "If he's hunkered down, maybe, but—"

Eric stepped away and addressed the room. "We're going to do two rescue teams. I will lead one, Pauline the other. Our focus is to get the injured down. If anyone's able to stay and help look for Gerald, let us know."

Dunk shook his head. "I'm taking Connor down."

Patrick caught the hard, exhausted set of Dunk's jaw. It wasn't all about loyalty to Connor. It was about disgust at Gerald, too. "I'm with you, Dunk." They'd made a good team so far, and Patrick wanted to keep a close eye on Connor.

Henry said, "I'll help with Wes. Gill, you in?"

Gill nodded, already gathering supplies. "All in."

Lewis said, "I'll stay up here overnight to search for Gerald. We have some daylight left today and can start again at first light if we don't find him."

The two Muckleshoot men looked at each other. Dougie shrugged. Ralph nodded.

"We'll stay with you," Ralph told Lewis.

Outside, the wind rattled the hut and packed the windows with a fresh layer of frost and debris. Patrick thought of Susanne, the way she questioned this part of his life, the part that needed the mountains and the challenge. He wondered if he should have stayed home or at the very least not brought Wes and Henry here. They'd very nearly ended up just three more bodies in the glacier, another ghost story passed around the hut when a batch of climbers asked, "You ever seen anyone die up here?"

And the answer would be, "Yes, more times than you'd like to think."

Was that Gerald's fate?

In the mountains, sometimes people don't get to choose their own ending. Patrick knew that now more than ever.

CHAPTER TWENTY-SEVEN: EARN

Buffalo, Wyoming
August 25, 1978

Perry

Perry sat in the locker room with his helmet in his lap and his jersey sodden with sweat, feeling every scrape and bruise as a point of pride and a tally of its cost. The win hadn't even sunk in yet. It had been a messy, almost-impossible fourth quarter, comeback, and he'd played a part in it. A *real* part.

He'd told himself he'd remember every second, but the details were already blurring. The only things that stood out were biting his own tongue, the sweat in his eyes, and the thwump of the ball against his hands when he'd blocked a punt. He'd felt it rattle his arms and heard the crowd screaming. Then all that mattered was chasing the ball before anyone else got it.

Coach strode in, his steps slapping the tile. He clapped a beefy hand on the chalkboard. "You boys earned this one. Buffalo Bison, one and oh. You know what that means?"

A ragged chorus shouted, "We're number one!"

Coach laughed. "Means you get to taste a win, and you get to want it again. But before you start thinking you're hot stuff, let's remember something." His gaze swept the benches. "Let's talk about the play that turned the whole damn game around. Who saw that blocked punt?"

A couple of the seniors pounded their fists on their pads, yelling "Flint!" and "That's my guy!"

Coach pointed at Perry. "Let's hear it for the Baby Wolverine. You saved us from a world of hurt, kid."

The locker room exploded in howls, someone giving a high-pitched "Awoooo!" that sounded more like a coyote than anything else, but the effect was electric. Perry ducked his head and felt his cheeks burn, but he couldn't stop himself from smiling.

The coach quieted the room with a whistle. "But let's get this straight. You block a kick like that, you hit like that, you're no one's baby. Not anymore." He let the words settle, then grinned. "From now on, you're just Wolverine, understood?"

A louder, more coordinated chant this time, half the team slapping their lockers, the others pounding the benches. "Wolverine! Wolverine! Wolverine!"

Perry tried to file every detail away so he could tell his dad about it later. He wished his family could have been in the stands to see his big play.

Coach had finished his speech and postgame chaos resumed, everyone talking at once. Some guys peeled off their pads, some hit the showers, and a few just sat on the bench, reliving every play. The concrete echoed with the clack of cleats and the steady drone of the old locker-room radio, tuned to the scores in other games.

As Perry reached for his towel, a pair of linemen wedged into the space on either side of him. Both had arms like pork shoulders.

"Hey, Wolverine." Billy thumped Perry on the back. "You're not dating that new girl Bijou, are you?"

Perry laughed, the question catching him off-guard. "We're just friends. I barely know her."

Chuck snorted. "Not what I heard, man. Someone said you were making out after school yesterday."

He felt his face flush. "We were just talking."

"Sure. Talking." Billy's eyebrows waggled. "You got Jillian on the hook, too? Or is that just a rumor?"

The world wobbled for a second. "Who?"

Dave grinned, teeth crooked and stained from grape soda. "Jillian. Word is she likes her men small and wild."

"Yeah, right." Perry snorted. "I'm not going with either of them."

Chuck made a show of crossing himself. "That's a shame, man. Gotta play the field while you're a hero."

He shook his head, but he was grinning. The fact that people even cared was weird. He kept his answer light. "I just want to play football."

They left him alone, retreating to a pack of sophomores who were arguing about a play in the third quarter.

Perry ducked into the showers for a lukewarm rinse, then pulled on jeans and the only clean shirt he had in his bag. He folded his number thirty-seven jersey and tucked it into with the rest of his stuff. He tied his laces, then hoisted his bag and headed for the exit. The locker room had mostly cleared, save for a few guys lingering to call home or change bandages. Perry decided not to call his mom for a ride. He could just walk to the hospital since she'd said she would be there with Trish.

Coach stood by the doorway, clipboard in hand. "Nice job out there, Flint. You'll remember this one. You need a ride?"

"Thank you. I'm walking back to the hospital." He waved and slipped out the side door.

The stadium, mostly empty, seemed like an entirely different place after a night game. The field glowed in a bubble of light, but outside the circle, shadows crowded in. The bleachers creaked and popped. The smell of popcorn and cigarette smoke still hung in the air.

He cut through the fence, following the path that would spit him out near the street. He ran through the game in his mind again, replaying every second, walking slowly. He felt sore in a good way, like he'd earned his place.

As he neared the sidewalk, he paused and glanced over his shoulder. The parking lot was mostly empty. Perry hugged the edge of it. A couple of upperclassmen loitered near a pickup, passing a bottle back and forth, but they ignored him. He kept going, head down, trying to look like he was cool.

He was almost to the end of the lot when he heard a sound. A footstep? The echo made it hard to tell if it was real or just the slap of his own sneakers against the pavement. He stopped and listened. It was gone. No one was there.

He started again, this time walking faster. The footsteps had made him a little nervous. They reminded him of his wary feeling before the game when he'd thought that man had been watching him. It had been the kind of day where bad things happened. He glanced over his shoulder. Still nothing. The hairs on his neck bristled, which was dumb. It was the stadium parking lot on a Friday night. Of course there were people here, and people made noises, including footsteps.

He heard them again. This time, louder. Closer. He turned, spinning a full circle, but the lot still looked empty around him. He let out a half-laugh. "Get a grip," he muttered.

He reached the sidewalk, crossed over to the hospital side, and for a moment he relaxed. The streetlights there were better, and the hospital sign glowed blue and white at the end of the block. He was almost safe.

The next second, something heavy smashed into the back of his head. The world flipped, then spun, then all the lights went out.

CHAPTER TWENTY-EIGHT: SNAP

Mount Rainier, Washington
August 25, 1978

Patrick

Patrick wasn't sure how long he'd been dozing in the back of the van, but it was the uneven rattle of the wheels over the last gravel patch of the access road that woke him. His head thunked against the window, and for a heartbeat he thought he was still mid-fall on the glacier, bouncing as he slid, his left shoulder in agony. His eyes popped open and his heartbeat slowed when he realized where he was. He tried to rotate his shoulder with partial success and not insignificant pain. Outside the world was a blue-black bruise, streaked with cloud. The only lights were from Paradise Inn, the sodium-orange glow of the visitor lot, and, directly in front of them, the strobing red and white of an ambulance.

He blinked, eyes gummy. The vehicle wasn't even parked yet, and already two paramedics jogged up to meet them. The entire van, full of battered climbers and tired guides, groaned in unison.

"Showtime," said Wes, who had not let go of his left forearm since they'd left the high camp.

Patrick tried to get his brain in order. He remembered the mountain, the good but also more than he wanted to, the bad. His team's equipment failure, their slide, the avalanche, Wes's injury. Discovering the long dead climber. Connor almost dying at the summit and now pale as wax, slumped against the window in the front passenger seat.

The guides got out of the Suburban first. Eric, his face a wind-chapped mask, counted heads, then went to the back and hauled out the largest of the battered duffels. Pauline intercepted the paramedics and gave a rapid-fire report on Connor's altitude symptoms, loss of consciousness, and fall.

The climbers opened the doors to the back seat. It was late enough that most tourists had retreated indoors, leaving a pine-scented silence broken only by the sound of the ambulance's engine.

"I'm looking forward to a real bed," Henry said, and gave Patrick a slap between the shoulder blades. Henry's headache had broken, but he looked like hell, and the lines in his face were deep trenches.

Patrick clambered out after him, legs rubbery, then turned to help Wes. His friend had refused to let an ambulance be called for him, insisting that Patrick could take care of him. Patrick had relented since he'd assessed that Wes didn't have an injury which waiting for more comprehensive treatment would worsen. If he had a break, it was at worst a non-displaced fracture which had snapped back into place. The cost of delay was pain, and if Wes was willing to pay it, it wasn't for Patrick to overrule him unless when he worked on stabilizing it in the Inn he discovered a complication he didn't expect. And, if he did, he would drive Wes to the hospital himself.

The ambulance was parked at an angle, engine running, lights flashing. The medics had already flipped on their work lights, casting long beams onto the pavement. One of them, the older of the two with gray hair poking out from his knit cap, pointed at Connor and said, "That him?"

Eric nodded. "Connor Patton. Yes. He's awake, but not right."

The paramedic grunted and took over, opening the front passenger door and barking instructions. "Let's go, Connor. Can you walk, son?"

Connor mumbled, "Yeah," but didn't move.

Dunk came around and tried to lift him, but Connor's legs didn't cooperate, and the medic had to catch his elbow to steady him. They bundled Connor onto a gurney, strapping him down as gently as they could. The second medic, a woman with a harsh scar across her nose, set about taping an oxygen line to his face and clamping a finger monitor to his hand.

Pauline motioned the other climbers toward the side entrance of the inn. "You guys should get some hot drinks, chow, showers, and beds. But first, Dunk and Patrick, can you come with me?"

Patrick didn't know how she could be so brisk after what they'd just done, but he followed her toward the ambulance, where the medics were prepping for departure. Connor's eyes were open.

Pauline said, "Dunk, can you give them his medical history? Allergies, prior head injuries, anything like that. And Patrick, I'd like you to give them your medical assessment of what happened on the mountain. "

Dunk rattled off a few things. No chronic illnesses, no known history of seizures. He apologized for not knowing more.

Patrick added, "He showed symptoms of ataxia and possibly acute mountain sickness for at least three hours before he collapsed." He went through the details and how Connor had done on the descent.

"Good enough," said the medic. He scribbled it on his report, then called into the radio. "Bringing patient to St. Joe's. ETA, one hour."

They loaded Connor into the ambulance. Dunk left with Gill, Wes, and Henry for the inn, but the doctor in Patrick made him stay behind. Even with oxygen now, he didn't like how Connor looked. He heard the sound of footsteps and turned.

It was Gerald. He was alone, hands in his pockets, watching the ambulance. "Who's in there?"

Patrick hesitated, then said, "You made it down, Gerald. That's great."

Gerald looked away. "I couldn't wait up there all day for you guys to get down."

"You look rough," Patrick said. "You need anything? Food, water?"

"Nothing," said Gerald, his voice flat. "Who's in there?" he repeated.

"Connor."

There was a silence then. Patrick waited for Gerald to say something else, but he just stood there, shifting his weight from foot to foot.

"Is Dunk inside?" Gerald finally asked.

"Yes," Patrick said. "Everyone's inside. You going in?"

"Not yet." His eyes flicked to the road, then back to Patrick. "You know, Connor was just along for the ride, but he couldn't say no. Never could. Not to anyone. I don't completely blame him for what he did. But at the end of the day, I have to stick by my commitment."

Patrick tried to make sense of it. "He's lucky you care about him," he said.

"I care about finishing what I started," said Gerald. "That's all."

Patrick nodded and headed toward the lobby.

Behind him, he heard scuffling noises. A primal scream.

What the heck? He turned.

Gerald was lunging into the back of the ambulance wielding an ice axe.

CHAPTER TWENTY-NINE: DEFEND

Paradise, Washington
August 25, 1978

Patrick

For half a heartbeat, Patrick's brain didn't register what he was seeing. Gerald, frozen for a split second, one boot on the running board, the other already airborne, ice axe overhead, about to bring it down on Connor's torso as he lay strapped to a gurney.

There was a sound. It was raw, guttural, and more animal than human. Only then did time resume its normal speed. Patrick launched forward with a wild reach, his own hand closing around Gerald's arm as the axe arced down. The head of the tool grazed Connor's parka, tearing a flap, then struck the gurney's steel frame with a metallic chime.

The blow should have been enough to stop Gerald cold, but he seemed to have a superhuman reservoir of strength. He twisted and tried to bring the axe around for another shot. Patrick crashed into his shoulder, nearly bowling both of them into the driver's side of the front seat. The world telescoped down to a mess of elbows, fists, and hot breath. Patrick was exhausted from summitting. Compared to him, Gerald had plenty of fight left in him.

"Jesus!" someone yelled from the front.

The two EMTs dove into the back at the same time, crashing past the gurney. One caught Gerald at the waist, the other pinned his left wrist to the floor. Patrick used his full body weight on Gerald's back, forcing his shoulder flat and wrenching the axe away. Gerald wrenched his head and neck around and tried to bite the nearest human, which was Patrick. He was luckily just out of range.

"Hold him! Hold him" the female medic barked as she reached for a webbed orange restraint strap.

Gerald snarled, spat, then went slack. He panted, snorting like a bull. Patrick had his knee in the center of the man's back. He wanted to say something. *What is wrong with you? Have you lost your mind?* But instead he concentrated on keeping the man's arm twisted away from any weapons.

The axe clattered on the van's floor, the spike now dull with red. *Connor's blood? No, not blood,* Patrick realized. Just a streak of red paint from the gurney.

Connor said, "What the hell? Did you guys see what he tried to do to me?" His words sounded clearer. Adrenaline, probably.

"You deserved it and worse, you traitor," Gerald said, projecting spittle with each word.

With practiced speed, the female medic buckled Gerald's wrists behind him, lashing them to a handle bolted to the ambulance wall. She leaned in, her face inches from Gerald's. "If you so much as twitch, I will narc you right here, clear?"

Gerald's eyes were glassy, his lips peeled back in a silent snarl. He blinked but didn't answer her.

The older medic, his face red and trembling, had to reset his glasses twice before he managed to radio for police backup. "This is Lander Base. We have a code black, repeat, code black. Violent subject, armed but subdued and restrained. We are parked at Paradise Inn lot, immediate response needed. Over."

Pauline, who'd been at the lodge entrance corralling stragglers, sprinted over. She scanned the scene, took in the chaos, then locked eyes with Patrick. "Are you okay?"

"Fine. Connor, are you okay?"

Connor lifted his head, face pale. "He missed me. I'm fine."

Patrick shook his head. "Barely. Dear God. He would've split your head like a coconut."

"The only thing better would have been his balls," Gerald muttered.

The female medic, already shifting into triage mode, said, "He still needs to get to the hospital. Let's roll. The subject is restrained. He'll be fine. We'll radio to redirect the cops to meet us."

Her partner nodded. "You're right." He crawled back into the driver's seat.

She hopped out the back, Patrick right behind her, then she slammed the ambulance doors and disappeared around to the passenger side.

Patrick stepped away, breathing hard, the adrenaline making his hands shake. He watched as the van fishtailed out of the lot, lights strobing off the slicked pavement.

Pauline said, "What the hell was that about?"

He wiped his hands on his windbreaker, still tasting the coppery tang of fear in his mouth. "I don't know." He thought about what Gerald had said. "Either he had some kind of grudge against Connor or just went crazy. He tried to brain him with an ice ax. I guess he would have if I hadn't stuck around. I just barely managed to knock his aim off."

"How terrifying!"

Patrick nodded. "It was. Thanks for saving Connor's life up there."

"Thank you for saving it down here."

They headed toward the warm light leaking from the inn's lobby.

The walk felt longer than it should. Each step, the image of Gerald's face flashed in Patrick's mind. He wondered what would drive a man to do that, to attack with such intent.

Inside, the empty lobby Pauline bid him goodbye. Patrick paused. His multiple brushes with death made him want to hear Susanne's voice before he did anything else. He headed toward the pay phone.

The young woman at the front desk who had checked Patrick in the night before called out to him as he passed. She was on the phone, hunched over a notepad, her face flushed with urgency. When she saw him, she covered the receiver and called out, "Are you Patrick Flint?"

He blinked. "That's me."

She looked relieved. "I thought so. There's a call for you. It's urgent." She held out the phone. "It's your wife."

Urgent? That didn't sound good at all. Patrick's throat tightened. For a second, he could only stare at the phone, as if it were a rattlesnake. He took it, bracing for impact.

"Susanne?"

She answered on the first breath. "Patrick. Oh, thank God. Are you safe?"

He squeezed the receiver. "I'm fine. There was, um, well, something happened, but I'm okay. How are you?"

There was a pause. "I'm fine. But Trish."

Patrick felt like his insides had just jumped off the top of the Empire State Building. "What about Trish? Is she okay?"

"She was hit by a car. She had surgery. Dr. John said she'll be fine. Perry was with her, but he wasn't hurt—" Susanne's voice cracked, and the rest came out as a sob. "I need you home."

He closed his eyes. A million questions ran through his mind, but all of them would delay leaving. Dr. John said Trish would be fine, so he asked only one. "What happened to her?"

"A compound fracture of both leg bones."

It was serious, but she was in good hands, and barring a rare complication, extremely unlikely to be life threatening now. Painful, a slow recovery, and still with potential long-term problems, but not as life altering as an injury to her head, neck, back, or internal organs, like her spleen. He swallowed down a big lump in his throat. "Oh, Susanne. I'm so sorry. I'll leave now. I'll be there as fast as I can drive. Is there anything else you need me to know or do before I get Wes and Henry and go?"

The line went quiet. "Perry. He's starting tonight. I sent your father to watch him so I could be with Trish."

There were so many reasons to question his choice to be in Washington this week. Perry's first game as a varsity starter. Neither parent had been there. It wasn't nearly as important as Trish's wellbeing, but it still stung. "Thank you for sending Dad."

"Hurry, okay?"

"I promise I will. I'm sorry, and I love you." He hung up, feeling his legs go hollow. This changed everything. He, Wes, and Henry had planned to stay the night to rest and recover, but they had to get on the road. *Trish. Susanne. Perry.* Waves of guilt crashed over him. He should have been home. He should be there now.

CHAPTER THIRTY: SEARCH

BUFFALO, WYOMING
AUGUST 25, 1978

Susanne

FLUORESCENTS HUMMED FROM ABOVE, electronic cicadas slowly driving Susanne crazy. Her stomach growled. She couldn't remember whether it was dinner, lunch, or breakfast she'd last managed to eat. She sat in the recliner next to Trish's bed, cross-legged with her shoes off, staring at the plastic pitcher on the tray. Every so often, a nurse would come in to check Trish's pulse and pain level, but not Kathy, who had gone off shift a few hours before.

Trish slept with her mouth slightly open now. Susanne's hands were in her lap, and she clenched and unclenched them. She'd tried reading *Good Housekeeping* magazine, twice, but the words swam. It was easier just to watch Trish.

The phone at the bedside rang.

For a heartbeat, Susanne thought it was Patrick, calling from Washington. She had forgotten to tell him about Vangie losing the baby. Vangie hadn't wanted to tell Henry, but didn't he deserve to know? She jumped up and grabbed the phone receiver.

"This is Susanne Flint," she said, breathless.

"This is Joe." Gone was the conciliation she'd heard in his voice earlier.

"You okay?" she asked.

"I was better before I drove across town for nothing."

"What? Did Perry not play?"

"Oh, he played all right. Helluva game. Blocked a punt even."

"That's great! So, what's wrong?"

"What's wrong is I went all that way for nothing. Where's the boy?"

Her throat tightened. "He didn't go home with you?"

"No," Joe said, voice sharp. "I stayed through the end of the game, then I got to talking with some fellas I was sitting with. When I got to the locker room, no Perry. His coach said he was walking to the hospital."

Susanne's mouth went dry. "How long ago was this?"

"An hour or so. Is he there?"

She clutched the neck of her blouse. "He's not here."

There was a long, spiky silence. Joe was never at his best with ambiguity. "Well, he's not with me."

She caught a tremor in his voice. "He'll turn up," she said, but it tasted like ash. "Maybe he's with friends?"

"If he is, he owes me an apology. I'm going to bed. But, uh, call me when he turns up."

"You do the same if he shows up at home."

He made a harrumphing noise.

She hung up, then stood for a moment, trying to will herself back to calm. Maybe Perry was in the cafeteria. Maybe he was in the family room, asleep in a chair. Maybe, maybe, maybe, but every maybe drove her a mile closer to panic.

She hurried out, checking the nurse's station first. A red-haired nurse was manning the desk. Susanne had only met her once. Becky.

"Have you seen my son?" Susanne asked. "He's fourteen, blond, a little beat up from a football game?"

Becky shook her head. "Want me to check the ER?"

"Yes, please. Anywhere and everywhere."

While Becky dialed, Susanne walked to Vangie's room. She looked inside. Vangie was asleep. Perry wasn't with her. Not that she'd expected him to be. He hadn't even known Vangie was in the hospital.

She went back to Trish's room, moving faster now. For a wild second Susanne wanted to wake her up, to ask if she remembered anything, if she'd seen Perry. But that was crazy. Susanne had been with her the whole time.

The hospital was quiet, the only noise the clink of a cart in the hallway and Trish's monitor. Susanne paced, hands worrying each other. She thought about Perry as a toddler, how he would vanish from playgrounds. They'd search frantically for him, fearing the worst, only to find him behind the trash cans or up in the highest part of the jungle gym. Not lost, never lost, just hiding.

The phone in the room rang, jarring her out of the memory. She grabbed it. "Hello?"

It was Becky. "No sign of him in the ER or the cafeteria. He's not in any of the waiting rooms, either. Do you want us to page him?"

"Please."

"Okay. I'll call you if we find him."

"Thank you." Susanne set the phone in the cradle.

She waited for the page. The ancient loudspeaker crackled and echoed through the halls. "Perry Flint, please report to the main desk. Perry Flint, come to the main desk."

For long minutes she let herself hope it would do the trick, that Perry would materialize, sheepish and hungry, with some half-baked excuse.

After ten, she gave up. No Perry.

She checked the time. Past eleven. Her pulse was starting to race, the inside of her skull buzzing with what-ifs and could-bes. With the car that had crashed into Trish and very nearly into Perry. Of Bella loose. Of Perry starting that night, beating out the kid whose father had threatened Perry.

She could search more, and she wanted to call Patrick. Maybe she could catch him before he left for home. Those things had to wait, though. It was time to bring in the police. And the officer she trusted most just happened to be one of her best friends.

Hands trembling, she picked up the phone and called Ronnie's home number as her lips moved in prayer.

CHAPTER THIRTY-ONE: RETURN

PARADISE, WASHINGTON
AUGUST 25, 1978

Patrick

AFTER PATRICK HUNG up the phone with Susanne, he turned, intent on finding Henry and Wes. He didn't have far to go. Wes was seated on a bench across the lobby, his arm cradled against his chest in its sling. Henry paced nearby.

Patrick almost ran over to them. "We need to leave," he said without preamble. He'd have time to tell them about Gerald and Connor later. "Trish got hit by a car. She's had surgery. I'm sorry, but I've got to get home."

Henry stopped pacing. "Jesus, Patrick. When did you find out?"

"Just now." Patrick ran a hand through his hair. "Let's pack and go. You guys can sleep on the road."

Wes stood, wincing as the movement jarred his injured arm. "I'll grab my stuff."

"No, you sit," Patrick said. "We'll get it."

"Room 212." Wes handed him a key. "I have a small duffel. Stuff everything in the bathroom into it. Everything else is packed or with me from the climb." He nodded at his backpack on the floor by his feet.

Patrick nodded, then turned to Henry. "You okay?"

Henry's face was still pale, but his eyes were clear. "More than. And I'm driving."

"Your head. You need to sleep."

"I'm driving," Henry repeated, firmer this time. "Your daughter's hurt, you're a terrible driver even when you're not distracted, and Wes has one working arm. I'm the best option we've got."

Patrick didn't have the energy to argue. "Fine. I'll grab your bags, too, so you can load our climbing gear in the Suburban. I left it unlocked." His theory was that if there was nothing to steal in a car, there was no reason to break out the windows. No self-respecting car thief would steal a gold Pontiac Lemans anyway. "Everyone meet back out there in fifteen minutes."

He raced upstairs to his room, heart hammering against his ribs. Every second felt precious now, every moment away from Buffalo a betrayal. He should have been there. He should never have left. The guilt was a physical weight pressing down on him as he threw clothing and gear haphazardly into his duffel, then did the same for his friends.

Back in the parking lot, Henry and Wes were already waiting. The night was brisk and clear, a stark contrast to the storms they'd battled all day on the mountain. The stars seemed almost mocking in their brilliance.

Henry took two of the bags hanging off Patrick's body and sore left shoulder and threw them in the back. He slammed the rear door. "Let's move."

Patrick helped Wes into the backseat, arranging the pillows they'd brought from home to stabilize his arm.

"I'll work on that arm on the way," Patrick said, climbing into the passenger seat. "I want to do a better job of immobilizing it."

"I'm fine for now," Wes said. "Let's just get us home."

Henry started the engine. "It's a seventeen- or eighteen-hour drive without stops. I'll need you to trade off with me some, Patrick."

Patrick nodded, already calculating. "We should trade every few hours to stay fresh and alert." They'd need gas, coffee, maybe a quick stop for food. Every minute counted. He glanced at his watch. It was just past ten. That would put them home before five the next day.

As Henry pulled out of the parking lot, Patrick stared at the shadow of Mount Rainier against the night sky. Just hours ago, standing on its summit had seemed like the most important thing in the world. The events of the day had created a pile that outweighed the achievement by a long shot.

He closed his eyes, trying to pray, but all that came was a desperate, wordless plea. The guilt crashed over him in waves.

Hang on, Susanne. I'm coming home.

CHAPTER THIRTY-TWO: WAKE

Bighorn Mountains, Wyoming
August 26, 1978

Perry

Cold. That was the first thing Perry felt. Cold seeping through his clothes, pressing into his skin. Then the pain hit. A throbbing, pulsing ache at the back of his skull that made the world spin even with his eyes closed. He tried to open them, but they seemed stuck with something crusty and dry. After several more tries, he opened them to slits. Where was he? How long had he been here? Why didn't he know?

The night sky glowed faintly above him, stars pricking through a webbed ceiling of pine branches. His cheek pressed against something hard and gritty. Dirt, maybe pine needles. A strong smell was right under his nose, like dirt but older. He tried to move his arms, found them working, though heavy. Very heavy. His right arm was pinned underneath him. His left hand came up to touch the back of his head. His fingers came away sticky and dark.

Blood. His blood.

Panic surged through him, overwhelming the pain. He strained to hear anything human. Cars, voices. But there was only the soft rustle of wind and the distant hooting of an owl. No headlights. No streetlights. No houses. No hospital. No stadium.

The stadium. That's where he'd been. The football game. His blocked punt. Coach calling him Wolverine and telling everyone that he was no baby wolverine anymore.

He tried to sit up, and the world tilted violently. His stomach clenched, and he fought down the urge to vomit. Everything hurt. His head was the worst, but his ribs ached, his side, his back. Had he been in a car crash? He didn't think so. He remembered walking from the stadium, heading toward the hospital to see Trish and his mom.

Trish. The car had hit her. The Bronco. The man.

Perry blinked, trying to clear his vision. He had to get up. Had to find help. Had to get back to his family.

He tried again to sit up, rolling to his side first, using his elbows for leverage. The pain in his head spiked, white-hot, making his vision a night sky of fireworks. He waited for it to pass, then pushed himself to a sitting position.

The clearing around him came into focus, but it seemed to move like waves under a boat. Trees. Lots of them. Pines mostly, tall and dark against the night sky. Rocks and undergrowth. A small open space where he lay. No path. No road. No sign that anyone had ever been here except him.

"Help," Perry tried to call, but it came out as a hoarse whisper. He swallowed, winced at the dryness, and tried again. "Help! Help me!"

His voice sounded thin and small, swallowed by the forest. Emptiness crushed in on him, and for a terrible moment, he felt like crying. But he wasn't a little kid anymore. He was the Wolverine now. He had to be tough.

Again, he tried to figure out how he'd gotten here. The last thing he remembered was toward the hospital. Then... nothing. Just blankness where his memory should be, and then waking up here, wherever here was.

The back of his head. The blood, the throbbing. Someone must have hit him. Like the car had hit Trish. But who? And why bring him out here?

Perry gingerly touched his head again, finding a raised, tender lump in his matted hair.

He needed to stand up. Needed to find his way back to town. He was wearing the same clothes he'd put on after the game. Jeans, sneakers, a t-shirt. No jacket, because it was August and hot as fire. Yet where he was now, it was pretty cold. He checked his pockets. Empty. No wallet. No change. The moon gave just enough light to see by, a thin crescent hanging low but not blocked by the mountains. Because the mountains were clearly where he was. The cold air. The forest around him.

Mom would be worried sick. The thought gave him a jolt of determination. *Get up. Find your way home.* If he could see the stars, maybe he could figure out which way was north.

Perry braced himself against the ground and tried to push up to his knees. The movement sent a fresh wave of pain through his skull and a surge of nausea to his stomach. He paused, breathed through his mouth in short gasps, waiting for the spinning to stop.

When it slowed enough, he tried again. Knees first. Then one foot planted. Then pushing up, using a tree trunk for support. The world swooped and swayed around him, but he managed to get upright, leaning heavily against the rough bark.

Standing made his head hurt even worse. Each beat of his heart sent pulsing pain through his skull. He pushed off from the tree, took one shaky step, and nearly fell. His balance was off, the world tilting and swaying with each movement. It was like the time he'd spun around thirty times for a game of pin-the-tail-on-the-donkey at his friend John's birthday party. Only a hundred times worse. *And John was dead. Had been for a long time.*

He took another step. Then another. Each one sent spikes of pain through his head, but he kept going. Five steps. Ten. He was making progress, though painfully slow.

"Dad," he whispered. "Dad, what would you do?"

His dad always knew what to do. But his dad was on a mountain in Washington, and Perry was alone in the dark.

A memory flashed. His dad teaching him about using stars to navigate. The Big Dipper. Follow the pointer stars to the North Star. But which way was home? Buffalo could be in any direction. And these were mountains—the Bighorns, probably. The mountains covered hundreds of miles.

Perry's foot caught on something, and he stumbled. The sudden movement made his stomach heave. He doubled over, retching. Nothing came up but bile. His stomach was empty. The vomiting made his head hurt even worse. He spat, trying to clear the sour taste from his mouth, and wiped his lips with the back of his hand. The world was spinning faster now, trees blurring into a dark smear against the starlit sky.

Keep moving, he told himself. Just keep moving.

He took another step, then another. Each one felt like walking on a ship's deck in a storm. Maybe he'd find a trail. Maybe it would lead to a road.

Perry focused on that hope. He put one foot in front of the other. Twenty steps. Thirty. The trees were thinning out a little. Maybe there would be a clearing ahead where he could see better, figure out which way to go.

His shoe slipped on a patch of pine needles, and he went down hard on one knee. The impact jarred his whole body, sending a fresh explosion of pain through his head. The world tilted sharply, like a roller coaster off its tracks.

Black spots danced in his vision. The trees around him seemed to bend and sway, though there was barely any wind.

"No," he gasped. "No, no, no."

If he went down completely, he knew he wouldn't be getting back up. Not right away. The world was spinning too fast now, the stars making streaks across the sky. He tried to keep his eyes open, but the lids felt weighted.

"Help," he tried once more, but his voice was barely audible even to himself.

He slumped forward, catching himself on his hands before he faceplanted into the dirt. The pain in his head had become all-encompassing, blotting out every other sensation except the cold. So cold.

His arms gave out, and he collapsed onto his side. The rough ground pressed against his cheek, but he barely felt it now. Darkness crowded the edges of his vision.

His last conscious thought was of his family. Mom at the hospital with Trish. Dad on Mount Rainier with Wes and Henry. None of them knew where he was. None of them could help him.

Then the darkness swallowed him, and he knew nothing more.

CHAPTER THIRTY-THREE: BURN

Buffalo, Wyoming
August 26, 1978

Trish

Trish became aware of heat like fire ants marching through her veins. She opened her eyes to the dim hospital room, the fluorescent light in the hallway casting just enough glow through the cracked door for her to see the shadowy outlines of the medical equipment around her. Something was wrong. Her body felt like it was burning from the inside out. Her hospital gown was sticking to her sweat-slicked skin. The brace on her leg felt like a furnace, trapping the heat inside.

She turned her head, expecting to see her mother's sleeping form in the recliner beside the bed, but the chair sat empty, the thin hospital blanket crumpled in a heap on the seat.

"Mom?" Her voice cracked, barely audible even to herself. The clock on the wall read two seventeen. Morning or afternoon? The darkness outside the window suggested early morning.

Trish pushed herself up on her elbows, wincing as pain shot through her shoulder. Just the slight movement made her feel short of breath and sent a wave of dizziness washing over her. For a moment, the room tilted dangerously. She squeezed her eyes shut. When she opened them again, the room had steadied, but the heat remained.

Trish reached for the plastic cup of water on the bedside table, but her fingers trembled so badly she knocked it over. The cup tumbled to the floor. *Great. Perfect.* She leaned back against the pillows, her breaths shallow.

Her thoughts drifted back to the accident. The blue car, the squeal of tires, the sensation of flying through the air. She remembered pushing Perry, the split-second decision that saved him and landed her in this hospital bed. Was he hurt? Was that why her mom was gone?

No, that doesn't make sense. Perry was fine. Bruised, but fine. He'd gone to play in his football game. But if not Perry, then what? Her dad, maybe? The thought sent a spike of fear through her chest. Climbing Mount Rainier was dangerous. Her mom had been worrying about it all summer.

Trish fumbled for the call button, her fingers slipping on the plastic as she pressed it repeatedly. Each second of waiting seemed to stretch into a minute. Her chest felt heavy. Beads of sweat rolled down her temples.

"Hello?" she called, her voice stronger this time. "Is anyone there? I need help."

The silence that answered her was unnerving. Weren't hospitals supposed to be busy, even at night? She pressed the call button again, holding it down.

Just as she was about to try calling out again, the door swung open. A nurse Trish didn't recognize stepped in, clipboard in hand. She was older than Kathy, with steel-gray hair pulled back in a tight bun, and wire-rimmed glasses perched on her nose.

"You rang?" the nurse asked, her voice businesslike but not unkind.

"My chest hurts, and I'm really hot," Trish said, suddenly feeling childish about the complaining. "And I spilled my water. I'm sorry."

The nurse approached the bed, glancing down where the cup had fallen. "Don't worry about that. Let's check your temperature." She pulled a thermometer from her pocket.

"Where's my mom?" Trish asked as the nurse slipped the thermometer under her tongue.

The nurse raised a finger, signaling for Trish to be quiet while the thermometer did its work. Trish didn't like strange hands on her or an unfamiliar face looking down at her with clinical detachment. Where was Kathy, with her gentle touch and kind smile? Where was her mother?

After what felt like an eternity, the nurse removed the thermometer. As she read it, her expression changed, brows drawing together in a frown.

"What is it?" Trish asked. "Is something wrong with me?"

The nurse looked from the thermometer to Trish, then back again, as if confirming what she was seeing. "Your temperature is 103.2," she said, her voice taut.

"How bad is that?" Trish asked, though she already knew the answer from the nurse's face.

"It's concerning, especially post-surgery." The nurse set the thermometer aside. "How long have you been feeling this way?"

"I don't know. I just woke up." Trish watched as the nurse got out a stethoscope and pressed it against Trish's chest.

"Breathe deeply for me."

Trish did as she was told. Drawing a breath wasn't easy. It was like a weight was pressing down on her chest.

The nurse nodded, making a note on her clipboard. "Any pain elsewhere? Headache? Nausea?"

"My head hurts a little," Trish admitted. " And I feel kind of dizzy."

The nurse placed a cool hand on Trish's forehead, then checked her pulse at her wrist.

"What about my mom?" Trish asked again. "She was here when I fell asleep."

The nurse straightened up. "I don't know. I just came on shift an hour ago." She glanced at her watch, then at the door, as if calculating something. "I'll get a doctor to take a look at you."

"What's wrong with me?" Trish asked, her voice rising.

The nurse began adjusting the IV drip attached to Trish's arm. "We'll have to wait for the doctor to tell us," she said, her tone like a kindergarten teacher. "Did you feel this warm before you fell asleep?"

Trish tried to remember. Everything about the day was fuzzy. "I was kind of out of it from the surgery. It's hard to say."

The nurse nodded, making another note. She moved to the sink and dampened a washcloth, then returned to place it on Trish's forehead. The cool cloth provided momentary relief, but within seconds it was as warm as her skin.

"I'll page Dr. John, too," the nurse said, replacing the cloth with a fresh, cool one. "He's not in the hospital right now, but he'll want to know about this. We may have to wait a bit on the other doctor. He was with another patient when you paged me." She straightened Trish's sheets with brisk efficiency. "Try to rest. I'll be back soon." The nurse moved toward the door, her rubber-soled shoes squeaking.

"Wait," Trish called after her. "Please find my mom. She wouldn't have left unless something was wrong."

But the nurse was already gone, the door swinging shut behind her. Trish was alone again.

She stared at the ceiling, trying to make sense of it all. There was no way she was going to be able to rest. The room spun again, and she closed her eyes against the vertigo. It was hard to think clearly. She needed water, needed her mom, needed answers.

Outside her room, footsteps approached—multiple sets, moving quickly. Voices murmured, too low for her to make out the words. Then silence again.

"Hello?" she called, her voice wavering. "Is anyone there?"

No response.

Trish fumbled for the call button again, pressing it repeatedly to no avail.

She wished she could get out of bed and go find someone who could tell her what was going on. But her leg was immobilized. She was a prisoner to the bed.

The door swung open again, and a doctor she didn't recognize stepped inside followed by the same nurse. The doctor was young, much younger than Dr. John, with dark circles under his eyes and rumpled scrubs.

"Hello, Trish," he said, moving to her bedside. "I'm Dr. Wilson. I'm covering some shifts while Dr. Flint is out."

"Dr. Flint is my dad."

His eyebrows went up. "Oh. Okay, then. Nurse Matthews tells me you're running quite a fever."

"Where's my mom?" Trish asked.

Dr. Wilson glanced at the nurse, then back at Trish. "How about we focus on getting your fever down first, then we'll find her," he said. "Let's take a listen to those lungs."

As he reached for his stethoscope, Trish grabbed his wrist. "Please," she said, her voice breaking. "Where is she?"

The doctor hesitated, exchanging another look with the nurse. "I don't know," he said finally. "But what I do know is that we need to address your fever right away. Okay?"

It wasn't okay. Nothing about this was okay. But Trish released his wrist, letting him listen to her lungs.

"Your chest feels heavy?"

"Yes."

He nodded. "Wind, water, wound, walking, wonder drugs. The five Ws. Most of the time it's wind," he muttered.

"What?"

"Just running through a checklist," he said. "Have you been coughing?"

"No."

"I don't hear any wheezing," he said. He lifted her wrist. His lips moved as he watched a clock on the wall. After about ten seconds he released her arm and started muttering again. "Heart rate isn't higher than I'd expect." He looked up at the ceiling. "No transfusion. No catheter. Really too soon for a wound infection. A little soon for deep vein thrombosis or pulmonary embolism, and she's awfully young for it." He frowned, then made eye contact with her again. "I need to look at your legs."

"Okay."

He raised her gown and studied both her thighs, even getting Nurse Matthews to help so he could see the back of them, which was a painful ordeal.

"All righty then. We're going to run some tests, and I'll need to get that brace off to take a proper look."

"Tests for what?"

"All kinds of things, but most specifically deep vein thrombosis."

Whatever that was. When he didn't explain, she didn't ask. She was too tired and too worried about where her mom had gone.

"I'm going to go order the tests," Dr. Wilson said, straightening up. "Nurse Matthews will stay with you."

"Wait," Trish called as he turned to leave. "Please find my mother. She wouldn't have left my room this long unless something was wrong."

Dr. Wilson paused at the door, his expression unreadable. "I'll see what I can find out." His tone suggested it was an empty promise. Then he was gone.

The nurse busied herself with Trish's IV bag, avoiding her gaze. The silence stretched between them.

"If you know something about my mom, just tell me," Trish said quietly.

Nurse Matthews sighed, finally meeting her eyes. "I really don't know anything specific," she said. "But there was some commotion earlier. Police officers coming and going. I saw her talking to them."

Police officers. Had they found out who did this to her? "Why were they here?"

The nurse attached a new IV bag and adjusted the drip. "I'll be back in a moment," she said, avoiding the question entirely. "Try to relax. Getting agitated will only make you feel worse."

"Please," Trish called after her as she moved toward the door. "Find my mother! Tell me what's happening!"

But the nurse was already gone.

CHAPTER THIRTY-FOUR: CARRY

BUFFALO, WYOMING
AUGUST 26, 1978

Susanne

THE HOSPITAL CAFETERIA lights buzzed overhead like angry wasps, casting a sickly yellow glow over the scratched Formica tables. Susanne stared at the untouched coffee in her Styrofoam cup, watching the surface shimmer with each tremor of her hands. Two in the morning, and her son had been missing for nearly five hours. The weight of it pressed against her chest, making each breath a conscious effort. She needed to stay alert, needed to think clearly, but exhaustion tugged at her like an undertow, threatening to pull her under.

The coffee had grown cold, a skin forming on its surface. She couldn't remember when she'd poured it. Time had become elastic, stretching and contracting. She forced herself to take a sip anyway, grimacing at the bitter, tepid taste. The normalcy of drinking coffee gave her something to do with her hands, even if she wasn't sure whether the caffeine would do any good.

Where is my son? The question circled her mind like a vulture. A fourteen-year-old boy doesn't just vanish. Not in Buffalo... unless someone takes him. The thought sent another wave of nausea through her stomach. *No.* He had to be with a friend. She'd called several of them earlier. She would make more calls.

She pressed the heels of her hands against her eyes, trying to force back the tears that threatened. Crying wouldn't help find him. It wouldn't change what had happened to Trish. It wouldn't bring Patrick home any faster.

Patrick. When she'd called earlier, the desk clerk at Paradise Inn had said he'd just driven away. That meant he was on his way home, which is what she wanted, but it also meant that she was alone in this until he arrived.

She pushed back from the table, the metal legs of the chair screeching against the floor. The sound was jarring in the empty cafeteria. The night shift cook glanced up from behind the counter, then quickly looked away.

The hallway outside was quiet, the overhead fluorescents dimmed for the night, casting long shadows that stretched and yawned along the corridor. Susanne walked with purpose toward the nurses' station. She needed to make more calls, and she couldn't do it from Trish's room. Her daughter needed rest, and Susanne couldn't bear the thought of Trish overhearing that her brother was missing. Not yet. Not while she was still recovering from surgery.

The nurses' station sat empty except for Becky, the red-headed nurse who'd helped earlier. She looked up as Susanne approached, her face softening with sympathy.

"Any word?" Becky asked, voice low.

Susanne shook her head. "I need to use the phone again, and a phone book if you have one."

"Of course." Becky pushed the telephone across the counter, then retrieved a slim telephone book and sent it over, too. "Take as long as you need."

Susanne flipped through the pages. She didn't know all the kids on the team. Just a few. Her hands trembled as she dialed the first number. The phone rang five times before a groggy voice answered.

"Hello?" The man sounded disoriented and annoyed, as anyone would be at two in the morning.

"Jim, it's Susanne Flint. I'm sorry to call so late." Her voice caught. "Perry is missing. I need to know if Chuck has heard from him or has any idea where he might go."

The line went quiet for a moment. "Missing? What do you mean missing?"

"He disappeared after the football game. No one's seen him since. The police are looking, but I thought maybe..." She trailed off, the enormity hitting her anew.

"I'm so sorry. Hold on, I'll get him."

After a minute, she heard muffled voices in the background, then the sound of the phone changing hands.

"Mrs. Flint?" Chuck's voice was thick with sleep. "I haven't seen Perry since the locker room after the game. Is he really missing?"

"Yes." The word felt like glass in her throat. "If you hear from him, or think of anywhere he might go, please call the hospital or the sheriff's department right away."

"I will. I promise. Do you want me to call around, you know, and, like, ask other people?"

“That would be great. Thank you.”

She hung up and immediately dialed another number. The Millers. Then the Prestons. Then the Hendersons. Each call followed the same pattern—shock, concern, questions she couldn't answer, and ultimately, no revelations. With each negative response, the knot in Susanne's stomach tightened. The list of Perry's friends and teammates dwindled. So did her hope.

By the fifth call, Becky had set a fresh cup of coffee beside her, this one steaming hot. The small kindness nearly broke her.

"Thank you," she managed.

Becky nodded. "Dr. Wilson and Eleanor are checking on Trish now. I was about to come find you."

"Is something wrong?" Alarm shot through her, fresh and sharp.

"Her temperature's up. He wants to check the incision site."

Susanne stood so quickly she knocked the phone off its cradle. "I need to get back to her."

"One minute." Becky laid a gentle hand on her arm. "Make your calls first. Trish is in good hands, and getting worked up won't help either of you."

She was right, of course. Susanne took a deep breath and picked up the phone again. She had one more call to make before she returned to Trish.

Ronnie answered on the first ring, her voice alert despite the hour. Of course, she was at the station, so there was no reason for her to sound sleepy. "Harcourt."

"It's Susanne. Any news?"

“Hey, Susanne.” A pause. "Nothing concrete yet. All hands are on deck searching, including volunteers. I’m combing through vehicle registrations. We've got roadblocks set up on all the major roads out of town."

"That's not enough." Susanne's voice rose, drawing a concerned look from Becky. She lowered it again with effort. "It's been over five hours, Ronnie, not a trace of him. I’ve called every friend and teammate I can think of. I should be out there helping look."

"Susanne, listen to me." Ronnie's tone was firm but gentle. "The best thing you can do right now is stay with Trish. And we need you somewhere we can find you if—" She caught herself. "When we have news."

"You don't understand. I can't just sit here and wait."

"I do understand." Something in Ronnie's voice shifted. "You’re my friend, and I love you. But this is our job, Susanne. Let us do it. We’re going to find him."

"I'm his mother!"

"And that's why you need to be strong and stay put. If Perry shows up at the hospital looking for you, someone needs to be there. And if Trish wakes up asking questions, she needs her mother."

Susanne closed her eyes, fighting against the logic she didn't want to accept. Then she remembered Trish had spiked a fever. Maybe Ronnie was right. "Has anyone checked the baseball field behind the school? Or—"

"Yes. That and more. Coach Cantrell is riding with one of my deputies, pointing out every spot Perry might go."

A sob threatened to escape, and Susanne swallowed it back. "What if someone took him, Ronnie? What if it's the same person who hit Trish?"

Ronnie's voice was careful, measured. "I need you to consider something, because anything is possible. Kids his age sometimes take off when they're upset. He could have gone somewhere to think and fallen asleep."

"He wouldn't do that. Not without letting someone know. He knew how distraught I was already."

"I hear you. And we're not ruling *anything* out, but we are starting with the leads you, Trish, and Perry gave us earlier." Ronnie paused. "To that end, I do have a little bit of news. We tried to pick up Larry Childs' father for questioning. His name is Gentry."

"And?"

"He's recently released from prison in Oklahoma. Repeat instances of violent assaults. It's why his wife and son moved here. To get away from him. But as soon as he was out he followed them here."

"What did he say?"

"We haven't been able to find him. His ex-wife has no idea where he is either. But... "

"But?"

"He does drive a 1970 blue Bronco."

Susanne felt her breath catch in her throat. "It's him. He'll know where Perry is!"

"It could be him. Or not. We also tried to talk to Dabbo Kern and Jimmy Gross. We haven't been able to find them either. But we're on it, and we have BOLOs out for all three of them. Now, have you talked to Patrick yet?"

At least it was progress, if only a little. "No. He's on his way home from Washington."

"Okay. Listen, with Perry missing, we're a little concerned about Trish, more than we were before. With every available officer looking for Perry, I've asked the hospital security guard to start including your hall multiple times on each round he makes."

"You think she's in danger here?" The blood drained out of her face.

"I just want to be careful. It's another reason that it's important you stay there. Keep an eye out, and I'll call you the second we know anything. I promise."

After hanging up, Susanne stood still for a moment, held in place by the weight of helplessness. She wanted to scream, to run out into the night and call Perry's name until her voice gave out. Instead, she straightened her shoulders and headed back to Trish's room. A uniformed security guard was just passing by as she reached it, and he saluted her. She nodded at him, not sure whether his presence made her feel better or worse.

The door was ajar, and as she approached, she could hear a man's voice, calm but firm. "We need to get this off right away. Her temperature's still rising."

Susanne pushed the door open to find an unfamiliar doctor and an older nurse she didn't know hovering over Trish. The nurse was setting up a tray of instruments while the doctor examined the top of the brace where it ended above Trish's knee. Trish was awake, her face flushed with fever, eyes glassy and frightened.

"Mom?" Trish's voice was small, uncertain.

Susanne was at her side in an instant, taking her hand. "I'm here, sweetie. I'm right here."

"Where were you?" There was accusation in the question, and something else. Fear.

"Making some calls." Susanne brushed damp hair from Trish's forehead. "I'm sorry I wasn't here when you woke up."

The doctor looked up. "You're Mrs. Flint?"

"I am."

"I'm Dr. Wilson. This is Eleanor Matthews."

"Nice to meet you both."

Eleanor nodded.

Dr. Wilson said, "We need to remove the brace and check Trish's wound site."

"What's wrong?" The words sent a chill through her. "Is it serious?"

"We're not sure yet," he said, his tone neutral in the way Patrick would use when he didn't want to alarm her but needed to convey urgency. "But whatever it is, we've caught it early, and we're going to take care of it."

"This may hurt," he told Trish. "I'm going to move slowly and gently. Try your best to hold still."

Trish's grip on Susanne's hand tightened. "Is it because of the accident?"

"Sometimes patients run a fever after surgery," Dr. Wilson explained as he began unstrapping the brace. "It's not uncommon, and there could be multiple reasons, as benign as her having a cold. So it's impossible to say what caused it until we know what it is."

Trish flinched and whimpered, and Susanne leaned closer, maintaining eye contact. "Look at me," she said. "Just focus on me."

Dr. Wilson worked the brace open, and Nurse Matthews helped him hold it that way.

"I don't see anything that looks worrisome here," Dr. Wilson said, examining the surgical site. "I'm still going to irrigate the wound, apply a topical antibiotic, and we'll start IV antibiotics in case of a bacterial infection. My best guess is that she's got a virus, but we won't take anything for granted."

Susanne watched as he worked, her mind splitting between the plights of her children. She felt stretched thin, like a piece of taffy pulled to its breaking point. Where was Patrick when she needed him most? The thought wasn't fair—he hadn't known this would happen—but it came unbidden all the same.

"Mom?" Trish's voice pulled her back. "You look weird. What's wrong?"

Susanne forced a smile. "Just tired, honey. It's been a long night."

"Is it Dad? Is he okay?"

"He's fine. He's on his way home."

Trish seemed to accept this, turning her attention back to Dr. Wilson as he cleaned the wound. The antiseptic he used made her wince, but she didn't cry out.

Trish's eyes were heavy with exhaustion and fever. "Will it hurt when I try to walk?"

"You won't be walking on it for a while," he said. "Not until we're sure you don't have complications and cast you up."

As Dr. Wilson and Nurse Matthews worked together to refasten the brace to Trish's leg and elevate it on pillows as the IV antibiotics dripped steadily into her arm. Trish gritted her teeth. Sweat broke out on her forehead.

"There," Dr. Wilson said. "You're strapped back in."

Susanne looked out the window, at the darkness beyond the glass. "Please, Patrick," she whispered, too low for anyone else to hear. "Please hurry home. I need you. We all do."

Dr. Wilson began explaining the treatment plan, but the words washed over Susanne like waves, leaving no impression. All she could think of was the clock on the wall, ticking away the minutes. And with each tick, her fear grew stronger.

"Mrs. Flint?" Dr. Wilson was looking at her expectantly. "Did you hear what I said?"

She blinked, forcing herself back to the present. "I'm sorry, could you repeat that?"

"I said we'll be watching Trish closely over the next few hours. I apologize in advance. It won't be a restful night."

"Of course." She nodded mechanically. "Whatever she needs."

As the doctor and nurse left the room, Susanne settled into the chair beside Trish's bed, reaching out to hold her daughter's hand again. Trish's eyes were closed now, her breathing uneven but steady. The fever had exhausted her.

Susanne closed her eyes for a moment. For all the practical ways in which she needed Patrick—his steady presence, his problem-solving mind, his unwavering belief that everything would be okay—she needed his arms around her more.

She found herself calculating time and distance in her head. Patrick had left Rainier yesterday evening. If he drove straight through, stopping only for gas and quick breaks, he might make it back by late afternoon.

That was still more than twelve hours away.

Twelve hours of not knowing where Perry was.

Twelve hours of facing Trish's medical crisis.

Alone.

CHAPTER THIRTY-FIVE: LIMP

Coeur d'Alene, Idaho
August 26, 1978

Patrick

Patrick knelt on the gravel shoulder, the small flashlight clenched between his teeth casting just enough light for Henry to finish tightening the lug nuts. The spare tire looked pathetic. A skinny, temporary thing that belonged under a go-kart, not a Suburban loaded with three grown men and their gear.

The first hints of dawn were just beginning to lighten the sky, turning black to navy blue. His watch read five thirty-seven a.m. They'd been driving since leaving Rainier, stopping only once for gas, coffee, and a bathroom break. A moment's inattention, a pothole that appeared out of nowhere in the pre-dawn darkness, and they'd blown the right front tire somewhere between Coeur d'Alene and the Montana border.

His shoulder throbbed, but that pain was insubstantial compared to his worry about Susanne and the kids. The call from Susanne kept replaying in his head. Trish was stuck in a hospital bed two states away while he was on the side of a highway in Idaho with a tire that looked like it might give out before they crossed the next county line.

"Almost done." Henry gave the wrench a final twist. He grunted as he worked, his movements slower than normal. The altitude sickness that had plagued him on the mountain was gone, but thirty-six hours of minimal sleep had taken a toll.

Patrick removed the flashlight from his mouth. "Will it hold?" The question came out rougher than he intended, his voice sandpaper-raw from exhaustion. It had been his turn to drive for the last two hours.

Henry rocked back on his heels, wiping his hands on a dirty t-shirt that had been repurposed as a rag. "It'll get us somewhere. Not sure it'll get us all the way to Montana much less Buffalo."

Wes sat on the Suburban's bumper, his left arm immobilized in the sling which Patrick had reinforced with long twigs he'd gathered at their last gas stop. In his opinion, it was likely Wes had a non-displaced fracture. He'd cast it when they got back to Buffalo after an x-ray for confirmation. The problem was the pain, which Wes was keeping to a dull roar with Tylenol.

"Why's that?" Wes asked.

"It's a donut," Henry said. "They're designed to get you ten, maybe twenty miles to the nearest service station."

Patrick squinted at the eastern horizon. This was his fault. He hadn't checked the spare in the Suburban. "What's the nearest town down the road with a tire shop?" Patrick asked, already doing the mental calculations of time lost.

Henry shrugged. "No idea. But it's Saturday, and it's not even six yet. Nothing's gonna be open for hours."

Patrick felt his jaw clench. Hours. If the donut flatted, they could be stuck for God knew how long. Every minute they delayed was another minute he was away from his family when they needed him. He pushed himself to his feet. The movement sent a sharp jolt through his injured shoulder, forcing him to brace against the car with his good hand.

"You okay?" Wes asked.

"Yeah."

Wes clearly didn't believe him. "You should let me drive for a while."

"With one arm?" Patrick forced a tired smile. "I'd rather take my chances with the donut."

Henry finished packing away the jack and wrench. He gave the temporary tire a skeptical look. "The car manufacturer should be ashamed for putting this thing in a car this size. It doesn't even feel safe."

Patrick stared down the empty highway. No headlights in either direction. Just the lonely stretch of blacktop disappearing into the hills ahead and behind them.

Wes said, "We don't have much choice. Unless you want to steal a tire off someone's car."

The dark joke hung in the air. None of them laughed.

"How far do you think we can push it?" Patrick asked.

Henry kneeled, examining the spare more closely in the growing light. "Depends on how fast you drive, how much weight's in the car, the road conditions." He shook his head. "It's not made for this, Patrick."

"I know that. But this isn't my area of expertise. If you had to guess, how far?" Henry did a lot of his own tire repair work on his ranch. The trucks, the tractors. He knew more than Patrick.

"Fifty miles? Maybe? And that's if we're lucky and drive like we've got eggs under the gas pedal. We're still close enough to Coeur d'Alene that one of us could walk back, get a wrecker, and have it tow us to a tire shop."

Which wouldn't be open. Patrick did the mental math. Fifty miles would get them... nowhere near where they needed to be. The sky was lightening by the minute. Soon the heat would be oppressive, the side of the highway a dangerous place to be stranded. Patrick stared at the eastern horizon.

"We keep going," Patrick said, the decision crystallizing in his mind. " We'll drive slow and hope the spare holds until we find an open service station."

"And if it blows?" Henry asked.

"Then we deal with it," Patrick said. "But we don't split up, and we don't wait around for hours."

A semi-truck roared past, the wake of air rocking their Suburban. Henry squinted after it. He sighed, then nodded. "Okay. We push on. But we're stopping at the first open service station we see."

"Deal," Patrick said, relief flooding through him.

Wes stood, adjusting his sling. "I'll check the map. Maybe there's a town within range."

Patrick walked to the edge of the shoulder. The empty highway stretched before them. In the growing light, he could make out the jagged silhouettes of mountains against the sky.

"All right," Henry said, patting his back once. "Let's get this show on the road. I'll drive again. You need to rest." Patrick started to protest, but Henry cut him off. "I had a solid nap. I've got this."

The logic was sound, even if Patrick hated the idea of not being behind the wheel. He relented with a nod. "Two hours. Then we switch."

Henry smiled, a tired expression that didn't reach his eyes. "Deal."

They returned to the car, where Wes had the map spread across the hood. "Looks like Thompson Falls is about forty miles over the Montana line," he said, tracing the route with his finger. "Might have a service station."

"Forty miles," Henry repeated. "The donut should make that, if we're careful."

Patrick hoped it would. Had to believe it would. They couldn't lose any more time.

CHAPTER THIRTY-SIX: NAVIGATE

Bighorn Mountains, Wyoming
August 26, 1978

Perry

Perry's eyes fluttered open to bright sunlight warming his face. He lay there, the throbbing in his skull keeping time with his heartbeat. The world no longer spun like it had last time he woke, but his mouth tasted like dirt and copper pennies. He tried to swallow and found his throat sandpaper dry. He wasn't sure how long he'd been out. The sunlight told him it was morning. At least it wasn't cold anymore. August in the Bighorns could get chilly at night, but the days warmed quickly.

He moved his fingers first, then his arms. They worked. Next came his legs. Still attached, still functioning. His t-shirt was stiff with dried sweat and rusty brown from his blood. The back of his head felt like someone had taken a hammer to it, but the bleeding had stopped. Dried blood matted his hair to his scalp in a crusty mess that pulled when he shifted his weight.

Slowly, carefully, he pushed himself up to sitting. The world tilted for a second, then settled back into place. He was much better than he'd been in the middle of the night. He recognized the mountainous terrain. The Bighorn Mountains he assumed. He'd been up here enough times with his family that he was familiar with them, but he didn't know them like the back of his hand.

His brain cycled back. What was the last thing he remembered before he'd woken up out here? He'd been... At first he got nothing, then events started coming back to him. The football game. Coach calling him Wolverine. Walking to the hospital to see Trish. Then nothing.

Perry touched the back of his head again, wincing at the tender lump, as he looked around. The clearing around him was maybe thirty feet across. Rocky ground with patches of scrubby grass and pine needles. He looked for landmarks, anything familiar, but saw only trees and the edge of a rocky outcropping to his left.

He pushed himself to standing, his legs shaky but holding. He scanned the ground. Where he'd been lying, the grass and dirt were disturbed, showing the imprint of his body. But nearby were tire tracks. Wide ones, from something bigger than a car. *A truck, maybe. Or a Bronco.* His stomach flipped at the thought.

He stepped closer, his sneakers crunching on pine needles, fighting dizziness. The tracks were in a patch of softer soil. Two parallel lines where tires had rolled right up to the edge of the clearing. The prints showed a Y-shape. Whoever it was had turned around and headed back out.

Perry followed the tracks, moving as quickly as his battered body allowed. His head pounded with each step, but he pushed through it. The tracks led him through a narrow gap between pines, down a gentle slope covered in loose rocks that shifted under his feet, and he had to steady himself against tree trunks more than once.

The tracks grew fainter where the ground hardened, but he could still make them out. Fresh. Recent.

He kept following them. As he walked, a question played on repeat in his mind. Who had done this to him? It seemed like he'd been knocked out, driven up into the mountains, and left for dead. Had it been the man who hit Trish with the Bronco? He thought back to the night before. He hadn't seen a Bronco in the stadium parking lot.

He did remember something, though. A man watching during warm-ups. Sunglasses. Brown hair curling at the ears. No mustache.

Perry had been sure the Bronco driver had a dark mustache. Trish insisted he was clean-shaven. They couldn't both be right, unless...

Unless there were two men. One driving the car that hit Trish, another watching Perry at the game. Or maybe it was the same man, but he'd shaved the mustache off.

He groaned. All the thinking wasn't helping his head.

He would focus on getting out of here. Worrying about what had happened wouldn't save him. Being smart might. He looked up at the mountains again searching for landmarks. He was many miles from Buffalo, that much was certain. High in the mountains. Deep enough into the backcountry most kids his age would have trouble finding their way out, especially with a head injury.

But Patrick Flint had taught his children how to navigate in the wilderness.

Dad would be proud if he could see me now, he thought. Then another thought. Maybe his dad would be looking for him. Maybe everyone was. Mom would be frantic. She would call Ronnie. The thought made him feel better.

The tire tracks became harder to follow, appearing only in scattered patches of softer ground. They turned down an incline. Perry's foot hit a loose rock. He stumbled and grabbed a pine trunk to steady himself. His hands came away sticky with sap. He wiped them on his jeans and kept going.

The slope flattened out, and Perry found himself at the edge of another clearing. This one was larger, with patches of dead wildflowers amongst dry grass. And there, cutting a line through the far side, was a gravel road. Relief washed through him so intensely his knees nearly buckled.

The tire tracks continued across the clearing, heading straight for the road. They were clearer here, pressed into the soft earth. Hope built in Perry with each step. A road meant people. Maybe not right away, but eventually.

When he reached the spot where the tracks met the road, he could see where the vehicle had veered off the gravel, flattening grass and leaving dark gouges in the earth. Off roading in motorized vehicles was illegal in the national forest. Not that whoever had grabbed him cared much about breaking laws, obviously.

Perry stood in the middle of the empty road, looking both ways. It disappeared around bends in both directions. No signs. No markers. The road could lead anywhere. He could pick the wrong direction and end up walking further into the wilderness, further from help.

His stomach cramped with hunger, and he doubled over, pressing his hand into his gut. His throat burned. He needed to find water soon or he'd be in real trouble. Dad had drilled that into him. Water first, shelter second, food third. But which way? It could be heading anywhere.

Perry closed his eyes, trying to think through the pounding in his skull. What would Dad do?

The sun. Dad had taught him how to navigate by the sun. East and west, sunrise and sunset. It was morning, and the sun was still low in the sky. That meant it was rising. East.

And Buffalo was on the eastern side of the Bighorns. So, if he headed toward the sun, he'd be going in the right general direction. He might not hit Buffalo directly, but he'd reach the eastern foothills eventually. Find a ranch, a house, something. Better yet, a paved road.

Perry looked down at the gravel road again, then at the sun filtering through the trees. If he took a right, he'd be walking toward the sun.

Right meant east. East meant Buffalo. Buffalo meant home.

Perry turned right and took his first step down the gravel road, the sun warm on his face, guiding him forward. Each step hurt, but he would make it. He had to.

Wolverines, he told himself, *don't give up.*

CHAPTER THIRTY-SEVEN: QUIT

Buffalo, Wyoming
August 26, 1978

Trish

Trish opened her eyes to the same ceiling tiles she'd been staring at all night. Twenty-four of them, arranged in a grid above her bed. She'd counted them at least a dozen times as staff came and went, monitoring her fever. Her leg throbbed with each heartbeat, a constant reminder of everything that had gone wrong.

She didn't need to look to know her mom was there. The gentle sound of pages turning, the faint scent of coffee gone cold, the occasional tired sigh.

"You're awake." Her mom's voice came from the left, followed by the creak of the vinyl hospital chair and the rustle of a magazine being set aside. "How are you feeling?"

Trish turned her head. Her mom looked like she'd aged five years overnight. Her usually bouncy hair hung limp around her face. She wore the same blouse as yesterday, now wrinkled from sleeping in the chair.

"Like I got hit by a car." Trish tried for humor, but her voice came out raspy and weak. "Then got put in the oven. Except that I also have chills and body aches." She sneezed. “And my eyes itch.”

Her mom’s face tightened at the joke. She reached for the plastic cup on the bedside table and held the straw to Trish's lips. "Small sips. Dr. Wilson says your fever's down a little this morning."

The water tasted metallic, like it had been sitting too long in pipes, but Trish drank gratefully. "What time is it?" she asked when she'd had enough.

"Just after eight. You've been sleeping on and off since they changed your bandages."

Trish glanced down at her leg then at the IV line snaked from her arm to a bag of clear liquid hanging beside the bed.

Her mom busied herself adjusting Trish's blanket, smoothing it over and over. "Kathy brought breakfast by earlier, but I turned it away. I didn't want to wake you. Are you hungry? I can see if they can bring something now."

The thought of food made Trish's stomach turn. "No. I don't think I could eat anything."

"You need to try so you can keep your strength up."

"Maybe later." Trish shifted, trying to find a comfortable position. Every movement sent a dull throb through her leg. "Has anyone called Ben?"

Her mom paused in her fussing, a brief hesitation that Trish might not have noticed if she hadn't been watching so closely. "No, not yet. With everything happening so fast, I haven't had a chance to get home."

"He's probably worried. If he's heard anything at all." Trish stared at the window, where sunlight slanted through half-drawn blinds. "He was supposed to call me last night. Maybe Grandpa Joe told him."

“I don’t think he was home.”

“Then he really will be worried. It’s like I stood him up.” Trish’s voice rose an octave on that last bit.

"I'll call him as soon as I go home," her mom promised. "I need to head back soon anyway to get some clean clothes and make sure your grandfather hasn’t given Fergie away."

"Is Grandpa Joe okay?" Trish frowned.

"He's fine. Just being himself." Her mom’s smile was strained. “You know how he is.”

Trish did know. Her grandfather was perfectly capable of feeding himself, but he acted helpless without someone to do everything for him. She couldn’t understand how her sweet, gentle grandmother had put up with him for so many years.

Her mom continued. "He went to Perry's game last night. Your brother blocked a punt and played very well.”

“Did they win?” Trish thought about the cheerleading squad. It was their first home game, too. The other cheerleaders had been crazy excited. Her? Not as much. She hoped they did well, though. With her not showing up, they had to know she was in the hospital. Would they start visiting? Maybe she didn’t want to see anyone. Perry had told her she looked like she’d dived headfirst into a gravel pit.

“I believe they did."

"Where is Perry? Is he at home?"

Another pause, longer this time. Her mother's hands stilled on the blanket. "I'm not sure right this minute," she said, then followed up quickly. "How's the pain? Do you need me to call Kathy?"

That wasn’t an answer, but Trish was too exhausted to push for more information. Perry was probably watching film or whatever football players did the night after a game. "It's not too bad right now."

Her mom nodded. She looked so tired. Drained really, like someone had pulled a plug from the wall socket and let all the energy flow out of her. The dark circles under her eyes told a story of a night without rest, and there was something in her expression that Trish couldn't quite place. Something beyond exhaustion. Something like fear.

"Mom, you look awful," Trish said, immediately regretting her bluntness. "I mean, you should get some sleep while you're home. I'm just going to lie here anyway."

Her mom managed a weak smile. "Such a charmer. Must get that from your father."

"Seriously, Mom. I'm fine. You know the nurses will be checking on me like every ten minutes."

"I'll go home soon." Her mom fussed with the water pitcher, refilling Trish's cup even though it was still half full. "Just want to make sure your fever stays down a bit longer. I plan to visit Vangie on my way out, too, if she's still here."

"Visit her?" Trish studied her mother's profile. The way her hands trembled slightly as she poured the water. The way her eyes darted to the door whenever footsteps passed in the hallway. Something wasn't right.

"Did I not tell you?"

"Tell me *what*?"

"I guess with your fever and all, I didn't. Vangie is a few rooms down. She, uh—"

"Mo-om, what is it?"

Her mother set the pitcher down. "You have to swear to keep this a secret. It's a grown-up thing."

"I will."

"She was pregnant, and she lost the baby. Had a miscarriage."

"Oh, no! And she's here without Henry."

"Yes. It's very sad."

"I guess if I'm not supposed to know you can't give her my thoughts and prayers."

"Correct. But I appreciate it on her behalf." Her mom gave her a half smile.

"Has Dad called?" Trish asked.

"Not yet. He's probably driving through Montana by now."

"I guess we'll see him today then."

"Yes, we will." Her mom's smile didn't reach her eyes.

Trish let her head sink deeper into the pillow. Even this short conversation had worn her out. She closed her eyes, just for a moment, and drifted in a haze that wasn't quite sleep but wasn't wakefulness either. The sounds of the hospital floated around her. The squeak of rubber-soled shoes in the hallway, muffled conversations, the rhythmic beep of monitors. All of it seemed distant, like it was happening in another world.

A sharp clatter yanked her back to full consciousness. Trish's eyes flew open to see a girl with braided red hair struggling to hold an enormous bouquet of flowers and a mylar balloon that proclaimed GET WELL SOON in glittery letters. The noise had been Marcy knocking over a metal basin as she tried to navigate the cramped hospital room.

"I totally meant to do that," Marcy said, her voice loud in the quiet room. "Wanted to make sure you were awake."

"Marcy," Trish's mom stood, relief evident in her voice. She got up and went to hug her. "The flowers and balloons are so pretty."

"Hi, Mrs. Flint. Yeah, it's nice when your parents own a florist shop. My mom put these together for me first thing."

"Hey, Marcy." Trish tried to push herself up to a sitting position. Her mom quickly adjusted the bed controls, raising the head so she didn't have to strain. "Those for me?"

"No, they're for the other cheerleader who got mowed down by a car," Marcy said, rolling her eyes. "Of course they're for you, dummy." She set the flowers on the side table and tied the balloon to the bed rail. "Everyone signed the card. Even Jillian, who insisted on being included when she heard about it."

"That's... nice." Jillian was the last person Trish wanted to think about or have anything to do with.

"You'll never guess who brought her when she came to sign it last night."

"Not Dabbo!"

"Bingo, and with his evil sidekick Jimmy."

"You didn't happen to see what he was driving, did you?"

"Um, yeah. It was blue. An old Scout or Bronco or something."

Trish's stomach lurched. The vehicle that hit her could have been Dabbo's. He had dark hair and no mustache like the driver. It wasn't out of the question. "Oh, my God."

"What?"

"Guess what ran into me?" She didn't wait for an answer. "A blue car like a Bronco or Scout."

"No way!"

"Way."

"They hate you. I hope the police are going to talk to them."

"I think they are."

"Good." Marcy perched on the chair beside the bed. "So, how bad is it? Cindy told everyone you were probably going to lose your leg, but I told her she's full of it."

"She is full of it," Trish confirmed. "It's just broken. But the doctor says it'll heal." Eventually, she thought but didn't add, crossing her fingers.

"You should have seen Cindy at practice yesterday," Marcy leaned in, her voice dropping to a stage whisper. "She was practically glowing. Kept going on about how you're tragically sidelined—her exact words. I think she's worried you're going to beat her out for homecoming queen, although I don't know why she thinks you being in a car wreck will prevent that." She cocked her head. "Unless the vote was tomorrow. Your face. Dang, girl."

Trish groaned. "Is it really bad?"

"It's not really good."

Trish's mom cleared her throat. "I'm going to get another cup of coffee. Can I bring you anything, girls?"

"I'm good, Mrs. Flint, thanks!"

Trish said, "I'm fine, Mom."

As soon as her mom stepped out, Marcy leaned in even closer.

"Okay, now tell me the real story. What the heck happened? Everyone's saying different things."

Trish sighed. "There's not much to tell. Perry and I were walking toward the side entrance to the school. This car came out of nowhere."

"Was it aiming for you?"

"Maybe? I can't be sure."

"That's so scary!"

"It was. So, then I pushed Perry out of the way, and boom—here I am."

"Holy crap." Marcy's eyes widened. "You're like a real-life hero. Did you see who was driving? Was it really that guy with the mustache that Bijou's been telling everyone about?"

"I don't know. It happened so fast." Trish frowned. She really didn't remember a mustache. "Wait, what has Bijou been saying? And how do you even know her? She's new, and she's a freshman."

"I have the same lunch period as her and Perry. She's cool. She just said that there's some creep in a blue Bronco who's been hanging around the school." Marcy waved a hand dismissively. "Anyway, you should have heard Davy at lunch yesterday. He was telling everyone how he's going to visit you and bring you his letterman jacket to wear while you recover."

Despite feeling like garbage, Trish couldn't help but smile. Davy was the quarterback, and he was cute. It was flattering. But her heart was taken. "He wishes."

"I know, right? Oh! And Mr. Baldwin told everyone that you were one of his best students and would probably be valedictorian, which made Connie turn green."

The gossip should have interested Trish more than it did. Normally, she'd be hanging on every word, mentally filing away each detail to analyze later. But now, with her leg throbbing, her eyes burning, her body aching, and an itch that threatened to turn into a sneeze at any second, it all seemed distant. Like something from another life.

"What about the game?" Trish asked, more to keep the conversation going than from any real interest. "Did I miss anything important?"

"Just Cindy throwing a fit because we didn't nail the new routine at halftime. She said we have to run laps at practice Monday because we couldn't get the timing right. Like who died and made her queen of the world! Except I guess as captain she does have a little bit of say in it." Marcy bounced a little on the edge of the bed, then caught herself when Trish stiffened and winced. "Sorry! I forgot about your leg. Anyway, we're going to start working on the homecoming routine this week."

"I don't think I'm going to be back in time for homecoming," Trish said. Dr. John had put her recovery well past any of the fall cheerleading events.

Marcy's face fell. "But that's weeks away. Surely you'll be better by then?"

"Dr. John said I'll be out all fall. I mean, Marcy, my whole tibia broke and was sticking out of my skin. They had to screw it back together."

"Months?" Marcy looked stricken. "You'll miss the whole season!"

Trish felt something shift inside her chest. A weight that had been there for longer than she wanted to admit. "Actually, I was thinking..." She took a deep breath. "I might quit cheerleading altogether."

The words hung in the air between them. Marcy's mouth opened, then closed, then opened again. She looked like a fish that had suddenly found itself walking through a shopping center.

"Quit?" she finally managed. "You can't quit! You love cheerleading! Plus, we're doing it together. It's a best friend thing."

Did she love it, though? Trish wasn't so sure anymore. "I don't know, Marcy. This whole thing has made me think a lot." She gestured vaguely at her leg. "Maybe it's a sign."

"A sign to quit something you've worked at all summer?" Marcy shook her head vigorously, her braids swinging. "No way. That's the painkillers talking."

"What does it matter, anyway? I'll be out all of football season, which is practically the only reason for being on the squad. At least part of the basketball season. You've got Cindy. She's the captain. And they can bring up an alternate if the squad feels lopsided."

"It doesn't matter who has the captain title. The squad needs you. I need you!" Marcy's voice rose. "Who's going to keep Cindy from turning practice into her personal dictatorship? Who's going to remember all the counts when she gets confused? Who's going to stretch with me and help me with my jumps?"

Trish sank deeper into her pillows. The pain medication made her head feel cottony. "I know my parents don't like quitters," she said quietly. "But maybe this is different. Maybe this is knowing when to let go."

"I'm with your parents. It's not letting go, it's giving up," Marcy insisted. "And for what? Because of some stupid accident? You earned this."

"I don't think I want it anymore," Trish admitted, the words coming out in a rush. "I've been thinking about it all summer, even before this happened. I'm not sure I ever really wanted it. I just did it because..." She trailed off, unsure how to explain the complicated tangle of expectations, emotions, and assumptions that had guided her choices.

"Because what?" Marcy pressed. "Because it's awesome? Because we have the best time together? Because you're good at it?"

"Because it was expected," Trish said simply. She'd tried out for the squad when she was broken up with Ben. People had encouraged her. Her parents thought it would bring her out of her introverted shell. It's what pretty girls were supposed to do, to be popular. Her mother had been a cheerleader.

Marcy stared at her, genuinely confused. "Who expected it?"

"Everyone. My mom. The school. Girls like us." Trish gestured between them. " That's just how it works."

"That's such bull—" Marcy caught herself, glancing toward the door where Trish's mom might return any moment. "That's not true." Marcy's expression shifted from confusion to something like panic. "Don't do this, Trish. Please. Just take the time you need to heal and then come back. The squad won't be the same without you."

"The squad will be fine," Trish said.

"You're my only real friend on it. It won't be the same without you," Marcy repeated, her voice smaller now. "Promise me you'll at least think about it more before you decide? Don't make any big decisions while you're all..." She waved her hand vaguely. "Drugged up and stuff."

A soft sound from the doorway made them both turn. Trish's mom stood there, coffee cup in hand, tears streaming silently down her face.

"Mom?" Trish struggled to sit up straighter. "What's wrong?"

Her mom's free hand flew to cover her mouth, but it wasn't enough to hold back the sob that escaped. The coffee cup tilted dangerously.

"Mrs. Flint?" Marcy jumped up from the bed, alarmed.

The cup slipped from her mom's grasp, hitting the linoleum floor with a splash of brown liquid. But she didn't seem to notice or care. Instead, she sank into the nearest chair, her whole body shaking with the force of her crying.

"Mom!" Trish tried to reach for her, but the movement sent pain shooting through her leg. "What happened? Is it Dad? Is he okay?"

Her mom shook her head, unable to speak through her tears.

"I'll get a nurse," Marcy said, backing toward the door.

But Trish's mom raised a hand to stop her. "No," she managed between sobs. "No, I'm—" Another sob cut her off.

Trish had never seen her mother like this. Not ever. Cold dread washed over her, drowning out even the pain in her leg.

"Mom, please," she begged. "What's happening? You're scaring me."

"I'm sorry." Her mother's face crumpled, and fresh tears flowed.

She opened her mouth, tried to speak, but only another broken sob emerged. "It's just all hitting me. And... I've just talked to your father."

CHAPTER THIRTY-EIGHT: REEL

St. Regis, Montana
August 26, 1978

Patrick

Thirty minutes earlier:

The donut spare made a high-pitched whine as Patrick eased the Suburban into the tire shop's parking lot, the sound like a dying animal giving its last desperate cry. They'd nursed the pathetic excuse for a tire through sixty miles of Montana highway, driving so slowly that semi-trucks blasted past them with horn blares. Patrick's injured shoulder throbbed, and the knot in his stomach had grown with each mile that separated him from Buffalo, from Trish in her hospital bed, from helping his wife and holding her in his arms.

"Made it," Henry said, his voice rough with fatigue. "Barely."

"Thank God," Wes mumbled from the backseat, where he'd been dozing fitfully, his broken arm cradled against his chest. The sling looked dirty and inadequate in the morning light.

Patrick eyed the neon OPEN sign flickering in the window of Thompson's Tire & Service like it was the Holy Grail. The lot was empty except for them, no waiting customers to delay the repairs they desperately needed.

"Stay put," Patrick told Wes. "No point in all of us getting out."

Wes saluted with his good arm.

The morning air was already warm, promising another scorching August day as Patrick and Henry approached the shop. Patrick's legs felt wooden, like they belonged to someone else after so many hours cramped behind the wheel. A bell jangled as Henry pushed open the door.

Inside smelled of rubber and motor oil, the familiar scent of all tire shops everywhere. A thin man with grease-stained hands looked up from behind the counter.

"Help you fellas?"

"We need a tire," Patrick said, not bothering with pleasantries. "Right front. And we're in a hurry."

The man whose name was Thompson, according to the patch on his shirt, eyed them both, taking in their rumpled clothes and exhausted faces. "Let me guess, you're rolling on a donut?"

"Unfortunately," Patrick replied.

Thompson walked over to the window and peered out at their Suburban. "Yeah, those little donuts aren't meant for real driving. What size you need?"

Patrick gave him the size. Thompson nodded, running a hand through his thinning hair. He gave Patrick a few price point options. Patrick picked one of the cheapest.

Thompson said, "Take about twenty minutes to get you fixed up."

"How much?" Patrick asked, already reaching for his wallet.

"Seventy-eight dollars with mounting and balancing."

Patrick winced. The price was steep. They had no choice, though. "Fine. Can you start right away?"

"Sure thing. Just pull her into bay two and leave the keys."

Thompson gestured toward the service area. "There's coffee in the waiting room if you want it."

"Actually," Patrick said, "I need to make a couple of phone calls. Long distance. I'll pay for them."

Thompson raised an eyebrow. "Phone's for customers, but long distance—"

Patrick pulled out his wallet and extracted a twenty and a five. "This cover it?"

The man pocketed the bills with a nod. "Phone's on the wall there. Help yourself."

Henry went outside to move the car while Patrick stared at the phone, suddenly nervous about what he might learn when he called. He didn't pick it up.

When Henry returned, he looked at Patrick expectantly.

"You want to call first?" Patrick asked.

Henry nodded and picked up the receiver. "Thanks. I should check on Vangie."

Patrick stepped back to give him privacy, pretending to examine a rack of windshield wipers while Henry dialed. From the corner of his eye, he watched his friend's face, noting the exact moment Henry's expression changed from tired to concerned. Henry's shoulders stiffened and his voice dropped to a near-whisper.

"When?" Henry asked into the phone. Then, "Is she still at the hospital?"

Patrick moved farther away, giving Henry space, but he could still hear fragments of the conversation. Behind him, he was dimly aware of the service bay door opening, the sound of their Suburban being driven inside.

"...How bad?... Oh, Jesus... No, I understand... Tell her I'm... Soon as we can..."

By the time Henry hung up, his face had lost its color beneath the stubble and grime of their journey. He stood motionless, staring at the wall behind the phone as if he could see through it to Wyoming.

"Henry?" Patrick approached cautiously. "What is it?"

Henry turned, his eyes wet. "Vangie lost the baby."

Patrick felt the words like a physical blow. "God, Henry, I'm so sorry."

"She started cramping yesterday afternoon. Passed out in the kitchen. One of the hands found her and called an ambulance." Henry's voice was flat, controlled, but Patrick could see the effort it cost him. "She's still at the hospital. She called and told them she was fine, but..."

"Do you need to call her?"

Henry nodded. "But I don't have the number."

"I know it by heart." Patrick dialed. The line clicked and hummed, the distance between Montana and Wyoming stretching out in electronic pulses. When a crisp female voice answered, he identified himself and asked for Vangie's room. He listened, then hung up. "She was discharged fifteen minutes ago."

Henry's shoulders slumped.

Patrick gripped his friend's arm. "We'll get you home as fast as we can."

Henry nodded, his jaw working. "Why didn't she call me?"

Patrick had no answer for that. "I'm sorry."

"Your turn to call," Henry said, clearly not wanting to talk about it further.

Patrick took the receiver, his hand shaking slightly as he dialed the hospital number again. He probably shouldn't have hung up, but he had wanted to give Henry all his attention.

The same female voice answered. "Buffalo Hospital, how may I direct your call?"

"This is Dr. Flint again. I need to speak with my wife, Susanne. She should be in my daughter Trish's room."

"Hello, Dr. Flint. I'm sorry your daughter is our guest, and about, um, your son. One moment, please."

Before Patrick could ask what she meant, he was on hold. Surely he'd misheard her? What was wrong with Perry? His heart rate accelerated to Olympic caliber sprinting. The seconds stretched as he waited. He clutched the receiver so tightly his knuckles turned white.

"Patrick?" Susanne's voice came through, tinny and distant but unmistakably hers.

"Susanne, thank God." Relief washed over him, followed immediately by renewed worry at the strain he heard in her voice. "How's Trish? Is she okay?"

"She's..." Susanne paused. "There's something wrong. It was a compound fracture, you know, and she had surgery. Now she has a fever and chest pain. They were worried about something like a DMV or—"

"DVT?" Patrick's doctor brain kicked in. Then his brain went to pulmonary embolism, and he felt sick.

"Yes. Dr. Wilson says it would be very unusual if she has one. He hasn't found anything so far. He thinks it's more likely she has a virus unrelated to the surgery, but he's still keeping a close eye on her."

Patrick felt his lips moving with no sound coming out. He interrupted the impulse and refocused on Susanne. "I'm so sorry I'm not there." The words felt inadequate, guilt settling heavy on his shoulders. He hated having to trust this Dr. Wilson, who'd only been brought in to cover Patrick's days off. Had he gone through all the five Ws? "Has Dr. John come in?"

"They're consulting him by phone."

That made Patrick feel better. A little. He had no choice but to trust the medical professionals who were there and to get home as fast as humanly possible. "We're getting the tire fixed. Long story. Slight delay. We'll be on the road again in twenty minutes. Expect us by six. But there's something else I need to know. The receptionist mentioned something about Perry."

There was a silence. A long silence. Then he heard a sob.

"Susanne?" he prompted. "What aren't you telling me?"

He heard her take a shaky breath. She lowered her voice to a whisper. "Patrick..." Her voice broke. She tried again. "Patrick, Perry's missing."

The world seemed to tilt beneath his feet. "What do you mean, missing?"

"He disappeared after his football game last night." Susanne's words came out in a rush now, as if she'd been holding them back and couldn't any longer. "Joe went to watch him play, but when he went to pick him up, he was told Perry was walking to the hospital. But he never arrived here. No one's seen him since. The police have been searching for him all night."

Patrick's throat closed up. He couldn't breathe. Couldn't speak. The coffee machine in the corner gurgled and hissed, the sound unnaturally loud in the sudden silence of his mind.

"When?" he finally managed. "When exactly did this happen?"

"Around nine-thirty last night. After the game. Patrick, he's been gone for nearly twelve hours." Susanne's voice cracked again. "Volunteers are helping search. They've set up roadblocks. They've checked everywhere he might go." He could hear the tears in her voice. "I've called everyone, Patrick. No one's seen him. I'm so worried he's been taken by whoever hit Trish."

The implications of her words hit him like a fist to the gut. This wasn't Perry staying late at a friend's house or losing track of time at the arcade. This was something else. Something worse.

Patrick's mind raced through possibilities, each one worse than the last. Had Perry gotten lost? Been kidnapped? Hit by a car like Trish? Was he injured somewhere, unable to call for help? The image of his son lying hurt and alone made him dizzy with panic.

"Does Trish know?" he asked, struggling to keep his voice steady.

"No. She's asleep, but I'm in her room, and I'm whispering so she won't overhear. But she's asking questions. She knows something's wrong."

Patrick turned to find Henry watching him, concern etched across his tired face. Beyond him, Wes had made his way into the shop and stood by the coffee machine, his good arm supporting his injured one.

"We have to go," Patrick said, his voice sounding strange to his own ears. "We have to get home now."

Susanne said, "Patrick, you've been driving all night. Please be careful. I need you here in one piece."

"I will. We'll take turns." Patrick's vision tunneled, focusing on the peeling paint of the wall in front of him. "We'll be there as fast as we can."

"Just be careful," Susanne repeated. "I can't..." She didn't finish the thought.

"I will. I promise. We'll find him, Susanne."

The last thing Patrick heard as he hung up was his wife's sobs. He stood motionless, his hand still resting on the receiver. The shop sounds faded to a dull roar in his ears. All he could see was Perry's face the morning he'd left for Mount Rainier. Sleepy-eyed at the breakfast table, mumbling goodbye around a mouthful of cereal. Patrick had ruffled his hair, told him to behave for his mother, to try his hardest at practice, and how sorry he was to miss his first game. Had he told him he loved him? He couldn't remember.

"Patrick?" Henry's voice came from far away. "What happened?"

Patrick turned, his movements wooden. "Perry's missing."

"Missing?" Wes stepped closer. "What do you mean?"

"He disappeared after his football game last night. No one's seen him since." The words felt unreal coming from his mouth. "Twelve hours. My son has been missing for twelve hours, and I wasn't there."

Henry and Wes exchanged a look. "We'll find him," Henry said, his voice firm despite his own grief. "We'll get home, and we'll find him."

Patrick nodded, but inside he was collapsing, a building with its support beams suddenly removed. His hand trembled as he ran it through his hair. His son. His little boy. His determined young man. Out there somewhere, maybe hurt, maybe scared, maybe—

No. He couldn't let his mind go there.

"The tire," he said suddenly, turning toward the service bay. "We need to get on the road."

Thompson appeared from behind a stack of tires. "Just mounting it now. Five more minutes."

"Make it three," Patrick said, his voice hardening. "We need to go. Now."

The tire man must have seen something in Patrick's face because he nodded without argument. "Yes, sir. Fast as I can."

CHAPTER THIRTY-NINE: PRESS

Buffalo, Wyoming
August 26, 1978

Perry

Perry's legs burned with each step, the stones and dried roadbed crunching under his sneakers in a mocking rhythm. The morning sun beat down on his exposed neck, his t-shirt offering little protection against the growing heat. He'd been walking for hours, or maybe it just felt that way. But he kept moving. East meant Buffalo. Buffalo meant home. One foot in front of the other.

His tongue was sticking to the roof of his mouth, and each swallow was a painful reminder of how desperately he needed water. Perry scanned the roadside for any sign of a creek or one of the ditches carrying irrigation water down from the reservoirs. His dad's voice echoed in his mind. *You can survive three days without water, but it gets dangerous after the first.* He wasn't sure how long it had been. Definitely eighteen hours. Maybe more if he'd lost a day while he was unconscious.

The road curved around a rocky outcropping, then straightened again, disappearing into the distance. No cars. No people. Just endless potholes and pine trees. The mountain backroads were rough, and this one was worse than most.

He paused, bending forward with his hands on his knees. Black spots danced at the edges of his vision. *Don't pass out. Not here.* He took three deep breaths, then straightened up. His head throbbed in time with his heartbeat, the lump where he'd been struck feeling hot and tight against his scalp.

"Just keep going," he muttered, his voice cracked and unfamiliar.

He crested a small rise in the road, and a flicker of movement caught his eye. About fifty yards ahead, something large and dark walked into the road. Perry froze mid-step, his heart leaping into his throat.

A bear.

Not a cub, either. An adult black bear, its shoulders hunched as it sniffed the road. He'd seen black bears before, but never alone, and usually from a vehicle. Was it male or female? Female was worse because of the possibility of cubs. But either option was bad if he surprised the animal. This was the start of heavy feeding season as the bears prepared for hibernation.

Dad's voice again. *If you see a black bear, don't run. Stand your ground or back away slowly. Make yourself look big.*

Perry's legs trembled beneath him. The bear hadn't noticed him yet, preoccupied with something at the side of the road. He knew he should make noise now, while he was still a good distance away. That way the bear wouldn't feel threatened and could just go on its way. But his voice seemed stuck in his throat, his limbs locked.

The bear's head swung up, nose working the air.

It had caught his scent.

Perry's heart hammered against his ribs. His fingers tingled with adrenaline. The bear stared directly at him now, its small eyes fixed on this strange, two-legged intruder.

"Hey bear," Perry finally managed, his voice trembling and weak. He lifted his arms, stretching them to the sky. He tried again, louder. "Hey bear! I see you! Go away!"

The bear rose onto its hind legs. Grizzlies might be larger and scarier, but a full-grown black bear was still intimidating, and Perry was definitely intimidated.

"I'm just passing through!" Perry waved his arms over his head to make himself look bigger, even as he took a small step backward. "Not here to bother you!"

For several excruciating seconds, the bear remained upright, swaying slightly as it evaluated this strange, noisy creature. Then, with an almost casual motion, it dropped back to all fours, turned, and ambled off the road into the trees.

Perry's knees nearly buckled with relief. He waited another five minutes, making sure there were no cubs and that the bear was truly gone before continuing. His already parched mouth had gone completely dry with fear, and the adrenaline dump left him feeling even more exhausted than before.

The terrain grew more difficult as the morning wore on, too. The road rose and fell, winding and twisting so often that Perry couldn't tell if he'd gained or lost elevation. His calves and thighs burned with the effort. Sweat trickled down his back, soaking his t-shirt. He'd reached the point where he knew he'd give anything for a drink of water. Anything for the familiar comfort of his room, his bed, his mom's voice calling him down for breakfast.

What was his family doing right now? Were they looking for him? Mom must be worried sick. The football team would be expecting him at Monday's practice. Coach would wonder where his Wolverine had gone. The thought of his nickname gave him a fresh burst of determination. Wolverines don't quit. He pushed on.

By early afternoon, clouds had gathered on the western horizon. Dark, ominous towers of gray and charcoal that grew and spread with alarming speed. Perry watched them approach, his stomach knotting with dread. A thunderstorm was the last thing he needed right now, but they were common in the mountains, especially in the afternoon. *Water, though. That would be good.*

The wind picked up, bringing with it the smell of rain and what Perry thought of as lightning. The temperature dropped so fast that goosebumps rose on Perry's sweaty arms. Thunder rumbled in the distance, a low, threatening growl.

He needed shelter. Lightning struck high points, and right now, he was the highest thing in the road and clearing beyond. The tree line was thirty yards away. Not ideal, but better than nothing.

Perry veered off the gravel, picking his way through tufts of tall grass and uneven ground toward a stand of pines. The first fat drops of rain splattered against his face just as he reached the trees. Within seconds, the sky opened up, rain coming down in sheets so thick he could barely see ten feet ahead.

He huddled at the base of a large pine, drawing his knees to his chest. His t-shirt was drenched in minutes. The ground beneath him turned to mud, soaking through his jeans. At least the rain meant he could deal with his thirst. He tilted his head back, letting the rainwater drop into his mouth from the boughs. It tasted of pine and dirt.

A jagged bolt of lightning split the sky, so bright it left an afterimage burned into his eyes. One-one-thousand, two-one-thousand. CRACK! The thunder shook the ground beneath him, and Perry flinched, curling into a tight ball.

Another flash, closer this time. No time to count before thunder exploded overhead, the sound so loud it seemed like his teeth rattled. The hair on his arms stood up, static electricity making the air feel thick and dangerous. It reminded him of a thunderstorm along Big Goose Creek up in Walker Prairie a few years back, when he and his dad had taken shelter under a rock overhang. He wished his dad were here with him now.

"Please stop," he whispered, though whether he was talking to the storm or God, he wasn't sure.

Lightning blazed again. This time it struck a tree less than fifty yards away. The crack of splitting wood was lost in the deafening thunder. The scent of burning pine filled the air, acrid and sharp. Perry scrambled away from his sheltering tree, suddenly aware that it might be a lightning rod rather than protection. A fire hazard, too. Lightning was a major cause of forest fires during the dry season, August and September mostly. It might be raining now, but he knew it wouldn't last long. If a lightning-struck tree was still smoldering, it could ignite.

He ended up huddled in a shallow depression, rain pounding his back, mud squelching beneath him. Each breath came in a gasp. Every few seconds, lightning illuminated the forest in harsh, blue-white flashes.

It felt like hours, though it was probably only twenty minutes before the storm began to move on. The lightning grew more distant, the thunder less immediate. The rain didn't let up for a few more minutes, but at least he wasn't about to be electrocuted.

When the storm finally passed, Perry emerged from his hollow, soaked to the bone and shivering, teeth chattering. His sneakers squished with each step, and his jeans chafed against his legs. The mud made the trek back to the road difficult, his feet slipping with every other step.

He reached the gravel road again and turned in the direction he'd been walking. Now he was wet and cold, and the road even worse as runoff deepened trenches past storms and snow melt had carved into it. The road wound downhill for a stretch and grew pretty steep. Twice he slipped and fell, the second time skinning his palms as he caught himself. Small rocks embedded themselves in his skin. He winced as he picked them out, leaving tiny pinpricks of blood behind.

Then the sound of an engine cut through the post-rain silence. Perry's head snapped up, hope surging like an electric current. A vehicle! Coming up from behind him! He turned, scanning the road eagerly. Then fear gripped him. He was completely isolated. What if it was the person who'd taken him and dumped him out here? He wouldn't recognize them. He'd have no way of defending himself.

A pickup truck appeared around the bend, moving slowly, almost waddling through the muddy, torn-up road. Perry waved his arms frantically. The truck had to stop. Had to see him.

The driver did see him. Perry could make out the shape of a man behind the wheel, his face turning to track Perry as the truck approached. Perry waved more desperately, his heart racing.

The truck slowed even more. Perry's face split in a relieved grin.

Then the driver gunned the engine, swerving around Perry and continuing up the road without even tapping the brakes. Mud splashed from the tires, splattering Perry's already filthy clothes.

"Hey!" he shouted, his voice breaking. "HEY! STOP!"

But the truck was already disappearing around the next bend, its taillights gleaming briefly before vanishing entirely.

Perry stood in the middle of the road, arms still half-raised. A knot formed in his throat, hot and painful. He swallowed it down. Don't cry. It won't help anything. Keep going.

He trudged onward. The encounter left him feeling more alone than before. He'd been seen—actually seen—and still left behind. He was just a kid. Well, teenager, but he didn't look threatening. How could someone just leave him out here? *Could it be the person who dumped me?* If so, at least he hadn't stopped to finish Perry off. It was small comfort, though.

The afternoon stretched on, the sun occasionally breaking through the clouds to steam the moisture from the road. Perry's clothes began to dry, stiffening with mud and sweat. His legs moved mechanically, one foot in front of the other on autopilot.

The distant growl of another engine barely registered. He didn't even look up this time, not wanting to face another rejection, too numb to feel scared about who it might be. But the sound grew louder, different from the truck. Higher pitched, more of a whine than a rumble. A motorbike.

Despite himself, Perry turned. The bike came into view, a rider hunched over the handlebars. Perry raised one weary arm in a half-hearted wave, not really expecting a response.

The motorbike slowed slightly as it passed. It was a small one, made for trail riding. The rider's helmeted head turned toward Perry, and for a moment, hope flared again. Then the bike accelerated away, the rider never looking back.

Perry didn't even have the energy to feel disappointed this time. He just kept walking.

His sneakers had worn blisters on both heels, each step a fresh burst of pain. His empty stomach had given up growling and now just ached hollowly beneath his ribs. The sun tracked across the sky, beginning its westward descent.

And then the road changed.

Perry almost didn't notice at first. His eyes had been fixed on his feet for the past hour, watching each step to avoid further falls. But suddenly, there was thick gravel on the roadbed, which had been mainly mud and packed dirt for hours.

He looked up, blinking in surprise. The gravel road had ended at a T-intersection with a paved highway. An actual highway, with painted lines and everything and a sign that read HIGHWAY 16. The road linking Buffalo across the Bighorn Mountains with Ten Sleep, Worland, and beyond.

A small, desperate laugh bubbled up from his chest. Civilization. He'd reached civilization. Tears pricked at his eyes, but he blinked them away.

Now he just had to figure out which way to go. Left or right? This section of the highway didn't look familiar. He looked up at the sun, trying to orient himself. It was mid-afternoon, maybe three or four o'clock. The sun hung in the southwestern sky, no longer a reliable east-west indicator, especially since the roads tended to wind, and what appeared eastward in one section might end up going west.

Perry frowned, his battered brain struggling to think clearly. Both directions would eventually lead to towns, to people, to help. But which would get him to Buffalo?

He tried to remember the map in his dad's truck. The Bighorns were crisscrossed with dirt and gravel roads. If only he could figure out what road he'd come from, he'd know where on Highway 16 he was now.

He would have to go with his gut. His dad had taught him that instincts were nature's way of connecting the mind to a wisdom beyond human understanding. He hoped that was right.

So, he turned left. The pavement felt strange beneath his feet. Smooth. Forgiving. His feet didn't move around in his shoes. His blistered heels thanked him, and he walked with renewed energy.

The road curved gently through the trees, following the natural contours of the mountain. Perry kept to the narrow shoulder. The shadows were growing longer, stretching across the asphalt like dark fingers reaching for him.

Then he heard the steady approach of an engine coming from ahead of him. Perry stopped, watching the bend in the road, waiting for the vehicle to appear.

A car rounded the curve, sunlight glinting off its windshield. It was a big and blue. For a terrifying moment, Perry thought it was a Bronco—the car that had hit Trish, the car driven by the man who might be responsible for his current predicament.

His heart stuttered in his chest. He should hide. Should dive into the trees and wait for it to pass. But his legs refused to move, rooted to the spot by exhaustion and the desperate need for help. It wasn't a Bronco, he realized as it drew closer. But it was definitely blue and a similar shape.

Too late to run now. The driver of the vehicle had spotted him—its speed decreased, brake lights flashing briefly. Perry's mouth went dry again, fear coursing through him like ice water. What if the man who had hit Trish and nearly him had switched cars? What if this was how it ended, after all he'd survived?

The vehicle slowed further, pulling onto the shoulder about twenty yards ahead of where Perry stood frozen in indecision. The engine cut off. The driver's door opened.

Perry held his breath as a man stepped out. The light was behind him. A baseball cap shadowed his face.

It could be anyone. It could be help, or it could be the opposite.

Perry stood rooted to the spot, unable to run, unable to call out. The man took a step toward him, his features still obscured by the cap's brim.

Then he raised his head, and Perry saw his face.

CHAPTER FORTY: REUNITE

Buffalo, Wyoming
August 26, 1978

Patrick

Patrick barreled through the hospital doors, ignoring the startled looks from people milling near the reception desk. His heart hammered against his ribs as he navigated the corridors. He was close. So close to his family. He rounded a corner and brushed past an orderly, heading for the nurses station nearest where he thought Trish would be.

As he ran up on it, he shouted, "Where's Trish?"

"Dr. Flint!" Eleanor Matthews shouted the room number back at him as he passed. Her voice faded behind him.

He didn't slow down. Henry had dropped him and Wes at the entrance, telling Patrick he would have someone from his own ranch follow him back to town with the Suburban. Patrick had barely heard him, already running before the car had fully stopped, while Wes made his way in to get his arm x-rayed.

Patrick spotted the room number. There was a security guard leaning against the wall outside the door. He nodded at the man.

"Whoa. Not so fast." The security guard stepped in front of him. "Who are you?"

"Patrick Flint. That's my daughter in there."

"Patrick!" It was Susanne's voice inside the room.

The guard stepped aside and Patrick pushed through the door. There she was—Trish, braced leg propped up on pillows, the head of her bed elevated, her face pale but her eyes bright and alert.

"Dad!" her face lit up.

Patrick crossed the room in three long strides and leaned in to put his arms around her, careful of the IV line taped to the back of her hand. She felt smaller somehow, more fragile than the teenager who'd waved goodbye to him nearly a week ago. Her arms wrapped around his neck, and he breathed in the familiar scent of his nearly grown baby girl.

"I'm here, sweetheart." His voice cracked on the words. "I'm so sorry it took so long."

"Doesn't matter." Trish pulled back, eyes scanning his face. "You look terrible, Dad. I thought Mom looked bad, but you have her beat. Of course, I think I probably win."

Patrick laughed. "Thanks. It's been a long couple of days." His gaze swept over her, the doctor in him automatically cataloging her condition—skin tone good, eyes clear, respiration normal. "You do look a little beat up, though. How do you feel?"

Before Trish could answer, Susanne's soft voice came from behind him. "Her fever broke this morning. She's been feeling sick." As if on cue, Trish sneezed. "They think it was just the onset of a virus. Bad timing that scared us all to death."

Patrick turned to find his wife, her face drawn with exhaustion but her eyes bright with unshed tears. "Susanne." He said her name softly. Reverently.

She crossed to him, and he pulled her into the embrace with Trish, the three of them like shipwreck survivors clinging to a life raft.

Patrick felt Susanne's tears dampening his shirt, her shoulders shaking with silent sobs. He tightened his grip, one arm around each of his girls, and fought back his own tears.

"I came as fast as I could," he murmured into Susanne's hair. "God, I'm so sorry I wasn't here."

They stayed like that for a long moment, the three of them tangled together. Finally, Susanne pulled back, wiping her eyes with the heel of her hand.

"They're sure she doesn't have deep vein thrombosis or a pulmonary embolism?" Patrick asked.

"Dr. Wilson is quite confident."

"How bad was the fever?" Patrick asked, still holding Trish's hand.

"Bad enough that Dr. Wilson was worried." Susanne's voice was steady now, but Patrick could read the lingering fear in her eyes. "Her temperature got up to 104.3."

Patrick nodded as Trish sneezed again. "God bless you."

"It hurts to sneeze. But I guess that's better than the alternatives were. They had to take off the brace," Trish said, gesturing toward her leg. "And it hurt like hell—heck," she corrected, glancing at her mother.

"I think you've earned a few hells after what you've been through," Patrick said, squeezing her hand. He reached out to touch her forehead, a gesture as old as her childhood, checking for fever. It was almost normal. "I'll take a look at your chart later. I want to read everything myself."

"Always the doctor," Susanne said.

Patrick wanted to ask about Perry. Before he could get Susanne to walk into the hall with him, the door opened again, and Patrick turned, expecting to see a nurse or perhaps Dr. Wilson himself. Instead, Deputy Ronnie Harcourt stood in the doorway, her uniform wrinkled and hair from her usually neat braids electrified around her face. But it wasn't Ronnie who made Patrick's heart stutter in his chest.

It was the figure behind her.

CHAPTER FORTY-ONE: GATHER

BUFFALO, WYOMING
AUGUST 26, 1978

Patrick

IT WAS PERRY. Standing there in hospital scrubs that were too big for him, a white bandage stark against his blond hair, his face bruised but his eyes bright and alert.

Patrick froze, unable to process the sight before him. After a day imagining the worst, the reality of his son standing there short-circuited his brain.

"Perry?" The name came out as a whisper.

Perry gave a small, lopsided smile. "Hi, Dad."

Patrick moved before he realized what he was doing, crossing the room in two strides and sweeping Perry into a bear hug. He lifted him clear off the ground, squeezing him so tightly that both Perry and his shoulder protested.

"Easy, Dad! You're going to break my ribs!"

Patrick loosened his grip but didn't let go, one hand coming up to cradle the back of Perry's head, carefully avoiding the bandage. "You're here. You're okay." He couldn't seem to form more complex thoughts, his entire being consumed by the reality of his son, solid and alive.

"I'm okay," Perry confirmed, wriggling free. "Just tired. And my head hurts."

Patrick kept a hand on his son's shoulder. He looked between Susanne and Ronnie, questions tumbling over each other in his mind.

"One of the search volunteers found him walking along Highway 16," Ronnie said, answering the unasked question. "About four miles west of Deer Haven Lodge. Sheriff Westbury brought him straight here."

"When?" Patrick managed, his voice rough.

"About two hours ago," Ronnie replied.

Susanne moved to Perry's side, wrapping an arm around his shoulders. "Tell your dad what you told us, honey."

Perry looked down at his feet, then back up at Patrick. "I don't really know what happened, Dad. I was walking to the hospital after my game, and something hit me from behind. When I woke up, I was in the mountains somewhere. Like, really in the middle of nowhere."

"You don't remember who took you? Or where they took you?" Patrick asked, his doctor's mind already cataloging Perry's symptoms. Potential concussion, memory loss, the risk of internal injuries.

Perry shook his head, wincing slightly at the movement. "It was dark when I woke up the first time. I passed out again. When I woke up for real, it was morning, and I was alone. I found a road and just started walking. Tried to head east, like you taught me."

"Smart boy," Patrick said, his voice thick with emotion.

"We're going to need a full statement from Perry," Ronnie said, leaning against the doorframe. "And we might take him back up to see if we can track back to where he was dumped. There could be evidence, though that storm today probably washed most of it away."

"Storm?" Patrick asked.

"Big thunderstorm hit the mountains this afternoon," Ronnie explained. "Perry said he got caught in it."

Perry nodded. "It was pretty bad. Lightning hit a tree right near me."

Patrick's stomach clenched at the thought of his son alone in a violent mountain storm, concussed and lost. If he ever found out who had done this to his boy, he would make sure they paid. They would pay, and pay, and pay. "You hiked through that?"

"No, I found a low spot," Perry said with a shrug that was pure teenage bravado.

Trish spoke up from her bed. "Perry's a regular Daniel Boone, Dad. Apparently, he hiked for miles, fought off a bear, and survived on rainwater and his own stubbornness."

"A bear?" Patrick's eyebrows arched.

"It wasn't that dramatic," Perry said, shooting his sister a look. "The bear saw me and left. And it was only like, I dunno, ten miles of hiking. Maybe."

"With a concussion," Ronnie added. "Kid's got your determination, Patrick."

Patrick grinned at his son. "Chip off the old block."

"And he's smart like his mother."

"Even better."

"I do have news for everyone. We picked up Gentry Childs. The one who threatened Perry."

"Threatened him?" Patrick said.

"Perry beat Larry Childs out for a starting position. His father threatened Perry after a practice. He's just off a stint in Oklahoma State Prison for assault and battery, too. Go on, Ronnie." Susanne rolled her hand.

"As I told you last night, he drives a 1970 blue Bronco. It has a dent on the front right fender that is consistent with hitting Trish, but inconclusive. And he has no alibi for last night when Perry was taken or when Trish was hit."

"It was him! Over a game! That's so... so... ridiculous."

"And yet still so awful."

Patrick frowned. "Are you sure it was him?"

"Not yet. Childs is our top suspect now. He denies doing either thing, He denies doing either thing, of course, but without an alibi, he's a strong suspect. We had enough to arrest him, but not enough to be sure. That's why we're needing Perry's statement and the additional evidence from the crime screen. We're getting a search warrant for his Bronco, too."

Patrick had caught up. "A violent loser with no alibi who threatened my kid and is driving the right vehicle."

"It's too early to say we've got him, but... "

"But you think you've got your guy."

Ronnie touched the tip of her nose.

"What about Dabbo and Jimmy?" Trish said.

"We talked to them. They have alibis."

"And Bella?" Susanne said.

"No evidence that she's even still in the state."

It was a lot, and nothing was conclusive. Patrick knew he couldn't rest easy until the sheriff's department was sure the person behind bars was the right guy, the one who'd hurt his kids. Still, this Gentry Childs did seem the most likely candidate. At some point, Patrick had to trust local law enforcement to do their job, admittedly a hard one. The memory of the Buffalo police targeting Susanne for Whitney Saylor's murder haunted him, though. They didn't let up on her until he and Susanne had found the killer for them. It made full trust difficult.

He pulled Perry close again, overcome with a fresh wave of gratitude. He would put his worries aside. His family was here, safe under one roof. The magnitude of what could have happened—what nearly happened—was overwhelming. Both of his kids attacked. Both of them hurt.

"Hey, speaking of the position I beat Larry out for," Perry said, pulling away to look up at Patrick. "I blocked a punt, Dad. Coach called me the Wolverine. And we won!"

Patrick laughed, the sound surprising even himself. Leave it to Perry to focus on the football victory in the midst of everything else. He'd always been obsessed with the game. "That's amazing, bud. I'm so proud of you." His face sobered. "And I'm so sorry I missed it. I should have been there."

"It's okay," Perry said. "I knew you were doing something important."

Important. The climb seemed so trivial now, so selfish. What was standing on the summit of Rainier compared to being here when his family needed him? "Not as important as you."

"So how was it?" Perry asked, his eyes lighting up. "Did you make it to the top? Was there snow? Did you see any crevasses? Was it as hard as you thought it would be?"

Patrick shook his head, smiling despite himself. "There'll be plenty of time to talk about the mountain later." He squeezed Perry's shoulder, then felt the back of his son's head. "That's quite a bump you've got there. Have you been examined properly? X-rays? CT scan?"

Perry rolled his eyes. "Dad, I'm fine. They already did everything."

"Who did? What did they check for? Did they rule out subdural hematoma?" Patrick fired the questions rapidly, his hands already moving to examine Perry's pupils, checking for signs of increased intracranial pressure.

"Subdural what?"

"Brain bleed."

"Dr. Wilson checked me out," Perry said, squirming away from Patrick's probing fingers. "He said we're getting the family discount today. I've got a concussion but probably nothing worse. I can go home with you."

"I want Dr. John to look at you, too," Patrick said firmly. "I don't even know Dr. Wilson."

Perry groaned. "Dad, come on. I'm fine. I hiked for miles. If I had a brain bleed or whatever, I'd be dead by now, right?"

"Not necessarily," Patrick began, his voice slipping into lecture mode. "Subdural hematomas can develop slowly, and symptoms can be—"

The door opened once more, cutting off Patrick's medical explanation. Dr. John stood there, his white coat rumpled and his glasses low on his nose. Ronnie was just behind him, having apparently slipped out to fetch the older doctor.

"Thought I heard the worried father voice of Patrick Flint," Dr. John said, his weathered face breaking into a smile. "Good to have you back."

"John." Patrick stepped forward to shake his hand. "Thank you for taking care of my family. Both of them," he added, glancing from Trish to Perry.

"Dr. Wilson did most of it. But all in a day's work," Dr. John moved toward Perry, medical chart in hand. "Let's have a look at that head of yours, young man. Your father won't rest until I've cleared you, and frankly, neither will I."

Perry sighed dramatically but submitted to another examination with the resignation of someone who knew resistance was pointless. As Dr. John checked Perry's pupils and reflexes, Susanne slipped her arm around Patrick's waist, leaning into him.

"You look dead on your feet," she murmured. "When did you last sleep?"

"I caught a few hours in the car while Henry drove," Patrick said, wrapping his arm around her shoulders. "I'll be fine."

"You're not fine," Susanne countered. "None of us really are. And I won't be until I'm absolutely sure they have the right person locked up."

Patrick leaned his forehead down to hers. What could he say to reassure her? He felt exactly the same way.

CHAPTER FORTY-TWO: IGNITE

Buffalo, Wyoming
August 28, 1978

Perry

Perry savored the last bite of his mom's chicken spaghetti, the cheesy white sauce and tender noodles a welcome change from hospital food. His head still ached where someone had bashed it, but the pain had faded to background noise. He felt sure he'd be ready to play in the game next weekend.

"More spaghetti, Perry?" His mom held out the serving bowl, a hopeful look on her face. She'd been like that since he'd been snatched. Constantly offering food, checking on him, finding reasons to touch him.

"No thanks, Mom." Perry patted his stomach. "I'm stuffed."

She nodded and set the bowl back on the coffee table, which had been turned into a makeshift dining surface. Paper plates, plastic cups, and serving dishes covered every inch. Trish was lounging in

Dad's recliner, laid back with her leg propped up. Since she was unable to move to the table, they'd brought dinner to the living room instead.

Grandpa Joe sat in the armchair opposite Trish, scraping the last bits of sauce from his plate. "You should have seen this boy at the game last Friday." He pointed his fork at Perry. "Broke through that line like he'd been shot out of a cannon. Best blocked punt I've ever seen."

Perry felt his face grow warm. "It wasn't that big a deal," he mumbled.

"The hell it wasn't," Grandpa Joe said, ignoring his mom's pointed look about the language.

Henry chuckled from his spot on the couch. "Sounds like you've found your calling, Perry."

"Speaking of calling," Wes said, waving his fork around with his good arm, "your dad here was calling for his Lord and savior when that avalanche nearly took us out." His other arm was in a cast.

"I was not." His dad grinned.

"Tell us about the mountain, Dad," Perry said, leaning forward. "Was it awesome?"

His dad shared a look with his mom that Perry couldn't quite interpret. "It was something else. Beautiful. Terrifying. Like nothing else on earth."

"You made it to the top, right?" Perry prompted.

"He did," Henry confirmed, bouncing little Hank on his knee. The toddler giggled, grabbing for Henry's nose. "Wes and I didn't. Not after we nearly died up there."

Vangie swatted her husband's arm. "Don't say it like that. You're going to give me nightmares all over again."

"What happened?" Trish asked, adjusting her position in the recliner. She'd been quiet most of the evening. In addition to her surgery, she had been sneezing and coughing for a few days but was starting to feel better.

Dad set his empty plate aside. "We were roped together when our guide went off the trail, which pulled me off and then Henry and Wes. Then somehow we came unclipped from him."

"Lewis," Wes supplied. "He didn't have much of a bedside manner."

" We were sliding toward a crevasse."

Perry's eyes widened. "How'd you stop?"

"Your dad dug his ice axe in so hard I thought he'd dislocate his shoulder," Henry said. "Stopped all three of us."

"Then, when we were climbing back out, the snow shelf above us broke loose and caused an avalanche," Wes added, his voice dropping dramatically. "Thought we were goners for sure."

Perry frowned. "What did you do?"

"We hunkered down, covered our heads, and prayed," his dad said. "The main slide missed us by maybe ten feet. Close enough to feel the wind off it."

"That's when this fool tried to keep climbing with a broken arm," Henry said, nodding toward Wes.

Wes shrugged his good shoulder. "I had no choice. But at least I was better off than the dead guy that we found."

"What?" Trish said, her voice a squeak. "You found a dead guy?"

His dad said, "Someone who'd been lost up there years ago. The avalanche uncovered him, poor soul."

"Holy smokes," Perry said. "That's wild."

"It was sobering."

"Tell them about the crazy guy with the ice axe, Doc," Wes prompted.

His dad's expression darkened. "That was something else entirely. A climber named Gerald had some kind of breakdown and tried to attack his buddy Connor with an ice axe. Would have killed him if I hadn't been there to stop it, with the help of some EMTs."

"Why would he do that?" Perry asked.

"We don't know." His dad exchanged glances with Henry and

Wes. "Mountain climbing can push people to their mental limits, though."

"People just snap sometimes," Wes said, his tone serious for once.

Little Hank chose that moment to break free from his father's lap, running circles around the coffee table with squeals of delight. The tension in the room dissolved as everyone laughed at the toddler's antics.

"Speaking of people snapping," Henry said, his voice quieter as the laughter subsided, "any word on the guy they think hit Trish and took Perry?"

The room fell silent. Perry stared at his empty plate, uncomfortable even thinking about what had happened to him and Trish.

"Gentry Childs. Nothing concrete," his dad replied. "The tire tracks Perry found in the mountains were washed away by the rain. Without a clear description or physical evidence, the case will be circumstantial. Ronnie has been hard at it, though, and she's convinced it's him. In fact, that's why she and Jeff weren't able to bring Will and join us. She's working extra shifts on this."

"I still don't remember much," Perry said, feeling like he'd failed somehow. "Just waking up in the mountains. The rest is blank."

His mom reached over to squeeze his hand. "Your dad told you memory loss is common with head injuries."

"And Bella Crooke?" Vangie asked, catching little Hank as he barreled past. "Any sign of her?"

His dad shook his head. "Sheriff Westbury said they found her name on the passenger list for a flight out of Denver to Houston. From there she could have gone anywhere. Even out of the country. They've got alerts out, of course." He trailed off, the implication clear. Bella was gone.

"Good riddance," Grandpa Joe muttered.

"If she never comes back, I won't complain," Trish said, shifting in the recliner and looking uncomfortable.

Perry nodded in agreement. The thought of facing that woman in court, of having to relive what happened on Cloud Peak knotted his stomach up tight. "I don't want to testify."

"None of us do," his dad said, his jaw tightening. "But if they find her—"

"I know," Perry interrupted. "We'll do what we have to."

His mom stood suddenly, plastering on a bright smile that didn't quite reach her eyes. "Who's ready for dessert? Patrick made huckleberry ice cream."

"Homemade?" Kathy perked up. "I haven't had that since I was a kid."

"Perry's favorite," his dad said with a wink.

Perry felt a genuine smile spread across his face. Things weren't back to normal. They might never be completely normal again. But sitting here with his family, with the promise of his dad's homemade ice cream, it felt like maybe they'd be okay.

"I'll help," he offered, starting to rise.

"You sit. You're still recovering." His mom waved him back down. "Your father can help me."

His parents walked to the kitchen, and conversations resumed in the living room. Wes was telling Joe about some fishing spot on Clear Creek. Trish, Vangie, and Kathy were discussing when Trish might return to school. Henry had his hands full trying to corral Hank, who seemed determined to climb the bookshelf.

It was chaos. It was normal. It was family.

For the first time since waking up alone in the mountains, Perry felt truly safe.

PERRY'S DAD returned carrying a large plastic bowl of homemade ice cream with deep purple huckleberry swirls. Nobody made ice cream like his parents. Rich and creamy with just the right sweetness, the wild huckleberries adding bursts of tangy flavor that store-bought ice creams could never match. Grandpa Joe perked up at the sight, his perpetual scowl softening. Even Trish, who'd been picking at her dinner, smiled.

"The freezer just finished, so it should be perfect." His dad passed the serving spoon to his mom.

She scooped ice cream and passed Perry the first bowl. He dug in immediately. The cold sweetness hit his tongue, the flavor so intense it made him forget about his headache for a second. "This is heaven. Worth getting kidnapped for."

The room went silent. Perry froze, spoon halfway to his mouth, realizing the others were staring at him. "Sorry. Bad joke."

His mom's expression was pained, but his dad reached over and squeezed Perry's shoulder. "Joke if it helps," he said. "But maybe give us a few more weeks before the kidnapping humor, okay?"

Perry grinned and focused on his ice cream instead.

"You think I can get the recipe?" Kathy asked, breaking the awkward silence.

"Family secret," his dad said with an exaggerated wink. "Flint men have been making this ice cream since my grandfather's day."

"With a few modern improvements," his mom added drily. "I doubt your grandfather had an electric ice cream freezer."

"True enough." His dad laughed. "But the recipe's the same."

Wes held up his bowl. "I'll need another serving for proper analysis. You know, to see if I can reverse-engineer the secret."

"In your dreams, Braten."

His mom refilled Wes's bowl anyway.

Trish was scraping the bottom of her dish. "Did you put vanilla extract in this batch, Dad? Tastes different."

"Good different or bad different?" his dad asked.

"Good. Really good." Trish held out her bowl for seconds, too.

A sharp bark from the front of the house interrupted the dessert analysis. Ferdinand had been banished outdoors where he wouldn't beg for food.

"What's got into him?" Grandpa Joe grumbled as another volley of barks erupted, these more urgent than the last.

"Maybe a rabbit in the yard," Henry said.

The barking grew more frantic. A low growl followed, then another explosive series of barks. Perry had heard Ferdinand bark plenty of times. At delivery men, at passing cars, at shadows that turned out to be nothing. This was different. This was his something-is-very-wrong bark.

"I'll check on him." Perry set his empty bowl on the coffee table. His head protested as he stood too quickly, but he ignored it. Ferdinand was more his dog than anyone else's, so it was his job.

"Tell that mutt to pipe down," Grandpa Joe called after him. "Some of us are trying to enjoy our dessert in peace."

Perry made his way through the living room toward the front entryway. The barking grew louder, more insistent. The dog was at the front door now, claws scrabbling against the wood, whining between barks. As he passed the big living window, he looked out and saw the back of a vehicle driving away.

"Oh my gosh! There's a blue car out front like the one that hit Trish!" He shouted.

"But that guy is in jail," his mom said.

"Jimmy and Dabbo. Dabbo has a car like that." Trish was shaking her head.

"Where did you hear that?"

"From Marcy. She saw them. Remember the horse manure in the bag and how I saw a car like that driving away? It was them. I know it was. The prank calls, too. Half of me still thinks it was Dabbo that ran me down."

"I thought you didn't recognize the man behind the wheel," their mom said.

"I didn't get a close enough look. But what I saw wasn't clearly *not* him. And if Jillian was their alibi, or if they were each other's alibis, well, then I just don't believe them."

As his parents quizzed Trish, Perry moved onward toward the door. "It's okay, boy," Perry soothed. The dog was still going nuts. Uneasiness prickled his skin. Ferdinand wasn't the type of dog to make this big of a fuss over nothing. Not at their door. Never scratching it.

Maybe this had all been about the vehicle.

Then why didn't he stop barking when it left?

Perry noticed something odd. The area in front of the door felt warm. Too warm with the air conditioner blowing air down from the vents right above it. He reached for the doorknob to let the dog in but jerked his hand back immediately.

The metal was hot. Not warm. Hot.

Perry stepped closer, squinting at the bottom of the door. A faint orange glow outlined the gap between door and threshold. Ferdinand's barking and whining reached a frenzied pitch but somehow sounded muffled.

"Dad?" Perry called, his voice strangely calm despite the adrenaline suddenly flooding through him. "Dad, I think you need to see this."

"What is it?" There was mild curiosity in his tone.

Perry placed his palm flat against the door panel, then snatched it back. The wood was hot enough to be uncomfortable. Through the door, he heard a strange, soft crackling sound.

"The door's hot," he said, louder this time. "Really hot. So is the doorknob."

"Coming."

He backed away and saw wisps of black smoke curling through the gap at the top of the frame.

"Dad!" This time his voice cracked with urgency. "The door's on fire! The house is on fire!"

Everything paused for a silent beat, then the living room exploded with noise. A dish and utensil clattered to the floor, Trish gasped, and his mom shot to her feet, knocking over a TV tray.

His dad rushed over and touched the door and the knob. "Everyone out the back door, now!" His dad's voice was commanding. "Henry, help Trish! Wes, get Joe! Susanne, call the fire department! Kathy, help Vangie and Hank!"

Perry stood frozen, watching as the thin line of orange beneath the door brightened and expanded. Ferdinand continued barking frantically on the other side. On the burning porch. He wasn't scratching the door anymore.

"Perry!" His father's hand closed around his arm, yanking him back toward the living room. "You, too. Move out!"

The smoke detector in the hallway began its shrill, piercing wail.

CHAPTER FORTY-THREE: TRAP

Buffalo, Wyoming
August 28, 1978

Susanne

Susanne's world narrowed to a single point of focus when Perry's words registered. *The house is on fire.*

She knocked over the TV tray holding the plastic bowl of ice cream as she sprang to her feet, her mind making rapid calculations. How long had the door been burning? How quickly would the flames spread? Where were the keys to the truck? Her gaze swept across the faces of her family. Trish immobile in the recliner, Perry wide-eyed with shock, her father-in-law stunned into silence. But it wasn't just them. They had a house full of guests, too.

Three exits. Front door, back door, garage. Go, go, go.

"Everyone out the back door!" Patrick's voice cut through her racing thoughts. "Henry, help Trish! Wes, get Joe! Susanne, call the fire department! Kathy, help Vangie and Hank! Perry, move!"

The smoke detector penetrated the frozen moment, galvanizing

Susanne into action. She lunged toward the kitchen where the wall phone hung beside the cabinets. Her fingers fumbled with the receiver, jamming it against her ear.

Nothing. No dial tone. Just dead silence.

She jiggled the cradle frantically. "The phone's dead!" she shouted, her voice barely audible over the shrieking alarm.

Patrick appeared by the table, his face tight with controlled panic. "I used a towel on the doorknob, but the door won't budge. The back door's on fire, and it won't open either. I'm checking the garage."

Susanne's stomach lurched sickeningly. Two exits blocked. She slammed the useless receiver down and rushed after Patrick, who was already yanking on the door that connected the house to the garage. It didn't open. He tried again, putting his shoulder into it, his face reddening with effort.

"It's stuck," he growled, then pressed his palm flat against the door panel. He jerked it back immediately. "Hot. This one's burning too."

"All the doors?" Susanne's voice sounded distant in her own ears. "That's not possible."

Patrick met her eyes, and in that moment, she saw the truth they couldn't bring themselves to say aloud. This wasn't accidental. Someone had deliberately trapped them inside and set fire to their house. But who? Bella was gone. Gentry Childs was in jail. Who had done this?

"Windows," Patrick said simply, already moving.

Susanne followed him back to the living room, where chaos had erupted. Joe was arguing with Wes about what to do next while Henry had lifted Trish, cast and all, into his arms. Kathy was gathering Hank from Vangie, who looked pale but composed, her hands steady as she passed the child over then stood and took him back.

She's still weak from that horrible miscarriage.

"Doors are all blocked," Patrick announced, his voice cutting through the noise. "We need to go through a window. Henry, get Trish to the master bedroom window. It's the largest."

"What about Ferdinand?" Perry asked, his face ashen. "He's outside!"

"That's good. Dogs are smart," Susanne said, squeezing Perry's shoulder as she passed. "He'll run from the fire. We have to focus on getting everyone out." There was no choice. The smoke was already thickening near the ceiling, curling down the walls in gray tendrils.

Perry nodded, swallowing hard. "I'll open the upstairs windows. I've climbed down the tree out front before."

Susanne followed Patrick down the hallway toward their bedroom, her mind cataloging resources and escape routes. The fire extinguisher was in the kitchen, but with three doors already in flames, what good would it do?

Patrick was already at the bedroom window, yanking at the latch. She picked up the bedroom phone to see if it worked. Silence was all she heard from the receiver.

"What the hell?" Patrick muttered. He'd opened the latch and tried to open the window without any success. He tried again, bracing himself and pushing with all his strength.

Susanne moved to help him, adding her muscle to his effort. The window didn't move one iota. "Why won't it open?" she gasped.

"I don't know. Let's try another one." Patrick was already moving toward the second window in their bedroom.

Henry appeared in the doorway, Trish in his arms. "Where do you want her?"

" We can't get the windows open." Patrick wrestled with the second window. "This one's stuck too."

"I'll take her back to the living room and come help you."

Susanne ran to the guest bedroom across the hall. Same result. The window unlocked but wouldn't slide up. Panic bloomed in her chest.

She heard Perry's voice from the staircase. "Dad! The windows upstairs won't open!"

Patrick joined her in the guest room and examined the window frame closely. "They've all been sealed," he said, his voice tight with anger and disbelief. "Somehow. I can't tell with what."

"When? Who would—" She couldn't complete the thought.

"Same person who set the fires," Patrick answered grimly.

Kathy stuck her head in the door. "None of the kitchen or living room windows will open either," she said, her nurse's training evident in her calm efficiency despite the fear in her eyes.

Henry appeared behind her, and Patrick said, "We need to break one, Henry. The shatterproof glass won't be easy."

"Fireplace tools. I'll get them," Susanne suggested, already going for them.

The smoke was noticeably thicker now, hanging in a gray pall near the ceiling. Susanne ducked instinctively as she hurried back into the living room. Kathy was by the front windows, yanking up futilely. Wes steadied Joe, who looked bewildered. Vangie cradled Hank close to her chest, the child's face buried in her neck.

Susanne grabbed the small hatchet from its place beside the fireplace tools. As she turned, she caught Trish's terrified gaze from the couch, where Henry had deposited her.

"Mom?" Trish's voice was small, younger somehow. "What if we can't get out?"

"It's going to be okay," Susanne promised, wishing she could believe it herself. "We're going to break a window."

She met Patrick back in the main bedroom, hatchet in hand. He took it from her, moving to the big window.

"Stand back," he ordered, raising the hatchet over his head.

The first blow landed with a dull thud rather than the expected crash of breaking glass. The hatchet bounced off the window, barely leaving a mark.

Patrick stared at the unbroken pane in disbelief. "What the—"

He swung again, harder this time. A small crack appeared, radiating out a few inches, but nowhere near enough to create an opening. Again and again he struck, his face reddening with effort and frustration. The window, designed to withstand break-in attempts, surrendered only tiny spiderweb cracks with each impact. The new windows they'd installed just that summer. The ones Patrick had been so proud of for their energy efficiency and security features.

"Shatterproof," Henry said grimly. "We need a sledgehammer or a battering room."

"In the garage," Patrick said. "Let's try the hatchet on the back door." Patrick was already trotting that way. "Maybe we can chop through it."

Susanne followed him through the thickening smoke to the kitchen. It was becoming difficult to breathe the hot, smokey air, and her eyes stung.

Patrick approached the back door cautiously, testing it with his hand before positioning himself.

The hatchet hit the wooden door with a satisfying clunk, but Susanne's hope quickly vanished. The door was solid oak, two inches thick. The blade was barely nicking it. Even with the hatchet, it would take too long to create an opening large enough for everyone to escape.

"Too thick," Patrick confirmed after several blows, his breath coming in pants. "We'd need hours."

The smoke detector's wail was joined by a second alarm, then a third, as detectors in other rooms activated. The air was growing visibly hazier. Susanne could feel the heat building, not just from the doors but from the walls themselves, as if the entire structure was being consumed from the outside in.

"We're trapped," she whispered, the reality of their situation hitting her with physical force.

Patrick grabbed her shoulders, his eyes intense. "No. There's always a way out. We just have to think. What about the attic vent?"

"It's tiny as I remember, but we should check."

"The old root cellar!" Trish shouted. "Dad, remember the door in the basement that goes out to the cellar?"

Susanne's heart leapt. "The root cellar. Of course." She couldn't believe she'd forgotten it. She'd been down there just last week. "But the hatch was stuck. I tried and I couldn't get it open."

Patrick ran toward the doorway down to the basement. "Henry, you're with me and Susanne. The rest of you, stay together in the living room. If the smoke gets worse, get down on the floor where the air is clearer."

Susanne caught Kathy's eye. "Wet towels," she instructed. "Get them from the bathroom. Put them over your faces, especially the children and Joe. And Trish—she can't move easily with that cast."

"We've got it," Kathy assured her, already moving toward the hallway bathroom.

"Be careful," Vangie added. "We can't afford any more broken bones right now."

Patrick was already descending into the darkness below, flicking on lights as he went. Henry followed, with Susanne close behind. The basement air was clearer, though tendrils of smoke were beginning to seep through the floorboards above.

"It's that way," Patrick said to Henry, pointing to the far side of the big room where a narrow door led to the root cellar. He hurried over, unlocked it, and yanked it open, revealing a passageway. "Flashlight," he muttered, patting his pockets.

Susanne remembered she'd removed the one she kept on the shelf outside the passageway door when she went into the cellar. She'd taken it upstairs with her, then what? She closed her eyes. She'd brought it back down here, but she'd put it on the bookshelves behind her. She ran over and got it. "Here." She clicked it on and pointed it down the passage, the beam illuminating the dusty space.

The three of them moved quickly through the narrow corridor, Patrick stooping slightly under the low ceiling. The air smelled of earth and dampness, a stark contrast to the acrid smoke above. At the end of the passage, they came to the cellar.

Susanne directed the flashlight beam upward, locating the hatch in the ceiling that opened to the backyard. It was made of steel, about three feet square, with a handle bolted to the underside.

"There it is," Patrick said, relief evident in his voice. "Our way out."

Susanne shone the light directly on the hatch.

He ascended a few of the steps then positioned himself under it, reaching up and placing his palms against it. His shoulder protested, but he ignored it. "At least this one isn't hot."

With a grunt, he pushed upward.

The hatch didn't move.

He repositioned his feet, bracing himself better, and pushed again with greater force. Still nothing.

"Let me help," Henry offered, moving beside him. Together, the two men strained against the hatch, muscles cording in their necks and arms.

It remained firmly closed.

"It might be sticking from disuse," Susanne suggested, though dread was pooling in her stomach.

Patrick shook his head, breathing hard from the effort. "Maybe so. But it feels like it's being held down from above, too. Like something heavy is on top of it."

The implications struck Susanne like a physical blow. Had someone blocked this exit, too? A someone who had known and thought of everything?

Henry wiped sweat from his forehead. "Maybe if we—"

A crash from upstairs interrupted him, followed by shouting. Perry's voice carried down to them. "Dad! The living room ceiling is on fire!"

Patrick's eyes met Susanne's, and she saw in them a reflection of her own terror. The house was burning around them. Every exit was blocked. Time was running out.

CHAPTER FORTY-FOUR: UNMASK

Buffalo, Wyoming
August 28, 1978

Patrick

Patrick's heart seized at Perry's words. The living room ceiling was on fire. Time was short. Smoke would soon fill the entire house, followed by flames consuming everything and everyone in their path.

"Susanne, we need to get everyone down here. It's too dangerous upstairs," he said.

Her eyes were huge. "But what if you can't—"

"We can."

She nodded, whirled, and ran back into the basement with the flashlight, leaving Patrick and Henry in near darkness, illuminated only by the dim light filtering down from the basement.

While Henry caught his breath, Patrick planted his feet more firmly against the earthen floor and threw his weight upward again, shoving against the metal hatch with every ounce of strength he possessed. The muscles in his shoulders and back screamed in protest, but the hatch remained immobile.

"It won't budge," he grunted, easing the pressure for a moment to catch his breath. Sweat trickled down his temples despite the coolness of the root cellar.

Henry positioned himself beside Patrick, his face grim. "Together again. On three."

They counted off and pushed simultaneously, straining upward until Patrick felt the veins in his neck bulging and his injured shoulder screaming in pain. The hatch creaked and shifted upward slightly, giving them hope, but then settled back into place with a dull thud.

Patrick heard more shouting from upstairs, but he couldn't understand what was being said. The smoke detectors had fallen silent, which was worse than their shrieking. It meant they'd either been disabled by the heat or the smoke was too thick for them to function properly. Either way, it wasn't good news. Patrick hoped Susanne had the group on their way downstairs.

"Whoever did this was thorough," Henry said, wiping sweat from his face with his sleeve. "Sealed the windows, blocked the doors, and now this."

"We're not giving up," Patrick declared, though panic clawed at his insides. His family was up there. Trish, immobile. Perry, already injured from his kidnapping. His father with his bad heart. "There has to be a way."

"Everyone is coming." Susanne reappeared, the flashlight beam dancing across the earthen walls as her hand shook slightly.

Patrick looked around the small cellar, but the shelves held only preserved foods in glass jars, gardening supplies, and empty containers. "If I had a lever that could fit in the lip of the hatch..." He trailed off, frustration building. "But all my tools are in the garage."

"Trish opened it a few days ago."

"What?" Patrick turned to her. "How?"

"She pried it open with your claw hammer."

He exhaled heavily. “Which is with my tools.”

Susanne's eyes lit up. "I think I saw it in the laundry room yesterday. Trish never put it back up."

"For once, I'm thankful for teenage disorganization," Patrick said.

Susanne was running. She called over her shoulder, "I'll be fast."

"Be careful!" Patrick said. "Stay low, under the smoke!"

The flashlight beam bounced away with her again.

"If that hatch is bolted from the outside—" Henry began.

"It's not," Patrick cut him off, unwilling to entertain the possibility. "It's just stuck, or something heavy was placed on it." He ran his fingers along the edge of the hatch, feeling for any give. "We'll get it open."

The seconds stretched like hours as they waited, the sounds of the fire growing louder overhead. Creaking wood. The pop and hiss of timbers surrendering to flames. The muffled voices of their family members down the corridor in the basement.

A part of Patrick wanted to abandon the hatch and race back to be with Susanne, with their children, even if it meant facing the flames together. But logic overruled emotion. Their best chance, their only chance was through this cellar. He wondered if they could dig out and tested the earthen ceiling with his hands. It was hardpack. They had no shovel. But if they had to try, they would. He started mentally reviewing the items upstairs they could use.

HE WAS INTERRUPTED when Susanne reappeared again, rushing down the passage, the flashlight bobbing wildly. In her hand was the claw hammer, its metal head gleaming in the light.

"I got it," she panted, thrusting it toward Patrick. "The kitchen's filling with smoke, though. Everyone’s in the basement now, but the ceiling up there—" She swallowed hard. "It's bad, Patrick. The ceiling beams are starting to show."

Patrick took the hammer, its weight reassuring in his palm. If they had to make another trip upstairs to find makeshift digging tools, it would have to be soon. "This will work. Let's do this, Henry."

He positioned himself under the hatch again, this time with the hammer angling so its claw end could slip into the narrow gap between the hatch and its frame. It took a few tries. The gap was barely wide enough, but finally, he managed to wedge the claw in.

"Here we go," Patrick said, gripping the hammer handle with both hands. He pulled downward, using the leverage to force the hatch upward. The wood creaked in protest.

"It's moving," Henry observed. "Let me help."

Henry positioned his hands on the hammer handle alongside Patrick's, and together they pulled, muscles straining, teeth gritted against the effort. The hatch gave another inch, then stuck again.

"Something's definitely on top," Patrick gasped. "But I can feel it sliding to the side. We need more tilt. Pull harder!"

They redoubled their efforts, the veins in their forearms standing out like ropes. Patrick felt something in his injured shoulder give way, but he pushed through the pain. If his rotator cuff hadn't been torn before, it was now, but nothing mattered except getting that hatch open.

With a sudden snapping sound, the hatch lifted another few inches.

"It's unstuck!" Susanne cried.

Henry quickly jammed his shoulder against it, preventing it from falling back into place.

"I can see through the gap out to the ground," he reported. "Looks like rocks around the hatch. Someone piled landscaping rocks on top of it."

"Good try," Patrick muttered. "But they're not going to win."

He moved the hammer to a slightly wider part of the opening and pulled again. This time, the hatch rose enough for Henry to get his hands around the edge.

"I've got it," Henry grunted. "One more good push."

Together, they heaved upward. The hatch suddenly flew open with surprising force, sending a cascade of small rocks tumbling into the cellar. Patrick ducked, shielding his head as pebbles rained down around them.

"You did it!" Susanne cried, her voice tight with relief.

Patrick wasted no time. "I'll go up first and make sure it's clear." He hoisted himself through the opening, his hands finding purchase on the damp earth surrounding the hatch. As his head cleared the cellar, fresh air hit his lungs, cool and sweet compared to the increasingly smoky basement.

He went the rest of the way up the stairs, quickly scanning the backyard. No sign of an intruder, just Ferdinand barking frantically from the far side of the yard. The night was lit by an orange glow as flames licked at the rear windows of his home, smoke billowing from under the eaves.

"All clear!" he called down. "Henry, send them up one by one. I'll help from here."

He reached for Susanne's hand as she came out.

"Go to the front yard and get everyone to congregate there," he instructed. "Make sure everyone stays clear of the house."

She nodded and took off running around the side of the building.

"Vangie next," Henry called from below, helping her from behind.

Hank came after his mother, the toddler wide-eyed and frightened but thankfully quiet. Patrick helped with Hank and directed Vangie to the front yard. Then came Wes. Patrick could see the pain in his friend's face, but Wes didn't utter a sound.

One by one, they emerged from the cellar. Kathy, Joe, and then Perry, whose face was streaked with soot and sweat. Each person's escape eased the vice grip of fear around his heart, but the hardest was still to come.

"Trish is next," Henry called up. "This is going to be tricky."

Susanne reappeared at Patrick's side, kneeling beside the hatch opening. "I'll help. The others are safe in the front yard."

Together, they reached down as Henry carefully walked Trish up the steps. The brace made maneuvering difficult, and Patrick could see the pain etched on his daughter's face as they tried to angle her through without bumping the injured leg.

"I'm sorry, sweetheart," he said as Trish let out a whimper. "Almost there."

"Just get me out," Trish said through gritted teeth. "I can handle it."

With careful coordination, they managed to maneuver her through the opening, Trish biting her lip to keep from crying out as her leg scraped against the edge of the hatch.

"Henry, come on!" Patrick called.

Henry's lank frame appeared in the opening. As soon as he was clear, Patrick did one more head count, then slammed the hatch shut, as if sealing off the nightmare they'd just escaped.

Patrick joined them in the front yard. Everyone was huddled together, watching in stunned silence as the Flints' home was devoured by flames. The fire had spread rapidly and was now engulfing most of the house. The heat was intense even from where they stood, forcing them to back away.

Kathy reappeared, panting and bent over on her knees. "I ran to the neighbors and they'd already called the fire department. They're on their way."

For whatever good it will do. It was too late to save the house.

Patrick did another quick head count. He couldn't help it. He was consumed with the need to be sure no one was left behind. Everyone was there. Everyone except the dog.

That's when Patrick heard Ferdinand's barking intensify so much that it was loud enough to hear even with the flames. It had changed from alarm to aggression. Patrick turned toward the sound, spotting the dog at the edge of the property where Patrick had noticed him right after he came through the hatch.

"Ferdie is worked up. I'm going to go get him," he told Susanne.

"I'll come, too," Perry said.

Patrick held up a hand. "Stay here with your mom and sister. All of you stay together."

He trotted across the property to the agitated dog. What he found when he got closer made his jaw drop and kicked his racing heart rate up another gear.

Ferdinand had someone pinned to the ground, paws on their chest, from what Patrick could see in the flickering light cast by the burning house. The Irish wolfhound was as sweet as they came, but he was big, heavy, and strong.

Patrick ran faster. He closed in on the dog and could soon make out more details. Ferdinand had his teeth buried in the front of a denim jacket, holding a struggling figure down on their back with the weight of his body. The person was dressed in work clothes. Under the jacket, they were wearing jeans, boots, flannel shirt, and a baseball cap pulled low, obscuring their face.

A man, he thought, but on the small side, which was good. Patrick was going to have to take over this job from his dog and restrain the guy. This was likely the person who had trapped them in the burning house.

"Ferdie, stay!" Patrick commanded.

The dog growled and maintained his grip. The man quit moving.

Patrick knelt beside the figure, feeling a rage as pure and bright as the fire. He snatched off the baseball cap, revealing short dark hair spilling over the guy's face. *He matches the kids' descriptions.*

But then the guy tossed his head, which swept the hair from his face.

Patrick did a doubletake. It was a woman's face partially obscured by short, dark hair.

He was a *she*.

Recognition hit him like a physical blow, even absent the long blonde ponytail this woman used to wear, back when she was Trish's cheerleading coach.

"Bella Crooke," he breathed.

Her eyes, cold and calculating despite her vulnerable position, met his. "Dr. Flint," she said, her voice oddly calm given the circumstances. "I see you managed to find your way out."

"You set fire to our house," Patrick said, the reality of it still sinking in. "You tried to kill my entire family. Our friends."

"You should have stayed on your mountain. You should have *died* on your mountain."

Patrick's hands shook. He wanted to wrap them around her throat.

He reached for Ferdinand's collar instead of Bella's neck.

"Ferdie, let her go," he said, giving the collar a tug.

The dog reluctantly let go of Bella's jean jacket, backing up a few steps while maintaining a watchful stance, growling low in his throat, hackles raised.

Pulling him off her was a mistake. As soon as Ferdinand's clamp on her was released, Bella shot up with shocking speed. Her hand disappeared behind her back and reappeared holding a small revolver.

She pointed it at Patrick as she scrambled backwards, keeping the gun trained on him the whole time.

"Whoa!" he said, putting his hands up at his shoulders.

When she was out of his reach, she stopped. "Don't move," she said, her voice steady.

Patrick stood stock still, acutely aware that Ferdinand was poised to lunge again. If the dog attacked her, Bella would shoot him without hesitation. "Bella, put the gun down. The police are on their way."

Her face twisted into something ugly. "I still have plenty of time to kill every member of your meddling family first and be long gone by the time they get here."

"That won't bring back your husband's artifacts," Patrick said, trying to keep her attention on him. The last thing he needed was her to rush the group, firing into their midst. They wouldn't hear her coming. They probably wouldn't even hear him if he yelled a warning.

"They were mine," Bella hissed. "Mine by right. Whitney Saylor was stealing them. Everything that happened after that was her fault."

"*You* killed *her*."

"Not according to the jury. But she did have it coming."

"You tried to kill the rest of us on Cloud Peak. But you didn't, thanks to my son."

"I thought he was actually dead when I left him."

For a moment, Patrick's brain was paralyzed. Then reality came rushing at him. "You. You took Perry. You dumped him in the mountains." The person with the most motive to kill Perry was Bella. It had always been her.

"Of all of you, he has the most to answer for to me. He deserved to suffer and die slow," she said, as if discussing something as mundane as the weather.

Patrick burned with rage. Back on Cloud Peak two months before, when it seemed certain Bella would kill Patrick and Wes, it was Perry who had stopped her with a sling shot. Literally, a sling shot. Patrick was so proud of that boy.

And this woman had kidnapped him and left him for dead.

He glared at her. "That's two times he's bested you, then. Three if you count tonight, since he's the one who noticed the fire in time for us to get out."

Before Bella could respond, Patrick heard a familiar voice far to close. "It was her, Dad! Bella was the man who hit Trish!"

Perry was right behind Patrick.

"Speak of the spawn of the devil," Bella said.

The gun. The gun in Bella's hand. All she had to do was pull the trigger, and Perry would be gone.

Patrick turned and shoved his son back. "Perry, go to your mom."

Perry didn't move. "But Dad, it was her. Dressed as a man. I see it now. She was following us. And then—"

"Perry, she has a gun. Go. Now. Tell everyone Bella is here and wants to kill them all. Make them leave. That's an order!"

Perry hesitated, then he spun and ran. There was no gunshot. Patrick heaved a sigh of relief. Perry was safe, and now Bella didn't have the element of surprise with his friends and family anymore.

Patrick turned back and locked eyes with her.

"So much for plan B. Well, it's been lovely catching up, but I guess I'll be going now." She took a step backward.

Ferdinand growled low in his throat. Bella's gun hand twitched toward the dog.

"Ferdie, stay," Patrick ordered, his voice taut.

Sirens wailed in the distance. Fire trucks or police, he couldn't tell. Bella's head jerked toward the sound, momentarily distracted.

"It's over, Bella," Patrick said. "Drop the gun."

Ferdinand's growls intensified.

Her eyes refocused on him, cold and empty. "Nothing is over," she said flatly. Then she backed away, the gun never wavering from its aim at his center mass. "Tell your little shit of a son he won't get lucky again."

Before Patrick could respond, she fired at him, but not fast enough to beat Ferdinand, who leapt toward her with his bulk and knocked her to her knees. She let out a piercing scream.

Her shot was knocked off target just enough that the bullet hit Patrick in the shoulder instead of in the middle of his chest, the difference between pain and death.

Still, the sound he made as he fell was primal, and Ferdinand raced back to his side. The dog whined and nosed him, urging him up. Patrick groaned. He didn't have time to give in to pain. He struggled to his knees. He had to stop Bella.

But by the time he was back on his feet, clutching his left arm, Bella was already disappearing into the trees. Patrick took a step to follow but stopped himself. Going after an armed woman who'd already tried to kill him twice that night was suicide, especially in the dark and with his vulnerable family still at risk.

He looked at the ground where Ferdinand had tackled her. Blood speckled the grass, visible even in the dark. He turned to his dog. *Don't let it be, Ferdie.* He felt all over the excited animal.

But Ferdinand was intact. The injured party was Bella Crooke.

He fell to his knees and hugged him, bad shoulder be damned. "Good dog, Ferdie. Good dog."

He just prayed Bella was injured enough.

CHAPTER FORTY-FIVE: REBUILD

Buffalo, Wyoming
September 3, 1978

Patrick

Patrick settled into the leather chair beside Susanne, their knees touching in silent reassurance. Her face showed the strain of the past week or so, but her eyes remained clear and determined. They'd lost nearly all of their possessions, but they still had what mattered most. Each other, their children, and their dog and horses.

After living as vagabonds since the fire, Max's office felt like a sanctuary. The county building's air conditioning hummed steadily, a stark contrast to the crackling of flames that consumed their home and still echoed in Patrick's dreams. It was definitely far more comfortable than the Sibley Ranch bunkhouse where they'd been holed up until moving into a hotel last night.

Max shuffled the papers on his desk, his eyes serious behind wire-rimmed glasses. "I appreciate you both coming in. I know it's been a hell of a week."

"Feels like a year." Patrick looked down at his left arm, which was in a sling and still hurt. Luckily, Bella's bullet had gone straight through and out the other side of the fleshy part of his shoulder. It had caused no further damage than he'd already done getting the cellar hatch open. A torn rotator cuff was a small price to pay for getting everyone out alive.

"Fair enough." Max nodded. "You know why I asked you to come see me. I have some news about Bella Crooke that you'll want to hear."

Patrick felt Susanne tense beside him. She'd been jumpy since the fire, startling at unexpected sounds and checking door locks twice, sometimes three times. He couldn't blame her. The knowledge that someone had meticulously planned to trap and burn them alive wasn't something a person got over quickly.

"They caught her accomplice," Max said. "A man named Charles Becker, goes by Chickie. Airport security nabbed him at Denver International trying to board a flight to Mexico using a fake passport."

"An accomplice?" Susanne leaned forward. "She wasn't working alone?"

Max shook his head. "Nope."

"How did you figure that out?"

"It's convoluted, so bear with me. It starts with Bella telling Patrick she was the one who kidnapped Perry. From there, the logic goes like this. If the blue Bronco at the school meant to hit Perry, which seems likely since Trish pushed him out of its path, and Bella had a reason to hurt Perry and in fact *did* later that day, then it was *probably* Bella driving that Bronco at the school. To completely make the logic leap, we had to see if she owned one or had access to one. But the cops had stopped reviewing registration records when they found Gentry Childs owned one, given that he was such a great suspect."

Patrick nodded. "That makes sense. What did you find?"

"Well, we couldn't tie her to ownership of a Bronco."

"That's disappointing."

Max held up his hand. "We found that Chickie Becker is the proud owner of a 1971 blue Ford Bronco."

Susanne shook her head. "But who is he? I've never heard of him."

"I'll bet you've seen him. He came to the courtroom every day of her trial."

"The guy in the back row with the graying blond ponytail? The one that wore the same Grateful Dead t-shirt every day?"

Patrick had noticed the same person before he left for Mount Rainier.

"Yeah, that's the guy. He was already known to us. He'd struck up a pen pal relationship with her when she was in jail. Then he started visiting her. We asked around and learned he'd been calling her his girlfriend."

"Was he?"

"I suspect only in his own mind. By the time we went to pick him up, he was gone. We had a search warrant for the Bronco, though. We found Bella's driver's license in the floorboard, and Perry's athletic bag in the backseat."

"You got him."

"Well, enough to get an arrest warrant for conspiracy attempted murder. We put out a BOLO on him. Denver airport security did a fine job recognizing he was using a fake passport. When they detained him, they matched him to the picture we'd circulated of him."

Patrick rubbed his chin, shaking his head. "If only they'd have caught Bella the same way."

"I know. Anyway, Becker is plenty mad at Bella, who he says skipped out on him. He believed they were running away together. Once he realized that all the heat that was coming his way, his attorney negotiated a plea deal in exchange for information."

"Will he still serve time?"

"Yes. Even better, he gave us the whole story about the fire at your house. Your former house."

Patrick's jaw tightened. "Tell us."

"According to Becker, they spent a few days preparing." Max flipped open a folder, though he didn't seem to need to reference it. "They sealed the windows with construction glue while you were away from the house. Cut the phone lines. The night of the fire, they placed metal bars with knob clamps on every exterior door—something that required a great deal of pre-planning and preparation." Max's tone was gentle but factual. "Once they had everything ready, he manned the getaway car, and she splashed gasoline on the wooden doors and lit them up."

"How did they get in our house, though? *When* could they have had that much access to it?"

"Becker said they started as soon as Bella got out and continued while Trish was in the hospital. Then they just had to work around Joe's comings and goings and naps."

Patrick pictured Bella moving around their property, methodically setting the stage for their death. He swallowed hard, fighting the fury that threatened to overtake him. "I can't believe they went through all of that to try to kill us."

"He said they hadn't even known the Sibleys and Wes would be there."

Susanne put her hand over her chest. "It was a spontaneous, last-minute gathering. We were celebrating the arrest of Gentry Childs. Of the threat to our kids being removed. Little did we know. What terrible, terrible luck."

"He was almost gleeful about it. Until he got to the part of the story where he was waiting down the road for Bella after the fire, and she never showed up."

"What did Becker say about the attacks on Trish and Perry?" Patrick asked.

"He's claiming that was all Bella. Obviously, he doesn't match the description of the Bronco driver. You saw Bella at your house dressed as a man with short dark hair, and her body type is similar to the description of the driver. At least with respect to Trish. There were no witnesses to Perry's abduction."

"She admitted to me she'd taken Perry, and Perry identified her as the driver of the Bronco that hit Trish. We know what she did."

"And now we have some evidence to back up what you and Perry saw and heard. Which is optimal, for when this goes to trial someday."

"What about her whereabouts?" Susanne asked. "Any sign of her?"

"Not yet." Max leaned back in his chair. "But we'll find her. Becker gave us a list of her contacts, places she might go, aliases she might use."

Susanne's brow furrowed. "I don't understand something. The police told us she took a flight to Houston right after the jury verdict. How was she here?"

"We now believe someone else traveled under her name," Max explained. "She never left Wyoming, as far as we can tell. And she's likely not using her own name anymore."

"She's put us through hell. Please keep us posted if she's located."

"Oh, I will. I promise."

Patrick was nodding, absorbing everything. Then he lowered his hands to each thigh, making a slapping sound. "On a different but related subject, I got a call from Eric at TMI yesterday. He runs the guide company we used on Mount Rainier. They finished investigating our fall there, the one where we came loose from the tether to our guide. I think it will be of interest to you." With Patrick's close, almost familial relationship to Max, he'd already shared what had happened to Wes, Henry, and him on the climb.

Max raised an eyebrow. "I didn't know they were investigating it. Do tell."

"Lewis, our guide, claimed it was equipment failure, but the investigation found nothing wrong with any of the gear." Patrick paused, remembering the gut-wrenching slide toward the crevasse, the way the rope had detached from Lewis at exactly the wrong moment, and their near-death experience not once but twice as a result. "They overheard him on a phone call. He was telling someone that he'd tried his best but hadn't counted on how tough and lucky the Wyoming climbers were."

"Jesus," Max muttered. "That sounds really bad."

"TMI turned him over to the police. They told him they were going to get his bank accounts. He copped a plea deal in exchange for info lickety split after that." Patrick's voice hardened. "It turns out that Bella hired him to kill Henry, Wes, and me. To make it look like a climbing accident."

Susanne's hand found his, her fingers cold against his palm. They'd known Bella was vindictive, dangerous. But the scope of her plans, the patience with which she'd pursued her revenge even from inside a jail cell, was still difficult to comprehend.

"That's another charge to add to the list," Max said grimly, making a note. "Attempted murder on multiple counts."

"There's more from TMI," Patrick said. "Although it doesn't pertain to this case, it goes to show just how messed up the last week has been. One of the climbers, a guy named Gerald, attacked his buddy Connor with an ice axe."

Max's eyes popped. Patrick hadn't told him that story yet. "You're kidding me?"

"Connor was sick on the summit attempt which I'd assumed at the time was altitude sickness. He was so sick that he fell and would have died if our guide hadn't rescued him. After Gerald tried to kill him with the axe, the police thought the illness was suspicious. They found poison residue in one of Connor's water bottles. And his crampons had been sabotaged—the front points filed down just enough to compromise traction."

"And I was just worried you'd get hurt," Susanne murmured. "People were trying to kill each other left and right. That's crazy."

"It gets even wackier. Gerald had had a fight with another climber at Camp Muir. They think he picked the fight as an excuse to stay there, so he could hustle down the mountain and escape during what he hoped would be Connor's fatal summit attempt. Then he learned Connor had survived, and he lost it and tried to finish the job with the axe. He was apprehended immediately, so he'll be facing some serious charges."

"Any idea why he did it? That's usually the most interesting part," Max said.

"Connor was sleeping with Gerald's wife. His soon-to-be ex-wife. Her choice, not his."

"Did he confess to any of it?"

Patrick shook his head. "Not yet."

"Sounds like Rainier brings out the best in people."

"The mountain is unforgiving. With minds and bodies." Patrick paused, remembering the body they'd found in the crevasse. "Speaking of which, we found a dead climber up there. Our fall triggered an avalanche that uncovered him in a crevasse. I took his watch, and they were able to use it to identify him. He was lost in an avalanche fifteen years ago. I hope it brings his family some closure."

A moment of silence filled the office. Patrick could hear the tick of the clock on the wall, the distant sound of phones ringing somewhere deeper in the building. All three of them understood the limbo of not knowing and the pain of loss.

"Are you finished?" Max asked. "Because I have one more thing, and I saved the best for last."

Patrick glanced at Susanne, who shrugged. "We're finished."

Max smiled, the expression transforming his usually serious face. " One of the jurors from Bella's trial complained that the foreman was really aggressive, and that made us suspicious."

Patrick nodded. They all remembered the shock of that verdict, the way it had felt like justice thwarted.

"That led to us uncovering evidence that Bella bribed the jury foreman." Max's smile widened. "Five thousand dollars to steer the jury toward a not guilty verdict."

Patrick stared at him, the implications sinking in. "So that means—"

"The verdict is vacated. No double jeopardy." Max closed the folder with a decisive snap. "When we find her, and we will find her, Bella Crooke will be retried on the original first-degree murder charge, not just the newer attempted murders, and we also have the option of charging her with bribery and pursuing that conviction."

Susanne gasped softly. "So, Perry won't have to testify against her? About what happened on the mountain?"

"Not at the murder trial." Max nodded. "The evidence from the original crime is enough. We'll convict her this time. Your son can put her behind him."

Relief washed over Patrick, so powerful it momentarily stole his breath. Perry had been through enough. "Now all you have to do is catch her." *Before she fulfills her vow that Perry won't get lucky next time.*

"We'll get her," Max promised, his expression turning serious again. "It's just a matter of time."

Patrick squeezed Susanne's hand, feeling something like hope stirring for the first time since the fire. Bella was still out there somewhere, but she couldn't hide forever. And when they found her, she would finally face justice for everything she'd done. Not just to the Flints, but to Whitney, the Sibleys, Wes and Kathy, and everyone whose lives she'd damaged in her selfish pursuit of what she believed was hers.

"She won't hurt anyone else," Susanne said softly, as if reading his thoughts.

Patrick nodded. "No, she won't." He wasn't sure if it was a statement or a promise, but he meant it either way.

PATRICK BALANCED the paper sack of burgers and fries in one arm while Susanne fished the hotel key from the purse hanging from her shoulder. Her other hand clutched a drink carrier with four milkshakes, chocolate for Perry, strawberry for Trish, and vanilla for the adults. The fast food wasn't ideal, but after the meeting with Max, neither of them had the energy to deal with a proper restaurant. Besides, the kids never complained about burgers.

They'd already dropped his father's off in the room next door. A murdering house arsonist hadn't been enough to chase Joe Flint back to Texas.

The door swung open to reveal Perry sprawled across one of the double beds, math textbook open in front of him. Trish sat propped against the headboard of the other bed, her braced leg extended, crutches beside her, and a history book balanced on her good knee.

"Food's here," Patrick announced, setting the bag down on the small round table by the window with its view of eighteen wheelers in the back parking lot.

Perry closed his book with a decisive snap. "If I look at one more algebra problem, my brain might explode."

"Drama queen," Trish said.

Patrick helped her maneuver from the bed to one of the chairs at the table, where she put her leg in another chair. The hotel room was cramped for four people, especially with Trish's leg requiring extra space, but it was clean and safe, two qualities that had taken on new significance since the fire. Insurance was covering their stay while they sorted through the rubble of their home and made plans to rebuild. Ferdinand had stayed at the Sibleys' ranch after they left, where he had room to run and a temporary extra-large doghouse that Henry had built in one afternoon.

"How was the meeting with Uncle Max?" Perry asked, unwrapping his burger with the focused intensity of a starving teenager. Patrick's sister wasn't married to Max, yet. It seemed likely. If they ever broke up, the moniker would become awkward.

Patrick and Susanne exchanged a glance. "Good," Patrick said, distributing napkins. "Really good. They caught Bella's accomplice."

"Her boyfriend helped her," Susanne added, settling into her chair. "He's the one who told them how they set up the fire."

"Are they any closer to finding her?" Trish asked, dunking a fry in ketchup.

"Not yet," Patrick admitted. "But Max seemed confident they will."

Susanne changed the subject, her voice deliberately lighter. "How was school today? First week back going okay?"

This sparked a lively discussion of teachers and assignments, the normal rhythm of their family dinners continuing despite the hotel setting. Patrick watched his children as they ate. They'd been beaten up by their ordeals. It had taken a toll on both of them. But they were healing. They were strong.

When the burgers were reduced to empty wrappers and the fries to a few salty crumbs, Patrick leaned back in his chair, savoring the last of his vanilla shake. "Okay, family meeting time. Let's talk about some decisions we need to make."

"I want to apply to UAS," Trish said immediately, as if she'd been waiting for this opening. "The University of Alaska Southern. They have a great marine biology program."

Patrick raised an eyebrow. "Alaska? That's pretty far, honey."

"I know it's far," Trish said, fidgeting with her straw wrapper. "But their program is exactly what I want. And... well, Ben's there."

Patrick exchanged another glance with Susanne, reading the mix of concern and resignation in her eyes. They'd both known this was coming.

"Your mother and I have been talking," Patrick said carefully. "We'd like you to apply to the University of Wyoming as well as UAS. Keep your options open."

Trish's face brightened. "Really? You're not saying no?"

"We're not thrilled about you following a boy across the country," Susanne admitted. "But after I saw a flyer that came in the mail for you—"

"You looked at my mail? That's a violation of my privacy!"

"I only saw the return address on the envelope. I didn't open it.

But make no mistake that where your well-being is concerned I have no qualms with violating your privacy."

Trish started to pout then seemed to think better of it.

"Anyway, I went to the library and did some research. It's a good school. I saw the marine biology program, and it looks interesting. Your dad and I talked about it and we're not totally opposed. Just promise us you'll seriously consider all your options when the time comes."

"I promise," Trish said, reaching across the table to squeeze her mother's hand. "And I already started the UW application, too. But they don't have marine sciences."

Patrick smiled. His daughter had always been one step ahead of them. "There's something else we should discuss. Your cheerleading sponsor called yesterday after practice."

Trish shifted uncomfortably. "Yeah, about that. I decided to quit the squad."

Susanne just nodded. "We think that's a wise choice, given your recovery timeline. You couldn't cheer for months anyway."

Trish looked genuinely relieved, as if she'd been bracing for disappointment instead of support.

"My turn for news," Perry said, wadding up his burger wrapper and tossing it into the trash can. "I told Jillian I have a girlfriend, so she'd stop flirting with me all the time. It was getting uncomfortable."

Patrick tried not to smile. Perry's discomfort with Jillian's attention had been obvious to everyone except Jillian herself. "And does this fictional girlfriend have a name?"

Perry's freckled face flushed pink. "Well, that's the thing. She's not exactly fictional. I'm kind of going with Bijou now."

"Going with?" Susanne repeated, eyebrows raised. "As in dating?"

"Mom," Perry groaned. "Don't make it weird. We just talk and stuff. "

"She's nice," Trish offered. "Smart, too."

"Well," Patrick said, "Maybe we can invite her over to dinner so your mother and I can meet her."

"Da-ad. Nooo. We're not serious. That would be so embarrassing," Perry said.

Patrick laughed. "We'll see."

"I have some news too," Susanne said, rescuing Perry from further teasing. "I talked with Professor Seth yesterday. He arranged for Sheridan College to give me generous class credits to continue my research work. I'll be working for him for free, but it gets me closer to finishing my degree."

"That's fantastic," Patrick said, genuinely pleased. Susanne had put her education on hold for years to raise their family. Her return to school had been a friction point in their lives at times, but he'd come to realize how important it was to her. He was fully onboard now.

"I'm almost done with Kathy's wedding dress alterations too," Susanne added. "Thank goodness she had it at her house instead of ours. I can't imagine how she would have handled things if it had burned up three weeks before the wedding."

"Speaking of the wedding," Patrick said, "Wes asked me to be his best man yesterday. I said yes, of course."

"As if you would have said anything else," Susanne smiled.

A comfortable silence fell over the table, broken only by the rattle of the air conditioner and the revving of an engine in the parking lot. They had survived. They were together. And despite everything, they were finding their way forward.

"There's something else we need to discuss," Patrick said. "The money from Whitney Saylor."

Patrick had come into possession of two million dollars that a shady character had paid Whitney for the Egyptian artifacts Bella believed were rightfully hers. Because the sale was illegal, the buyer had denied being involved. When Patrick told Ronnie about it, she'd said finding money wasn't illegal, and urged them to keep it and do some good with it. He and Susanne had put most of it in a trust for charitable donations. They'd been having fun as a family choosing how to dole the money out.

"I was thinking," Patrick continued, "that we should donate some money to the Muckleshoot tribe's education fund. In Whitney's name. She would have climbed with them if Bella hadn't killed her. One of them helped bring Wes down the mountain after his injury. I really liked the guy, and he told me some of the programs they're having trouble funding for their youth. It really touched me."

"I think that's perfect," Susanne said softly.

"I'll bet Whitney would have liked that," Trish agreed. "Even though she made some bad choices, like taking those artifacts and trying to sell them, she wasn't all bad."

"All in favor?" Patrick asked, raising his hand. Three more hands joined his, the vote unanimous.

"One last piece of news," Patrick said, meeting each of their eyes in turn. "I called TMI this morning and canceled my reservation for their Aconcagua expedition in January."

"What?" Perry's jaw dropped. "But that's one of the Seven Summits!"

Patrick nodded. "I know. But I realized something on Rainier. The mountains will always be there, but my time with you won't." He reached across the table, taking Susanne's hand. "I'd rather hike trails I can share with my family than stand on summits alone. Wyoming has enough mountains to last me a lifetime."

Tears formed in Susanne's eyes. The silence that followed was full of understanding, love, and the unspoken acknowledgment that they had nearly lost everything.

"Besides," Patrick added with a grin, "our new house won't build itself. I think I'll have my hands full right here irritating contractors in Wyoming."

"To our new house," Susanne said, raising her milkshake cup in a toast.

"And to us," Patrick added, his heart full as they clinked their paper cups together.

For you, my love.

ACKNOWLEDGMENTS

When I got the call from my father that he had metastatic prostate cancer spread into his bones in nine locations, I was with a houseful of retreat guests in Wyoming while my parents (who normally summer in Wyoming) were in Texas. The guests were so kind and comforting to me, as was Eric, but there was only one place I wanted to be, and that was home. Not home where I grew up, because I lived in twelve places by the time I was twelve, and many thereafter. No, home is truly where the heart is. And that meant home for Eric and me would be with my parents.

I was in the middle of writing two novels at the time: *Blue Streak*, the first Laura mystery in the What Doesn't Kill You series, and *Polarity*, a series spin-off contemporary romance based on my love story with Eric. I put them both down. I needed to write, but not those books. They could wait. I needed to write through my emotions—because that's what writers do—with books spelling out the ending we were seeking for my dad's story. Allegorically and biographically, while fictionally.

So that is what I did, and Dr. Patrick Flint (aka Dr. Peter Fagan—my pops—in real life) and family were hatched, using actual stories from our lives in late 1970s Buffalo, Wyoming as the depth and backdrop to a new series of mysteries, starting with *Switchback* and moving on to *Snake Oil, Sawbones, Scapegoat, Snaggle Tooth, Stag Party, Sitting Duck, Skin and Bones,* and *Snow Ghost.*

I hope the real life versions of Patrick, Susanne, and Perry will forgive me for taking liberties in creating their fictional alter egos. I took care to make Trish the most annoying character since she's based on me, to soften the blow for the others. I am so hopeful that my loyal readers will enjoy them, too, even though in some ways the novels are a departure from my usual stories. But in many ways they are the same. Character-driven, edge-of-your-seat mysteries steeped in setting/culture, with a strong nod to the everyday magic around us, and filled with complex, authentic characters (including some AWESOME females).

I had a wonderful time writing these books, and it kept me going when it was tempting to fold in on myself and let stress eat me alive. For more stories behind the actual stories, visit the blog on my website: http://pamelafaganhutchins.com. And let me know if you liked the novels!

Thanks to my dad for advice on all things medical, wilderness, hunting, 1970s, and animal. I hope you had fun using your medical knowledge for murder!

Thanks to my mom for printing the early manuscripts (over and over, in their entirety) as she and dad followed along daily on the progress of the first few books.

Thanks to my brother Paul for the vivid memories that have made Perry such an amazing fictional kid.

Thanks to my husband, Eric, for brainstorming with and encouraging me and beta reading the *Patrick Flint* stories despite his busy work, travel, and workout schedule. And for moving in to my parents's barn apartment with me so I could be closer to them when they needed us.

Thanks to our five offspring. I love you guys more than anything, and each time I write a parent/child (birth, adopted, foster, or step), I channel you. I am so touched by how supportive you have been with Poppy, Gigi, Eric, and me.

To each and every blessed reader, I appreciate you more than I can say. It is the readers who move mountains for me, and for other authors, and I humbly ask for the honor of your honest reviews and recommendations.

Thanks mucho to Bobbye for the fantastic *Patrick Flint* covers.

Snow Ghost editing credits go to Karen Goodwin. You rock. A big thank you as well to my proofreading and advance review team.

SkipJack Publishing now includes fantastic books by a cherry-picked bushel basket of mystery/thriller/suspense writers. If you write in this genre, visit http://SkipJackPublishing.com for submission guidelines. To check out our other authors and snag a bargain at the same time, download *Murder, They Wrote: Four SkipJack Mysteries*.

BOOKS BY THE AUTHOR

Fiction from SkipJack Publishing

THE *RUNAWAY SERIES*:

Dead Water (*Runaway #1*)

THE *PATRICK FLINT* SERIES OF WYOMING MYSTERIES:

Switchback (*Patrick Flint #1*)

Snake Oil (*Patrick Flint #2*)

Sawbones (*Patrick Flint #3*)

Scapegoat (*Patrick Flint #4*)

Snaggle Tooth (*Patrick Flint #5*)

Stag Party (*Patrick Flint #6*)

Sitting Duck (*Patrick Flint #7*)

Skin & Bones (*Patrick Flint #8*)

Snow Ghost (*Patrick Flint #9*)

Spark (*Patrick Flint 1.5*): *Exclusive to subscribers*

THE *JENN HERRINGTON* WYOMING MYSTERIES:

BIG HORN (*Jenn Herrington #1*)

WALKER PRAIRIE (*Jenn Herrington #2*)

RED GRADE (*Jenn Herrington #3*)

THE *WHAT DOESN'T KILL YOU* SUPER SERIES:

Wasted in Waco (*WDKY Ensemble Prequel Novella*)

The Essential Guide to the What Doesn't Kill You Series

Katie Connell Caribbean Mysteries:

Saving Grace (*Katie Connell #1*)

Leaving Annalise (*Katie Connell #2*)

Finding Harmony (*Katie Connell #3*)

Seeking Felicity (*Katie Connell #4*)

Emily Bernal Texas-to-New Mexico Mysteries:

Heaven to Betsy (*Emily Bernal #1*)

Earth to Emily (*Emily Bernal #2*)

Hell to Pay (*Emily Bernal #3*)

Michele Lopez Hanson Texas Mysteries:

Going for Kona (*Michele Lopez Hanson #1*)

Fighting for Anna (*Michele Lopez Hanson #2*)

Searching for Dime Box (*Michele Lopez Hanson #3*)

Maggie Killian Texas-to-Wyoming Mysteries:

Buckle Bunny (*Maggie Killian Prequel Novella*)

Shock Jock (*Maggie Killian Prequel Short Story*)

Live Wire (*Maggie Killian #1*)

Sick Puppy (*Maggie Killian #2*)

Dead Pile (*Maggie Killian #3*)

The Ava Butler Caribbean Mysteries Trilogy*: A Sexy Spin-off From *What Doesn't Kill You

Bombshell (*Ava Butler #1*)

Stunner (*Ava Butler #2*)

Knockout (*Ava Butler #3*)

Fiction from Bookouture

Detective Delaney Pace Series:

HER Silent BONES (Detective Delaney Pace Series Book 1)

HER Hidden GRAVE (Detective Delaney Pace Series Book 2)

HER Last CRY (Detective Delaney Pace Series Book 3)

HER Forgotten SHADOW (Detective Delaney Pace Book 4)

HER Burning LIES (Detective Delaney Pace Book 5)

HER Cold HEART (Detective Delaney Pace Book 6)

Juvenile from SkipJack Publishing

Poppy Needs a Puppy

George Finds a Friend

Nonfiction from SkipJack Publishing

The Clark Kent Chronicles

Hot Flashes and Half Ironmans

How to Screw Up Your Kids

How to Screw Up Your Marriage

Puppalicious and Beyond

What Kind of Loser Indie Publishes,

and How Can I Be One, Too?

Audio, e-book, large print, hardcover, and paperback versions of most titles available.

ABOUT THE AUTHOR

Pamela Fagan Hutchins is a *USA Today* best selling author. She writes award-winning mystery/thriller/suspense from way up in the frozen north of Snowheresville, Wyoming, where she lives with her husband in an off-the-grid cabin on the face of the Bighorn Mountains, and Mooselookville, Maine, in a rustic lake cabin, when they aren't traveling the world for his work assignments or spending time on their catamaran in the British Virgin Islands. She is passionate about their large brood of kids, step kids, inherited kids, and grandkids, riding their gigantic horses, and about hiking/snow shoeing/cross country skiing/ski-joring/bike-joring/dog sledding with their Alaskan Malamutes.

If you'd like Pamela to speak to your book club, women's club, class, or writers group by streaming video or in person, shoot her an email. She's very likely to say yes.

You can connect with Pamela via her website
(http://pamelafaganhutchins.com)
or email (pamela@pamelafaganhutchins.com).

PRAISE FOR PAMELA FAGAN HUTCHINS

2018 USA Today Best Seller
2017 Silver Falchion Award, Best Mystery
2016 USA Best Book Award, Cross-Genre Fiction
2015 USA Best Book Award, Cross-Genre Fiction
2014 Amazon Breakthrough Novel Award Quarter-finalist, Romance

The Patrick Flint Mysteries

"Best book I've read in a long time!" — Kiersten Marquet, author of *Reluctant Promises*

"*Switchback* transports the reader deep into the mountains of Wyoming for a thriller that has it all--wild animals, criminals, and one family willing to do whatever is necessary to protect its own. Pamela Fagan Hutchins writes with the authority of a woman who knows this world. She weaves the story with both nail-biting suspense and a healthy dose of humor. You won't want to miss *Switchback.*" -- Danielle Girard, *Wall Street Journal*-bestselling author of White Out.

"*Switchback* by Pamela Fagan Hutchins has as many twists and turns as a high-country trail. Every parent's nightmare is the loss or injury of a child, and this powerful novel taps into that primal fear." -- Reavis Z. Wortham, two time winner of The Spur and author of *Hawke's Prey*

"*Switchback* starts at a gallop and had me holding on with both hands until the riveting finish. This book is highly atmospheric and nearly crackling with suspense. Highly recommend!" -- Libby Kirsch, Emmy awardwinning reporter and author of the *Janet Black Mystery Series*

"A Bob Ross painting with Alfred Hitchcock hidden among the trees."
"Edge-of-your seat nail biter."
"Unexpected twists!"
"Wow! Wow! Highly entertaining!"
"A very exciting book (um... actually a nail-biter), soooo beautifully descriptive, with an underlying story of human connection and family. It's full of action. I was so scared and so mad and so relieved... sometimes all at once!"
"Well drawn characters, great scenery, and a kept-me-on-the-edge-of-my-seat story!"
"Absolutely unputdownable wonder of a story."
"Must read!"
"Gripping story. Looking for book two!"
"Intense!"
"Amazing and well-written read."
"Read it in one fell swoop. I could not put it down."

What Doesn't Kill You: Katie Connell Romantic Mysteries

"An exciting tale . . . twisting investigative and legal subplots . . . a character seeking redemption . . . an exhilarating mystery with a touch of voodoo." — *Midwest Book Review Bookwatch*
"A lively romantic mystery." — *Kirkus Reviews*
"A riveting drama . . . exciting read, highly recommended." — *Small Press Bookwatch*
"Katie is the first character I have absolutely fallen in love with since Stephanie Plum!" — *Stephanie Swindell, Bookstore Owner*
"Engaging storyline . . . taut suspense." — *MBR Bookwatch*

What Doesn't Kill You: Emily Bernal Romantic Mysteries

"Fair warning: clear your calendar before you pick it up because you won't be able to put it down." — *Ken Oder, author of* Old Wounds to the Heart

"Full of heart, humor, vivid characters, and suspense. Hutchins has done it again!" — *Gay Yellen, author of* The Body Business

"Hutchins is a master of tension." — *R.L. Nolen, author of* Deadly Thyme

"Intriguing mystery . . . captivating romance." — *Patricia Flaherty Pagan, author of* Trail Ways Pilgrims

"Everything about it shines: the plot, the characters and the writing. Readers are in for a real treat with this story." — *Marcy McKay, author of* Pennies from Burger Heaven

What Doesn't Kill You: Michele Lopez Hanson Romantic Mysteries

"Immediately hooked." — *Terry Sykes-Bradshaw, author of* Sibling Revelry

"Spellbinding." — *Jo Bryan, Dry Creek Book Club*

"Fast-paced mystery." — *Deb Krenzer, Book Reviewer*

"Can't put it down." — *Cathy Bader, Reader*

What Doesn't Kill You: Ava Butler Romantic Mysteries

"Just when I think I couldn't love another Pamela Fagan Hutchins novel more, along comes Ava." — *Marcy McKay, author of* Stars Among the Dead

"Ava personifies bombshell in every sense of word. — *Tara Scheyer, Grammy-nominated musician, Long-Distance Sisters Book Club*

"Entertaining, complex, and thought-provoking." — *Ginger Copeland, power reader*

What Doesn't Kill You: Maggie Killian Romantic Mysteries

"Maggie's gonna break your heart–one way or another." *Tara Scheyer, Grammy-nominated musician, Long-Distance Sisters Book Club*

"Pamela Fagan Hutchins nails that Wyoming scenery and captures the atmosphere of the people there." — *Ken Oder, author o*f Old Wounds to the Heart

"I thought I had it all figured out a time or two, but she kept me wondering right to the end." — *Ginger Copeland, power reader*

BOOKS FROM SKIPJACK PUBLISHING

FICTION:

Marcy McKay

Pennies from Burger Heaven, by Marcy McKay

Stars Among the Dead, by Marcy McKay

The Moon Rises at Dawn, by Marcy McKay

Bones and Lies Between Us, by Marcy McKay

When Life Feels Like a House Fire, by Marcy McKay

R.L. Nolen

Deadly Thyme, by R. L. Nolen

The Dry, by Rebecca Nolen

Ken Oder

The Closing, by Ken Oder

Old Wounds to the Heart, by Ken Oder

The Judas Murders, by Ken Oder

The Princess of Sugar Valley, by Ken Oder

Gay Yellen

The Body Business, by Gay Yellen

The Body Next Door, by Gay Yellen

Pamela Fagan Hutchins

THE JENN HERRINGTON SERIES OF WYOMING MYSTERIES:

BIG HORN (*Jenn Herrington #1*), by Pamela Fagan Hutchins

WALKER PRAIRIE (*Jenn Herrington #2*), by Pamela Fagan Hutchins

RED GRADE (*Jenn Herrington #3*), by Pamela Fagan Hutchins

THE PATRICK FLINT SERIES OF WYOMING MYSTERIES:

Switchback (Patrick Flint #1), by Pamela Fagan Hutchins

Snake Oil (Patrick Flint #2), by Pamela Fagan Hutchins

Sawbones (Patrick Flint #3), by Pamela Fagan Hutchins

Scapegoat (Patrick Flint #4), by Pamela Fagan Hutchins

Snaggle Tooth (Patrick Flint #5), by Pamela Fagan Hutchins

Stag Party (Patrick Flint #6), by Pamela Fagan Hutchins

Sitting Duck (*Patrick Flint #7*), by Pamela Fagan Hutchins

Skin & Bones (*Patrick Flint #8*), by Pamela Fagan Hutchins

Snow Ghost (*Patrick Flint *9*), *by Pamela Fagan Hutchins*

Spark (Patrick Flint 1.5): Exclusive to subscribers, by Pamela Fagan Hutchins

THE *WHAT DOESN'T KILL YOU* SUPER SERIES:

Wasted in Waco (WDKY Ensemble Prequel Novella): Exclusive to Subscribers, by Pamela Fagan Hutchins

The Essential Guide to the What Doesn't Kill You Series, by Pamela Fagan Hutchins

Katie Connell Caribbean Mysteries:

Saving Grace (Katie #1), by Pamela Fagan Hutchins

Leaving Annalise (Katie #2), by Pamela Fagan Hutchins

Finding Harmony (Katie #3), by Pamela Fagan Hutchins

Seeking Felicity (Katie #4), by Pamela Fagan Hutchins

Emily Bernal Texas-to-New Mexico Mysteries:

Heaven to Betsy (Emily #1), by Pamela Fagan Hutchins

Earth to Emily (Emily #2), by Pamela Fagan Hutchins

Hell to Pay (Emily #3), by Pamela Fagan Hutchins

Michele Lopez Hanson Texas Mysteries:

Going for Kona (Michele #1), by Pamela Fagan Hutchins

Fighting for Anna (Michele #2), by Pamela Fagan Hutchins

Searching for Dime Box (Michele #3), by Pamela Fagan Hutchins

Maggie Killian Texas-to-Wyoming Mysteries:

Buckle Bunny (Maggie Prequel Novella), by Pamela Fagan Hutchins

Shock Jock (Maggie Prequel Short Story), by Pamela Fagan Hutchins

Live Wire (Maggie #1), by Pamela Fagan Hutchins

Sick Puppy (Maggie #2), by Pamela Fagan Hutchins

Dead Pile (Maggie #3), by Pamela Fagan Hutchins

The Ava Butler Caribbean Mysteries Trilogy*: A Sexy Spin-off From *What Doesn't Kill You

Bombshell (Ava #1), by Pamela Fagan Hutchins

Stunner (Ava #2), by Pamela Fagan Hutchins

Knockout (Ava #3), by Pamela Fagan Hutchins

MULTI-AUTHOR:

Murder, They Wrote: Four SkipJack Mysteries,

by Ken Oder, R.L. Nolen, Marcy McKay, and Gay Yellen

Tides of Possibility, edited by K.J. Russell

Tides of Impossibility, edited by K.J. Russell and C. Stuart Hardwick

JUVENILE:

Poppy Needs a Puppy, by Pamela Fagan Hutchins

George Finds a Friend, by Pamela Fagan Hutchins

NONFICTION:

Helen Colin

My Dream of Freedom: From Holocaust to My Beloved America, by Helen Colin

Pamela Fagan Hutchins

The Clark Kent Chronicles, by Pamela Fagan Hutchins

Hot Flashes and Half Ironmans, by Pamela Fagan Hutchins

How to Screw Up Your Kids, by Pamela Fagan Hutchins

How to Screw Up Your Marriage, by Pamela Fagan Hutchins

Puppalicious and Beyond, by Pamela Fagan Hutchins

What Kind of Loser Indie Publishes, and How Can I Be One, Too?, by Pamela Fagan Hutchins

Ken Oder

Keeping the Promise, by Ken Oder

www.ingramcontent.com/pod-product-compliance
Lightning Source LLC
LaVergne TN
LVHW010639110826
845149LV00014B/2894

9781956729474